The Devil's Breath

Graham Hurley is a writer and television producer. Many of his documentary films have won awards. His six part ITV series, *In Time of War*, marked the tenth anniversary of the Falklands Campaign. He is co-director of *Project Icarus*, a charity active in health education. His novels, *Rules of Engagement* (1990), *Reaper* (1991), *The Devil's Breath* (1993) and *Thunder in the Blood* (1994) are all available in Pan paperback.

By the same author:

Rules of Engagement
Reaper
Thunder in the Blood
Sabbathman

The Devil's Breath

Graham Hurley

PAN BOOKS

First published 1993 by Macmillan London Limited

This edition published 1993 by Pan Macmillan Limited
a division of Pan Macmillan Publishers Limited
Cavaye Place London SW10 9PG
and Basingstoke

Associated companies throughout the world

ISBN 0 330 32683 X
Copyright © Graham Hurley 1993

The right of Graham Hurley to be identified as the
author of this work has been asserted by him in accordance
with the Copyright, Designs and Patents Act 1988.

9 8 7 6 5 4 3 2

A CIP catalogue record for this book is available from
the British Library

Typeset by Cambridge Composing (UK) Ltd, Cambridge
Printed and bound in Great Britain by
Cox & Wyman Ltd, Reading, Berkshire

To Mum and Dad
who never lost faith
and Woody
who kept scoring the
goals

Whenever possible, troops should regard poison gas as simply another battlefield hazard. Given thorough training, and constant vigilance, there is no reason why casualties from gas attack cannot be kept to an absolute minimum. Vernacular use of phrases like 'Old Chokey' and 'The Devil's Breath' should be actively discouraged.

War Office directive
November 1917

The terrible thing about terrorism is that ultimately it destroys those who practise it. Slowly but surely, as they try to extinguish life in others, the light within them dies.

Terry Waite
February 1992

Prelude

6 May 1990

'An Israeli agent comes to the house. Here, in Ramallah. His name is Shlomo. He's young. He looks European. He's a handsome man. Always he wants to know about the *moharebbin*, the terrorists. Always, he asks about them. He wants me to tell him what I know. In return, he says, my son will be released from the prison. One day, I tell him some things. Not much. I don't know very much. But I give him some names. He goes away. I never see him again. And, yes, my son is released. Two weeks later, my son is killed. By the *moharebbin*. They come for him in the evening, and they tie him up, and they drag him through the streets behind a car until he is dead. I go to the *moharebbin*. I demand to know the truth. Why have they killed my son? They say that the Israelis have told them that my son has betrayed the *Intifada*. That my son has given them information. I say, which Israelis? Shlomo, they say. The blond one . . .'

The old man, Abu Yussuf, looked up, exhausted by his story, by the memories interred beneath the short, bitter sentences, by the image of his dead son, encrusted with blood, sprawled amongst the refuse in an alley behind the city's market. The dogs had been at him overnight. Part of his leg, below the knee, was missing.

The stranger across the table said nothing for a moment. He'd arrived in Ramallah the previous evening. He said he came from the Gulf, but he spoke the harsh, accented Arabic of Damascus. He'd stayed barely half an hour, just long enough to sip sweet tea, and share the old man's grief, and make the offer.

'Well?' he said at last. 'Will you take it? Will you do the job?'

The old man looked at him. The job. The offer. The chance to make it right again. He'd thought of nothing else since the stranger had risen from his table, thanked him for the tea and held him briefly by the shoulders, before walking out into the night. His wife said he'd be mad to take it, to get involved. Life was hard. You grew to expect such things. And anyway, they had two other sons.

Now the old man studied his hands for a moment. They were still dirty from the garage, and they shook slightly as he accepted another cigarette. He inhaled deeply, letting the smoke spread inside him, calm again. He'd loved his son, his smile, his quickness. When the Israelis let the place open, when they gave the kids a chance, he'd tried to study at Bir Zeit University. One day he might have made something of himself, got away from this place. Now, though, he was dead. Another grave in the dusty field behind the hill. Another curling photograph on the bare concrete wall.

The old man looked up. Outside, in the narrow street, kids were selling lemons they'd stolen from the market. He listened for a moment. They were laughing.

The stranger stirred and looked at his watch. The old man got up and turned away. After a while he began to nod, his hand reaching down for the table, holding on to it for reassurance.

'OK,' he said at last, 'I'll do it.'

*

Three months later, on 14 August 1990, in the hall of a large Victorian house in west London, a secretary stooped to the doormat and collected the day's post. Amongst the litter of envelopes was a brown Jiffy bag with a handwritten address and an 87p stamp.

She took the post upstairs to her office and ran the mail through the desk-top X-ray analyser. The Jiffy bag contained a video-cassette. Bending to the black and white screen, she could see the oblong shadow of the plastic case, the tightly wound spool of tape. She opened the bag and took out the cassette. Finding no accompanying note, she frowned and checked the address again. No doubt about it. Godfrey Friedland, 67 Sidmouth Place, SW10.

Friedland saw the cassette mid-morning, between meetings.

The pictures had been shot hand-held, the camera always moving, a twitchy finger on the zoom lens. They showed the boot of a car, a tangle of pipework, some kind of tank. A hand kept opening and closing the boot lid. Then the camera dipped below the bumper, and the screen went black for a moment as the auto-exposure fought to compensate, and then there was a grainy, out-of-focus shot of exhaust-pipes. The shot lingered for ten seconds or more, the hand still shaking, making the point. Exhaust-pipes, someone was saying. Not one exhaust-pipe, but two.

The screen went briefly black again, then the camera was inside the car, focusing down on the dashboard. A hand suddenly appeared, an oldish hand with brown, thick, gnarled fingers, pointing at a switch on the dashboard. The switch was white, and clearly out of keeping with the rest of the dash. The finger withdrew and then reappeared again, tapping the switch. Look, said the finger. Look at the switch.

Another brief moment of black, then a final image, Manhattan, late afternoon, the famous skyline shot from a moving car across the East River, the sun way over to the south, bits and pieces of Queens sliding past in the foreground. The shot went on for a minute or more, a car radio on the soundtrack, then – abruptly – the camera cut and the screen went black for the last time.

The secretary bent to the video-player and began to rewind the cassette. The man behind the desk grunted and reached for the nearer of two telephones. He punched in a number from memory and listened for a moment or two before the call was answered.

'It's arrived,' he said briefly, 'though God knows what it means.'

*

A day later, a man in his early forties walked into the Manhattan Plaza, a discreet, expensive hotel four blocks south of New York's Central Park. He carried a brief-case and a small overnight bag. One of the women behind the long curve of the reception desk glanced up and greeted him by name. The man returned her smile and checked that she'd confirmed the booking.

Lightly tanned, neatly dressed, he had a faint but perceptible West Coast accent. The woman took an impression of his charge-card and assigned him the usual room on the ninth floor.

Later that night the man asked for room service. He ordered an omelette with a light salad, which he ate alone. He made three telephone calls, one of them overseas. An hour before midnight he placed a fourth call, ringing a Manhattan escort agency and asking for a particular girl by name.

The girl arrived, by cab, thirty minutes later. She took the elevator to the ninth floor. Normally, as one or two of the staff well knew, she stayed for an hour or so. On this occasion she didn't reappear at all.

Next morning, at nine-thirty, one of the housekeeping crews arrived on the ninth floor and began to clean the rooms. The door to Room 937 was shut but not bolted. When knocks and polite enquiries produced no response, the maid opened the door with her pass-key. The curtains in the room were still drawn. The room was quite empty. There was a very bad smell.

The maid called again, then walked in, pulling back the curtains. The big double bed had been slept in. The sheets were crumpled and there were two sets of clothes neatly folded across the back of the three-seat sofa. The maid paused for a moment, puzzled, then crossed the room towards the shower. The shower door was shut, but the smell was much stronger here. It was a distinctive, heavy odour, impossible to ignore. It smelled the way certain tenements smelled on a very hot day in high summer, of bad plumbing and loose bowels and no spare dollars for air freshener.

The maid paused again, unnerved, then pushed the door. The door opened. Inside, on the floor, were two bodies. Both were naked, folded over each other in a random, almost childlike way. There was no blood. No bruising. No sign of obvious violence. Just the bodies, their legs and arms entangled, a man and a woman, as if asleep. The woman's hand lay inches from the side of the bath. Beside it, discarded, an aerosol.

The maid looked closer, at last recognizing the smell for what it was. The man must have messed himself. She could see it, smeared and caked down the inside of one of his thighs. It was everywhere, between his legs, on the floor, on the woman, everywhere. There was vomit, too, pooled behind the door. The place stank.

The maid swallowed hard, and turned and began to retreat, but as she did so she felt a strange sensation in her head. She reached out for support, surprised, and fell over an arm of the sofa. Sprawled on the carpet, she tried to crawl towards the door, her eyes beginning to hurt, the room slipping out of focus. She opened her mouth to scream, but nothing happened except a strangled gasping noise as her lungs fought for air.

Dimly, miles away, she saw feet in the corridor outside. She tried to lift her head from the carpet, to beg for help, to sound an alarm, to get some relief from this sudden, terrifying pain in her chest, but as the feet paused, and turned, and stepped into the room, the last of the daylight flickered and died, and she began to drift away.

The smell, she thought. That terrible, terrible smell.

*

That same day, in London, a man in his early thirties appeared on the steps of the Israeli Embassy in Palace Gardens. He wore a lightweight tan raincoat and carried a slim leather brief-case. He looked at his watch, glanced up and down the busy street, and then set off in the direction of South Kensington.

Ten minutes later, on a quiet corner of Queen's Gate Gardens, he consulted his watch again, pausing at the kerbside. Then he began to cross the road, quickening his step. As he did so, a black Mercedes saloon stopped about 50 yards away. A man got out of the passenger seat. The car drove away.

The man from the Embassy crossed the road, heading south. The passenger from the Mercedes intercepted him. They met outside a row of antique shops. They began to talk. Voices were raised. The man from the Embassy, impatient, shook his head and turned to go. As he did so, the other man drew a small hand-gun. He fired twice. The man from the Embassy fell to the ground. The other man knelt over him and fired twice more, at point-blank range, into his head. Then he pocketed the gun, picked up the brief-case, and walked quickly away in the direction of Gloucester Road tube station.

The man from the Embassy lay still. Blood was seeping from one ear.

Minutes later, a news photographer on a nearby assignment arrived. Someone had phoned his news editor, and he in turn had come through on the photographer's mobile. Now he parked his car across the road and slipped a Nikon from the glove-box. He circled the body quickly, ignoring the tiny group of silent onlookers, rationing himself to the obvious camera angles. The pictures showed a man in a tan raincoat lying in the street. He might have been drunk or he might have been asleep. Except that most of the back of his head had simply ceased to exist.

His work complete, the photographer ran back to his car and bent to his mobile phone. He was still deep in conversation when the first of the squad cars appeared at the top of the street. Ten miles away, at his paper's new offices in Docklands, the news editor heard the wail of sirens down the phone.

'Don't hang about,' he said. 'Get the stuff back here now.'

The photographer acknowledged the order with a grunt and slipped his car into gear. Driving away, he took one last look at the body on the pavement. Something had been bothering him about the face in the viewfinder, something strange, something out of keeping. Now he realized what it was. The expression on the dead man's face was a smile.

Book one

16 August 1990

1

Two hours after dawn, finally asleep, McVeigh lay in the big double bed, dreaming of Nanda Devi.

Half a lifetime in the mountains told him that the south-west route would be the best, a line of dots he'd plotted time and again on the photos he scissored from his mountaineering magazines. He smiled at the thought, surfing up and down through semi-consciousness, picturing the long six-day approach march, the dozens of rickety little bridges, the chuckling ribbons of icy water tumbling down from the high peaks, the long line of sherpas, their backs bent, the muscles of their legs knotted under their enormous loads.

At 11,000 feet, they'd establish base-camp. The air would be thinner here, slowing progress. To begin with, first time out, years back, the feeling of altitude had been unnerving, a strange and troubling experience, nature's way of telling you to go home. You got dizzy. You felt sick. Strength became a memory. Then you began to adjust, and something magical happened to the blood, and one morning you woke up and you discovered that you weren't quite so tired, and when you pulled back the tent flap and inspected the shape of the next 6000 feet – the frieze of mountains, the soaring peaks, the snow smoking off the higher ridges – then you were glad again, and hungry for it.

McVeigh stirred in the cluttered little bedroom, remembering it all, comforted. Nanda Devi was a dream, 25,000 feet, the highest mountain in India, the seat of the goddess, a destination, the end of a journey he'd probably never complete. Too bad. Even dreaming about it was enough to remind him how real life could be, how fragile it was, how unimportant you really were. Mountains, all mountains, were like that. They took everything you had and gave you back yourself. That's why you did it.

That's why you climbed. Mountains were special. And Nanda Devi, the shadow inside his head, was the most special of all.

A door opened down the hall. There were footsteps, a light, a face at the door, a lunge across the duvet, the sweet, warm, familiar smell. McVeigh grinned, his eyes still shut. Kids were as good as mountains. Better, sometimes.

'Billy?'

The boy giggled, rubbing his nose against McVeigh's, cupping his face in his hands, feeling the overnight stubble on his father's chin. For eleven, Billy was still small, still a child. His mother, McVeigh's ex-wife, put it down to forgetfulness. 'He forgets to eat,' she kept saying. 'Just never gets hungry.'

Now at seven in the morning, Billy was already dressed for the recreation ground, a couple of acres of stony turf at the posher end of Hornsey. Mid-morning, his football team were due to meet for the first of the pre-season training sessions, an hour or so of exercise, ball skills and hectic five-a-side. Billy had been playing for them for two seasons now, and McVeigh – never a team player – had encouraged the boy as much as he could. Most weekends, assignments permitting, Billy stayed over at the flat, and McVeigh would take him to the games, home or away, roaring what little advice he had from the touch-line. The experience had brought its own share of surprises. One of them had been a warm parental glow, a real sense of pride, when Billy started scoring goals. Another, more recently, had been Yakov.

McVeigh peered at his son in the curtained half-light, trying to push the name away, trying to forget.

'Looking forward to it?'

'Yeah.'

'Lotsa goals?'

'Millions.' He grinned. 'Squillions.'

'Better than last year?'

'Much.'

'How do you know?'

'Yakov says.'

The boy reached forward and bit the end of McVeigh's nose. McVeigh winced with pain, holding the boy tight, wondering

whether this might not be the time, now, with a whole day to
get over it, but the boy wriggled free, a blur of West Ham
colours, lunging for the door, footsteps down the hall, then the
sound of manic laughter from the first of the morning's TV
cartoons.

McVeigh lay back, gazing at the door, thinking yet again of
Yakov. He'd first met the man before Christmas. He'd noticed
him three or four times on the touch-line, watching the kids
play football, a tall guy, younger than McVeigh, loose-limbed,
well dressed, white Burberry, expensive slacks, his face half-
hidden by folds of cashmere scarf. At first, naturally curious,
McVeigh had put him down as the parent of one of the wealthier
kids, Highgate or Hampstead, but when he'd mentioned it to
Billy, the boy had shaken his head. Dunno, he'd said, doesn't
belong to us.

A week later, a wet Saturday in December, the two men had
found themselves side by side on the muddy touch-line. They'd
talked about the game, about individual kids, who was good,
who wasn't. To McVeigh's amusement, the man had singled out
Billy as a real prospect, good ball skills, physical courage, a
huge appetite for goals. McVeigh had thought that a bit strong,
and said so, but the stranger had shaken his head, reproachful,
almost stern, repeating what he'd said. He spoke good English
with a trace of an accent. He had a strong, open face and a mass
of curly black hair. He said he'd once played football himself,
semi-professionally, at home in Tel Aviv. He said he'd been
that rare animal, an unselfish centre-forward. He said he could
have been really good, only he shared too many goals with
other players, lacking the killer instinct. And with this last
phrase, he'd held out his hand, introducing himself, offering a
name to go with the sudden, almost childlike grin.

'Yakov,' he'd said, 'Yakov Arendt.'

The relationship had prospered. With a nudge from McVeigh,
Yakov had made his number with the team's manager. He said
he lived near by. He loved football. He'd been watching the
team for a while. He had a little spare time. Could he possibly
help?

Next week, he turned up in an old, much-used Nike track-suit. The kids, cautious at first, watched him strip off. Ten minutes or so on the pitch and the job was his. He played football the way he talked, with a deceptive languor, moving sweetly over the muddy pitch, perfect ball control, perfect balance, riding tackle after tackle, finding space for himself where none existed, setting up the showier kids with passes of rare elegance. They loved him for it: the goals he enabled them to score, the way he taught them to play, out-thinking the opposition, making the ball do the work, baiting traps, inflicting defeat after defeat.

Billy, especially, worshipped the man. At the boy's insistent invitation, he began to come back to the flat, sharing toast and Marmite and pots of tea in front of the ancient gas fire. McVeigh liked him too, his warmth, his obvious enthusiasm, the gentle fun he made of himself, the sense of apartness he carried with him, nothing fretful, nothing heavy, just a good-humoured awareness of being slightly at odds with the rest of the world.

After a while, he'd begun to talk a little about himself. He had a wife, Cela, back in Tel Aviv. He carried photographs of her, a small, cheerful, attractive woman in her early thirties, with huge, shadowed eyes and jet-black hair. They had a tiny apartment in Jaffa, near the old quarter. They'd been married for six years, and he missed her more and more, and one day soon, God willing, he might go back. Quite what he was doing in London, Yakov never made clear. McVeigh had his own ideas – the accent, the nationality, the *look* of the bloke – but he himself moved in a world where the questions always outnumbered the answers, and he respected the man's reticence.

Lately, high summer, the league season over, the three of them had spent a little time together, spontaneous excursions, mostly at Yakov's suggestion. A couple of fine weekends had taken them out of London in Yakov's car. He owned a red MGB convertible, a recent acquisition he treated with enormous pride, and he drove it fast, outside lane on the M4 overpass, Billy wedged in sideways on the tiny back seat, his huge grin partly masked by the Ray-Bans he always stole from Yakov's jacket pocket. The last time they'd been west, a hot Sunday in late July, they'd ended up at a small village in the Thames

Valley. Yakov had seemed to know the place. He'd taken them to a pub by the river. He'd ordered burger and chips for Billy, and they'd sat outside in the sunshine, watching the swans paddling by. His plate empty, Billy had drifted across to a play area where a couple of older kids were kicking listlessly at a plastic football, and the two men had sat at the table, McVeigh talking about Billy's new school. Listening, Yakov had nodded, watching the boy make a goal with two careful piles of T-shirts. After a while, he'd looked at McVeigh.

'You miss being married?'

'No.'

'You regret being married?'

'No.'

'You ever see your wife?'

'Not properly. Not to talk to. Just . . .'

McVeigh had shrugged, looking at Billy again, installed between the goal-posts. It was the first time the two men had ventured on to this kind of territory. After dozens of conversations about kids and football and the smallprint of living in London, it had seemed abruptly intimate. Yakov had smiled, saying nothing, and McVeigh had reached for his glass, swallowing the last of the beer.

'Find the right woman,' he'd said, 'and you're a lucky man.'

'I know.'

McVeigh had looked at him, puzzled by a new note in his voice, something unmistakably wistful, something close to regret.

'I thought—' he'd frowned '—you and Cela?'

'Yes?'

'I thought—' he'd shrugged, embarrassed '—it was all great.'

'It is. That's the problem.'

'What do you mean?'

'It *is* great. Very great.'

'Is . . . that a problem?'

'Yes.'

'Why?'

McVeigh had looked at him, waiting for an answer, some kind of explanation, but Yakov had simply shaken his head,

17

that same quiet smile, an expression of impenetrable sadness, and then he'd stood up, calling to Billy, taking the spin off the boy's pass with a deft flick of his foot, redirecting it to one of the older youths.

A week later, McVeigh was still brooding on the conversation, certain that Yakov had wanted to tell him something, half-convinced that he should phone up, suggest a quiet pint, just the two of them, no Billy, but in the end he'd done nothing about it, telling himself that he'd got it wrong, that the man had simply been lost for words, one too many shandies, that the moment had come and gone and meant very little.

Until three days ago, when every newspaper in the country carried pictures of a body sprawled in a Kensington street. One leg was in the gutter, and the head was at an odd angle, but the half-smile on the man's face gave the lie to the Israeli Embassy's careful evasions. Yakov Arendt. The wizard in the Nike tracksuit. The Sunday drinker with something on his mind.

McVeigh shuddered and turned over, shutting his eyes again. He had yet to break the news to Billy. And still, even now, he hadn't got a clue how to do it.

*

The incident at the Manhattan Plaza Hotel was still in the hands of the New York Police Department when the American Embassy in Amman, Jordan, received a small brown envelope from a youth on a motor-cycle. The youth left no name and offered no further point of contact. The envelope was addressed, in typescript, to the President of the United States.

It was opened by one of the Embassy's senior attachés. He read the two typed paragraphs twice and then reached for the phone. Halfway through dialling he put the phone down and ran upstairs to the Ambassador's office. The Ambassador, he knew, had a crisis meeting scheduled for noon. The meeting was to include top members of the Jordanian administration and a cousin of the King. Since the Iraqi invasion of Kuwait, two weeks back, there'd been lots of crisis meetings. It was 11.45.

The Ambassador read the note, shook his head, read it again. An active service unit had entered the United States. They were presently established somewhere on the East Coast. Soon they would be moving to New York. They were under Headquarters Command. They had been training for their mission for many months. Their mission would answer American aggression in the Gulf. It would remind US citizens that war, if it came, would be total. Total war included the indiscriminate, unannounced use of chemical weapons. A further communiqué would follow. The note was signed 'The Martyrs of 7th June'.

Encrypted at the highest security classification, the contents of the note were on a desk in Washington, DC before the first of the Ambassador's guests drove in through the Embassy gates. The gates, recently installed against possible kamikaze attacks, were blast-proof and electronically controlled. The attaché who'd first read the note watched them swing shut behind the big limousine. Ironic, he thought, remembering the terrible threat behind the letter's last paragraph. One hundred and ninety thousand dollars' worth of hi-tech engineering. And it wouldn't make a cent's worth of difference.

*

In Washington, the note from Amman was preserved – eyes only – until the arrival of the named addressee. Normally Sullivan was at his desk in the West Wing of the White House by 7 a.m. On this particular Tuesday, after a crippling day in London and an overnight flight back, he was two hours late.

Sullivan hung his coat on the back of the door and sank into the big leather chair behind the desk. An early shower had caught him as he stepped out of the car. His hair was still wet. He gazed down at the note without reading it. Impending war, as he was beginning to understand, played havoc with the ageing process. Already, after a fortnight of crisis management, of back-to-back meetings and helicopter dashes to Andrews Air Force Base, he felt several hundred years old. His wife, as concerned and patriotic as the next administration spouse, was beginning to make impatient noises about nuclear strikes, an eye for an eye, the importance of getting the whole damn thing buttoned up before her precious husband succumbed to the incessant deadlines and self-destructed. Who knows? he thought. Had Saddam Hussein kept his hands off Kuwait, they might even now be back-packing along the more remote Yosemite trails, three weeks of wilderness they'd been promising each other for nearly two years, a chance – at last – to shed a little of the bulk that seemed to come with the job. Some hope.

He reached for the note and read it. Lifting the phone, he checked with the decrypt office in the basement of the Executive Office Building across the street. He made another call to a New York number, briefer still. Then he picked up the note and walked along the blue-carpeted corridor to the Oval Office. The President had been at his desk since dawn, one eye on the CNN transmissions piped through to the middle of the three televisions installed beneath the big framed painting of Gettysburg. Rumour was, the President never slept. Didn't need to. Mistrusted the stuff.

The decrypt from Amman passed across the desk. The President read it, fidgeting with a pencil as he did so. Then he looked up.

'What do we know about this business in New York?'

'Nothing, sir. Yet.'

'OK. So let's have us find out.'

'It's in hand. They're checking now. They'll phone.'

There was a long silence. The two men looked at each other. Then the President ran a tired hand over his face. Soon now he'd be going back to Maine, a little fishing, a little sunshine, a little fun. It was important to try to kid the rest of the world that life went on as normal. Even with the Middle East about to blow up. The President looked down again at the note.

'What's the worst?' he said.

'The worst?' Sullivan frowned. 'The worst is, that it's true.'

'And?'

'And . . .?' He shrugged. 'We close New York.'

The President gazed at him. Fatigue, or some trick of the light, had somehow flattened the planes of his face. He looked terrible.

'You serious?'

Sullivan nodded.

'Yeah.'

The President looked at him some more. Then he shook his head.

'We can't,' he said. He brooded for a long moment, turning in his chair and staring out of the window. 'That's what the bastard wants. And that's why we can't do it.'

One of the three telephones on the President's desk trilled softly. He lifted it to his ear. He was still staring out of the window, the pencil between his teeth. He listened intently for a full minute, then he put down the phone without a word. He looked at Sullivan across the desk and nodded at the telephone.

'It *is* true,' he muttered. 'They ran the full analysis this morning. Takes a while in New York.'

'Are they sure?'

'You bet.'

Sullivan nodded slowly but said nothing. The President looked at him, a moment of frank appraisal, then got up and walked to the window. After a while, Sullivan cleared his throat. 'We need a fireman,' he suggested. 'Someone to take care of this.'

The President nodded, grunting assent. Then he turned back into the room. He was frowning.

'Like who?' he said.

Sullivan thought for a moment, trying to resist the temptation to play the old White House game. Instant decisions were the currency of most administrations, including this one. They were supposed to demonstrate a certain macho domination over events. They were supposed to put you where the job description said you should be. In control.

'Someone good,' Sullivan said carefully. 'Someone solid.'

'Sure.'

'Someone who's worked in the Middle East. Knows the ground. Knows the Israelis . . .'

The President nodded again, the impatience evident in his voice. 'You bet.'

'Someone . . .' Sullivan shrugged, running out of words.

The President looked at him a moment, distracted by some passing thought, then he began to frown again, leaning forward, stabbing the air with his finger, suddenly urgent. 'Listen, John.

21

Whoever picks it up, it has to be tight. And it has to be quick. The invisible mend. With me?'

Sullivan blinked. Even thirty years' citizenship couldn't, just sometimes, keep the Irish out of his voice. It was there now, exhaustion mostly, and real concern. 'That's freelancing,' he said quietly.

The President nodded. 'Damn right.'

'The Chiefs'll hate it. The Chairman, too.'

'Who says they'll ever know?' The President paused. 'Who says they even *deserve* to know?'

The President shot Sullivan a look. August 2nd, the day the Iraqis invaded Kuwait, had left the United States high and dry. None of the Intelligence services had predicted it was going to happen, and when it did, the Chiefs of Staff in the Pentagon had precious little in the drawer to deal with it. It had taken Saddam just four hours to seize Kuwait City. Yet for days afterwards in Washington, the President and the military had sat at opposite ends of the city, stewing quietly, wondering what in God's name they could do. After years of supporting Iraq, the President felt utterly betrayed.

'Tight,' he said again, '*real* tight.'

Sullivan nodded, the point made, the argument over.

'You want to meet this guy? Whoever he is?'

'No.'

'You want me to handle it?'

'Yes.'

'You sure, sir?'

'Yes.'

Sullivan nodded again. Personal contacts were usually essential for the President. People didn't exist for him unless he'd actually met them. The fact that this normally iron rule was not to apply was itself significant. Whoever he found, whatever his name, the guy he'd task was to be totally out of channels, totally his own man, the ultimate freelance. Sullivan shrugged, his orders clear, the reservation in his voice quite gone. 'OK,' he said.

The President stared at him for a moment, then strode across the room, back towards the desk. In ten hectic days, with the Iraqi army massing on the Saudi border, peering south, eyeing

20 per cent of the world's oil reserves, he'd banged heads and bent arms, and committed the world's most powerful nation to the defence of King Fahd. He'd ordered carrier attack groups into the Persian Gulf. He'd mobilized a quarter of a million troops. And now he was close to slipping an economic noose around Saddam's neck in the shape of binding UN sanctions against the Iraqi regime. In response, Saddam had annexed Kuwait, closed Iraq's borders and taken thousands of foreigners hostage. Some of them – lots of them – were American. That was bad enough. But what was far, far worse – now – were the two brief paragraphs still lying on the desk.

The President picked up the decrypt. The implications were terrifying. New York. A weekday. Five p.m. The height of the commuter hour. One of the main thoroughfares. Hundreds of cars. Thousands of pedestrians, shoppers, office workers, *kids* for Chrissakes, totally innocent, totally unawares. And they had the stuff. He knew they had the stuff. The guy up in New York had said so. He'd said it was industrial grade. That was the phrase he'd used, just now, on the phone. Industrial grade. One hundred per cent. The real McCoy. As good as anything to come out of Dugway or the Rocky Mountain Arsenal. And it wouldn't stop there, either. If they did it once, they could do it again. And again. And again. Until no one with any brains left would *ever* risk New York. An entire city. America's finest. Empty. The Big Apple. Gone.

The President let the decrypt flutter to the desk. It landed, as it happened, upside down. He stared at it for a moment.

'Find your guy and get him to Tel Aviv,' he said. 'The Israelis know more about these bastards than we ever will. Tell them they're on the team. Tell them we'll take care of the rest of it.'

'Rest of it?'

'Yeah . . .' The President looked at him a moment, then gazed out of the window again. 'Saddam.'

※

McVeigh sat in the Crouch End branch of McDonald's, spooning sugar into a lukewarm cup of coffee. He'd told Billy about Yakov an hour ago. He'd freed up half a day, and collected the kid from school and broken the news as casually as he could, in

23

a traffic jam on Muswell Hill. His plan was to keep the thing as low-key as possible – no drama, no big announcement, just a word or two about an accident, something entirely innocent, something that might have happened to anyone. Put this way, McVeigh hoped the news might simply come and go, the simplest explanation for Yakov's abrupt departure from the football field. He was completely wrong.

Billy sat across from him. His burger was untouched. 'What happened?' he said for the second time.

McVeigh glanced round, uncomfortable. The place was full of kids, mothers, prams, shopping. There was lots of laughter from a birthday party in the corner. He'd have chosen somewhere else for a real conversation. Not here. McVeigh glanced across at Billy. The boy hadn't taken his eyes off his father's face. He wanted an answer.

'I don't know,' McVeigh said.

'Yes, you do.'

'I don't.'

'It was in the papers.'

'How do you know?'

'A boy told me. Jason.'

McVeigh looked at him for a moment, then nodded, conceding the point. Jason was the team's goalkeeper. His father owned a small corner shop. The shop sold papers. Sometimes Jason helped behind the counter. McVeigh toyed with his coffee. Not even sugar made it taste right.

'He was shot,' he said slowly. 'Someone shot him.'

'Who?'

'I don't know.'

'Why did they shoot him?'

'I don't know.'

The questions came to an end. Billy sat completely still, more still than McVeigh could ever remember, his face a mask, no trace of emotion. McVeigh reached out for him, trying to comfort him, trying to say in some simple, direct way that he was truly sorry, but the boy withdrew his folded arms, tucking them in against himself, a warning for McVeigh to keep his distance. McVeigh looked him in the eye, trying to move the conversation along, playing the parent, trying to coax the boy out of the hole he was digging for himself, but the questions still lay on the table between them. Why did Yakov die? And who killed him?

Abruptly, McVeigh changed tack.

'Have you talked to your mother about this?'

'No.'

'Why not?'

'She didn't know him.'

McVeigh nodded, trapped anew by his own questions. Part of him was beginning to understand what it was that made Billy such a good centre-forward, why he scored so many goals. The boy was utterly determined. He never took his eye off the ball. Yakov again, exactly his analysis. McVeigh frowned.

'You think I should know how he died? Who did it?'

'Dunno.'

'You think I should try and find out?'

He glanced up. The boy was still looking at him, expressionless, unblinking. 'Yes,' he said at last.

'Why?'

'Because he was our friend.' He glanced suddenly at his father. 'Wasn't he?'

McVeigh nodded slowly. A woman at the next table was trying to spoon-feed a baby and listen at the same time. He wondered what she made of their conversation. He looked at Billy again.

'So how would I do that?' he said. 'How would I go about it?'

Billy shrugged. 'Dunno,' he said. 'That's what you do, isn't it? Find out things?'

McVeigh smiled for the first time, amused by the small truth of his answer. He picked up the coffee cup and risked a second mouthful. Billy was still watching him, still waiting. 'Well?' he said.

McVeigh frowned. There was something in the boy's voice that he couldn't quite place. At first it sounded like hostility, something close to bitterness, then he realized that it was something else entirely. Without using the words, the boy was indicating a responsibility, telling him what he should do. Yakov had died. There had to be a reason. He'd been a friend of theirs. So it was McVeigh's job to find out. McVeigh put the coffee down.

'OK,' he said. 'My turn.'

'What?'

'My turn. My turn to ask questions.'

Billy shrugged again. 'OK,' he said.

McVeigh looked at him for a long moment.

'Say I found out why he died. Who did it. Who shot him . . .'

'Yeah?'

'What difference would it make?'

'*Difference?*' The child stared at him, the stare of someone who can't quite believe their ears.

McVeigh leaned forward. 'Yes. Why should I do it? Why should anyone?'

'Because . . .' Billy's eyes widened with a sudden anger. 'Because he's dead. Because they shot him. Because . . .' His voice faltered a moment, racing ahead of what he was trying to say, 'because he was so *good*.' He clung on to the word for a moment, then – for the first time – he looked away, down at the yellow styrofoam box with the cold burger and the limp thatch of shredded lettuce. He picked at a chip for a moment, inconsolable, then his head fell forward into his hands and he began to sob, his whole body shaking, pushing McVeigh away when he reached across the table, trying to comfort him.

Afterwards, back outside, it was raining. Billy sat in the passenger seat of the car, staring ahead, his face quite blank again. McVeigh fumbled for the ignition. He wanted to reassure the boy, to tell him that everything would be all right, that he'd probably make a few enquiries, find out what he could, call in a favour or two. Instead, on an impulse, he suggested they drove across to Upton Park. West Ham were playing a pre-season friendly. He'd seen it advertised in the paper. They could have doughnuts at half-time, and Coke. Billy was still staring through the windscreen. He didn't appear to be listening. 'I want to go home,' he said numbly. 'Please.'

*

Ron Telemann left his wife's BMW on the fourth floor of the 'M' Street Colonial parking lot, and walked two blocks to the address his secretary had typed on the index card. The call, she said, had come through at 10.57. The meeting was scheduled for noon. On no account was he to be late.

Already sweating in the sticky heat, Telemann glanced at his watch and quickened his step through the start of the lunch-time crowds. His secretary had been lucky to find him at all. Three days into his annual leave, he'd been minutes away from leaving Washington and driving south, the kids in the back of the beaten-up old Volvo, the windsurfer and the rubber dinghy on the roof, a fortnight's provisions in the back, his wife leafing through the Rand McNally, looking for yet another route to the tiny North Carolina resort they'd been visiting for nearly a decade. 'Sullivan,' his secretary had warned when he'd exploded on the phone. 'The man says do it, you do it.'

Telemann rounded the corner of 'K' Street and crossed the road on the green light. He'd met Sullivan on a number of occasions, a big, heavy-set White House staffer, a rising star with the Bush crowd. He'd put in good solid years at State during the sixties and early seventies, buffered himself with a small fortune from real estate during the Carter presidency, and worked his ticket back to the centre of the Republican admin-istration under Reagan. Now, word was he'd made himself irreplaceable at the NSA, acquiring a desk at the White House and a nice view of the Ellipse. Telemann's previous dealings with Sullivan had left him acutely wary. The guy was Irish. A lot of what he said was blarney. But he had real muscle, the kind that comes with age and good connections, and he never hesitated to use it. With Telemann's own career in the balance, it was probably worth being half a day late on the beach.

He checked the address against the card in his pocket. The fourth floor belonged to a prominent firm of Washington attorneys. Telemann recognized the name from way back. Sullivan, he knew, had once been a partner there.

Telemann took the elevator to the fourth floor where a secretary led him through the cool, open-plan office. At the end of the office was a door. The secretary knocked once and walked in. Sullivan sat in a big recliner behind a desk. He looked exhausted and a good deal fatter than Telemann remembered. Even six months, he thought, can make a difference.

Sullivan looked up. The secretary had gone. 'Better here,' he said, 'than the White House.'

'Sure.'

'Quieter. No fucking interruptions.'

'You bet.'

Telemann hesitated for a moment, then sat down. Sullivan studied him for perhaps a minute, the usual treatment, the small close-set eyes, the pudgy face, the tie-knot never quite in place. Then he began to talk, his voice low, confidential, an implicit invitation to join the boys, shut the door, put his feet up. He outlined what was really happening in the Gulf, the insider's brief, the story behind the headlines, the big meaty hands describing the shape of the coming alliance against Saddam. He detailed the pressure-points, the places where they were putting on the real squeeze, the speed with which the Iraqis had understood the likely consequences. And finally – utterly logical in the sequence of events – he told Telemann about the morning's decrypt from Amman, two brief paragraphs which had brought the Administration to a thoroughly nasty bend in the pike.

Telemann followed the story without comment. With these guys, you never hurried things. Reacting off the top was third-grade stuff, your first and last mistake. Sullivan watched him, leaning back in the big recliner, playing with a paper-clip, waiting for a response.

Telemann at last obliged. 'A hit squad,' he said carefully.

'Correct.'

'Iraqi-based.'

'We can't say that.'

'But Iraqi-funded.'

'We assume so.'

'With orders to hit New York.'

'Yep.'

'With several gallons of Tabun GA.'

'You got it.'

Telemann nodded. It seemed, on the face of it, a logical proposition. Pinned down in the Gulf, threatened by the biggest war-machine on the planet, you struck elsewhere. And where better than New York? The First World's golden city? Home of the UN? Home for all those sanction-backing diplomats?

Telemann blinked, looking at Sullivan again. Tabun GA was nerve gas, civilization's waking nightmare, the weapon that even the Nazis had refrained from using. It got to you in seconds, tiny droplets of the stuff, the thinnest mist. You breathed it in, or it penetrated your skin, or it found some other way to get at you. You gagged. You staggered. You began to choke. Telemann shuddered. His knowledge of the chemistry of Tabun was crude in the extreme, but even the threat was enough, the simple phrase 'nerve gas', the thought of the muscles cramping tight, all control gone, the body decoupled from itself, death a merciful release. He looked at Sullivan afresh. News like this you didn't share. Not unless you had some other end in view. Telemann drew in a long breath and held it for a moment before letting the air out slowly, the softest of whistles. August on the beach was fast receding.

'So what do you want?' he said.

Sullivan tipped forward, towards the desk. For a moment, Telemann thought the chair was going to collapse. It didn't.

'We want you to find them,' he said carefully, 'and stop them. Quietly. Quickly. Nobody the wiser.' He paused. 'We want you to talk to your Israeli friends and anyone else you think might help. You'll have every asset we can give you, short of publicity. You'll have stand-alone status and unlimited reach. Logistically, you're looking at a blank cheque . . .' He paused again, fingering the paper-clip, trying to bend it back into shape. Telemann watched him, letting the phrases sink in, promises of a kind he'd never heard in his life.

'Why me?' he said at last.

Sullivan considered the question. Then he tossed the paper-clip towards the bin. It missed.

'Because you're smart,' he said, 'and difficult, and speak the right language.' He paused for a moment, 'And we were impressed by your CIA paper, too. That took guts.' He paused again, reaching for another paper-clip.

'Thanks,' Telemann said drily.

'Anything else?'

'Yeah . . .' Telemann looked away a moment. The question had been bothering him for a while, and as soon as he'd framed it, he knew it was directed at himself as much as at Sullivan. Ambition was a fine thing. But even his had limits. He looked up again. 'Tell me,' he said, 'do I have any choice?'

Sullivan gazed at him for a long time, the beginnings of a smile on his face. Then he shook his head. 'No,' he said. 'The word on the President's lips is duty.'

*

Godfrey Friedland arrived at the Ritz Hotel thirty minutes late. The traffic in Central London was jammed solid, the second grid-lock in less than a month, and the cab up from Fulham had finally dropped him nearly a mile away. The walk had done him no good whatsoever. At fifty-eight, for the first time in his life, he was beginning to feel his age.

He walked into the hotel and took the lift to the sixth floor. MI6 had kept a suite for nearly a decade now, a permanent arrangement heavily subsidized by a leading Tory Party backer. Friedland knew the arrangement well. One of his last jobs at MI6 had been to draw up a schedule of regular electronic sweeps.

He paused in the corridor and knocked at the door. A voice told him to come in, a voice he recognized. The man from Number Ten. Ross.

Friedland opened the door and stepped into the suite. He hadn't been here for nearly a year, not since the last big crisis, but nothing had changed. Still the same fake Louis-Quinze chairs. Still the same heavy brocade, with the thick pile carpet and the hideous velvet curtains. Ross, sitting at the conference table, waved him into a chair. He didn't bother with a hand-shake or even the courtesy of a formal greeting.

Friedland took off his coat, folding it carefully over the back of a chair, taking his time. Had he stayed in the Service, he'd doubtless be still outranking Ross, even though the young civil servant had become a Whitehall byword for preferment and a certain steely arrogance. As it was, though, he'd elected for the offer of early retirement, placing his own interpretation on the series of covert meetings he'd attended with a tiny coterie of Smith Square luminaries. Then, back in '82, the deal had been quite explicit: in return for generous 'support', he was to put his knowledge and his contacts at the service of the Downing Street private office. Post-Falklands, with the wind filling the Tories' sails, he was to ride shotgun on the heavyweights of the Intelligence Service, providing independent guidance and advice to an administration with an almost pathological mistrust of the established machinery of government. He was to be permanently on call, at the end of a telephone or a fax, a bottomless source of second opinions. In practice, this arrangement meant premises of his own, regular consultancy fees and a certain maverick satisfaction with his new-found freedoms. At last he could say what he liked about whom he liked. He could form his own opinions, offer his own judgements. He could subject raw data to the kind of coldly objective assessment that had long been a memory in mainstream Intelligence. To his own amusement, in the parlance of his trade, he'd been 'turned'.

Now, though, there was Ross. The man looked up and offered a thin smile.

'What did you make of the video?'

Friedland shrugged. Light conversation with the likes of Ross had never been his forte.

'A man in a car,' he said, 'making a series of points. Not too difficult to follow.'

'You understood it?'

'Out of context?' He shook his head. 'No.'

Ross nodded, letting the silence between them make his point. The currency of the game they played was knowledge. And he, as ever, was banker. He glanced down at the pad. 'The video came via the Consulate in Nicosia. Simply handed in.'

'By whom?'

'No one knows.'

Friedland nodded. He knew Nicosia well. He'd served there

31

for a while in the mid-sixties, running agents into the Middle East. It was very tatty. He'd rather liked it. He looked across at Ross. 'If someone's sending a message,' he said lightly, 'there have to be other elements. I can't build a sentence out of your video.'

Ross nodded. 'There are. Or at least we think there are.' He paused for a moment, then told Friedland about a rumour they'd picked up from a diplomatic source in Tel Aviv, the emergence of yet another Palestinian terror group, totally unknown, new faces, new name.

Friedland looked at him. 'What is it?' he said. 'What's the name?'

'Seventh June.'

'Just that?'

'Yes.'

Friedland nodded slowly, drawing the obvious conclusion. June 7th 1981 was the day the Israelis had bombed the Iraqi nuclear reactor, waves of F-16s wheeling over the top-secret site on the outskirts of Baghdad, reducing the place to rubble. Nine years later, with the Iraqis back on the nuclear threshold, Saddam Hussein now offered the Palestinians fresh hope of driving the Israelis into the sea. Small wonder they were doing their best to help him.

Friedland made a note of the name of the new group, then glanced up again. 'So,' he said, 'we have a man with a tank in his boot. And we have some interesting plumbing. And we have a false exhaust-pipe . . .' He paused, frowning. 'We also have a nice view of Manhattan, and a brand-new Palestinian terror group . . .' He fell silent, his pen poised, his eyes gazing at the heavy folds of curtain. Outside in the street, the traffic was beginning to move again. He could hear the buses grinding down Piccadilly. Strictly first gear. Ross was looking at him carefully. The exchange was developing into a seminar. 'The Iraqis may have the bomb,' he said slowly. 'As you well know.'

'Yes.'

'So what else do they have?'

Friedland at last took his eye off the curtains, favouring Ross with a blank stare. If it pleased the younger man to patronize him, so be it.

'Gas?' he said mildly.

'Exactly.' Ross looked at him, saying nothing more, refusing to elaborate, waiting for Friedland to catch up.

Friedland, compliant as ever, obliged. 'The Iraqis have nerve gas,' he said slowly, 'and the Palestinians have a new terror group . . . and someone in New York has a tank in his car boot, and probably a diffuser too, and a video-camera to show the world . . .'

'Quite.'

'So—' Friedland frowned. '—we might reasonably infer . . . might we not . . . that whatever they've got planned for Manhattan . . .?' He broke off and shrugged, letting the point make itself. The Americans were sending troops into Saudi Arabia. The Prime Minister would doubtless follow suit, and when that happened, Oxford Street would be as legitimate a target as Broadway. Friedland looked at Ross and raised a single eyebrow.

Ross nodded. 'We need to know what we're in for,' he said. 'Best case. Worst case. And we want the thing kept tight. So—' he shrugged, gesturing round '—I thought we'd commission a little research.'

Friedland nodded, unsurprised. 'Research' was the usual euphemism, code for the neatly typed reports that Ross seemed to thrive on, a mix of gossip, speculation and hard Intelligence that Friedland was able to cull from thirty years in the field. Evidently, the reports gave Ross bullets for the gun he carried to the endless round of Whitehall meetings. It meant that Downing Street had sources of its own and didn't have to rely on the official briefings. The Intelligence establishment hated the practice. They thought it close to treason.

Friedland looked Ross in the eye. 'How soon?' he said.

'Very soon. As soon as possible.'

Friedland frowned. It was a difficult commission. Doing it properly would take weeks of analysis. 'Why don't you ask the Americans?' he said mildly. 'That might be productive.'

Ross looked at him, saying nothing, favouring the suggestion with a chilly half-smile. Then, abruptly, he stood up. 'Seventy-two hours,' he said, heading for the door.

*

McVeigh sat alone in his flat, the window half-open. The rain had gone now and the night was warm. Down the street, several houses away, the kids from the Poly were having a party. Heavy Metal. Iron Maiden. Mercifully low.

McVeigh reached down for his glass and swallowed a mouthful of Guinness. He drank rarely during the week. Clients didn't like it, and they had a point. It took the edge off you. It slowed you down. Tonight, though, was different. Tonight, for the first time he could remember, he'd lost Billy. The kid had gone away from him, in his head, where it mattered most. When McVeigh had dropped him off at his ex-wife's house over in Highgate, the child had barely said goodbye, turning up his cheek for the ritual kiss, his flesh cold to the touch. Then he'd run inside and slammed the door behind him, without even a backward glance.

McVeigh, hardened to most of life's surprises, had driven home with a pain in his belly, a thick, choking fury in the very middle of him, part grief, part something less easy to define. Outside the flat, he'd parked the car, let himself in, and retrieved his singlet and shorts from the line in the tiny square of back garden, then run north, against the gradient, twice his normal distance. At the top corner of Hampstead Heath, in the half-darkness of a London summer evening, he'd paused under the shadow of a copse of trees and done press-ups, sets and sets of them, first a hundred, then a pause, then a hundred more. The exercise and the run back had taken away the worst of the hurt, transforming it into a simple physical pain that he found infinitely more acceptable.

Fatherhood had never been easy, not when the child lived 4 miles down the road, yet each succeeding year it had become more and more important. Now, sitting by the open window, his bare feet on the sill, McVeigh knew the boy meant everything to him, the one part of his life he was determined to get right. Work had always been irregular, and he could never afford to turn jobs down, but whenever he was back home, Billy came to stay. At first, his ex-wife had muttered about routines and the inconvenience of it all, but McVeigh had fattened the maintenance he paid, knowing that money was a fair swop for something literally beyond price. The boy was his. He had the same brown eyes, the same blond hair, fine, short, dead-straight. He had the same laugh, the same way of holding his pen, his spoon. He ran like McVeigh, an easy lope, and lately his face had begun to change, shedding some of the puppiness of childhood, starting to acquire the square jaw and the high, angular cheekbones that McVeigh encountered every morning in the shaving-mirror. Billy was small for his age, but McVeigh had been that way too, and in the evenings, after football, when he sometimes fretted about it, McVeigh was able to grin, and give him a hug and tell him that yes, no question, he'd be at least 6 foot, just like his dad.

Now, emptying the last of the Guinness, McVeigh grinned again, the pain quite gone. The phone directory lay beside him on the floor. He reached down, switching on the small table-lamp, finding the number he wanted. Then he picked up the phone and dialled. The number answered at once, the embassy switchboard, a courteous male voice, lightly accented.

McVeigh closed his eyes, leaning back in the ancient leather chair, marvelling at how simple it all was, now that the boy had finally driven him to a decision. 'I'm a friend of Yakov Arendt's,' he said. 'And I'd like an appointment.'

2

That same evening, Tuesday 19 August, a small Cypriot-registered freighter called the *Enoxia* slipped up the River Scheldt from Vlissingen, puttered past the giant cranes of the new container terminal, entered the Tidal Basin and negotiated the tricky passage into one of the few remaining quays still used in Antwerp's inner harbour.

An hour later, a shipping agent arrived in an old Renault van and conferred briefly with the master on the dockside. An order was noted for fresh fruit and vegetables, a note made about a minor oil leak from one of the main bearings in the single prop-shaft. Arrangements were made to load a part-cargo at seven the following morning. The master was still trying to remember the French word for 'pesticide' when two of the half-dozen crew aboard shuffled down the gangway and headed for one of the nearby bars.

Past midnight, they were still there, sitting around a table playing cribbage. They were both Greeks, in their early twenties. One of them was quietly drunk, nursing his fourth glass of Stella Artois, playing his cards with a careless bravado, savouring this brief run ashore before the next leg of the voyage across the English Channel to Sheerness, and then the long haul south to the Maltese port of Valletta.

A stranger sat behind them at the bar, a slightly older man, Mediterranean, perhaps a little darker. In the smoky gloom, neither of the card-players took much notice. If they thought anything, they assumed he was – like them – a seaman, a thousand miles from home, killing time.

At half-past one, the stranger approached the table. He spoke to them in French. Neither man understood. He picked up the small bundle of notes in the middle of the table and pocketed them. Then he walked out.

The smaller of the seamen went after him. Outside in the street, he found the man at the kerbside, counting the notes, looking for a cab. The seaman tried to grab the notes. The stranger, a bigger man, solid, fended him off. The seaman kicked him hard on the side of the knee. The stranger folded the notes into his jeans' pocket and turned on the sailor, pinning him against the metal shutters of the shop next to the bar. Then he beat him senseless, with short, economical jabs to the body and head, one hand holding him steady, the other doing the damage, the shutters rattling with each new blow.

The incident was over in less than a minute. The Greek sailor slumped unconscious against the shop-front, his nose broken, his jaw shattered, his breathing barely audible to the frightened shipmate kneeling beside him on the wet cobble-stones, waiting for the ambulance. In the log of the local police station, a gaunt two-storey building 3 kilometres away, the incident formed a one-line entry in the midnight–6 o'clock shift. 'Assault,' read the terse, handwritten scrawl. 'No witnesses.'

Next morning, a big Mercedes truck arrived on the quayside. In the back, under a tightly roped tarpaulin, were 180 5-gallon drums. Each drum was painted red, with carefully stencilled warnings on the side and lid. The warnings, in English and German, read 'Pesticide. Dangerous Chemical. Handle with care'.

The loading took nearly two hours. By midday, the freighter had slipped her moorings and was pursuing the last of the ebb-tide towards Vlissingen and the open sea. On the bridge, behind the wheel, the first mate was still waiting for the replacement crewman to confirm the tally of drums onloaded from the Mercedes truck. On the dockside, there'd been some confusion. The manifest said 180. There appeared to be 181.

Passing the lighthouse at Walcheren, the new crewman finally appeared in the wheelhouse. He'd come through the agent, highly recommended. They'd been lucky to get him at such short notice. The first mate glanced over his shoulder and asked him the score. The new crewman, a young Dutchman with a radical crew-cut and tiny tattoos behind each ear-lobe, gazed out through the salt-caked bridge windows. 'One hundred and eighty,' he said thoughtfully. 'Like the manifest says.'

*

The interview in New York was, as the old man had been promised, merely a formality.

He took the train in from New Jersey, half-past ten, the worst of the commuter hour over. He walked the six blocks from Grand Central Station, keeping himself in the very middle of the sidewalk, trying to avoid the beggars lounging against the shiny, over-stocked shop-fronts. Just once, he stopped to check the map he'd been given and to re-read the letter. The interview was to take place at eleven-fifteen. He was to check in at reception and ask for Mr Aramoun. His work permit and his certificates, already sent with the job application, would be returned during the course of the interview.

The old man folded the letter into the pocket of his jacket and began to walk again. The jacket, brand-new, felt stiff and hot. His slacks, too, and the 100-dollar lace-up shoes and the diamond-patterned tie were all wrong. He felt like a parcel, ribboned and addressed by someone else. Abu Yussuf, he told himself for the hundredth time. That's your name. That's who you really are. Abu Yussuf.

The office building, number 1831, was on the corner of 18th Street and Avenue of the Americas. The old man paused outside, his head back, looking up at the sheerness of it, the unbroken wall of black glass. He began to count the floors, eyes narrowed against the brightness of the sun, but he gave up at forty, shaking his head, dizzy with the heat and the noise and the sour, slightly metallic taste of high summer in New York. Forty floors, he thought. And still less than halfway up.

He walked cautiously into the sudden cool of the reception hall. The place was walled in flecked grey marble. He was pursued towards the reception desk by the sound of his own footsteps, very loud. He was searched at a low rope barrier by a black security guard. The man looked into his eyes as the hands parted his jacket and raced lightly over his torso. He knows already, the old man thought. He knows I'm really Abu Yussuf. He knows the immigration papers are fake. He knows.

At the reception desk, he produced the letter again. The receptionist checked on a telephone and directed him to the wall of elevators. Listed beside the call buttons were the names of the tenant companies. There were dozens of them. He searched for the company on the sixty-fifth floor and found it almost at once. Impex (Beirut), it read. It looked new, cleaner than the rest, handsome lettering, white on blue.

Minutes later, calmer now, he sat in a corner office on the sixty-fifth floor stirring tiny pellets of saccharine into a cup of black coffee. Until now, he'd never tasted saccharine in his life, never dreamed that so much sweetness could come from such a tiny thing. It was an astonishment to him, a real discovery, one of the thousands of toys with which this strange, rich, eager society had overwhelmed him. Saccharine. Sweeteners. One hundred and fifty in a box, and less than a dollar fifty.

The man across the desk, Mr Aramoun, finished writing on the pad before him. He looked up, pocketing the pen. The two men had already shaken hands, a light, dry touch, a scent of after-shave, the smell of lemons. He spoke in Arabic, with a Lebanese accent. He smiled. 'You like New York?'

'Very much.'

Mr Aramoun looked at him, the smile widening. 'Not like Ramallah, eh?'

'No.'

Mr Aramoun eased back in the chair, turning it slightly, favouring the long chasm of 18th Street with a slightly proprietorial glance, the busy, successful New Yorker with the city at his feet. 'Very hot today. Stinking hot. Horrible month, August . . .'

The old man nodded, aware already of the role in which he had been cast, the recently arrived immigrant, one of the stateless brothers, the *dafawim*, orphans from the West Bank, victims of the Zionist storm, derided by Arabs and Israelis alike. Trash, thought the old man. He thinks I'm trash, just like the boy back in New Jersey thinks. He thinks I'm good for the janitor's job, good with the plumbing and the cable runs and mopping up the office spills. But not much else.

The old man put his hands together in his lap, aware of how big they were, how clumsy they must look in this huge office with its wall-to-wall carpet and its big pictures and its low crescent of padded leather sofa. Mr Aramoun bent briefly to a form on the desk, reaching for his pen again. Looking at the form, screwing up his eyes, the old man could just recognize his own writing.

'You've been here three months?'

'Yes.'

'You have a place to live?'

'Yes. In Newark.'

'Good place? Comfortable?'

The old man nodded, eager to please, thinking of the corner tenement, the plastic bags of refuse on the street outside, savaged by the neighbourhood cats, the endless flights of broken stairs, the smell of the place.

'It's fine,' he said. 'It's all I need.'

'And you plan to stay around? Put in some time with us?'

'Yes.' The old man did his best to smile. 'Yes, of course.'

Mr Aramoun nodded, making notes on the pad. The pen paused. He looked up. 'We have the whole floor here. That's twenty-three offices. We may expand some more. There's the place to be kept clean, there's help with security, there's help in the mail-room, there's help for the folk who take care of the catering operation, coffees, teas, all kinds of beverage.' He leaned forward. 'You think you can handle that?'

'Yes.'

Mr Aramoun nodded slowly. The old man waited. This was where the interview would lead. Ask about the money, they'd said. Complain a little. Haggle. He'll want you for nothing, so do it the New York way. Show him what you've learned in your three brief months. Don't make it too easy for him.

The old man coughed, already embarrassed. 'The money . . .' he began.

Mr Aramoun lifted a finger, cutting him short. 'It's low,' he said quickly, 'very low. I know that. But do a good job for us, and it'll get better . . .' He smiled. 'Much better.'

He got up and held out his hand, and the old man looked up at him, blinking, ready with his little speech, realizing suddenly that the interview was over, and the job was his, and his coffee was only half-finished.

The old man got up and shook the proffered hand, muttering his thanks, and made a tiny bow, backing awkwardly towards the door. Mr Aramoun turned away, one hand already reaching for the phone, telling him to fix a start date with the secretary in the office down the hall.

Afterwards, back at Grand Central, the old man found a pay-phone and called the number, as agreed. The number answered. It was the young boy again. Since he'd lost his job, he was always there. He never went out.

'The job,' the old man said gruffly. 'They liked me. I got it.'

*

Coming out of the Embassy, looking for a cab in the stream of traffic pouring down Palace Gardens, McVeigh was still thinking about Yakov.

He'd just spent half an hour with a youngish Israeli called Rafael in a sparsely furnished room on the third floor. Rafael, who'd evidently known and liked Yakov, had said he was sorry about his friend's death. It had come, he'd said, as a shock to all of them. Yakov had been working at the Embassy for nearly a year. His posting was due to end in the autumn. He'd been popular with his colleagues, a bit of a clown sometimes, but a man with a soul, too, a man who liked to shoulder the troubles of others, a man to go to when times got rough. Quite why he'd died was anyone's guess, but Rafael's own belief was that Yakov had been mistaken for someone else, someone perhaps not from the Embassy at all.

McVeigh had followed the low monotone without comment, only interrupting at the end to wonder who it might have been to pull a gun in a residential London square, broad daylight, *lunch-time* for God's sake, and execute a killing with such cold efficiency.

41

At this Rafael had nodded, suddenly sombre, his eyes straying to the window with its distant glimpse of Hyde Park. His voice fell even lower, a murmur, but the words he used and the shapes his hands made in the space between them left McVeigh in no doubt that London – Europe – was a jungle, a battlefield for international terrorists, most of them Arabs. In this ceaseless blood-letting, Israelis were often targets of simple opportunity. Killing Israelis, he said, was a day's work for a half-dozen Palestinian terror groups he could identify by name. It was a constant threat, a constant possibility, and if you happened to be Israeli, then you did what you could to avoid getting shot. But sometimes, just sometimes, they got lucky, and when that happened, and someone you knew and loved got killed, then it was horrible, like a death in the family.

Yakov had been a real friend, a special man, and now he was gone. His wife had already flown over from Tel Aviv. She'd returned to Israel only yesterday, with her husband's body in the hold of the big El Al 747. At the Embassy, during her visit, they'd done what they could to soften the blow. Mercifully, there'd been no children.

But as for the rest of it? Rafael had smiled, a smile of resignation, shepherding McVeigh towards the door. Scotland Yard were very good, he'd said. As a police force, they had the Israelis' genuine respect. If there was any possibility of finding whoever had killed Yakov – if – then they were the men to do it. McVeigh had hesitated at this, standing by the lift, wondering quite how to end the conversation, whether to reminisce about his son's dead friend, his passion for football, his talent with the kids, or to enquire a little more deeply into his real role at the Embassy, what he was there for, what he actually did. But when the lift rumbled upwards and the doors sighed open, and Rafael offered a handshake, all he finally managed was a smile and a muttered word of thanks. 'Nice bloke,' he said, as the lift doors closed between them. 'Real shame.'

Now, sitting in the back of a taxi heading east towards Victoria, McVeigh recognized the exchange for what it had really been: an expression of sympathetic regret, half an hour of routine condolence devoid entirely of the kind of information he'd come to find. Foolish, he thought, to expect anything else. Rafael, after all, had got it about right. The Israelis were permanently in a state of war. Here. In Europe. At home. Everywhere.

The taxi dropped him outside a pub in Buckingham Gate. The saloon bar was already crowded with lunch-time drinkers. Towards the back, the usual place, he found the man he'd come to see, the man he'd phoned first thing, home number, still in bed, his new wife already complaining in the background.

The man looked up and nodded a greeting. He was in his middle thirties, once athletic, now beginning to run to fat. The pint glass beside the folded copy of the *Daily Mail* was nearly empty. McVeigh reached for it and went to the bar. He ordered a plate of sandwiches and two packets of crisps. The other man eyed the crisps when he finally sat down.

'Fucking à la carte again?' he said, reaching for the beer.

They talked for nearly an hour. The other man, George, confirmed what little he'd told McVeigh on the phone. The Met had mounted an immediate investigation into the Queen's Gate killing and set up an incident room at the Yard. Given the circumstances, it looked political, so they'd pulled in a couple of blokes from the Anti-Terrorist Unit, and opened lines to the MI5 boys, and run traces on the more visible of the likely hit-men. All told, including the clericals, the team had numbered over twenty, and they'd got as far as a short list of four suspects when the bell had gone, and the referee had stepped into the ring, and it was suddenly all over.

At this McVeigh looked at him, bemused. Three difficult years in the Marine Corps Investigation Branch had given him a kinship with George, but recently he was beginning to wonder. Promotion hadn't come the way it should, and the drink was playing havoc with his language.

'What do you mean?' he said, 'referee?'

George eyed him over the rim of his glass. There wasn't much of his third pint left.

'It's all over,' he said. 'Fight's off.'

'Off?'

'Yeah, cancelled. Incident room's closed. Team's disbanded. Person or persons unknown. You know the way it goes.'

'But you hadn't even started.'

'Fucking right.'

'So how do they justify that?'

'You tell me.'

George tipped back the glass, emptying it, eyes looking for the big clock on the wall behind the bar. The glass back on the table, he slumped back in the chair, shoulders hunched, hands deep in the pockets of his raincoat. There was an etiquette in these meetings of theirs, gesture and response, but McVeigh made no attempt to pick up the glass.

'But why?' he said again. 'Tell me why.'

George shrugged. After three pints he got difficult. After four, it would be simple aggression. Once, in the Marines, it had been a laugh. Now, it had ceased to be funny.

McVeigh put the question a third time. 'Why?'

'Dunno.'

'Yes, you do. Or you'll have theories. Bound to.'

George shrugged. 'Suits fucking someone,' he said. 'But you tell me who.'

McVeigh nodded, pondering the proposition. 'Who's in charge?' he said, looking up.

George burped noisily and named a Detective Chief Superintendent they both knew, Harry Quinton, a slightly older man whose short-cuts were legendary but whose clear-up rate had earned the cautious admiration of the bosses on the eleventh floor. George drank with him sometimes, evenings, and played snooker at a smoky hall in Bethnal Green. Given the circumstances – a shooting in broad daylight, no real investigation – Harry would have had some definite thoughts about it all, and it was inconceivable that George wouldn't have had to share them.

McVeigh eyed the empty glass for a moment. It was half-past two. 'Harry . . .' he prompted.

George looked at him. 'Gutted,' he said. 'Well fucked.'

'But what did he say?'

There was a long silence. Then McVeigh got up and went to the bar. With the fourth pint he ordered a treble Scotch. George watched him carrying them back. He was forward now in the chair, his voice low, his body bent in towards the table. McVeigh put the drinks down between them. George ignored them. McVeigh took a second or two to place the new tone in his voice. It was anger. 'What's the interest?' he said. 'Why all this?'

McVeigh thought briefly of Billy. Explaining all that was complicated, and he wasn't sure that George would follow. He'd never been good with kids.

'I've got a client,' he said.

'Foreign?'

'No.'

'Domestic?'

'Very.'

'OK.'

George glanced round. The pub was beginning to empty. He beckoned McVeigh closer. McVeigh obliged, listening without comment while George told him what he knew. Harry, he said, had somehow pissed off the Israelis. He didn't know how, and neither did Harry, but the cooperation he'd been getting from Palace Gardens had been withdrawn. The bloke who'd died, Arendt, had evidently been a Mossad man. That was the way the MI5 boys had told it. He'd been Mossad since the mid-eighties, and good at it, a *katsa*, a Case Officer, one of only a handful world-wide.

McVeigh, listening, nodded. Mossad was the Israeli Secret Service. They were the best in the business, Israeli's eyes and ears. Some of the strokes they pulled were beyond belief. No wonder the man had played football with such guile.

George, glass in his hand, went on. Arendt had been Mossad, and Harry – at the very least – now had a motive. Whoever did it had a thing about Israeli spooks. Which only left about half a million Arab hit-men, every one of them longing for a Mossad notch on the butt of his gun. McVeigh nodded again, remembering Rafael, the Israeli at the Embassy, same theory, same conclusion. He frowned, watching George swallow the last of the Scotch. The beer was still untouched. 'So where's the catch?' he said. 'If it's all that simple?'

George looked at him for a moment, on the edge of some private decision. Then he leaned forward again. 'We had a witness,' he said. 'Bloke owns an antique shop. Off Queen's Gate Gardens. Saw the whole thing. Apparently there was a big argument beforehand. Before the bloke got stiffed.'

'What about?'

'He couldn't hear. Not properly. But that's not the point.'

'No?'

'No. The point is the language. The language they were using.'

'What was it?'

George hesitated again. Then he reached for the beer. 'Hebrew,' he said, wiping his lips.

McVeigh looked at him for a moment, weighing it up. Then he shrugged. 'So the Arab speaks Hebrew,' he said. 'Big deal.'

'This was *good* Hebrew. The real thing.'

'So?' McVeigh said again. 'The Arab speaks good Hebrew. So what?'

George gazed at him for a long moment, and McVeigh recognized the signs, the impatience, the hands beginning to clench, the fist coming down on the table, the beer dancing in the glass. Instead, though, George leaned forward again, another card to play.

'Two days ago,' he said, 'Harry gets a phone call. The investigation's dead in the water. The heat's off. He's back to fucking traffic offences. But the phone still rings.'

'Who is it?'

'Israeli woman. Arendt's wife.'

'What's she want?'

'A meet. She wants to meet Harry. She's got his name from the Embassy, or the press, or some fucking place, and she wants to buy him dinner. The works. Wheeler's. Lobster. Champagne. You name it.'

'So what happens?'

'What do you think happens? You know Harry. He loves all that. Loves it. So he goes. Meets the woman. Fills his face.

Expects . . . you know . . . something to happen . . . information . . . a name . . . a lead . . . someone to put in the frame . . .'

'And?'

'Fuck all. It's the *woman* does all the asking. She spends all night trying to find out how far Harry had got, where he'd been, who he'd talked to, all that. Says she wants revenge.'

'So what happened?'

'Harry tells her fuck-all. Gets pissed. Goes home. End of story.'

George took a long pull at the beer, and McVeigh watched him, trying to picture the scene, thinking about Harry Quinton, the appetite on the man, how greedy he was. 'Tell me something,' he said slowly. 'Did Harry try it on at all?'

'Of course.'

'And?'

'Nothing. Dead loss. Shame, really. Apparently she was something else . . .' George grinned for the first time, his mouth slack, his eyes bright. He was obsessed with women and had three failed marriages to prove it.

'So tell me . . .' McVeigh said. 'Tell me what she looked like.'

'The Israeli's wife? Harry's little widow?'

'Yes.'

George grinned again, remembering Harry's description, reminting the phrases, good as new. 'She was blonde. Tall. Not fat. Wonderful arse on her. Great face. Great lips, you know, just built for it. Big figure. Really big. Had Harry creaming his knickers . . . poor bastard . . .'

McVeigh looked at him for a while, letting the words sink in. Then he got up and thanked George for his time, and turned on his heel, heading for the door and the street outside, remembering Yakov's sheaf of photos, his wife, the small, attractive figure. The cap of jet-black hair, the big smile. Cela.

At the door he hesitated for a moment. Then he was away, out into the street and the bright August sunshine, smiling.

*

Telemann arrived at La Guardia late, the Eastern shuttle to New York delayed an hour on the tarmac back in Washington. 'ATC grid-lock,' the captain had told the passengers with a resigned apology. 'Second time this week.'

At La Guardia, Telemann was met by the guy he'd already conferenced on the secure line. In the flesh, he was quite unlike the impression he'd made on the phone. The voice had been deep, thoughtful, sure of itself, and Telemann had imagined someone older, bulkier, a little slow on his feet maybe, a little overweight. The figure by the baggage carousel was none of those things. He was small, thin, sallow, with a watchful expression and a hint of Latin blood behind the over-trimmed moustache and the soft brown eyes. He looked young, too, no more than thirty-five, a tribute to a man already perched in the upper reaches of the New York Police Department.

Telemann extended a hand, still not quite sure. 'Mr Benitez?' he said.

The other man smiled. 'Alfredo,' he said.

The two men shook hands, then walked quickly through the crowded concourse and out on to the pick-up area. At the kerbside was an unmarked Chevvy with a dent in the rear wing. Behind the wheel sat another man, black. Like Benitez, he wasn't wearing uniform.

They drove into Manhattan across the Triborough Bridge, then headed downtown on the East River Memorial Drive. At First and 30th, they pulled left into the Bellevue Hospital. They took the elevator to the basement and walked along the corridor to the morgue.

By now, Telemann had confirmed the worst of it. The incident at the Manhattan Plaza had been investigated by a small core-team of four. By the time the bodies had arrived at Bellevue and the autopsy procedures had been completed, the clinical trial had gone cold. The investigating pathologist could find nothing helpful in the way of residues or specific organ damage. The couple in the hotel bathroom had evidently died of respiratory failure, but no obvious causal mechanism had shown up.

So far so good, but there were two other pieces of evidence. One of them was the maid from Housekeeping who'd first discovered the bodies. She'd collapsed outside the bathroom, but survived. As best she could, she'd described her symptoms, and these had gone into the file. The other piece of evidence was an aerosol recovered from the bathroom floor. According to the label, it contained shaving-foam. It had been sealed inside a polythene bag and hand-carried to the NYPD forensic laboratories. Already suspicious, the investigating technicians had put on full protective clothing, including face-masks, before analysing the contents. The analysis had occupied four difficult hours, but by the end of the afternoon there was absolutely no doubt about their conclusions. The liquid inside the aerosol was dimethylaminoeth-oxy-cyanophosphinne oxide. The stuff was virtually colourless, with a faintly fruity smell. The standard military abbreviation was Tabun GA. Most people called it nerve gas.

Telemann followed Benitez into the morgue. Forty-five minutes in the car from La Guardia had already given him a respect for the man. He was quiet, thoughtful, undramatic. Days back, after the aerosol analysis, he'd already understood the need for discretion, for secrecy, for ring-fencing the investigation, keeping it away from the media, from the politicians, even from his own colleagues. Mercifully, the NYPD had never had to deal with nerve gas before. Nor, for that matter, had there ever been much call for measures against anthrax or hand-portable nuclear bombs. But these weapons existed, and the threat was therefore credible, and now that one version of the nightmare had come to pass, he'd known at once that the secret must – at all costs – be kept safe. In all, eleven people knew enough to make them a risk. Each one he'd seen personally, spent time with them, explained the public order consequences of loose tongues and wild rumours. The investigation, naturally, was proceeding. But the cause of death was still, in official terms, unknown.

The two men walked into an ante-room of the big six-slab autopsy theatre. The room was tiled entirely in white. The light was harsh from the overhead neon strips, and there was a strong smell of bleach. One of the walls was occupied by a bank of tall refrigerators. Benitez nodded a greeting to an attendant, murmuring a name, and waited while the man opened one of the fridge doors. Inside, racked on metal trays, were half a dozen bodies. The attendant pulled out a tray near the bottom. Inside the clear polythene bag was a man in his early forties. His head lay to one side, mouth slightly open, and except for the long autopsy incision his body was unmarked. He looked fit, well made, in good shape, though the tan on his chest and his legs was beginning to fade.

Telemann looked at him for several moments before turning away. Ten years in the CIA had taken him to places like these all over the world – the same smell, the same low background whirr from the big white fridges – yet he'd never quite got used to the sight of a corpse. Badly damaged, by a bomb or a beating or a cleverly worked traffic accident, and it was sometimes easier to cope with. But like this, a man asleep in a plastic bag, it was hard, and gazing down he knew yet again that it was true what they said. Look a dead man in the face and you see your own funeral, your own end.

Telemann shook his head and glanced up at Benitez. Most of the details he already knew. Lennox C. Gold. Forty-one years old. An avionics consultant from San Antonio Heights, California, a hands-on-engineer who'd smelled the big money and left the development laboratories in the San Bernadino Valley with a headful of knowledge and a firm bead on the upmarket end of the American dream. Much of his experimental work had been for Department of Defense programmes, some of them sensitive, and his commercial activities had twice rung bells with the security agencies. He'd been duly investigated and placed under surveillance, but on both occasions nothing much had turned up. The guy was greedy, and ambitious, and worked like a demon, but on all three counts that simply made him a good American. Telemann looked down at him again, wondering. 'The name . . .' he mused. '. . . Gold.'

Benitez glanced up. He'd been reading another autopsy report, something unrelated.

Telemann nodded at the body between them. 'Jewish?'

Benitez frowned. 'Sure.'

'Should that matter?'

'Maybe. You've seen the security reports. He's certainly been talking to the Israelis, but so he should. They're good customers.'

Telemann nodded. Lennox Gold had secured contracts with

two separate divisions of the Israeli Aircraft Industry. His speciality was Electronic Counter-Measures, ECM, the shell of hi-tech electronic emissions that cocooned the latest generation of fighter planes from the attentions of enemy missiles. In today's dog-fights, no pilot could survive without them. R & D-wise, the US still led the field, and Gold had the inside track. To the Israelis, always looking for the edge, his knowledge would have been invaluable.

Benitez looked thoughtful. He was still gazing at the body in the bag. 'You're looking for a motive?'

'Maybe.'

'You think he got too close to the Israelis?'

'It's possible.'

'Close enough for someone to want to kill him?'

Telemann shrugged but said nothing. No one from New York knew anything about the message from Amman. That, for the time being, was the tightest Federal secret of all. He nodded at the fridge. 'What about the girl?'

The attendant glanced at Benitez and slid out another tray, immediately above Gold's. The body in the bag was smaller, whiter. She had curly brown hair, shoulder-length, and a little of her lipstick had survived the attentions of the pathologist. She had a good figure, long legs, and her knees were slightly bent, drawn up towards her belly, a pose that lent her a strange innocence. The stitching on the long autopsy incision from her throat to her belly was as neat as Telemann had ever seen. Normally, no one put much effort into it. An autopsy, after all, wasn't something you ever survived. But the work on this girl was different. Someone must have seen what Telemann had seen. Someone must have cared.

Benitez was picking his teeth. 'Elaine Fallaci,' he said, 'Italian hooker. Successful. Freelanced for an agency on the Lower East Side. They work the diplomatic crowd a lot. That's serious money.'

'She live in town?'

'Sure. Small apartment. East 74th. Overlooks the Park . . .' He smiled. 'That's how good she must have been.'

Telemann nodded, his eyes still on the girl. Something about

51

her reminded him of his own wife, a decade and a half back, that summer they first met at the University of San Diego. He'd always regarded their life together as one of God's bigger miracles, infinitely delicate, infinitely precious. The fact that this girl was dead disturbed him more than it should. Mortality, he thought again. Hers. Mine. Laura's.

He glanced up at Benitez. 'You say he'd met her before?'

'A lot.'

'How many times?'

'Double figures.'

'Who says?'

'The agency.'

'They keep records?'

'Yes.'

'They give them to you?'

'Yes.'

'Why?'

'They want to stay in business.' Benitez smiled a thin smile. 'And the girls aren't keen on dying.'

Telemann nodded, accepting the point. 'You talked to the girls?' He nodded at the tray. 'They tell you anything?'

'Not much. It's quite common to keep a handful of steadies. Better the devil you know . . .' Benitez trailed off, still looking at the dead girl. Then he shrugged and glanced up at Telemann again. 'He was a businessman. Flew in regularly. Met people around town. Serious guy. Hard worker. Very straight up. Nothing kinky. Nothing violent. Treated her nice. Strictly cash. Two hundred bucks an hour. No hassling for deals . . .' He paused again. 'Shame about the aerosol.'

They exchanged glances and stepped back from the bodies, and Telemann heard the rumble from the rollers and the soft clunk of the door as they turned away and the attendant tidied up. Back outside the morgue, sitting in the car, Telemann wound down the window. The driver had disappeared inside the hospital in search of a Coke machine. For late evening, it was still very hot.

'The aerosol . . .' Telemann prompted. 'Anything fresh?'

Benitez nodded slowly. 'Yes,' he said.

'You've traced it?'

'Yes.'

Telemann leaned forward from the back-seat, his arms resting on the back of the driver's seat, cradling his chin. Three days' intensive work in Washington – page after page of eyes-only Intelligence clattering in over the secure data lines – had simply convinced him that the investigation was presently a matter of focus, of finding something tiny, something simple. Before he went to Tel Aviv, before he touched base again with his Mossad buddies, before he walked into the swamp, he had to make sure there wasn't something far more obvious staring him in the face. He smiled, looking at Benitez in the gathering darkness, knowing at last that he'd been right. There *was* something far more obvious. The goddamn aerosol.

'So,' he said, remembering the colour prints faxed up from New York, 'we have an aerosol. Supposedly full of shaving-foam. Actually full of nerve gas . . .' He paused. 'His? Or hers?'

'Neither.'

'No?'

'No.' Benitez was smiling now. 'The aerosol was in the bathroom before they arrived. Along with the soap and the shampoo and the shower-cap. The hotel supply them. It's part of the service.' He paused. 'Compliments of the management.'

Telemann nodded. 'So who services the room?'

'Cleaning crews. There are three of them. We pulled in the one that did Room 937 the day our friend booked in. Woman for Queens. Hispanic.'

'And?'

Benitez looked at him for a moment, then shook his head. 'Nothing. She says she did the room the same as always. Aerosols came out of a pack. Could have been any one of twenty-four.'

'You believe her?'

'Yeah.' He nodded. 'She was the one who discovered the bodies next day. Right there. In the bathroom.' He paused. 'Would you do that? If you knew?'

Telemann smiled, accepting the point. 'So what are you saying? Someone swopped them?'

'Yeah. After she'd fixed the room.'

'Knowing Gold had booked in?'

'Sure.'

There was a long silence. Telemann was frowning now, his chin in his hands, propped on the back of his seat. The night the girl arrived from the agency, it had been late. Gold had already eaten. The paperwork from room service proved it. The girl had gone up there, the usual booking, an hour or so, and they'd fucked on the bed a little and maybe gone to the bathroom, Gold still eager for it, a variation or two, her call, or his, still time on the meter, and there on the shelf, the complimentary white aerosol with the red and blue logo, menthol-fresh. She would have reached for it, and gone down on her knees and given him a squirt or two, decorating him maybe, or scrolling some nonsense across his belly, the way he probably said he liked it, but instead of the blobby dots of white foam, and another half-hour or so of lazy screwing, there'd been a thin colourless mist and the far-away smell of rotting fruit, and quickly – in seconds – that long paragraph of symptoms Telemann had by now committed to memory. The nose beginning to run. The tightness in the chest. The bathroom going dim around them, the edges of the shower blurring, the light beginning to fade. Then the first real struggles to breathe, their mouths wide open, their lungs gasping for air. Pretty soon now, their bodies out of control, they'd start to vomit. They'd head for the door. They'd get cramps. They'd fall to the floor, totally haphazard, all control gone. There'd be piss and shit everywhere. Then they'd start to convulse. Time-wise, the literature was explicit. In a hotel bathroom, the door shut, their bodies touching, the sweet intimacy of heavy sex, they'd have been dead in less than a minute.

Telemann nodded slowly, imagining it all, the most horrible, least graceful of ends. 'So where did it come from?' he said softly. 'Who put it in the room?'

'Kid from Housekeeping.'

'How do you know?'

'He had access to the room. He drew the key that day. Four o'clock. After the booking had come in.'

'You talked to him?'

'No.'

'Why not?'

'He's gone.'

'Gone where?'

'We don't know . . .' Benitez paused. 'He disappeared the same night. Didn't show next morning . . .' He paused again for a moment. 'One theory says he may have gone home. We're trying to check.'

'Oh?' Telemann looked across at him. 'Where's home?'

There was a long silence. Telemann could see the white teeth in the dark mask of Benitez's face. The man was smiling again.

'Baghdad,' he said.

3

For the second time in a week, McVeigh picked up his son from school.

He parked in the usual place, sitting in the battered old Escort a yard or so up the hill from the corner shop where Billy always stopped for crisps and a can of something fizzy. He'd already phoned his ex-wife, telling her not to bother with the school run, and they'd talked for a moment or two about what might be wrong with the boy. Billy had stopped talking. All the spirit, all the laughter had gone out of him. He was listless and disinterested. He was off his food. He'd even abandoned his nightly session in front of the television, feeding his library of football games into the video-machine, playing and replaying his favourite goals.

His mother had tried to talk to him about it, hoping to fathom this sombre new mood of his, but she'd got nowhere. The boy had simply listened to her questions, shrugged his shoulders and gone upstairs. Three evenings alone had convinced her that something was terribly wrong. Now she wanted to know what.

McVeigh, listening, had been tempted to tell her about Yakov, about what the Israeli had meant to the boy, but in the end he'd decided against it. One of the many reasons their marriage had finally disintegrated was McVeigh's job, his involvement in a world she neither understood nor trusted. Any suggestion that this same world might somehow reach out for Billy, too, would simply compound the problem.

Now, sitting in the car, McVeigh watched the first of the school-kids pouring out through the big brick gates. The school was private, a curious, off-beat little institution with a free-wheeling, progressive regime tailor-made for kids like Billy, with his father's talent for failing exams. Private education conflicted with everything that McVeigh believed in, and the fees were costing him a fortune, but even he had finally accepted the obvious. For Billy, at least, the place was a godsend.

The boy appeared at the school gates. He was alone. He glanced up and down the road, looking for his mother's white Citroën. Not seeing it, he began to walk up the hill, towards the corner shop. McVeigh slipped off the hand-brake, coasting slowly down the road, hugging the kerb. On the seat beside him was a can of Lilt and a packet of Bovril crisps. Billy saw the car and a brief smile ghosted across his face. McVeigh stopped. The boy got in.

They drove back along the usual route, Highgate Hill, Hornsey Lane. McVeigh asked him about school. The boy grunted, monosyllabic answers, the bare minimum. Outside the flat McVeigh stopped, killing the engine. Billy reached automatically for the door. The crisps lay untouched on the dashboard. McVeigh pulled him back. The boy looked startled for a moment, then resigned, already knowing what was to follow. McVeigh frowned, part-caution, part-irritation.

'Your mother's worried,' he said.

'What?'

'Your mum. She's worried. She thinks you're not well.'

'I'm OK.'

'I don't think you're right, either.'

'I'm fine.'

'You're not. And I know why.'

McVeigh looked at him for a moment, and the boy held his eyes for as long as it took to raise the colour in his cheeks. Then he shook his head, an expression of impatience or perhaps embarrassment. McVeigh leaned back against the car door, in no hurry. There was a dimension in this small moment of time that he understood all too well. Billy, his Billy, the face at the bedroom door, the grin on the pillow beside him, had collided with real life. And real life, with its inexplicable aches, its sudden pains, their causes, their effects, hurt.

Billy glanced across at his father, a hesitant, interrogative look, a question. McVeigh smiled, and reached for him, trying to put the answer into words. 'Yakov?' he suggested.

The boy said nothing, just nodded, agreeing. McVeigh grinned at him, trying to turn the corner, trying to change the mood. 'Want to know what I've done?'

Billy looked at him for a long moment, then shook his head. 'No.'

'No?' McVeigh frowned. '*No?*'

Billy fumbled for the door again. McVeigh stopped him. 'Why not?'

'Because . . .' Billy shrugged. 'I dunno . . .'

He trailed off lamely.

McVeigh, genuinely confused now, bent forward across the car. 'But, Billy,' he said, 'it's important.'

'What? What's important?'

'What happened. To Yakov.'

'I know.'

'Then listen, son. Listen.'

'Yes, Dad.'

'No, I mean it.'

'I know. I know you mean it. That's why—' He shrugged again. McVeigh, watching him carefully now, caught the tell-tale inflection, the voice still up, the thought stillborn.

'Why what?' he said softly. 'Tell me. Why what?'

'Why—' Billy gulped, a symptom McVeigh was at last able to recognize. Guilt. McVeigh leaned forward again, determined not to lose the advantage. Billy looked at him, defeated. 'Why I wrote the letter,' he said.

'What letter?'

'To Yakov's friends.'

'What friends?'

'At the Embassy. The place he works. They said it in the papers. They said he came from the Embassy. I looked it up. My friends helped me. I've got the address. I *wrote* to them.'

McVeigh nodded, following it all now, understanding it. 'And what did you say?'

There was a long silence. Then Billy grinned at him, the first grin in days, sunshine after the dark. 'I told them it was OK. I told them you'd find whoever did it.'

McVeigh looked at him. 'You told them *what*?'

'I said you'd—' he shrugged, delighted now, the secret out, his own little contribution, Yakov avenged '—I said you'd find the man, whoever it was—'

'And?'

'And kill him too.'

McVeigh blinked and began to protest, to frame another question, but Billy wasn't listening. He was out of the car and across the road, pushing in at the gate. He had the keys of the flat now, his own set, and he let himself in with another grin, tossed back over his shoulder, as his father locked the car and came after him.

Upstairs, Billy was sprawled in front of the television, fingering his way through the channels on the remote controller, still giggling. McVeigh asked him twice whether he'd been joking. Both times he said no. He'd posted the letter yesterday. He'd addressed it to Mr Ambassador. He'd written it out twice, once practice, once in fair, best handwriting, joined-up letters. He hadn't told his mother and he hadn't meant to tell McVeigh, but now his dad had found out, so it didn't really matter any more. The only thing that mattered was getting his own back on whoever had killed Yakov.

McVeigh stood in the doorway, teapot in one hand, kettle in the other, trying to compete with the kids from *Grange Hill*. 'You shouldn't have done it,' he said. 'You shouldn't have written.'

'But I had to.'

'No, you didn't.'

'Yes, I did.' He turned round, stretching lazily, the old Billy again. McVeigh looked at him for a moment, wondering what the Israeli diplomatic machine would make of a letter threatening constructive homicide from an eleven-year-old, knowing that – yet again – the boy was playing the Good Shepherd, penning him in, making the decision for him.

Grange Hill came to an end and the credits began to roll. Billy got up and said he was hungry. McVeigh returned to the kitchen. He had bread and jam, and half a packet of crumpets. Turning from the cupboard to start a question, he bumped into his son. Billy looked up at him, very close. 'You will find them, won't you? These men?'

McVeigh frowned for a moment, still in a muddle about the jam, whether Marmite might be better. Billy pulled out a stool and clambered on to it. He put his arms round McVeigh's neck, and McVeigh smelled the musty, slightly sour smell of the classroom. Billy asked the question, his nose touching McVeigh's. McVeigh shrugged. 'I dunno . . .' he said.

'No—' Billy held his eyes, refusing to let him go '—but you *will*, won't you?'

'I'll try.'

'And when you do?'

'Yeah?'

Billy raised two fingers, pressed together, the shape of a gun, and held them to his father's head.

'Bang,' he whispered, his mouth close to McVeigh's ear. 'Bang, bang.'

*

The fishermen finally deposited the small red drum marked 'Poison' on the quayside at Ramsgate, a cluttered little harbour on the eastern shoulder of the North Kent coast.

They'd spotted it shortly after midnight, low off the port quarter, most of it submerged in the confused lop of the cross-seas in the lee of the Goodwin Sands. One of the hands on deck thought it might be a mine, but in the glare of the big overhead lights it was difficult to be certain until they were close enough to read the heavy black stencil.

The skipper of the 40-foot trawler, a recent convert to ecological issues, supervised the capture of the drum. Lately, the Straits of Dover had begun to resemble the scene of a maritime disaster. Bits of rope, baulks of timber, assorted plastic debris, even whole containers came bobbing down the Channel on the flooding tide. At night especially, the larger objects could be lethal. When the weather and the trawl permitted, the skipper tried to do what he could.

The drum was secured to the side of the boat with ropes and

winched carefully aboard. When they berthed next morning at the fish dock in Ramsgate, it was the first object off. Midday, the night's catch already en route to the London markets, the skipper walked the quarter-mile to the harbour-master's office, reporting his find and staying just long enough to confirm that a reward was unlikely.

Later in the day, the harbour-master studied the drum. It was red, a little sturdier than usual, with the vertical seam double-welded, and thick welts around the top and bottom. There was a black diamond enclosing a death's-head on the side. Stencilled across the middle of the diamond, in heavy capitals, was the single word 'POISON'. Detailed information was normally coded beneath the warning, in keeping with international regulations, but in this case there was nothing. No ADR panel, no numbers to identify the specific contents or degree of risk. Simply two words in German at the bottom of the drum, '*Eigentum der . . .*', the rest of the sentence crudely painted over.

The harbour-master, who'd never seen a drum quite like this before, returned to his office and called the local fire service. He explained the situation and said he'd be glad for someone to take a look. He could see no leaks himself, but he'd prefer to be certain. The duty officer confirmed the details and promised to send an appliance. The call was logged at 15.53.

*

The old man, Abu Yussuf, turned his back on the hot glare of the street and stepped into the darkness of the garage. The place stank of oil and the sour tang of exhaust. With the light still off, he might have been back in Ramallah. He smiled, switching on the light and hanging his cap on the back of the door.

The tiny lock-up garage was three blocks from the tall row of Newark tenements that was, for the time being, home. He walked here every morning, already sweating in his overalls in the heat, soaking up time before he could start the new job in Manhattan. Quite why he'd been asked to secure the job, he didn't know. It had simply been orders, another terse phone call from Mohammad Kabbaul, the Damascus Arab, the one he'd listened to all those months ago back on the West Bank, the one who'd confirmed the way it had really been with his son, the one who'd promised him his very own helping of *jihad*. Holy war. Revenge.

The old man reached for a length of waste cotton and bent over the open trunk of the car. He'd chosen the car himself, a month and a half back, from a dusty street-corner lot over in Brooklyn. Kabbaul had come with him on that occasion and they'd taken a cab from Newark. Sitting in the back of the rattling Chevvy, the old man gazing out at the Manhattan skyline, Kabbaul explained what was to be done. They needed something anonymous, he'd said, something reliable. They'd take the car back to Newark, to a lock-up garage Kabbaul had rented, and there the old man was to start work. He was to install special equipment in the trunk. There had to be room in the trunk for a tank of liquid, some pipes, a pump and whatever else the old man might need. Kabbaul had said he was no engineer, but he thought it would have to be a big car.

It was. The old man had circled the used-car lot, looking at the models on display, the state of the tyres, the bodywork, the huge engines caked with oil under the propped-up hoods. Privately, he thought the prices outrageous, but Kabbaul had already told him that money didn't matter, and so in the end he'd chosen an '84 Oldsmobile for $2300, light tan, the long expanse of hood balanced by a huge trunk. It was the kind of car that littered the streets of Newark, or Brooklyn, or the Bronx. The old man had seen hundreds of them already, and knew it was perfect.

They'd driven the Oldsmobile back to Newark, the old man at the wheel. The car handled like a boat, swaying and yawing and dipping on the pot-holed roads. By the time they'd crossed Manhattan, he knew there was a problem with the rear shockers and made a mental note to do something about it, telling Kabbaul there'd be more money to spend. Kabbaul had shrugged the warning aside. 'It doesn't matter,' he'd said. 'You must make the car good for one journey. One journey only.'

The old man, confused, had asked why, negotiating the busy sliproad on to the New Jersey turnpike, half-listening while the

Arab told him what was to be done. Soon, he'd said, they'd take delivery of a sealed drum. In the drum would be a liquid. The drum was equipped with a special one-way valve. The old man's job would be to install the drum in the trunk of the Oldsmobile and figure out a method of getting the liquid out of the drum, turning it into some kind of mist, and piping it on to the streets outside. The old man, thinking already of the gear he'd use, how simple the proposition was, had asked about the liquid in the drum.

'What is it?' he'd said. 'What is this stuff?'

Kabbaul had said nothing for a moment, fingering the tarnished chrome trim around the door. Then he'd looked across at the old man. 'You remember Balata? The first time?'

The old man had nodded. Balata was a refugee camp near Nablus, an hour and a half north of Ramallah. The *Intifada* had started there after a two-day riot in Gaza. The old man hadn't seen it for himself, but the Israelis had applied the same tactics a thousand times since. Water-cannon. And riot sticks. And tear gas. And, when everything else failed, a sudden fusillade of bullets, totally indiscriminate, kids lying dead on the street. The old man had glanced across, safe now on the New Jersey pike.

'So what's the stuff?' he'd said again. 'The stuff in the trunk?'

'Gas.'

'What kind of gas?'

'Tear gas. The gas the Israelis use.'

The old man had nodded. The Israelis used the gas a lot, whenever there was trouble. He'd seen the spent canisters himself, lying on the street after yet another riot. Even empty, they still smelled vile, that sour, acrid, choking stench that reached inside your head and made your eyes burn, your tears fall. He'd been gassed himself, everyone had. It was the smell of early summer, the start of the season of riots, the hot, windy days when you only walked the streets with a damp handkerchief, something to cover your nose and mouth, just in case. The kids called it '*drat*', giggling. In Arabic, '*drat*' means farts, Israeli farts.

Pulling off the pike at the Newark Airport exit, the old man had brought the conversation to a close, one last question, aware of his own tiny role in this clever, clever plan of theirs. 'So I do the job in the trunk,' he'd said. 'What then?'

'Then we drive the car.'

'Where?'

'Here.'

'Here? In Newark?'

'No.' Kabbaul had nodded across to the left, towards the soaring cliffs of downtown Manhattan, a brief, contemptuous tilt of the head. 'There.'

Now, working in the airless garage, checking his seals, testing the wiring, the old man pondered the proposition again. The work on the car had been no problem. The drum of gas had yet to arrive, but he'd been given an empty replica. He'd examined the drum carefully. He'd never seen anything quite like it. It was heavier gauge steel than usual, and the vertical seam had been sealed with a double weld. The valve, likewise, was the work of someone who'd known what they were doing. It was heavy-duty, steel and brass, a 20-mm throat, properly seated.

His plans made, he'd measured the drum and built a retaining cradle in the trunk of the Oldsmobile, fitting it snugly against the rear bulkhead. He'd plumbed a route out of the drum, using 20-mm copper piping from a hardware store six blocks away. He'd bought a small, neat, high-pressure pump, and supplied it with a power-feed from the car's wiring-loom. From the pump, more piping led to a vaporizer he'd acquired from a garden centre up in Westwood. The stuff from the drum would be pumped into the vaporizer. The vaporizer would turn it into a thin mist. More pipe, galvanized steel, slightly larger bore, looped down from the vaporizer and disappeared through the floor pan of the trunk. Bracketed to the chassis of the Olds, it ran beside the car's exhaust-pipe, protruding slightly beneath the fender. To any passer-by, it looked like the work of an Olds enthusiast, some guy who wanted to stay ahead of the pack. Only the extra switch on the dash might invite unwelcome questions, but the old man had even done his best to camouflage this. 'Air Conditioning Boost' read the Dynotape label he'd stuck beneath the white switch. 'Depress to Activate.'

Looking at it now, he smiled. The label had been his idea, a late addition after he'd been able to view the video they'd made. It looked neater, more professional. He reached out and turned on the ignition. Then his finger strayed left, towards the white switch. The pump in the trunk began to hum, then the vaporizer cut in, and he walked round behind the car, looking down at the false exhaust-pipe. Only yesterday, he'd dismantled the one-way valve and filled the empty tank with water. Now he could see the fine mist of tiny droplets, a dark stain on the garage door, a metre or two from the back of the Olds. The stain spread and elongated. Water began to pool on the concrete floor.

The old man looked at it, wiping his hands on the cotton waste, feeling pleased with the job he'd done, how neat it was, how well it worked. Justice, he thought, remembering Ramallah again, the drifting clouds of tear gas, the faces masked by handkerchiefs, picturing the scenes at the kerbside over in Manhattan, smiling.

*

Sitting at his desk, Ross read the letter again. It was handwritten in a child's careful capitals. It was addressed to the Israeli Embassy, dated three days previous.

'Dear Mr Ambassador,' it began. 'Last week a friend of me and my dad's got killed. His name was Yakov. He was brilliant at football. He trained our team. Now my dad's going to find out who did it. My dad used to be in the Marines. He goes all over the world. He knows about guns and sometimes he carries one. I've seen it. When he finds the man, he'll kill him too . . .'

Ross paused, his finger on the last line. The letter, a photo-copy, had arrived in the midday bag from the Intercepts Office at Mount Pleasant, one of the derisory titbits the people at MI5 occasionally tossed his way. Mail addressed to a handful of key embassies was regularly screened, and some of it was permitted to filter through to Downing Street. Ross had always recognized the ploy for what it was, a gesture of contempt, an innocuous whiff or two of the real thing to keep the politicians happy, but he'd built a very successful career on other people's discarded opportunities, and now he sat back, gazing out of the window, wondering again about the man Arendt.

The killing itself had been brazen, broad daylight, Central London. The tabloids had run the pictures on the front page and there'd been plenty of outraged leaders about Middle Eastern terrorism spilling on to English streets. Elements in the Cabinet had been less than amused, and he'd seen memos urging a wide-ranging inquiry into the implications of Arendt's death. The latter had been firmly squashed by the Home Office, evidently at the request of the Israelis, and Ross now knew for certain that even the police investigation had, in the parlance, been allowed to wither on the vine. Quite why that should be so was anyone's guess, but Ross knew enough about the workings of the Intelligence community to suspect that it represented the settlement of some kind of debt. Someone important owed the Israelis. And now the favour had been returned.

Ross stood up and walked across to the big filing cabinet in the corner. The video was still in the bottom drawer. He loaded it on to the VCR and turned on the television. The images spooled through: the boot of the big American car, the tangle of pipework, the double exhaust, the gnarled old fingers pointing at the switch on the dashboard, then the view of Manhattan, the East River gleaming in the foreground, the big glass sweep of the UN building clearly visible. The screen went blank and he hesitated for a moment, one finger on the remote control, watching the pictures winding backwards, thinking again about the American, Sullivan.

He'd spoken to him twice in the last week. On both occasions the call had come from Washington, urgent decisions for the Cabinet about the military build-up in the Gulf. The Americans had abruptly rediscovered the merits of the United Nations, and they wanted a seamless stich-up in the Security Council. British cooperation was taken as read, and each of Sullivan's calls had simply added more items to the shopping list, but both times Ross had prolonged the conversation, wondering aloud about the terrorist threat, about the possibility of Saddam pre-empting the Americans and exporting the war to the West. He'd never mentioned the video directly, preferring to let Sullivan make the running, but the big American had only grunted at his suggestions, telling him he was paranoid, that the real war was in the Gulf, upfront, 100 per cent visible, the good guys versus the bad guys, yet another crusade for freedom and democracy. The terrorists were a fact of life, sure, but just now the only game in town was Desert Shield.

Ross, unconvinced, had pondered both conversations, certain that the Americans must have received a similar warning, maybe the same video, and now he returned to the desk, picking up the kid's letter, wondering whether there might – after all – be some kind of link between the killing of the Israeli and the pictures still spooling backwards on the VCR. What he needed, as ever, was a little independent advice, a little analysis untainted by either the Americans or, God forbid, the British Intelligence establishment. He studied the name on the bottom of the letter for a moment. The kid's father was evidently in the security business. He'd known the Israeli. He might respond to the right kind of invitation. Ross hesitated for a moment longer, then reached for the telephone. His secretary answered.

'Get me the Dorchester,' he said thoughtfully. 'Suite 701.'

*

Telemann met his wife, Laura, in a hotel room overlooking New York's Central Park. She'd flown north from Washington. The meeting was her idea, her request, a curt one-sentence telephone message left with the hotel's reception, awaiting Telemann's return. In fourteen years of marriage, he'd never seen her so angry.

'Don't bother me with secrets,' she said, 'because I won't listen.'

Telemann looked at her across the room. She was standing by the window with the light behind her. She was wearing a two-piece denim suit with a black cotton singlet underneath. She had open sandals, half-inch heels, and a light summer tan. With a hamper and a couple of towels, and the usual stuff for the kids, she could have been five minutes from the beach.

'I'm sorry,' he said again. 'It wasn't on the schedule.'

'It never is.'

'It's different this time.'

'That's what you always say.'

'It's true. It *is* different.'

'Why?'

Telemann sank on to the big king-sized bed and loosened his tie. Then he propped a pillow against the wooden headboard and lay back, closing his eyes. His eyes had been playing tricks again, losing focus, hurting. There'd been no result from the tests Laura had insisted he take, so he'd decided to ignore it.

She was still looking at him. 'Why?' she said again.

'That's a secret,' he said. 'And you hate secrets.'

He heard the soft clack-clack of her sandals as she crossed the room. Then she was sitting on the bed, looking down at him. He could smell her. Despite the anger, and the heat, and New York, she smelled great. He opened one eye, expecting a scowl, or tears, or worse. Instead, she was perfectly upright on the edge of the bed, with a detached, reflective look on her face, an expression of curiosity or perhaps regret, the storm quite spent.

'You want me to tell you about the kids?' she said quietly. 'Spell it out?'

Telemann shook his head. 'No.'

'How excited they were? Martha? Jamie? Bree?'

'No.'

She looked down at him for a long moment. 'If you weren't such a great father,' she said finally, 'it wouldn't much matter.'

'What does that mean?'

She shrugged. 'It means we'd just go off by ourselves. Like we always used to. We'd get by. Like we always did. We'd find some other orphans. God knows, America's full of them, especially vacation time . . .'

Telemann got up on one elbow, marshalling the old argument, the old excuse. 'I have a job,' he said. 'It's important. It's what we live on. What I do.'

'What you do is sit behind a desk and get pissed with it. With us. With everything.'

'Yeah, I know, but it's—'

'What?'

He looked at her for a moment, wondering whether it might be better to tell her. Not the details. Nothing that could burn him. But enough to get him off this particular hook. It's OK, he'd say, the problem's gone away, I'm out from behind the desk, I'm back in the field, where I always belonged. Instead, he reached out and took her hand.

'You should've,' he said. 'You should've gone to the beach. That's what you should've done.'

'We didn't want to.'

'Why not?'

'Because you weren't there. Because the kids had been planning it all for months and months, and thinking about it, and getting real excited. Us all for once. Us all, together. Hey—' she walked her fingertips along the back of his hand, an old gesture '—that a lot to ask for?'

Telemann shook his head, wondering why they hadn't had this conversation on the phone. There had to be more to it. Had to be. He kissed her hand and half-rolled on to his side. In a world of second and third marriages, endless buddy-talk of alimony, and lawyers, and guilt about the kids, this woman of his, this wife, had always been the very middle of his life, ground zero, the one person on God's earth without whom he couldn't function.

Lately, with the job, it had been more difficult. A dozen years with the Agency had given Laura a remarkable tolerance of midnight phone calls and crazy hours. Often, zilch notice, he'd been sent abroad, leaving her to cope. But that, somehow, had been OK. Working for the CIA, the Operations Director-ate, you expected it. Abrupt departures for the airport, scribbled notes from exotic locations came with the job. That kind of stuff was even, in its way, an excitement, something you could share, a curious form of aphrodisiac. But the last eight months had been different. Since Christmas, he'd been back in the Agency HQ at Langley full-time, wrestling with a desk and a promotion and a daily schedule of meetings. For the first time in his professional life, he'd collided head-on with company politics, inter-agency feuding and the constant games with the oversight committees up on the Hill. The experience had drained him more thoroughly than any field assignment he could ever remember. He'd hated it, the compromises, the sheer inertia of the place, and he knew that had made him a lousy husband. He'd come back to lead a regular life, to be home by seven every night, and it hadn't worked out at all.

He reached up for her and tried to pull her down. There was lots he wanted to say, but he wasn't sure that words were quite enough. She looked at him for a moment, resisting. He sank back on to the pillows, suddenly exhausted again, rubbing his eyes.

'I'm sorry,' he said. 'Tell the kids that. I owe them.'

'Yeah?'

'Yeah.'

Telemann closed his eyes again. They had three kids, all adopted. They'd tried for their own and failed. They'd had tests, both of them, and when the physicians finally confirmed that it was Telemann's fault, some problem with his sperm-count, they'd thought seriously about never having kids at all. But the marriage had matured and deepened, a big warm feeling, utterly secure, and they'd both wanted to share it, to spread the good news around a little, and so they'd gone to an agency and opened their lives to the counsellor, and waited a year or two and finally gotten a plump little half-caste called Martha. Two years later, from a slum in Detroit, came Jamie. Then Bree. At times, like any family, it had been difficult, and tiring, and chaotic. But never more than that. Until now.

Telemann opened one eye again, looking up. Laura was standing beside the bed. She'd taken off her jacket and was loosening the belt on her jeans. She began to take them off, wriggling out of them, kicking her sandals into the middle of the room. Then she pulled the singlet over her head and stood by the bed, looking down. She had wide shoulders, big breasts. She was beautifully made. Telemann watched her, the old excitement, his woman.

'Is it me?' he said. 'Or are you hot?'

She didn't look at him, didn't answer. She knelt on the bed beside him, half-smile, busy fingers, and began to unbutton his shirt down to the navel, her hands on his belly, teasing downwards, loosening the zip in his trousers, easing them off. He heard them fall softly to the floor. Then she was over him again, pulling down the cover of the bed, the sheets beneath, slipping out of her knickers, straddling him backwards, her head between his thighs, her hands beneath him. Naked, they made love, a long, wordless half-hour, lapping and sucking and nibbling on the big cool bed. Afterwards, her head on his shoulder, she traced the line of his upper lip with her forefinger.

'Pete phoned,' she said quietly.

Telemann nodded. Peter Emery was a friend from the Agency. He headed a section in the Analytic Directorate at Langley. He was brilliant, and gentle, and played the piano with a rare grace. Laura trusted him completely, an anchor for her errant husband.

Telemann looked down at her. 'And?'

'He said you'd been fired.'

'What?'

'He said you were out. He said he hoped we were coping.' She paused. 'He said he was sorry.'

Telemann was up on one elbow, blinking. 'Fired?' he said. 'When?'

'Yesterday.' She looked up at him. 'So why didn't you tell me?'

'Because I didn't know.'

He looked at her for a moment longer, wondering whether to pursue it now, get through to Emery on the private line, find out what was really happening. Then he remembered Sullivan, the last time they'd spoken, the terms they were offering, the way the job had to be framed. Out of channels, the man had said. Totally freelance. Totally deniable. No footprints. No paper chase. Not a single goddamn chalk-mark on a single fucking tree. He'd have a secure office and limitless back-up, but as far as the bureaucracies were concerned – State, Defense, NSA, FBI – Telemann was to become a non-person. He'd report directly to Sullivan and shed the rest of his professional life. At the time, preoccupied and slightly awed by the scale of the assignment, Telemann had simply agreed. That it might mean the formal end of his CIA days hadn't occurred to him. It was like waking up to snow in August. It was slightly unreal.

He looked at Laura again. 'You ask why they fired me?'

Laura nodded. 'Sure.'

'He tell you?'

'Yeah. He said you'd written some stuff about the Agency, why it screwed up so much. He said he'd read it. He said it was excellent. The exact word he used was sensational.'

Telemann nodded. His eight months at Langley had given him a focus for all his professional frustrations. For a decade, out in the field, he'd wondered why so many initiatives went wrong. Millions of dollars, thousands of man-hours, and important, indefinable things like loyalty and courage, all wasted, just piss in the wind. As a taxpayer, at the very least, he'd been obliged to act – *my* money, *my* effort. And so he'd named names, detailed specific operations, provided dates, locations, supporting evidence. After a day's pause for thought, he'd sealed the twenty-odd pages of typescript in a plain brown envelope and sent it to a top aide at the White House. Not via the mail-room at 1600 Pennsylvania Avenue, but by hand, after dark, to the man's home address. Afterwards, sitting in the car on a leafy street in north-west Washington, Telemann had wondered where the gesture might lead. Now he knew.

'Pete think I was dumb to do it?'

'No . . .' Laura hesitated.

'What, then?'

'He thought you were dumb to send it.'

Telemann nodded, rolling over, looking at her. 'And you? What do you think?'

Laura smiled up at him, her face still flushed. Then the smile faded and the other look came back, the look he'd noticed when she first came in, careful, appraising, reserved.

'Me?' she said. 'I don't care whether they've fired you. Or what you've done. I'm just wondering why we aren't all at the beach. If what Pete says is true.'

*

Godfrey Friedland toyed with his pencil, two-thirds of the way through the *Daily Telegraph* crossword, still wondering about McVeigh.

Ross had called mid-morning from the Private Office at Downing Street. The conversation, as ever, had been brisk. An associate from the Middle East would shortly be giving Friedland a ring. His name was Mr Al Zahra. He had substantial oil interests in the Gulf and elsewhere. He was incensed by the media coverage of the Queen's Gate shooting, and by the general assumption that the blame lay with one or other of the Palestinian guerrilla groups. It was, he said, a gross slander, and he'd crossed his suite at the Dorchester and lifted the telephone to tell the Government so. Normally, the Private Office secretariat would have shrugged the complaint aside, but circumstances made that course of action unwise. Mr Al Zahra had a deep pocket. He was generous with political donations. It would be a shame to disappoint him.

Friedland had made a note of the name, recognizing it at once, and enquired what he should do. Ross had grunted impatiently and told him to service the Arab as best he could. Seventy-five thousand pounds, he reminded Friedland, was a lot of money. A sum like that could matter if the next election was as sticky as the Treasury was beginning to suggest. He'd ended the conversation by enquiring about progress on the report. The seventy-two hours were up. Where was it? Friedland, still toying with the crossword, had fended him off. Enquiries were proceeding, he'd said. He'd be in touch.

Mr Al Zahra had phoned an hour later, a quiet voice, speaking perfect English. He'd apologized for taking a little of Friedland's time and had confirmed the gist of what Friedland already knew. The incident in Queen's Gate was, he'd said, a tragedy, but he'd been disappointed at the way the English newspapers had simply taken Israeli accusations at face-value. In a free country one might expect a little more of a free press. Doubtless the police would apply themselves to the task in hand, and perhaps one day they'd be able to give the lie to the Zionist slur, but the fact was that most of the damage had already been done, and time for setting the record straight was fast running out.

Friedland, listening, had agreed. But what did Mr Al Zahra want him to do?

At this, there'd been a brief silence. Then the Arab had returned to the phone, a little sharper, a little more businesslike. He understood that Friedland ran a security consultancy. He understood that he had access to investigators, to men of integrity who would take a spade to the earth and do a little digging of their own. Friedland had smiled at this, recognizing the elaborate metaphors, the extravagant courtesies, from his own years in the Middle East. Yes, he'd said, he knew such men.

The Arab had paused again, then given him a name. McVeigh, he'd said. A man called McVeigh. Friedland had scribbled the name on his pad, frowning, not recognizing it immediately.

'McVeigh?' he'd said.

'Yes. Pat McVeigh. He lives in North London somewhere. He works for a number of clients. He has a great deal of experience. Friends of mine speak well of him.'

Friedland had boxed the name on the pad, heavy lines, beginning to recall the name at last, an ex-Marine, Arctic and Mountain Warfare Cadre, a little outside the tight inner circle of Special Forces veterans on whom agencies like his own normally relied. McVeigh, he murmured to himself, writing down the Arab's telephone number and promising to put the two men in touch, Pat McVeigh.

Now, late afternoon, Friedland glanced at his watch. He'd found McVeigh's address through an associate. He'd phoned him. He'd established his availability. Soon, traffic permitting, he would arrive.

Friedland laid the crossword carefully to one side, got up and walked to the window. The street outside was empty. Soon, perhaps in an hour or so, the better class of secretaries and PAs would start returning home, those tall, well-educated girls with their Peugeot 205s and their pale, set faces, whose fathers could afford a flat in this area. He watched them most nights, stepping out on to the pavement, their groceries in the back of the car, plastic bags full of kiwi fruit, hand-wrapped cheeses and a bottle or two of Sainsbury's Pinot Noir. Occasionally, he tried to imagine the way their flats would look, their choice of decor, what kind of pictures they hung, what kind of sheets they slept between. The nights he worked late, he'd take a turn round the square before getting into his own car, walking slowly, a man at war with late middle age, risking a glance at a window or two. Many of the girls had boyfriends. They'd arrive in the middle of the evening for a meal. When it was hot, they never bothered to pull the curtains, and passing by he could hear the music, and the clink of glasses, and the low hum of conversation, the faces of those same stern secretaries softened by laughter and wine. Beside one basement flat in particular, Friedland sometimes paused, stooping to do up his shoe-lace. The table stood beside the window, and the girl often ate alone. She was small, thin-boned, sharp-featured. She often played Bruckner, the later symphonies. In a certain light, she reminded Friedland of his own daughter, still down in Sussex, still in the nursing-home, as addicted now to Methadone as she'd once been to heroin.

A taxi appeared at the head of the square. It stopped below the window. A tall, lean figure stepped out of the back, pausing to check the address and pay the driver. A face looked up, blond hair, cropped short, open-neck shirt, light cotton jacket, and Friedland instinctively withdrew into the shadows, sensing at once that it was McVeigh.

McVeigh stayed perhaps half an hour. Friedland thanked him for coming and made a careful note of what little the man was prepared to tell him. He'd been in the Marines for ten years. He was Arctic Warfare-trained and had done the Mountain Leader course. Latterly, after a fall in Norway and a particularly nasty fracture to his left leg, he'd transferred to the Investigation Branch. It hadn't been the kind of soldiering he'd joined up for, but he'd been surprised at his own interest in the job, and how good he'd been at it. The clerical back-up was hopeless, but so were most of the villains, so the thing had worked out OK in the end.

After the Marines, life had been dull. He'd tried to convert a passion into a way of life, tucking away some of his gratuity on the deposit for a small flat and investing the rest in a climbing consultancy. For a fee, he'd lead mountaineering parties anywhere on earth. The idea had been great, but the overheads were crippling and the recession had killed it stone-dead. For the last two years, in the absence of anything better, McVeigh had therefore gone back to doing what he knew best: investigative work, with a modest helping of physical violence.

Friedland, listening, had been amused. McVeigh, like so many of the Special Forces people, was nicely understated. But there was something else, too. A sense of irony and hints of a rogue mind behind the deadpan voice and the watchful eyes.

Friedland mentioned Al Zahra. McVeigh said he'd never heard of him. Friedland looked surprised. 'He says he knows you.'

'Does he?'

'Yes. He says you are very good. Highly recommended.'

'Who by?'

'Friends of his. Fellow Arabs. Chums.'

McVeigh nodded. He'd often bodyguarded for visiting Arabs, dividing his time between a table in the shadows of various Mayfair casinos and a chair in the upper corridors of some of Park Lane's more exclusive hotels. It was cheerless work, but it paid two fifty a day. For that money, he also ran errands, volunteering to collect what one young sheikh from Dubai called 'the groceries'. The groceries turned out to be a succession of expensive call-girls, some of whom McVeigh now knew moderately well. Maybe Al Zahra was from Dubai, too. Maybe it was his cue for yet another circuit of the flats off Shepherd's Market.

'What's he want?'

Friedland explained, briefly, what the Arab had told him on the telephone.

McVeigh listened, expressionless. Friedland got to the end of the story.

'So what *does* he want?' McVeigh said again.

Friedland shrugged. 'I don't know,' he said. 'You'll have to go and see him.'

'Tonight?'

'Half-past seven.' Friedland paused. 'He's expecting you.'

McVeigh looked at him for a moment, then glanced at his watch and nodded. 'Say I take the job,' he said, 'whatever it is . . .'

'Yes?'

'Who do I work for? Him or you?'

Friedland leaned back in the chair, smiling, remembering Ross's parting words. This bit, at least, was simple.

'Me,' he said. 'I want to know exactly what happens.'

McVeigh took a cab to the Dorchester. On the way, he thought about Friedland. He'd never met the man before, never heard of him. The address had been expensive and the office looked genuine enough, but there was something about the man, a strange diffidence, that disturbed him. Most of the agencies he worked for were run by 'Ruperts', recently retired Regular Army officers, late thirties, early forties, good regiments, good families, nice accents, well dressed, excellent connections, urban go-getters who trawled for the fat contracts and dished out the action to the Special Forces lads. It was good business all round, and McVeigh was glad for a slice of it, but Friedland didn't seem to fit that mould at all. Too old. Too battered. Too weary.

The taxi dropped McVeigh at the Dorchester. He took the lift to the seventh floor. The Arab had a suite at the end of the corridor. McVeigh knocked and stood carefully back. The door was opened at once by a youngish woman, Oriental, very black hair, expensive dress cut high at the neck. McVeigh introduced himself. Recognizing the name, the woman smiled, a minor alteration to the lower half of her face. McVeigh stepped inside. The Arab emerged from the bedroom, a small man, neat. He wore a blazer over a white silk shirt. There were Gucci loafers on his feet, and his grey slacks were perfectly pressed. He extended a hand and waved McVeigh into a chair, asking him whether he'd like a drink. McVeigh said no. 'You phoned a Mr Friedland,' he said, 'and Mr Friedland phoned me.'

The Arab inclined his head, glancing at the woman. She smiled at him, touching him lightly on the shoulder, fetching champagne from a small fridge. The champagne, already open, was a third gone. She poured two glasses and looked at McVeigh. McVeigh shook his head. 'No, thanks,' he said again.

The Arab touched glasses with the woman and sipped at the champagne. Then he told McVeigh what he'd already told Friedland. He was a wealthy man. He had a conscience. His Palestinian brothers were orphans in the Middle East, disinherited by the Israelis, penned into refugee camps, the men forced to find work away to feed their families. Fellow Arabs did what they could. There were numerous funds, many appeals. But the fact remained that the Palestinians had no homeland, no rights, no future. Half a million were crammed into the Gaza strip. Twice that number scratched for a living on the West Bank. And in the three years of the *Intifada*, no fewer than 60,000 children – *kids* – had been injured at the hands of the Israelis.

McVeigh followed the recitation without comment. The man was passionate. He spoke slowly, clearly, his voice never rising, but with each fresh statistic his body bent a little further forward on the long leather couch until he was nearly touching McVeigh's knee. His point made, he fell silent. The woman sat beside him, watching McVeigh.

McVeigh smiled peaceably. 'OK,' he said. 'What do you want me to do?'

The Arab looked at him for a moment, his eyes very black. Then he began to talk again, his voice even lower. An Israeli had been killed. It had been a tragedy. No one had been arrested. But to add insult to injury, the Israelis had only one name on their lips. They were judge and jury. Evidence, proof, was immaterial. To anyone sane, anyone Western, anyone non-Arab, it was obvious who was to blame. The Palestinians.

He paused again, the champagne untouched. 'Do you know how offensive that is?' he asked. 'To us? To me? To an Arab?'

McVeigh nodded. 'Of course.'

'Do you realize how bored we get? The same old tune? And how angry? Our people? Our land? Our children?'

'Yes.'

The Arab nodded slowly, still looking at him. The woman had turned away, curling her lip, shaking her head, a gesture of contempt.

McVeigh studied them both. 'So what do you want,' he said at last, 'from me?'

The Arab was silent for a moment, then he relaxed, letting his whole body go limp, leaning back on the couch, sipping again at the champagne. He smiled, apologetic. 'This man who died. His name is Arendt. Yakov Arendt.'

McVeigh nodded but said nothing. For as long as he could remember, he'd had a profound suspicion of coincidence. Things never simply happened. There was always a reason, a cause and a consequence. This belief had served him well. Twice, in the mountains, it had saved his life. Now he watched the Arab.

The Arab glanced up. 'I want you to find out about this man,' he said. 'I want you to talk to his friends. His wife, if he has one. Maybe his bosses, the people he worked for. I want to know how he died, and why he died, and maybe who killed him. People I know say you're very good. They say you know where to go, where to look.' He paused. 'I suggest you go to Israel. Israel is where it begins and ends.'

McVeigh frowned. 'Israel's a fair way,' he said slowly.

The Arab nodded, toying with his glass, rolling the stem carefully between two fingers. 'Five hundred pounds a day,' he said, 'plus expenses.'

McVeigh blinked. It was an absurd sum, nearly twice the going rate. It meant that Yakov Arendt had been a great deal more than a gifted amateur footballer. And it meant that finding out about him would be never less than dangerous. McVeigh studied the Arab for a moment, wondering who he really was, and why he was brokering the deal.

'I knew Yakov,' he said slowly. 'He was a friend of mine.'

The Arab inclined his head, a wholly ambiguous gesture, his

eyes still on McVeigh. 'Then I imagine there's no question about you taking the job,' he said softly.

'No?'

'No.' He shook his head, standing up, extending a hand. 'Where I come from friendship carries certain obligations . . .' He smiled. 'And this would be one of them.'

4

Back in Washington on the early shuttle from New York, Telemann drove to his new suite of offices on 'F' Street.

The offices were three blocks down from the Intelligence community headquarters near the old Executive Office Building beside the White House. The offices came with a large, capable woman called Juanita. Juanita was Sullivan's idea. She'd worked for him in a variety of posts. She was Puerto Rican, discreet, clever and totally loyal. She'd organize the office, answer the phone and access whatever facilities Telemann might need. She had Sullivan's clout and Sullivan's temper. Telemann had liked her on sight.

Now, nudging 20 m.p.h. on the Beltway, Telemann dialled Sullivan's home number on the mobile phone. The extra day in New York had locked the Manhattan Plaza investigation away for good. Benitez would keep looking, but the core-team was tiny. No chance, Telemann thought, that the story would leak any further.

Sullivan answered the phone. It was a quarter after six. He was already late for work.

'It's me,' Telemann said, 'I need the ULTRAS.'

Telemann slowed the car to a crawl as the commuter traffic thickened even more. ULTRAS were the daily digest of communications intercepts acquired and decoded by the National Security Agency out at Fort Meade. They were routed into the US from listening posts world-wide, and from specially assigned satellites. They came in buff files, edged in red. They were classified Top Secret. Sullivan was breathing hard on the phone. Telemann could hear him. Must have run in from the drive, he thought.

'You got 'em,' Sullivan said. 'They went to Juanita last night. You get choice cuts from the PDB, too. Courtesy the Chief.'

Telemann whistled, eyeing a break in the nearside lane. PDBs were the Presidential Daily Briefs, ten beautifully printed pages of premium Intelligence yield that had the tightest circulation of all. Only half a dozen men in Washington were cleared to read the Brief, and while Sullivan wasn't parting with the whole lot, it was the clearest possible indication of the status of Telemann's assignment. Access to the PDB was the Presidential arm around his shoulders. It meant they trusted him. And it meant they were waiting.

Sullivan was muttering something else, his voice low and blurry. Sometimes, from fatigue or anger or sheer laziness, he had trouble getting the words out. Telemann bent to the speaker. 'Pardon me?' he said.

'Analysis.' Sullivan raised his voice. 'We got you some help.'

'Who? What help?'

'Guy from the Agency.'

'Who?'

Sullivan's voice faded again, break-up on the transmission, and by the time the interference had cleared, he'd gone.

Telemann was downtown, his car parked, by seven-thirty. He walked the two blocks from the parking stack and took the elevator to the fourth floor. Juanita was already at her desk, a big woman, middle-aged, impeccably groomed. What little time Telemann had managed to spare for social chit-chat had gone nowhere. She'd moved north from Atlanta. She'd once worked for the Pepsi Corporation. There'd been a husband, maybe even kids, but now she lived alone, somewhere out in Silver Spring, riding the Métro to work every day. In this city, in every sense that mattered, she belonged to Sullivan. Now she smiled a welcome and picked up a small pile of mail. Beautiful hands. Long, scarlet nails. Telemann sifted quickly through the mail, standing by the desk. The promised ULTRA intercepts were nowhere. He glanced up.

'Stuff from NSA?' he said.

'In there. Waiting for you.'

Juanita indicated the smaller of the two inner offices. When

Telemann had left for New York, it had been empty. Now, evidently, someone had moved in. He frowned, began to pursue it, but Juanita was back at the big IBM, her fingers moving sweetly over the keyboard. Telemann hesitated for a moment, then crossed to the office door. He went in without knocking. The desk had been moved from the window to the darkest corner. Bent over a pool of light from an Anglepoise was a familiar figure: lightly striped shirt, blue braces, bony face, sallow complexion, the thin cap of hair beginning to recede from the huge forehead. He looked up. He had a pen in his hand, the 15-dollar Shaeffer that never left him.

Telemann grinned. 'Pete,' he said. 'Pete Emery.'

The other man smiled. 'Hi.'

'You on board? Mr Analysis?'

'Yep,' he said drily. 'Saddled and signed up.'

The two men shook hands. Juanita appeared with two polystyrene cups and a flask of coffee. Telemann reversed a chair, pulling it up to Emery's desk. It was still grey outside, the light diffused through the blinds. It felt, Telemann thought, slightly spooky. Two novices in some new religious order, picking their way, a strange mixture of excitement and dread.

'How did he sell it to you?'

'Who?'

'Sullivan.'

'He didn't. I was ordered over here. I didn't have a whole lot of choice.'

'They sack you, too?'

'Yeah. Sort of.'

'You object?'

'Not at all,' he said wryly. 'Peace and quiet. Regular salary. Security. Retirement benefits. Who needs it?'

He glanced down at the desk, and Telemann recognized the red-bordered ULTRA files. The computers over at NSA were programmed to recognize key words in the hundreds of daily pages of decoded intercepts. One of Telemann's first requests had been for Middle Eastern cable and telephone traffic, dating back to June. The stuff had come sieved through one of the big Fort Meade mainframes, and he'd been dreading yet more paperwork. Now, though, he didn't have to worry. As promised, Sullivan had solved his little problem. More to the point, he'd recruited one of the best brains in the CIA's Analytical Directorate.

Telemann looked up at Emery. 'You got the whole story?'

'Yep.'

'Believe it?'

'Yep.'

'Why?'

Emery hesitated for a moment, gazing down at the NSA reports, the long bony fingers riffling through the sheets of light blue paper. Then he looked up. 'Because it's simple,' he said. 'And effective. Plus it checks out.'

'Already?'

'Sure.' His eyes returned to the NSA intercepts. He lifted one from a separate pile near the phone. 'I had the data re-run,' he said, 'with new key words. Whole bunch of stuff.'

'And they came up?'

'Sure.'

'Lots of them?'

'Enough.'

Telemann nodded. 'Baghdad come up?' he wondered aloud, thinking of the kid who'd disappeared from the Manhattan Plaza, Benitez's little bombshell.

Emery watched him for a long moment. The light from the Anglepoise shadowed the planes of his face. 'No,' he said at last, 'it didn't.'

'Damascus?'

'Negative.'

'Tripoli?'

Emery shook his head again. Then he leaned back in his chair, hands behind his head, eyes studying a small crack in the ceiling beside the air-conditioning louvre. 'There's nothing outgoing from where you'd think to look first,' he said carefully. 'Nothing that I can find. Nothing obvious. But then there's no reason why there should be. Run a major operation, and you hide it under the biggest stones.' He looked at Telemann. 'Even the rag-heads would figure that.'

'Sure.'

'So—' the eyes were back on the ceiling again '—who else might be interested? Given the simple things? Like proximity?'

'Tel Aviv.'

'Yeah.' Emery nodded slowly. 'You bet.'

'You got stuff out of Tel Aviv?'

Emery nodded again. The eyes were closed now. He looked tired. 'A little,' he said. 'Enough.'

Telemann reached for his coffee and swallowed a mouthful. He'd first met Emery back in '81. Telemann had been running a covert liaison programme with the Argentinian Junta out of the Embassy in Buenos Aires. Argentinian military intelligence, G2, were obsessed with the Monteneros, up in Nicaragua, and their paranoia about Marxism extended to training a largish team of guerrillas in neighbouring Honduras. Emery, back at his desk in CIA headquarters in Langley, had mocked the operation from the start. Buenos Aires was 3000 miles away from Nicaragua. The Argentine generals were a bunch of fascist thugs. All they wanted was leverage in Washington. US interests would have been better served by the Mafia.

Telemann, an eager convert to the can-do ethic of the new administration, had flown back from Buenos Aires, enraged by what Emery was doing to his operation, by the latest acid memo from his desk. He'd stormed into Emery's office. He'd accused him of disloyalty, of betrayal. The row had gone on for most of the afternoon, ending in a bar in downtown Washington, with Emery at the wrong end of a bottle of bourbon but still smiling, still sceptical, still pointing out the difference between White House hype and genuine yield. We do Intelligence, he kept saying. We deal in facts. And to deal in facts you need three things. You need to source it. You need to prove it. And then you need to sit down awhiles and think about it.

In the end, he'd been right. As the decade developed, the CIA had become the tool of an administration bent on forcing its view on the world. Spread a map and the proof was there. The CIA supported right-wing tyrants around the world. Zia in Pakistan. Doe in Liberia. Marcos in the Philippines. Duarte in El Salvador. Look, Emery used to say, late in the evening in

Charlie's Bar, over in Georgetown, look at the deals we cut. Fancy guns, and the latest helicopter, and the world's best personal security, and a couple of million bucks. For what? For a foot in the door and a hand on the tiller. At this, with decreasing conviction, Telemann would say his piece about world communism and the global conspiracy, vintage Reagan, and Emery would smile, swaying gently on his bar stool, and pat him on the shoulder, his pet commando. 'Sure, buddy,' he'd say, 'you wanna get into bed with the slave owners, just you go ahead. Only never kid yourself who gets fucked . . .'

They'd become friends. Despite the differences in their age and temperament, despite their very different views of the world, they'd found it comfortable to be around each other. Emery, the older man, was a sceptic, almost Jesuitical, the perfect foil for Telemann. Telemann ran on 100 octane, always had. Emery favoured the slow lane, taking his time, enjoying the view, consulting the map from time to time to plot the most interesting route. He lived out in Maryland. He had a loveless marriage, no kids, and kept a sailboat on the Bay. Laura adored him, and so, in his own way, did Telemann. He was wise. You could trust the man, depend on him, and he cared, too. Recently, after three perfect days on the water, the kids had started calling him Uncle.

Now Telemann studied Emery across the desk. The surprise of finding him in the office had gone. In its place was a dim recognition of the kind of team Sullivan had put together. Telemann, at heart, had never stopped being a commando. His own brief spell behind a desk had proved it. He missed the action. He loved it out there. He knew he was good, and he was gratified that Sullivan had thought so too, but having the right guy at the sharp end wasn't enough. You needed someone at the heart of it, someone strong and experienced and independent enough to take a careful look at the bits of the jigsaw Telemann would shake on to the tray. That was Emery's talent. That was what he was doing in this dark little office. Emery would be his case officer. Emery would run him.

Now Telemann studied Emery across the desk. Already, the

man was poking at the jigsaw. Telemann nodded at the pile of intercepts. 'Our friends in Tel Aviv . . .' he prompted.

Emery nodded. 'I think they're watching,' he said carefully, 'but I don't know how much they can see.'

'But they'll know *something*.'

'Sure,' he smiled. 'Bound to.'

Telemann got up and walked to the window, peering down through the slats in the venetian blind. Four floors below, the traffic was backed up from the intersection. The Israelis had the tightest security service in the world, no question. The Middle East was theirs. In Intelligence terms, they practically owned it. They had priceless human-source assets all over. Damascus. Cairo. Baghdad. You name it. They took extraordinary risks, but the planning and the back-up were impeccable. Telemann had worked in Tel Aviv, and knew the Mossad headquarters on King Saul Boulevard, the ugly grey building with the discreetly armoured windows, and knew some of the agents, too. They were good. They were the best. They trusted nobody. They'd go to any lengths to secure a particular operation, achieve a particular hit. They were ruthless as hell and they seldom got burned. For years, Telemann's idea of heaven was to drive into the car park out at Langley and find the building full of Israelis. Only then, he'd always thought, would – could – the Agency really deliver.

Telemann stepped away from the window and returned to the desk. 'So what do we have?'

Emery glanced down and picked up a yellow legal pad. Telemann recognized the careful script, key words underlined, the odd exclamation mark.

Emery was frowning. 'There was some traffic into Hamburg last month . . .' he began.

Telemann nodded. Mossad loved Hamburg. They had a cosy relationship with the West German anti-terrorist police, a legacy from the Munich débâcle in '72, but of all the German cities Hamburg offered them the warmest welcome. Mossad kept a small permanent outpost there, housed in the fortified basement of the Israeli Consulate on Alsterufer.

Emery glanced up, then bent his head again and went on. 'We picked up a cable on the sixteenth,' he said, 'requesting information on a list of firms.'

'And?'

'There are seven companies, four of them German.' He peered at his own writing. 'Two of the others are Belgian. The other one's Dutch. They're listed, one to seven.'

'And what do they do, these firms?'

'They make chemicals of various kinds. Trimethyl phosphite, for instance.'

'Is that important?'

'It might be.'

'Why?'

Emery looked up. He wasn't smiling. 'Because trimethyl is an organic compound. Add potassium chloride and phosphorus oxychloride and you get Tabun GA.' He paused. 'These firms do the other chemicals, too. They sell the stuff for export. I guess Tel Aviv want checks on the major European ports. They're looking to establish channels, names, dates . . .' He paused again. 'End-users.'

Telemann nodded slowly, glad already that Emery was on the team, that he was spared a day and a half with the industrial chemists, that a chain of events was beginning to shape. He gazed at the paperwork on the desk. 'Anything else?'

'Yes.' Emery bent to the yellow pad again. 'There's another intercept. It's sourced from Vortex. They've been targeting the EEC negotiations in Brussels. This happened into the net a coupla days ago.'

'What is it?'

'It's a sign-off. Single phrase.'

Telemann frowned. 'And what does it say?'

'It says that number six went out through Antwerp. Three days ago.'

Telemann looked at the earlier intercept, the list of companies. 'Number six?' he queried.

Emery didn't bother checking. 'Littmann Chemie,' he said. 'Company in Halle.'

'Halle's East Germany. Or was.'

'Yep.'

'So why Antwerp? Why not Rotterdam?' He shrugged. 'Or Hamburg?'

Emery leaned back in his chair for a moment. 'Drive due west from Halle, takes you straight to Antwerp. It's a big port. Millions of tons of stuff. No one asks too many questions.' He paused. 'Ideal.'

Telemann nodded. 'So what do we have on the German company?'

'Nothing. Yet. They definitely produce the basic chemicals, but I've nothing specific.' He paused. 'The rest of the firms are in the same game. If it ain't chemicals, it's industrial plant, bits and pieces of the manufacturing process, expertise you'd need to make the stuff. From Baghdad, I guess it reads like a shopping list.'

Telemann rubbed his eyes for a moment, looking away, towards the window. Outside, the traffic was moving again. 'Antwerp . . .' he mused.

'Right.'

'And the Israelis have been there already. Is that what we're saying?' Emery looked at him for a moment, then his hand strayed to the pile of NSA intercepts. He lifted it several inches in the air, then let it fall to the desk. Telemann watched his coffee dancing in the cup.

'Electronic intelligence—' Emery shrugged '—There's a limit. What we need here is a good human source.'

Telemann looked at him. 'Me?' he said at last.

Emery nodded, reaching for his own coffee. 'Yes,' he said thoughtfully. 'You.'

*

It was three days before the harbour-master at Ramsgate heard news of his 5-gallon drum.

The local fire brigade had driven down the same afternoon, arriving within an hour of his call. They'd parked the big tender on the quayside and pulled on protective clothing before approaching the drum. Fishermen sorting out their nets had watched curiously as they bent over it, two men in one-piece yellow suits, the bulky breathing sets strapped to their backs, their faces half-hidden behind the clear perspex masks. They'd turned the drum over, squatting beside it, noting the skull and crossbones and the terse single word, 'Poison', and the painted-over line of German at the base, looking for extra information. As far as they could judge, the drum was in good condition. Inset into the lid was a heavy screw-cap. One of the fireman had flexed his fingers in the thick rubber gloves and tried it. It wouldn't budge.

The firemen delivered the drum to a warehouse on a trading estate at the back of the town. The warehouse belonged to the Highways Department. The drum stayed inside the secure container, parked between an air compressor and a neat row of traffic cones.

Eighteen hours later, a van from a company called Dispozall arrived at the Highways Department depot. Two men got out and inspected the drum. They had a brief conversation. Then one of them returned to the van and used the mobile phone to contact the local authority. Neither of them had ever seen a drum quite like this one. Better to ship it west, to the Waste Transfer Station at Newbury, than risk an on-the-spot analysis. The oil pollution officer, on the other end of the line, agreed. He'd raise the paperwork, and they'd take care of the rest of it.

Half an hour later, the contract authorized, he phoned the harbour-master. The two men had an occasionally difficult relationship. Information was one way of keeping it sweet.

'That drum of yours,' he said cheerfully, when the harbour-master answered, 'we've sent it away.'

'What for?'

'Analysis,' he said. 'No one's got a clue what's inside.'

*

By the time McVeigh arrived, mid-morning, the antiques shop around the corner from Queen's Gate was open. He stepped in through the door, closing it carefully behind him. A heatwave had settled on London, and already the temperature was in the eighties.

The shop appeared to be empty, and for a moment or two McVeigh browsed amongst the tapestries and the discreetly mounted brass lantern-clocks. There were very few pieces of furniture, but the stuff looked good. In the middle of the shop stood a large mahogany dining-table. There were eight chairs arranged around it, upholstered in pale yellow. McVeigh looked at it for a moment, trying to guess the price. Foreigners and royalty, George had told him on the phone, no riff-raff.

There was a movement at the back of the room and McVeigh glanced up. A small, slight man stood at an open door. McVeigh could see a flight of stairs, carpeted in red, behind him.

'Can I help you?'

McVeigh nodded, and crossed the room towards him. The man stepped out of the shadows. He looked sixty, maybe older. The suit was nicely understated, and a pair of gold-rimmed glasses hung by a chain from his neck. Latvian Jew, George had said. Third-generation import from Riga.

'Mr Enders?'

'Yes.'

'My name's McVeigh. I wondered if you could spare me a little of your time.' He paused. 'It's about last week. The shooting . . .' McVeigh inclined his head towards the door. Yakov had died ten paces down the street.

Enders eyed him for a moment, expressionless. 'Are you a policeman?'

'No.'

'A reporter?'

'No.'

'Then why are you here?'

McVeigh glanced round. He'd already decided on the table. Close to, the piece was beautifully preserved. The craftsmanship was exquisite, and generations of French polishers had given the surface a rare depth. McVeigh stood beside it, running his fingers along the reeded edge. Enders was watching him carefully. He hadn't moved an inch.

McVeigh glanced up. 'Chippendale?'

'Regency.'

McVeigh nodded, musing. There was a long silence.

'I understand you saw what happened,' McVeigh said at last. 'Before the bloke got shot.'

He glanced up. Enders had shuffled forward into the shop. His shoes were like the table, immaculate. He was still watching McVeigh, still waiting for some clue or other, some fragment of information that would explain this tall stranger with his battered leather jacket and his patient eyes. Then, abruptly, he nodded. 'Yes,' he said, 'I was here. In the shop.'

'Was the door open?'

'Yes.'

'Was there some kind of row?'

'Yes, there was.'

'And they weren't speaking English?'

'No.'

McVeigh nodded, looking at him, direct, appraising. 'What were they speaking?'

'Hebrew.'

McVeigh nodded again, and began to circle the table. A small, discreet card, handwritten, indicated the price. Fourteen thousand pounds. He picked it up and looked at it and then put it down again. Then he pulled a bunch of keys from his pocket and laid them carefully beside the card. There were two Yale keys on the big brass ring, sawtoothed on the underside, a statement of intent. Enders walked quickly across the thick Wilton carpet, light, soundless footsteps, no longer shuffling. He reached for the keys, and McVeigh stopped him, his own hand closing over the thin, pale fingers. Enders withdrew, as if he'd been scalded. 'What do you want?' he said. 'Why are you here?'

McVeigh looked at him. 'The man who died was a friend of mine,' he said carefully. 'I want to know what happened.'

'A friend?'

'Yes.'

'What kind of friend?'

McVeigh said nothing for a moment. Then he reached for the keys.

Enders watched him for a moment. Then he shrugged, weary. 'He got shot,' he said, 'your friend.'

'I know that.'

'The man pulled a gun and—' he shrugged again '—it was

such a shock. It was terrible. Here of all places . . .' He trailed off, and gestured hopelessly at the street, a tired, resigned movement of the right hand.

McVeigh was still watching him. 'He was a very close friend,' he said at last. 'I need to know whether he said anything before he was shot. Out there. In the street.'

'He didn't say anything.'

'I don't believe you.' McVeigh leaned forward across the table, his fingers splayed, aware of his own reflection in the deeply polished surface. 'So think about it. Think hard. Try and remember what he said . . .' He paused, recalling the chronology, the way the guy from Harry's team had detailed it on the Scenes of Crime report. 'Two men meet outside your shop. There's an argument. Voices are raised. Then one of them turns away. My friend. He steps across the street there, way across to the other side, and the other bloke goes after him. You're in here. The door's open. You see it all. So . . .' He paused, easing back, his fingertips leaving tiny sweat marks on the table. 'What did my friend say? Before he got shot?'

Enders looked at him for a long moment. Given a choice, McVeigh knew, he'd bring the conversation to an end. He'd phone the police, or try and throw McVeigh out, or simply turn on his heel and disappear up those perfectly carpeted stairs. But just now he didn't have the choice, and both men knew it. Enders closed his eyes for a moment. The keys lay between them, mirrored on the table. McVeigh was watching his hands. They were shaking.

'Your friend,' he began. 'What was his name?'

'Yakov. Yakov Arendt.'

Enders nodded, some private question answered, some fear stilled. His eyes were open now, looking at the keys. 'He said it would make no difference,' he said slowly.

'What would make no difference?'

'I don't know. He just said that and then . . .' He stared out at the road, the line of parked cars, gleaming in the sun.

McVeigh nodded, patient now, his voice softer, more intimate. 'OK. You heard what he said across the road. So now tell me the rest.'

Enders was still gazing out of the window. 'The rest?' he said vaguely.

'Yes. The argument. Here. On this side of the road. Outside your shop. Hear one, you'd have heard the other.' He paused. 'Wouldn't you?'

Enders looked at him for a moment. 'I didn't tell the police,' he began, 'but they said that wouldn't matter.'

'Who?'

'Your people. The Embassy people.'

'Oh.'

Enders looked at him, frowning, wanting confirmation.

McVeigh obliged. 'They won't come back,' he said. 'The police.'

'OK.' Enders nodded. 'They were arguing about the case. The brief-case. Your friend's case. The other man said it didn't belong to him. He said it wasn't his. He wanted your friend to give it back.'

'And?'

'Your friend wouldn't.'

'Why not?'

'I don't know.' He shrugged. 'He just wouldn't. "*Ney maas, li . . . ney maas, li . . .*" That was the phrase he used.'

'What does that mean?'

'It means—' He frowned, breaking off, looking McVeigh full in the eyes for the first time. ' "*Ney maas, li . . .*" You don't know what it means?'

'No.'

'You're not from the Embassy?'

'No.'

'But—' Enders shook his head, hopelessly confused '—you said he was your friend.'

'He was. But I'm still not from the Embassy.' He paused. 'Does that matter?'

Enders, ashen-faced, began to back slowly away, his eyes still on McVeigh's face, oblivious now of the keys, and the table, and the five-figure price-tag.

'Yes,' he said softly. 'Of course it matters.'

✳

Emery drove Telemann to Dulles International with an hour and a half to spare for the Sabena overnight to Brussels.

They'd spent most of the day in the office on 'F' Street, reviewing the hard data, ever-mindful of Sullivan's brisk mid-morning admonition on the dedicated point-to-point phone link with his White House office. 'I ain't into micro-managing,' he'd barked, 'but for Chrissakes keep it out of the hands of the Feds.'

Emery and Telemann had exchanged glances at this. Counter-terrorism within the USA was the responsibility of the FBI. Their beat. Their call. Yet here was Sullivan saying they had no right to a single fucking square inch of the picture. In one respect, of course, it made perfect sense. The FBI leaked worse than a sieve, always had, and if word of the Tabun threat got out, then the public order consequences would be awesome. But keeping it really tight, a handful of guys in an office on 'F' Street, had its downside. Whenever they needed back-up – Intelligence, analyses, technical information, simple footwork – then they had to acquire it piecemeal, covering their tracks, camouflaging the real thrust of the mission, turning themselves into the Intelligence equivalent of the stealth fighter. The latter image had been Emery's, a caustic aside, typically elegant, and Sullivan had loved it. Of course the fucking thing was risky, but risk-taking was an integral part of the job. Indeed, in most respects it *was* the job. That was the point he wanted to get across. That was why they'd been chosen. They had to give some to get some. There'd be limits, sure. But he'd bought their sense of judgement, and their love of the flag, and he knew – deep down – that they'd do a fine job. Just now, they owed it to him. Later, if there was such a time, America would owe them.

Afterwards, the line dead, they wondered aloud about how much he'd really told them, how much they really knew. It was perfectly conceivable that Sullivan had set up a number of discrete teams, cells, each one separately tasked, insulated laterally, need-to-know, sworn to secrecy. There might be one up in New York. Another in the Middle East. A third over in Europe. Telemann had tested him on the secure line. He was going to Brussels, he'd said, and Antwerp. Afterwards, he'd fly to Tel Aviv. There were leads to pursue, bases to touch, friendships to renew, debts to call in, arms to bend. He'd left it at that, deliberately vague, bread on the water, listening hard for any sign of wariness or alarm, but Sullivan had simply grunted his approval and wished him luck. Time belongs to the enemy, he'd said. The President had yet to receive a deadline, but doubtless it would come. US troops out of Saudi by such and such a date, or else. That was the whole point of the exercise. That was why the rag-heads were going to so much trouble. So, he'd said, let's go get the cock-suckers. Let's crank it up, move it on. Jesus, ride the fucking Concorde if you have to.

Now, twenty minutes out of Dulles, Emery went through it again. The Iraqis had a known nerve gas capability. They'd taken the decision to go chemical back in '74 when the Israelis refused to sign the Nuclear Proliferation Treaty. Wary of Israel, wanting parity, lacking the technical know-how to make a bomb of their own, they'd sensibly opted for the poor man's nuke: poison gas. They'd scoured the world for Arab scientists. They'd recruited engineers. They'd paid millions of dollars to Western firms for site plans and equipment. And by 1988, they were producing tons of the stuff a month, mainly mustard gas and nerve agents. Some of it they dropped on Iranian front-line troops during the eight-year war. More of it fell on the luckless Kurdish town of Halabja, killing thousands of women and children. The West, too late, imposed export bans on key constituent chemicals, but by the end of the decade, the Iraqis had acquired what they needed.

There were now five plants producing poison gas. The biggest, at Samarra, north of Baghdad, was huge. Telemann had seen the black-and-whites from the National Reconnaissance Office that very afternoon, sheaves of photos, perfect resolution, hand-carried across Washington in the big red folder marked TOP SECRET TALENT KEYHOLE. Spread out on the carpet beneath the window, they showed mile after square mile of plant and storage facilities, heavily masked by thick concrete revetments. The Iraqis had given the place a name, the

Muthanna State Enterprise for Pesticide Production, but it was nothing more than a blind. Every two-bit country with a chemical capability called the stuff 'pesticide'. It was simply a code, a convention, the blackest of jokes. Spray this on the bad guys, went the theory, and wipe them out for good.

And there was lots of it. Mustard came out of Samarra at the rate of 60 tons a month, and they'd been stockpiling for years. Of the nerve agents – Tabun and another gas called Sarin – there was admittedly far less, but in terms of strict lethality, that didn't matter. A dose the size of a cube of sugar would, given the distribution, kill two and a half thousand people.

'Delivery,' Telemann muttered, watching a distant 747 riding the glide-path into Dulles. 'They have to deliver.'

Emery nodded. His consumption of Camel cigarettes was peaking around fifty a day. Telemann had never seen him so fired.

'Sure,' he said. 'And there's a body in the Bellevue morgue says they can. That was smart. They knock off a guy who's been feeding the Israelis. And they send us a message, too.' He nodded again, approving. 'Neat.'

Telemann glanced across at him. 'You get any more on Gold?'

'Not yet. I've got guys on it now. IRS guys. One's out in LA crawling all over the estate. I told them they're owed.' He grinned. 'Big bucks.'

Telemann nodded. Investigators from the Internal Revenue Service were legendary, the enforcement equivalent of pit bull terriers. They could wreck a man's career in eight hours. They asked all the right questions for as long as it took, and they viewed sleep or weekends as a form of weakness. Telemann glanced across at Emery. Emery was trying to hide a yawn. Telemann reached forward and turned the air conditioning to cold boost.

'So tell me,' he said, 'where's the even money? They bring the stuff in? Or they brew it here themselves?'

'Bring it in. Dime to a dollar.'

'How?'

Emery shrugged, dipping his head for the last Camel and

crushing the empty pack. 'I'd say seaborne. A gallon or two slipped into a part-load. It wouldn't be difficult, and you might risk pressurization problems if you tried to air-freight it over. No—' he shook his head '—my guess is Boston, or New York, or one of those dinky little places up in Maine.' He paused. 'Department of Commerce are accessing some data, though we might get old waiting for it.'

Telemann nodded, gazing out of the window. He'd been away from the office most of the afternoon. Emery had picked him up at home. 'Anything new on Antwerp?'

Emery said nothing for a moment. Then he took a long deep pull at the cigarette and held it for a second or two. 'Yes,' he said, the car suddenly full of smoke again.

'What?'

Emery glanced at him. He wasn't smiling. 'Langley came through. Operations have some assets over in Brussels. Good local boys. Nicely placed.'

'And?'

'I gave them the dates. I asked them to bracket two weeks around the Israeli sign off . . .' He paused for a moment, picking a shred of tobacco from his lower lip. 'They had an odd little incident four days back. The local cops picked up a Greek guy in the middle of the night. Someone had been beating the shit out of him. He's still in hospital.'

'So what?'

A trace of a frown ghosted across Emery's face. He hated being hurried. 'The guy came off a boat. The *Enoxia*. Small freighter. She left Antwerp three days ago. I got them to check back. I asked for the manifest.'

'What was she carrying?'

'Amongst other stuff—' he paused '—pesticide.'

Telemann nodded. 'Was the Greek guy replaced?'

'Yep. They picked up a deckhand through the agent.'

'Who was he?'

'I don't know . . .' He looked across at Telemann. 'Yet.'

Telemann eased the seat an inch or two back and closed his eyes. 'You think I should talk to the agent?' He opened one eye and looked at Emery. Emery had already produced an envelope from his pocket. He laid it carefully on the dash.

'His address and phone number,' he said. 'And his name.'

'What do we know about him?'

'He's half-Flemish, half-Jewish. Brussels think he's *sayanim*.'

Telemann looked at the envelope for a moment, then closed his eyes again. If the shipping agent was a *sayan*, then he worked for Mossad part-time, one of a network of sympathizers worldwide. These were the guys who did it for Israel, the true believers, greasing the wheels of the Mossad machine. Often they were prominent local figures, trusted in their community. From time to time, on request, they provided funds, cover, safe houses, introductions, the countless favours that good Intelligence depended on. If he was *sayan*, if it was true, then it was the worst possible news. It meant that Mossad really was involved. It meant taking on the Israelis.

'Tough call,' Telemann murmured.

Emery glanced across at him, agreeing. 'The toughest,' he said.

Telemann pulled a face, knowing already that it was true. He'd been phoning contacts in Tel Aviv all morning, private numbers as well as the big headquarters switchboard on King Saul Boulevard, but so far no one had returned his calls. Personally, he'd always got on with the Israelis, kindred spirits, but he knew, too, that they had little respect for the CIA. The Americans, they thought, were barely in the game. They regarded them as amateurs, well intentioned, sincere, but hamstrung by their own naïvety, by the huge bureaucracies back in Washington, by the ceaseless need to answer to the politicians on the Hill. They pulled their punches. They thought too hard about democracy. They refused to meet like with like. In a wicked world, they behaved like virgins. The sun on his face, his eyes still closed, Telemann shook his head and sighed. Despite his birthright, and his passport, he had to agree. Too damn right, he thought.

Emery eased the big Chrysler off the pike and joined the feeder road that led to the airport. Telemann, upright in his seat again, could see the graceful tent-like shape of the terminal, and the tailplanes of the evening Jumbos waiting on the tarmac beyond. He'd made this journey hundreds of times, flying out, field assignments in Europe and the Middle East. More often than not, the operations had run into the sand, over-managed, over-controlled. For years, he'd chafed at the frustrations, the pages of careful ground-rulers, promising assignments wrecked by the senseless protocols. Now, though, the brakes were off. He had complete freedom, total responsibility. He could do whatever he liked to whoever he liked, just as long as he got a result. He thought of the Israelis again and wondered how he would cope. It wouldn't be easy. He knew it.

Emery slowed to join the queue for the departures ramp. Telemann felt inside his jacket pocket, checking for his passport and his ticket, automatic gestures, some small comfort. The car rolled up to the terminal building and coasted to a halt beneath the Sabena sign. Emery coughed. He had another envelope in his hand. It was small and white. He passed it across. 'From Laura,' he said. 'She made me promise.'

Telemann gazed at it. He'd seen Laura barely an hour ago. He'd driven over to the little white house in Maryland to pick up his bag. She'd packed it, like she always did. It was lying there on the bed, waiting for him. They'd spent a little time together. They'd talked about an autumn vacation. They'd said goodbye on the stoop, the kids too, little Bree all teeth and giggles.

He blinked, still looking at the envelope. 'What is it?' he said blankly.

'I don't know.'

Telemann reached for the envelope and opened it. Inside was a single sheet of paper, and a small flower. Laura pressed them between the pages of the kids' encyclopaedias. She was always doing them. They were never less than beautiful. Telemann looked at the flower for a moment. It was tiny, with purple leaves. He'd seen one before but he didn't know the name for it. He put it carefully to one side and unfolded the sheet of paper. A black porter had appeared with a trolley. His shadow fell over the car. Telemann bent to the paper, two brief sentences. 'I love you,' it went, 'and so do the kids. Which is why I don't think we can go on like this much longer.'

Telemann blinked and read the note again. Then he looked across at Emery. Emery was leaning against the door, one hand on the wheel, watching a Grey Line bus. He might have been a million miles away. Telemann gestured at the letter. 'You know about this?'

Emery's eyes left the bus. He looked at the letter. He didn't try to read it. Then he looked at Telemann. Telemann bent towards him, urgent now, his plane waiting, the Israelis waiting, God knows what in store. 'Do you?' he said. '*Do* you?'

Emery looked pensive for a moment, and Telemann had a sudden glimpse of it, the sailboat, the wide gleaming spaces of Chesapeake Bay, the photos the kids had taken, the whole family aboard, the picnic hamper, the half-empty bottles of wine, the wet towels draped over the boom, Bree naked, summer-brown, Emery at the tiller, inscrutable, his wife beside him, her smile. The older man was gazing out of the window again, his fingers softly tapping on the steering-wheel. The Grey Line bus had disappeared.

'Your plane goes at seven,' he said softly, 'and it's six already.'

*

Billy phoned McVeigh with the news. He'd been dialling the flat since four. He sounded pleased with himself, a little breathless, real excitement. 'Dad,' he began, 'I got it. I did it.'

McVeigh threw his leather jacket on to the sofa. He'd just come in himself. He hadn't seen Billy for two days, hadn't even spoken to him, and now he was going away.

'What, son? What've you got?'

'Picked. I got picked.'

'What for?'

'Hornsey Schools. They're training pre-season. We get shirts and socks and everything . . .' He paused, gulping with excitement. 'I'm the only one ever from our team. *Ever*, Dad. Isn't that brilliant?'

'Yeah. Wazza.'

'What?'

'Wazza. It means the same thing. It means brilliant.' McVeigh grinned. He hadn't used the old Marine term for years. Wazza. Billy was telling him about the training, who they'd be playing in the first game, how he'd been promised the centre-forward spot. '*Promised*, Dad. They promised me. Striker.' He paused. 'What do you think?'

'Wazza,' McVeigh said again, checking his watch. It was ten past seven. He told Billy well done and asked to speak to his mum. There was a bang as Billy dropped the phone and then a brief conversation in the background. When McVeigh's ex-wife came on, she sounded surprised. They rarely talked.

'It's me,' McVeigh said.

'I gathered.'

'Great news. About the boy.'

'Yes, it is. It's done him the world of good. He's almost normal again.' She paused, awkward. 'Was there anything else?'

McVeigh hesitated for a moment, then said that he was away for a while, on a job. He'd quite like to see the boy. It was seven. Why didn't they go out for a meal?

'He's eaten,' she said at once.

'I meant all of us.'

'Ah . . .' There was another silence, longer this time, and McVeigh pictured her standing by the phone amongst the Habitat furniture and the Afghan rugs and the heavy velvet curtains she'd inherited from her mother, trying to work out how to say no.

She returned to the phone. 'He's quite keen,' she said, reluctant.

McVeigh grinned again. 'La Dolce Vita,' he said, naming an Italian restaurant he knew she liked, 'I'll see you there in half an hour.'

McVeigh got to the restaurant first. He knew the owner, a small, talkative Italian from Naples. Like Billy, he was football-mad. They discussed the talents of Maradona for a minute or two, McVeigh pretending a knowledge he didn't possess, and the owner was still bodychecking around a line of empty chairs when Sarah appeared at the door. She was tall, a year older than McVeigh, with long blond hair. She spoke Knightsbridge English and wore expensive clothes with a practised languor. In the early days, transfixed by appearances, McVeigh had worshipped her.

Now he stepped forward and kissed her lightly on the cheek. Billy ran in from the car, tripping on the mat at the door. They sat at a table in the window, McVeigh on one side, Billy and Sarah on the other. Sarah sipped a Perrier water, looking wary. 'Nice surprise,' she said, without obvious enthusiasm.

They ordered seafood and a modest salad, pizza for Billy. A bottle of champagne arrived, and a huge glass of Coke. McVeigh poured the champagne and toasted Billy's news. The boy raised his glass of Coke, his eyes shiny. He said he thought he might play for England one day. Then he got up and excused himself, and disappeared towards the loo.

Sarah put her glass down. 'Who's Yakov?' she said carefully.

McVeigh explained. He said he'd been a coach with the football team. He'd taken the team to the top of their league, and he'd got on especially well with Billy. This season they might have done even better, only Yakov wasn't around any more.

Sarah was looking at him. 'Why not?' she said.

McVeigh took a last mouthful of squid and put his knife and fork down. 'He went away,' he said, not wanting to explain.

Sarah eyed him, cold, appraising. Then she frowned. 'It's funny,' she said, 'Billy's mentioned him a couple of times and . . .' She shrugged.

McVeigh was watching her carefully. He knew the signs. He knew when she was holding back.

'What?' he said.

'Nothing.'

'Yes, there is.'

She looked up at him quickly. 'For Christ's sake,' she said, 'you're not at work. I'm not some bloody suspect.'

McVeigh ignored the sarcasm. Sarah had never accepted the job he did. She thought it was grubby, demeaning, an excuse to mix with riff-raff. She'd married a Royal Marine, a tall, good-looking sergeant with real prospects, an NCO tipped – unusually – for a commission. It had been an unlikely pairing – her friends had called it quaint – but she'd had her reasons, and in the early days it had been fun. But then he'd fallen off a mountain and broken his leg, and the soldiering had disappeared, and the promotion with it. The marriage had survived another eight years, growing increasingly bitter. The night he'd left, she'd told him he was lazy and dull, no prospects, no guts, no ambition. He was totally selfish and had never cared less about anyone else in the world. McVeigh had remembered the description ever since, wondering whether it was true. Sarah's father had been a brigadier. She had a real problem with expectations.

McVeigh reached for his glass and emptied it. They'd been having a conversation. She owed him an answer. 'This guy Yakov,' he said, 'you were going to tell me something.'

Sarah shook her head, composed again. 'No,' she said, not bothering to hide a yawn. 'I was just thinking what a lovely name it was.'

Afterwards, the meal cut short, Billy came back to the flat with McVeigh. They'd had a brief conversation on the pavement outside the restaurant, the boy hopping up and down, pleading with his mother to let him spend the night at his dad's. He's going away, he kept saying. He won't be here for a bit. He can drop me off at school tomorrow morning. Reluctant, but boxed in, Sarah had finally consented, making McVeigh promise Billy would be in bed and asleep by ten o'clock. His school uniform he'd have to pick up in the morning. She left them with a nod and an icy thank-you for the meal, and McVeigh watched her getting into the white Citroën GTI, a good-looking woman in her mid-thirties, a total stranger.

Billy and McVeigh drove back to the flat. On the way, the boy burbled happily about the new season, the goals he'd score. As they joined the thin stream of traffic winding through Crouch End, he abruptly changed the subject, looking across at McVeigh, running his fingers up and down the empty champagne bottle the restaurant owner had given him as a souvenir.

'Where are you going, Dad?'

'Israel.' McVeigh glanced down at him. 'It's in the Middle East. It's where God came from.'

'Why? Why are you going?'

'On a job.' McVeigh smiled. 'For a man who's paying me lots of money.'

Billy nodded, absorbing the information. The car turned left. In twenty seconds, they'd be home. Billy looked thoughtful. 'Is it to do with Yakov?'

'Yes.'

Billy nodded and said nothing for a moment. 'He really is dead, isn't he?' he mumbled at last.

'Yes, son. Yes, he is.'

'I thought so.' He paused, solemn. 'It's a shame, isn't it?'

'Yes, it is.'

'He could have come and watched me play.' He frowned. 'What do you think he'd say? If he knew about it?'

McVeigh shrugged, turning into his road and coasting the Escort to a halt outside the flat. He reached for the ignition key and switched off the engine. Talking to Sarah again, sharing an hour or so with his ex-wife, had made him realize what a loveless adventure the marriage had been. The long winter nights when there was nothing left to say. The endless attempts to rekindle some kind of sex life. The drinking. It had all been so pointless, such a total waste of time, yet he'd go through it all again, every second of it, just for this, his son beside him, Billy, the world's best centre-forward, newly chosen for the Hornsey Schools Representative XI. He bent towards the boy, trying to find a word or two to express how he felt, how proud he was, but Billy's hand came out, stopping him, a caution. He was looking out of the window. He was looking up. 'Dad,' he said quietly, 'someone's in the flat.'

'How do you know?'

'I saw them.'

'Them?'

'Two people. Men. I saw them. I did.'

McVeigh looked at him for a moment, then told him to stay where he was, not move an inch, lock the doors. Billy nodded, still gazing up at the flat. McVeigh got quickly out of the car, checking for himself. His flat was on the first floor. There were three windows at the front. Two belonged to the living-room. The other one was the kitchen. The curtains were half-drawn in the living-room, the way he'd left them. The blind was down in the kitchen, nothing wrong there. He crossed the road and pushed in at the gate, wondering whether success had gone to Billy's head. Then he saw the front door. The front door was shared with the girls in the flat beneath. House rules, and the local crime rate, meant that it was always locked. Now, by an inch, it was open. The jamb around the lock was splintered.

McVeigh hesitated for a moment, then bent for an empty milk bottle on the step. Halfway up the staircase there was a right-angled turn. He took the turn quickly, on the balls of his feet, perfectly balanced, feeling the blood pumping, the old excitement. At the top of the stairs was his door. It was open. He hesitated again, listening for movement inside, hearing nothing but the tick of the water-heater and the steady drip of the kitchen tap he'd been meaning to fix. They're waiting, he thought. They've seen the car. They've seen me. And they're tooled up. And they're waiting. He looked at the bottle. Courage, he knew, had a great deal to do with calculation. You worked out the odds. You worked out the geography. You worked out what kind of shape you were in after a plateful of calamari and four glasses of champagne. And if you still did it, went for it, then you were either very brave or very stupid.

McVeigh grinned in the half-darkness. He could feel it coming, and in a curious way he was looking forward to it. He moved slightly to the left, bent slightly at the shoulders, then he was inside the tiny hall, pivoting right, sensing the figure behind the kitchen door, the long French chef's knife he'd bought only last week raised in readiness. He kicked at the door, a serious kick, smashing it back against the fridge. He heard a gasp of pain, and then there was a second shadow on the wall opposite, and the sound of splintering glass as he smashed the milk bottle against the door-frame and dug the jagged end into the face that lunged at him out of the darkness.

The man screamed with pain, clawing at the bottle, and McVeigh felt a rush of air as something heavy smacked into the wall beside his head. He ducked low, avoiding a second blow, and then drove hard, belly-height, head and shoulders, hoping to God the man didn't side-step, leaving him nowhere to go.

The man didn't, and McVeigh hit him squarely in the gut, hearing the air whistling out through his broken mouth. The man folded briefly, then bolted for the open door.

McVeigh turned, still holding the bottle. Then he was into the kitchen, tearing the door back, pulling at the figure behind, seeing the eyes, big, and smelling the sour prison smell of roll-ups and stale sweat. He raised the bottle, then hesitated a fraction of a second, long enough for the man to lunge for the stairs. He was black. He was young. He was medium-height. He was wearing jeans and a T-shirt. He clattered down the stairs, cursing, a flat London accent. His buddy was in the hall. They ran out into the last of the evening light, footsteps on the pavement, receding fast.

McVeigh stood at the top of the stairs, getting his breath back, making sure they'd gone. Then he turned back into the flat, circling the rooms, noting the usual damage, the drawers out, the wardrobe overturned, the cupboards emptied. Coming out of the bedroom, he heard footsteps on the stairs. He tensed and stepped back into the hall. He still had the bottle, the broken end slippery and wet with blood. He took a half-step forward, his arm raised, watching the angle in the stairs. Getting caught was foolish. Coming back was very silly indeed. This time he'd do the job properly.

The footsteps paused for a moment on the stairs. Then Billy was there, standing in the half-darkness. His eyes were wide and his arms was raised. He cast a long shadow for the single bulb in the hall downstairs. McVeigh stared at him, then started to laugh. In Billy's hand was the champagne bottle, the neck tightly gripped, the knuckles white.

McVeigh clattered down and lifted him up, aware, for the first time, of the blood on his own face. He held the boy the way he'd always done, from the early days, up close to him, cheek to cheek, nuzzling.

'Wazza,' he said softly. 'Bloody wazza.'

*

The old man, Abu Yussuf, looked at the boy across the garage.

'How do you know?' he said again. 'How do you know it's not a trap?'

The boy shrugged and turned away, a gesture of dismissal. Lately, he hadn't bothered to disguise his contempt. The old man was typical *samadin*, one of the passive ones, debris washed up from the tides that flowed back and forth across the Middle East, a Palestinian, coming from nowhere, destined for nowhere, an old man on whom it was pointless even wasting breath.

'It's not a trap,' he said.

The old man frowned. The boy had only just arrived, the usual three taps at the door. He'd brought a message from the Syrian. The stuff for the car was here, ready for collection. There was a rendezvous they had to keep, a car park to find, a big shopping mall up in Paterson. A guy with a white Pontiac had the stuff in his trunk. It was heavy. They'd need two of them to lift it. He'd only wait fifteen minutes. Maybe less. They'd have to go now.

The boy looked at his watch, then leaned back against the car. The air in the garage smelled funny. The old man must have been running the pump again, he thought. It's a toy. He's obsessed with it. He never leaves it alone. Typical *samud*. Brains made of jelly.

'So let's go,' he said. 'Now.'

The old man circled the car, watching him. The resentment showed in his face, his distrust of the boy, how uncomfortable he felt having him in his garage. Lately, the last day or so, he'd become convinced that the boy was watching him. He never talked about himself, where he'd come from. He never talked about his family, his mother, his brothers. He never discussed the struggle back home, how bad it was, how terrible to be driven to lengths like these. He never mentioned the Israelis, except to call them scum. In fact the only conversation they'd ever had revolved around the boy's job. He'd worked in a big hotel over in Manhattan somewhere. He'd earned hundreds of dollars a week. He'd done well.

Now the boy was opening the garage doors. The heat bubbled in from the street outside bringing with it the smell of garbage and bad drains. The old man followed him on to the sidewalk, blinking in the harsh sunlight.

'How far is Paterson?' he muttered.

'Half an hour.'

'When will we be back?'

The boy shrugged. 'Five,' he said. 'Six. I don't know. Why?'

The old man glanced back into the garage, the hot dark box that had become a kind of home. 'We'll need to test it,' he said. 'Make sure it works.'

The boy frowned. 'Test what?'

'The gas. The tear gas. We can do it with the door open. Later the better.'

The boy stared at him a moment, then began to laugh, remembering the stuff in the aerosol, what they'd told him it could do. '*Tear* gas?' he queried.

The old man nodded, and looked at his watch. 'You're right,' he said gruffly. 'We ought to go.'

5

The 5-gallon drum from Ramsgate arrived at the Newbury Waste Transfer Station on Friday 26 August. The analyst, as it happened, was abroad on leave. He reappeared two days later, tired and badly hung-over after an overnight flight back from Athens. There was a pile of paperwork on his desk and it was mid-afternoon before he got round to the Ramsgate drum.

The drum, still sealed inside a fire brigade container, was stored in a section of the warehouse reserved for suspected poisons. The shift leader had seen the death's-head symbol when the van arrived from Ramsgate, and had drawn the appropriate conclusions. The storage area, in a corner of the warehouse, was well lit, with windows on two sides.

The analyst studied the drum. It was stoutly made, thicker-gauge steel than usual. He could see no corrosion, no rust, no leaks. He and two other men lifted the drum from the secure container and walked it across the concrete floor towards the bench where he'd laid out his equipment. The weight of the drum suggested that it was full. He thanked the men and bent to examine the screw-cap on the lid of the drum. One of them, an older man, asked about the suit and mask he was supposed to wear. It was site regulations. The company was very strict. The analyst shrugged his advice aside. He still felt nauseous from the duty-frees he'd drunk the previous night. He'd wear the gloves and the thick rubber galoshes in case of floor spillages, but the rest he'd do without.

The older man said he was a fool and left the section. The analyst returned to the drum, studying it again, reading the notes supplied by the company's North Kent division, and the photostats of the fire brigade reports. In neither case was there any conclusion about what might be inside. The only clue was the half-line of German scrolled across the bottom of the drum. The analyst peered at the lettering. He knew a little German. 'Property of . . .' it went, then the rest of the line painted over. He looked harder. One or two of the letters were just discernible, slightly raised shapes under the layer of paint. He ran his fingertips over the word at the end, as if it were braille. There were five letters. One of them might have been an 'H'. He wasn't sure, couldn't be certain. He pulled on the thick rubber galoshes, bending down to tighten the laces. He reached for the gloves and wriggled his fingers inside. Then he stooped to the drum and tried to loosen the screw-cap.

It wouldn't give. He tried again, twisting hard, applying as much strength as he could muster. Still no movement. He turned to the work-bench and selected a small hammer. Corrosion, he thought. A little sea water under the lip of the screw-cap, the rust bonding it. Nothing that a whack or two with the hammer couldn't shift.

He began to tap the lid, working round it. The noise of the hammer made his head hurt. He completed the circle and turned the cap again. He felt it give, slowly at first, the barest movement, then it freed itself, turning easily between his fingers. He paused, tossing the hammer back on to the bench, then returned to the drum, removing the cap. He turned it over. There was a thin film of clear liquid on the underside. He bent low, peering into the drum, seeing the light reflected on the liquid inside. He sniffed, then sniffed again, trying to identify the smell. The smell reminded him of rotting plums.

He sniffed again, wondering why his eyes hurt so much, why the drum was slipping out of focus, what this terrible pain was in his chest, and seconds before the darkness came, it occurred to him that hangovers were never as bad as this, and that maybe – after all – he should have listened to the older man.

*

Telemann, who normally slept on west–east transatlantic crossings, sat by the window all night, a glass on the arm-tray at his elbow, trying to get the letter right.

By dawn, half an hour west of Ireland, he thought he'd finally succeeded. It wasn't angry. It wasn't pathetic. It wasn't bitter.

It simply detailed the way he felt, what it meant to him, the shock. He called the stewardess. He ordered his fourth bourbon. He took twenty minutes to drink it, watching the clouds beneath, pinked by the rising sun. Then he reached for the pad and read the letter again, and realized that he hadn't got it right at all. The thing was dead. It read like a medal citation. Grace under fire, determination to press on despite grievous wounds. He read it again, toying with the empty glass, then ripped the sheet from the pad.

At the airport, he'd watched Emery drive away. The older man had wished him good luck, *bon voyage*, but his eyes were cold and it wasn't at all clear which journey he meant. From a pay-booth in the terminal, Telemann had phoned Laura. Bree had answered. No, she'd said, Mummy was out, at the mall, shopping. Telemann had thanked her and told her that it was nothing important, nothing that couldn't wait until he got over to Europe, but there was another voice in his head, loud, crude, insistent, and whatever he did, there on the phone to Bree, or afterwards, joining the queue to check his luggage, he couldn't switch it off. Where had Laura really gone? Where had they agreed to meet? How much time did they give each other? What did they say? What did they do? And how often?

At Brussels Airport, Telemann stepped into the washroom by the baggage carousel before facing the day. Soaping his face in the mirror, he realized the kind of trap he'd stepped into, a trap of his own making. What you never did in the field was make assumptions. You never assumed you weren't being followed. You never assumed that rooms weren't wired, phones tapped. You never assumed that the casual acquaintance in the hotel bar, with his buddy-buddy smile and firm handshake, wasn't the guy they'd sent to burn you. That way, ever-sceptical, ever-alert, you survived. But private life, your own life, your wife and your kids, hell, that was supposed to be different. There were rules there, loyalties. You'd sworn an oath. You'd built a home and tried for kids, and finally made a damn good job of bringing up a bunch of other people's. You'd done it all, done it OK, better than OK, and now it was all ashes. The other guys, the guys he'd met in the office, in the field, maybe they had it about right after all. Whichever way you looked at it, however hard you tried, you got screwed. Telemann looked at himself in the mirror, a night's growth, the eyes reddened with booze and exhaustion. Laura, he thought. Of all people. Her.

He hired a car from the Hertz desk. He was travelling on a US passport under the name of Lacey. On the booking form, under the section headed 'Business Address', he scribbled a location in Chicago. The details had come through Juanita, the documents too. For cover, he was operating as a freelance journalist, working on assignment for a heavyweight magazine in the mid-West. He'd flown to Europe looking for background on a trade story. Would the tariff barriers close around the enlarged EC? Should the rest of the world brace itself for a trade war? The usual questions.

He drove north to Antwerp. He was there in less than an hour. The port area lay on the other side of the city, and he drove with his eyes half-closed, trusting the big blue signs, remembering the address of the police station which had handled the incident with the Greek sailor. Overnight, Emery would have cleared a path to his door, going out of channels, bypassing the normal protocols, ensuring that Telemann got the access he needed. It was one of the last things they'd discussed in the car, waiting in the drop-off zone, Laura's letter on the seat between them, and Telemann didn't have the slightest doubt that Emery would do as he'd promised, and grease the wheels. Work and pleasure, as he'd always insisted, were strictly incompatible.

At the police station, Telemann found the detective in charge. He didn't speak English. They talked for several minutes in halting French, and the detective confirmed that they had no leads on the attack. The Greek, he said, had been badly beaten. Whoever did it had known a great deal about physical violence. The doctors at the hospital said he was lucky to have survived.

Telemann nodded, making notes, aware of the man's curiosity, this small, dark, intense American, walking in from nowhere. The detective offered to drive him to the hospital, take him to the sailor, but Telemann said no thanks. He had the name of the ship, the date of the attack, the confirmation that the *Enoxia* had left the next day. The guy he really wanted to talk to was Vlaedders, the agent.

'You know him?' he asked.

The detective nodded. Everybody knew Vlaedders.

'What's he like?'

'OK. Rich.'

'Where'd he get the money?'

'From his business.' The detective laughed. 'Where else?'

Telemann looked him in the eye, long enough to know that the man wasn't bluffing, probably didn't know about the Israeli connection, if – indeed – there was one.

'Where do I find him?'

The detective reached for a phone book, confirming the address that Emery had already given him, and explaining how to find it. The detective looked at his watch. Vlaedders kept rich man's hours. If he wasn't at his office, he'd be at home. He gave Telemann another address.

Telemann drove away from the police station, following the detective's directions. He took the main road back towards the city, trying to avoid the trams that clanged noisily past. In the old quarter, several blocks away from the railway station, he found a car park. The walk to Vlaedders' office took less than five minutes. Telemann was awake now, alert, his mind emptied of everything but the next half-hour.

Vlaedders' office occupied the third floor of an old pre-war building beside a small hotel. Telemann went in, taking the stairs at a steady trot. Each landing was hung with fading water-colours, wide flat landscapes, candy-floss clouds. There was wooden parquet flooring underfoot. The smell reminded Telemann of school. Vlaedders' office door was open. Inside, a secretary sat behind a desk. She looked about ninety. Telemann introduced himself, using the cover name. He explained that he had no appointment with Mr Vlaedders, but would appreciate half an hour of his time. He was a journalist on assignment from the USA. He was researching a long piece on the prospect for European trade. Mr Vlaedders was at the sharp end. He must have seen all kinds of changes. It might offer a nice angle.

The secretary, who spoke excellent English, listened to him without comment. Then she got up and went into another office, shutting the door behind her. When she emerged again, she held the door open. 'He'll see you now,' she said. 'He has another appointment at three.'

Telemann thanked her and went in. Vlaedders was standing at the window. Expecting someone older, Telemann found a small, neat figure in his early thirties. He was wearing a dark, two-button suit, the jacket hung carefully over the back of his chair. He had thick, gold-rimmed glasses, and steady eyes, and an almost permanent smile.

He waved Telemann into a seat in front of the desk and sat down. Telemann explained who he was, what he'd come for. He sketched in enough background to justify the surprise call and then tried to narrow the focus. How long had Vlaedders been working in the shipping business? What kind of clients did he represent? Where were the real opportunities for a man who wanted to make serious money? What kind of changes would German reunification bring?

Vlaedders answered his questions one by one with an easy fluency. Like the secretary, he spoke perfect English. He knew a great deal about the shipping world. He indicated where the trends might lead. He agreed that reunification might make a major difference. Unless they were very foolish indeed, the Europeans would soon have the rest of the world by the throat.

The conversation went on, Telemann jotting the occasional note, Vlaedders watching him, ever-patient, ever-polite, the smile rarely leaving his lips. When Telemann enquired about particular cargoes, he conceded that there might be a problem. Bulk goods were sometimes a headache. Paperwork on finished products like televisions and fridges could be a nightmare. Telemann nodded, clearing the path ahead, picking his way carefully towards the Cypriot freighter, the consignment of pesticide, the source of the stuff.

'I understand you handle chemicals?' he said.

Vlaedders nodded. 'Sometimes.'

'Problems?'

'Occasionally. Sailors are born clumsy. Stowage isn't always

115

perfect. Containers are damaged in transit. You get gales. Bad weather—' he shrugged '—leaks.'

'Anything recent? Anything you can remember?'

There was a long silence, and Telemann wondered whether he'd overstepped the mark, changed gear too clumsily, hit a bump in the road. Vlaedders was still watching him. He had the expression of a man for whom life held few surprises.

'You want to know about the *Enoxia*?' he said. 'Is that why you're here?'

Telemann looked at him for a moment, then nodded. 'Yes,' he said.

Vlaedders smiled at him. Then he reached forward and took a single sheet of paper from a pad. He produced a pen from his pocket and scribbled a name and an address.

'There's someone a journalist like you ought to talk to,' he said, 'to save us both a great deal of time.'

Telemann nodded. 'Here?' he said. 'In Antwerp?'

Vlaedders looked at him for a moment or two, speculative, curious, bored with the game they'd been playing. Then he shook his head.

'No,' he said. 'You have to go to Hamburg.'

*

McVeigh finally found the Arab in a small restaurant in Mayfair. He was sitting alone at a small table at the back, reading a copy of *Newsweek*. He had a bread roll in one hand and a glass of something alcoholic in the other. He invited McVeigh to sit down.

McVeigh looked at him across the perfect square of white damask. 'I need some answers,' he said, 'and you may have them.'

'I may?'

'Yes.' McVeigh leaned forward across the table. 'Last night my flat was done over. Two guys. One white. One black. They were still there when I got back. They left shortly afterwards.'

The Arab nodded. 'Breaking and entering,' he said. 'Isn't that the phrase?'

'Sure. But explain this.'

McVeigh's hand went to his jacket pocket. He produced a

small metal object, about the size and thickness of a shirt button. Tiny whiskers of wire curled from one side, soldered in place. McVeigh put the object on the table-cloth. The Arab looked at it, reaching for another bread roll.

'It's a bug,' McVeigh said, 'I found it in the telephone.' He paused. 'My telephone.'

'You think these . . . men . . . put it there?'

'I know they did.'

'How?'

'The phone was still in pieces. When I had a good look round, there it was, on the floor, under the window.'

'Ah . . .' The Arab nodded. 'Telephone engineers.'

McVeigh said nothing, looking at him, the accusation plain in his face. He and Billy had spent hours putting the flat back together again. They'd finally got to bed past midnight, McVeigh swearing the boy to secrecy, all too aware of what might have happened had they both walked in together. Alone, he could cope with most of life's surprises. Having Billy around, it was very different. He was vulnerable.

McVeigh leaned forward, making his point, still angry. 'Checking up on me, were you? Making sure you get your money's worth?'

The Arab frowned, an expression of genuine pain. 'For £500 a day,' he said, 'I don't expect to be cheated.'

'Then why do it?'

'I didn't do it. Neither would I do it. My friend, we have a contract. You've agreed to find out certain facts, ask certain questions. A wise man makes his choice and then stands back. I expect results, Mr McVeigh. Not abuse.'

McVeigh looked at him for a long time. He was a good judge of character, of when someone was lying, and now he knew that he'd got it wrong, badly wrong. He sat back in the chair. 'I'm sorry,' he said, 'but I had to be sure.'

The Arab shrugged. 'It's OK,' he said, 'you made a mistake. Nothing worse.' He paused. 'I thought you were flying to Tel Aviv?'

McVeigh nodded. 'I am,' he said. 'Tonight.'

'Then shouldn't you be packing?' the Arab said mildly.

'Making your phone calls? Earning your money?' He paused again, his voice soft, the subtlest of reprimands.

McVeigh nodded again, getting up. He'd dropped Billy off at his mother's at eight, waiting in the car outside while the boy ran upstairs and looked through the drawer where he kept his secrets. He'd found the piece of paper in less than a minute, Yakov's writing, the address in Tel Aviv, the place where Yakov told him he could write. They had an apartment, he and his wife, an oldish place with a distant view of the sea.

McVeigh stood at the table for a moment. The Arab raised his glass.

'Shalom . . .' he said drily. 'And good luck.'

*

The first time she phoned, Emery said it was impossible. The second time, an hour later, she was in tears. He listened to her for perhaps a minute, and checked his watch. His car had been fitted with a secure mobile. He could work en route. He'd be out there within the half-hour. She wasn't to worry about lunch.

He drove fast, against the last of the late morning traffic, out through the lush acres of Chevvy Chase, out towards Rockville. Telemann had a house on the eastern edge of the town, modest white clapboard, big shuttered windows, extended out the back. It stood in half an acre of ground, mostly grass that Laura cropped weekly with an ancient power-mower. There was a barbecue pit, and a couple of apple trees, and a swing for Bree.

Bree met him in the drive, hearing the burble from the Chrysler's holed exhaust when Emery was still a hundred yards away, turning into Dixie Street. She ran out of the house and jumped up at him as he got out of the car. She was slightly retarded, and it showed in her eyes, a look of total trust, almost doglike. At ten, she could barely read or write.

'Peter,' she said, 'Uncle Peter.'

Emery kissed her, taking her hand and following her into the house. The house was cooler after the heat of the street. All the windows were open, and the curtains stirred in the breeze.

Laura emerged from the kitchen. She was wearing an old pair of Telemann's shorts and a singlet. Her legs were bare, and the strap had broken on one of her sandals. Every time she moved, the metal buckle banged on the wooden floor. She was carrying a tall glass, something golden topped with ice cubes. She gave it to him, kissing him as she did so. 'Apple and soda,' she said, 'no booze.'

Emery sipped at the drink and put his mobile phone on the window-sill. Bree clattered downstairs with a drawing book. She had two pens in her other hand, and she began to pull Emery towards the table. Laura shooed her away, promising a treat later. Then she glanced at the phone. 'I'm sorry,' she said quietly, 'I know you're busy.'

Emery shrugged and said nothing. He took her by the arm and led her to the sofa. She was a big woman, broad, well made. Kids suited her, and so did this house of theirs, the vessel that contained their lives. It was spacious, and chaotic, and friendly, a house without pretence or formality. It had resilience, and warmth, and character, so different to the neat, charmless apartment he and his wife tried to call their own. It was a big place, bigger than it seemed from the road, and Laura filled it all with her smile, and her laughter, and her limitless patience.

They sat together on the sofa, Emery sprawled against one arm, instantly at home. Laura sat beside him, her legs drawn up under her chin, the redness under her eyes barely visible beneath the summer tan.

'It's terrible,' she said, 'horrible.'

'What is?'

'Lying to him.'

Emery looked at her. The glasses he wore always made his eyes seem bigger. She'd noticed that. When they were off, he could look quite handsome. She reached forward and took the glasses off. Bree, watching from the stairs, yelped with pleasure and skidded across the floor and seized them. She put them on, circling the room, her hands out in front of her, feigning blindness.

Laura was still looking at Emery. 'So what do I do?' she said. 'Only it's driving me nuts.'

Emery yawned, apologizing at once. Laura took his hand.

'You're tired,' she said automatically.

'I am.'

'You working hard?'

'Yes.'

'Same job as Ron?'

'Yes.'

She nodded, knowing better than to push the questions. All that mattered were the symptoms, the fatigue, the lost tempers, the sleepless nights, the Tuinol in a neat pile on the locker beside the bed. She, above all, knew about those. How to mend empty bodies, broken minds.

'I love him,' she said absently. 'You know that.'

'Yes.'

She looked at him again, reaching for him, wanting the simple comfort of a hug, her head on his shoulder, her arms around his neck. Bree was still circling the room. She was singing now. She had a remarkable voice, high and soft and pure. It was the one thing in life she did really well, and she sang often. Emery had awakened to her sometimes in the early morning, sitting cross-legged on the end of his bed in the spare room, the door carefully shut behind her, his own infant Buddha. '*It's a little bit funny,*' she sang, '*this feeling inside . . .*'

Laura stirred. Her eyes were closed. The vein in her neck pulsed slowly, the morning's storm blown out, the tears quite gone.

'I nearly told him in New York,' she said quietly. 'That's why I went. I thought it was time.'

'And?'

'We made love.'

Emery looked down at her, stroking her hair. Her hair was thick, a rich auburn. She dyed it when she remembered to. It was greying gently underneath.

'Not a bad trade-in,' Emery said, 'under the circumstances.'

Laura said nothing for a moment. Bree had disappeared into the kitchen.

'Was I right?' she said at last, 'not to tell him?'

'You asking me?'

'Yes.'

'How should I know?'

'Because you know him and you know me. You know the kind of people we are. So—' she looked up at him '—you'll have a view. That's not a sentimental thing. It's not copping out. It's just the truth. You know the man. You're a good judge. So—' she reached up for him again '—help me. Tell me what you think.'

Emery nodded and said nothing, staring across the room at the open kitchen door. Bree's shadow lay across the white linoleum. She was trying to spell her own name on the fridge, a pile of red magnetic letters by her side.

'How sure are you?' he said at last.

'Very.'

'No grounds for doubt? No second thoughts?' He paused. 'Second opinions?'

She shook her head. 'None. We've been that way. You know we have.'

'So this is really it?'

'Yep.'

'Thought it all through?'

'Yep.'

'Do or die?'

She looked up at him and risked a small smile.

'Sure,' she said. 'You know the man. Do or die.'

*

Telemann was back at Brussels Airport by early evening. It was Friday evening, and the check-in desks were thick with Eurocrats commuting back to their weekend homes in London and Paris and Rome. Telemann returned the hire car and bought a Lufthansa ticket to Hamburg. The flight didn't leave for an hour and a half. He checked his bag and crossed the concourse to a bank of telephones. He checked his watch. In Washington, it was half-past twelve.

He dailled the operator and gave her the number and asked for a collect call, scanning the big overhead departures board. Thirty seconds later, Juanita was on the line.

'Hi,' he said, 'it's me.'

'I know. The operator told me.'

'This is a public booth. She tell you that, too?'

'No. But I figured it out just the same.'

Telemann hesitated for a moment. Using open lines and plain English was strictly left field. Nobody did it. Not unless you wanted to feature in an NSA intercepts digest, your name underlined for further action.

'Listen,' he said, 'I need to speak with Emery.'

'He's not here.'

'Where is he?'

'I dunno. But he has the mobile with him. You got the number?'

'Yeah.'

'Then I guess you phone it.'

She paused long enough to let him come up with a better idea, then Telemann heard the trill of another phone in the background and a smooth apology from Juanita as she put the caller on hold. Back on the line, she asked him if he was OK. He said he was, and hung up. He waited for a moment in the phone booth, lacking the strength, or perhaps the courage, to make the call. He was out of the office somewhere. It could be a million places. It could be Langley. It could be the attorney's place over on 'K' Street. It might even be the White House, Sullivan's real office, right up there in the dress-circle. It could be any of these places, but deep in his heart Telemann knew that it wasn't. Emery was where Laura was. Emery was with his wife.

Bree was back in the room when Emery's mobile began to ring. She was sitting on the floor in a puddle of sunshine, singing one of her favourite hymns, a Christmas carol she sang year-long, whenever she felt especially happy. She was singing it now. *'O come all ye faithful,'* she crooned, *'joyful and triumphant.'*

Emery reached over the back of the sofa and retrieved the mobile from the window-sill. Laura sat back, respectful, considerate. 'You want me to leave?'

Emery shook his head. 'No,' he said. 'Stay.' He lifted the receiver. He listened to the operator, 3000 miles away. He smiled. He said yes, he'd take the call. There was a brief pause.

Laura was watching him carefully, half-aware of what was happening, who was at the other end.

'Ron,' Emery said at last. 'Buddy.'

Hearing her father's name, Bree's smile widened even further. '*Come and behold him*,' she sang. '*Born the King of angels,*
O come let us adore him
O come, let us adore him
O come, let us adore him, Christ the Lord.'

Standing in the booth at Brussels Airport, Telemann held the phone away from his ear, blinking, unable to believe it. Bree. His daughter. Her song. On Emery's mobile phone. He shook his head, trying to dislodge the sound, hearing in the background another chord, deeper, a rumbling noise, the blood sucking noisily around his own body. This is madness, he told himself. Madness. I'm going mad. He lifted the phone again, hearing Emery's voice, hesitant, worried.

'Ron?'

Telemann looked out at the concourse, up at the departures board, anywhere, anything to empty his mind of that one overpowering image, Emery, Pete Emery, out in the little house on Dixie. He stared at the departures board, blinking again. For some reason, quite suddenly, he could see two of everything. Two destinations. Two flight numbers. Two take-off times. He rubbed his eyes. Double vision, he thought. Madness made real.

'Pete?' he mumbled.

'Yeah?'

'Where the hell are you?'

'Your place. With Laura. And Bree. You wanna word?'

The singing had stopped. Telemann swallowed hard. The balls on the man. No sign of panic, or guilt, or remorse. Not a single missed beat in that deep, slow voice of his. Straight buddy talk. Like he was in some bar in Georgetown, and Telemann had happened by, and Emery had called him in from the sidewalk, summoned the bartender and ordered up the usual pitcher.

'Some party,' Telemann muttered.

'What?'

'I said, some fucking party.'

'You OK? Tired? Hey—'

Telemann heard the noise of the phone changing hands. Then a new voice, softer, slightly wary, Laura. Telemann closed his eyes, letting his body sag against the corner of the booth. New York, he thought suddenly. That's why she came to New York. She meant to tell me. Only she didn't. Couldn't. Hadn't.

'Ron?'

Telemann looked at the phone. The man in the next booth was having a bad time in some other conversation. Telemann could hear him shouting in German, his finger jabbing at some imaginary assailant. His wife, Telemann thought. Another whore.

'Ron?'

'Yeah?'

'You OK?'

'Yeah.'

'What's happening?'

'Not much. You got Pete there?'

'Yeah.'

'OK. I need to speak with him.'

Telemann listened to the dialogue, his own voice, cold, and he marvelled at the control, the way this strange man in the booth had got himself in and out of such a difficult conversation.

Emery returned, laconic as ever. 'What gives?'

Telemann ignored the question, unfolding the piece of paper he'd got from Vlaedders. He read the name and telephone number down the phone. He was too far gone to worry about open lines. Open lines were for the birds.

'Reinhart Trumm,' he said again. 'Hamburg number. I'm flying there now. I'll phone you from Fuhlsbüttel. Run a check. I need to know.'

'Sure.' Emery paused. 'That it?'

'Yeah.'

'OK. Kisses from Laura. Take care now. Bye, buddy.'

Telemann gazed at the phone again, holding the receiver at arm's-length, hearing the click as the line disconnected. Care?

Kisses? Laura? *Buddy?* He turned on his heel, picked up his shoulder-bag and hurried towards the washroom across the concourse. As he did so, he looked up at the departures board, seeing double again, the second time in five minutes. He stopped and rubbed his eyes. He looked around. Everything was doubled, like a camera lens out of true. He took a series of deep breaths, eyes closed again, forcing the air deep into his lungs, counting slowly to thirty, and when he looked round again, his sight was perfect, the images no longer dancing. Odd, he thought, making for the washroom, wondering whether he still wanted to throw up.

*

Faraday's body stayed in the big mortuary fridge at Newbury General Hospital for an hour and a half.

The pathologist, summoned from her garden in Theale, arrived at 18.45. She read the accident report and conferred briefly with the casualty registrar. He told her that the drum of chemicals had been resealed, and the area decontaminated. Laboratory staff from the group's Analysis Division were now en route to the waste transfer station. They would remove a number of discreet samples and return to company head-quarters. A full report and analysis would be available within forty-eight hours.

The pathologist borrowed a small office beside the casualty area and telephoned the Newbury coroner. Without a formal request from the coroner's office, she wasn't allowed to proceed with a post-mortem. The coroner was out when she finally got through, but a clerk confirmed that so far there'd been nothing from the police on the incident, and consequently no plans for an inquest.

The pathologist put the phone down. She'd already visited the mortuary and had a look at the body. The attendants had removed Faraday's clothes and laid his naked corpse on one of the big stainless-steel tables. As she'd expected, there was no sign of external injury, except for some superficial abrasion on the forehead where he'd been dragged away from the drum by his feet. The real story was usually internal – the secrets yielded by the body's organs – but even here she knew she'd be lucky to find anything conclusive. There'd be no air left in the lungs to sample, nothing in the stomach that he might have swallowed. Death would be certifiable as respiratory failure, or heart failure, or both, but these terse phrases were of minor forensic value. Whatever had killed him would have left little, if any, trace. Perhaps the fatty tissue samples might respond to gas chromatography. Perhaps, like so many youngsters, he'd taken one sniff of solvent too many. But that, in view of his job, was unlikely.

She pondered the problem a little longer, watching the attendants in the mortuary wrapping the body in shiny white plastic. The label on the side of the drum had definitely read 'Poison'. It had been there in the reports, black and white. And the thing had been washed ashore, origin unknown, destination unknown, contents a mystery. The drum itself had evidently been a little out of the ordinary, reinforced top and bottom, heavier gauge steel than usual. She followed the attendants back into the fridge room and picked up the phone again, wondering how far to take it, whether to seek specialist advice. The number rang and rang, the switchboard busy, and after a couple of minutes she put the phone down again, glancing at her watch. There were still a couple of hours of daylight left. If she drove fast, she could be back amongst the roses by eight. The coroner would be back in his office tomorrow. Better to wait for a formal post-mortem.

*

Telemann stepped off the Lufthansa 737 at nine o'clock, Hamburg time.

The concourse at Fuhlsbüttel was nearly empty, a couple in the departures bar sipping a beer together before the late night flights took off, the odd businessman nursing a schnapps and a creased copy of *Die Zeit*. Telemann found a phone booth and used his ATT card to call Emery. It was mid-afternoon in Washington, and he was back at his desk in the office on 'F' Street.

Neither man wasted time with formalities. Emery had the details on a fax from Langley.

'Trumm's real name's Nathan Blum,' he said, 'he's a *katsa*.

He's been in Hamburg since April. Before that he was in Copenhagen . . .' He paused. 'He's spent time in South Africa and Buenos Aires. In fact he was there the same time as you . . .' He paused again, and Telemann could hear him chuckling. 'But the big news is Palestine. The guy used to be one of their point men on the West Bank. Speaks fluent Arabic. Took lots of scalps. So be careful, buddy. The man has a reputation.'

Telemann, memorizing the details as they spilled out of the phone, grunted. 'That all?'

'Yeah.'

'Anything else?'

'Not on this phone.'

Telemann nodded and said goodbye. He picked up his bag and made his way out of the building, looking for a cab. He'd phoned the number Vlaedders had given him from Brussels. A woman had answered, and Telemann had simply given her the facts, knowing that Vlaedders would already have been on the line. The name's Lacey, he'd said. I'm a journalist on assignment, and Mr Vlaedders suggests I talk to Herr Trumm. The woman had noted the details and promised to pass them on. Herr Trumm was in conference. She'd be able to talk to him within the hour. Herr Lacey should phone again.

Telemann stood outside the terminal building, yawning in the darkness. It was a hot night, with a fitful wind stirring the flags on a line of poles across the car park. Telemann could hear the halyards slapping against the poles.

He waited for another minute or so, then picked up his bag and began to walk slowly towards a line of cabs parked further down the terminal. Exhaustion had emptied him of everything but the simple imperatives of finding a bed and a shower, and a little peace. He'd shut his mind to Emery and Laura, and the fact that his marriage had hit the rocks. He'd done his best to erase the memory of his daughter's voice, the words carrying clear across the Atlantic. He'd even, for now, put aside the business in hand. Nathan Blum, the Israeli, would have to wait until tomorrow. Tomorrow, with a clear head after a decent night's sleep, he'd deal with it.

He lifted his arm to signal the nearest cab. As he did so,

another car parked in a bay across the road flashed its lights. He heard the engine start. It sounded like a diesel engine. The car began to move, pulling a tight U-turn, gliding to a halt at the kerbside. Telemann looked down. It was a Mercedes. Through the windshield, he could see two faces. One of them, behind the wheel, was a woman. She had a thin, angular face, hair pulled tightly back, a face he'd seen in a thousand magazines, the face of a model. She was looking up at him, smiling.

The passenger door opened and a man got out. He was wearing slacks and a short-sleeved shirt, open at the neck. His face was dark under a mass of curly blond hair. A smile revealed a set of perfect teeth. He extended a hand. 'Mr Lacey?'

Telemann nodded, the exhaustion gone. 'Yeah?'

'Reinhart Trumm. You telephoned from Brussels.'

The two men looked at each other for a moment, then Trumm opened the back door and bent for Telemann's bag. There was no discussion, no hesitation, simply the acceptance that Telemann would get in. Telemann did so, wondering why they were bothering with the formality of cover names. They checked the flights, he thought. A simple phone call.

Trumm put Telemann's bag in the trunk and got into the car. The woman engaged gear and eased the big Mercedes towards the airport exit. Telemann watched her from the back seat, quarter-profile, high cheek-bones, huge earrings, hair secured at the back with a knot of silk. She looked about thirty, possibly less. She smelled wonderful.

Telemann lay back against the dimpled leather. There wasn't much he could do, and they all knew it. The next hour or so belonged to them. They'd seized the initiative. They could dictate the pace.

Telemann yawned. 'Where are we going?' he said.

Trumm turned round, putting his elbow on the back of the seat. He was smiling again, completely relaxed. He might have stepped out of the shower after an hour or so of tennis.

'Hotel in town,' he said. 'Modest but clean.'

The Hotel Hauptstadt lay at the heart of the old city. Small, dark, undistinguished, it appeared to be empty. Telemann checked in at the desk and collected a key to a room on the second floor. The room was small and spotless. The duvet was turned down on the single bed, and the window offered a glimpse of the docks across the river. Telemann threw his bag on to a chair and sluiced his face under the tap. In the mirror, he wondered about having a shave but decided against it. They knew he'd just flown in. They knew he'd probably been awake for a couple of days. They were ahead of the game, and five minutes with mint-fresh foam and a Gillette razor wasn't going to change anything.

He joined them downstairs in a corner of the tiny bar. They were sitting at a table, studying a snack menu. When Telemann came in, they both got up. The Mercedes was still outside.

They drove west out of the city. The traffic and the houses thinned. Soon they were on an autobahn. Telemann, watching idly from the back-seat, saw signs for Elmshorn and Itzehoe. Twenty kilometres short of Brunsbüttel, the car slowed and left the autobahn. Apart from the occasional exchange between Blum and the woman behind the wheel, there was no conversation, no small-talk. The radio was on, the volume low, jazz classics, Quincy Jones, Stan Getz. Once or twice, curious, Telemann asked the kind of questions a visiting journalist might ask, drawing his cover around him, but the answers he got were no more than cursory, brief acknowledgements that he was riding in the car with them, a guest of sorts, and that they owed him the simple courtesy of a 'yes' or 'no'. Beyond that, neither of them was prepared to go. Federal Express, Telemann thought as the Mercedes slowed for yet another village. Couriers sent to the airport to collect the goods.

Beyond the village, they turned left. The road narrowed, no more than a track now, deeply rutted. In the distance, across the flat landscape, Telemann could see the lights of a ship moving slowly across the fields. He frowned, trying to make sense of the image, picturing the map of the area, the plains of Schleswig-Holstein stretching north and west towards Denmark. He blinked and rubbed his eyes, wondering whether this was yet another form of double vision, but the ship was still there, the red navigation lights high on the bridge, the dark silhouette of the hull, the row of port-holes aft, crew accommodation, softly lit from within. He hesitated, wondering whether to risk a question, realizing quite suddenly how tired he was, then he had it, the map again, the heavy blue line bisecting this neck of land, connecting the Baltic to the North Sea. The Kiel Canal, he thought. We're right up by the Kiel Canal.

Abruptly, the car swung left, along a dirt road and into the cover of a stand of trees. The car stopped. The woman switched off the engine, and for a moment there was silence. Then Telemann picked up another noise, mechanical, a low hum. Generator, he thought.

They got out. It was cooler here, the air fresher. Overhead, the trees stirred in the wind. Telemann peered into the darkness, following the woman as she picked her way through the long grass. There were lights through the trees, the generator sounded louder, there was the smell of manure and newly mown hay. On the other side of the trees was a small cottage. Beyond the cottage, shapes in the darkness, were a number of outbuildings. Listening hard, Telemann could hear the stirring of animals.

They went into the cottage, the woman knocking three times on the door and then letting herself in with a key. Inside, blinking in the sudden light, Telemann had the sense of a recent renovation: wooden beams exposed, expensive rugs on a newly laid wooden floor, carefully framed pictures, Kandinsky and Klee, twenties' classics. Despite the farmyard smells outside, the place belonged to someone altogether more metropolitan, someone with taste, someone who knew their way around the gentler pieces of Bauhaus. There was music, too, Brahms, the Violin Concerto.

Telemann followed the woman into the big downstairs living-room. A man in his sixties rose from an armchair in the corner. He was wearing shorts, knee-length socks and a khaki shirt. His skin was the colour of the darker stained pine panels. He had a long, deeply lined face, but his hair was still jet-black. He was lean and alert, a man with a lifetime's practice at looking after himself. He was smoking a pipe.

Blum crossed the room and shook the man's hand. Then he

turned to Telemann. The smile was back on his face, amused, gently sceptical, a man who had trouble remembering names. 'Mr . . .?'

Telemann hesitated a moment, wondering whether to bother with the fiction any longer. These people knew. He could sense it. The games were over. There were guys in New York with gallons of nerve gas, and scores to settle, and a delicate political point to make. US troops were pouring into Saudi Arabia. Time was running out.

Telemann shook the proffered hand. 'Telemann,' he said briefly. 'Ron Telemann.'

The man with the pipe studied him for a moment, still holding his hand, then he smiled. He spoke English with a heavy German accent. 'My name's Klausmann,' he said slowly. 'You may have heard of me.'

Telemann frowned, trawling his memory, looking for the index card. Klausmann, he thought. He shook his head, glancing across at Blum. The Israeli indicated an armchair beside a stack of expensive audio equipment. Telemann sank into it, still trying to place the name.

The woman appeared from the kitchen. She was carrying a tray. On it were two bottles of wine and a plateful of sandwiches. One or two of the sandwiches were beginning to curl. Telemann looked at them. They expected me earlier, he thought. An earlier flight.

The woman put the tray down and uncorked both bottles. She poured the wine. He accepted a glass and took a handful of sandwiches. They were some kind of *wurst*, thinly sliced, quite delicious. Telemann lifted his glass, a little revived, curious now, eager to see who'd make the running, which direction the conversation would take, where it might lead.

'*Prosit*,' he said with a smile, '*shalom*.'

The others lifted their glasses, amused by the toast. Then Blum leaned forward, abruptly businesslike. He indicated Klausmann with a tilt of the head, not taking his eyes off Telemann.

'You've come a long way,' he said, 'so we thought it better not to waste your time. Dr Klausmann is a chemist. He retired

131

three years ago. Now he lives here, in this house. Until reunification, he lived in the East.'

Telemann nodded, looking across at Klausmann, framing the obvious question, knowing already what the answer would be.

'Where?' he enquired politely. 'Where in the East?'

Blum looked at him for a moment. 'Halle,' he said, still smiling.

*

McVeigh arrived at Ben Gurion International Airport at half-past ten the next day.

The big El Al 747 was forty minutes late, delayed in a stack of circling aircraft. Sitting beside a window towards the back of the executive cabin, McVeigh looked down on the sprawl of Tel Aviv, trying to match the pattern of interlocking major roads with the city map he'd already committed to memory. The big roads were easy, Ben Yehuda and Dizengoff, running parallel to the seafront. There were beaches along the seafront, already dotted with sunbeds, and the long concrete arm of a marina.

The plane banked again, and the view of Tel Aviv changed, the south of the city suddenly visible, the old town, Jaffa, the walls of the ancient harbour, a single speedboat arrowing out to sea, the wake feathering away behind it. McVeigh gazed down at the deep blues and the dusty greys and browns, knowing that Jaffa was where he'd have to start, at the address in his pocket. Yakov's apartment.

The nose dipped, and the pilot eased back on the throttles, the whine of the engines changing note. McVeigh braced as the tarmac came up to meet the big Boeing, and the wheels bit, and the grass of the airfield, scorched brown by the heat, raced past. The aircraft shuddered under reverse thrust, and McVeigh reached forward for the paperback he'd tucked into the back of the seat. Inside the paperback was a postcard. It was unstamped. Billy had delivered it personally, by hand, the previous evening. McVeigh had found it on the mat.

Now, easing his seat-belt, he turned it over. On one side was a black and white photo of Gary Lineker. On the other, in careful capitals, was Billy's contribution to the next week or so.

Reading it, McVeigh smiled. No nonsense. No messing. Nothing fancy.

'Good luck, Dad,' it went. 'Come back soon.'

*

The analysts at the Dispozall group headquarters had a result on the Newbury sample by eleven-thirty, London time.

The Executive Chemical Officer, who'd supervised the last stages of the process, checked the read-outs a final time and returned to his office at the end of the bigger of the two laboratories. He'd not been briefed on the Newbury incident until he'd arrived for work at eight o'clock.

Wearing full protective gear, he'd spent the next three hours watching the analyst run the elimination tests, but he'd seen the colour of the stuff, and he'd heard what had happened out at Newbury, and twelve years' Army service told him the rest of the story. The result of the analysis, when it came, was the merest formality.

He closed the office door behind him and lifted the phone. A four-figure internal number took him to the group's managing director, three floors above. The man had been up half the night. He sounded knackered. The ECO extracted a sheaf of Kleenex from the box on the desk and mopped his face.

'That Newbury business,' he said briefly. 'It's nerve gas.'

'It's what?'

'Nerve gas. Tabun GA. It's bastard stuff. We need to deal with the rest of it sharpish. It's not nice.'

There was a long silence. The ECO gazed out through the glass walls of his office. The analyst was bent over the sample jars, sealing them again, totally airtight. Then the managing director returned. He sounded, if anything, even worse.

'We have a problem,' he said.

'You're right.'

'No.' He paused. 'I meant another problem.'

'Oh?' The ECO frowned. Tabun was a name from the doomsday brief. The amount he was looking at down the lab could take care of most of Greater London. Five gallons properly dispersed was enough to empty the British Isles.

133

'What's the matter?' he said. 'What's happened?'
'Newbury have been on. Half an hour ago.'
'And?'
'The stuff's gone.'

Book two

31 August 1990

6

The way Sullivan saw it, the message was for real. 'Kosher,' he said. 'For sure.'

The President looked at him for a moment across the long 25-foot conference table. Sullivan had flown up to Camp David by helicopter, arriving only minutes ago. Clambering out of the big Sikorsky, ducking in the downwash from the rotor, he'd followed one of the Marine guards across the landing-strip and down through the stand of pines to the Lodge. The President had been up at Camp David since Friday night. A principals-only meeting had just finished, the flasks of juice and the five empty glasses still sitting on the table. The President looked at him for a moment longer, then read the single sheet of paper again. Underneath the Kennebunkport tan, he looked tired and irritable.

'Amman again?'

'Cyprus.'

'When?'

'This morning. 09.14 Eastern Standard Time. Early evening in Nicosia.'

'Anything else come with it? Names?' The President paused. 'Any toll-free numbers we might call?'

Sullivan raised a smile at the joke, then shook his head. 'Nothing, sir,' he said. 'The way I heard it, the guy arrived on a motor-bike and left it at the gate. Same as last time.' He paused again. 'I'd have cabled the contents, but under the circumstances . . .' He broke off and shrugged.

The President glanced up for a moment, not hearing him properly. He seemed exhausted, his voice low. 'The bastard's capable of anything,' he said. 'Any damn thing. You see him on CNN last week?'

Sullivan nodded. 'I was there, sir,' he said gently. 'We watched it together.'

The President looked at him, frowning, and then nodded. 'Oh, sure,' he said. 'You were. I forgot.'

His hand reached for the flask of juice and he filled the nearest glass. Eight days ago, Saddam had appeared on television with a group of Western kids, effectively hostages of the Iraqi regime. One of them, an English boy, he'd talked to through an interpreter, benign, smiling, reaching across to touch and reassure the child, a father-figure, the very model of concern. The boy, plainly terrified, had done his best to hide his feelings, but the President, watching the big set in the Oval Office, had paled at the sight, his fists clenched, his face ashen. Sullivan had watched him across the room, knowing yet again that the crisis in the Gulf had become – for the President at least – a moral crusade. Black and white. Good and evil.

Now the President put the single sheet of paper on the table and sank into a chair. There was a long silence. Sullivan could hear the whine of a hoover outside in the corridor. The next meeting, he knew, was scheduled for late afternoon. The J-boys were arriving, the Joint Chiefs of Staff, breaking yet another weekend to keep the President briefed on the huge military build-up now flooding into Saudi Arabia. The President wanted the details, all the details, the name and composition of every last unit heading east. After the disasters of early August – the Intelligence people wrongfooted, the Pentagon in shock – he was determined to be the playmaker, the guy who called as many of the moves as possible.

A month into the crisis, it was beginning to work. The diplomatic noose was tightening daily. Twenty-two nations had pledged forces to the UN coalition. American forces in the Gulf now topped 100,000, with thousands more en route. And God knows, at last there were signs that the pressure was beginning to work. Only days ago, Saddam had offered to free the women and children he was holding in Baghdad. The price of their freedom – US withdrawal – was totally unacceptable, but none the less the news had drawn a small ripple of applause in

Washington's upper circle. The guy just blinked, went the word. We've got him by the balls and he's starting to hurt.

The President gazed around the table at the neat row of empty seats. His right hand strayed again to the message Sullivan had brought from Washington. The message was blunt. The President had four weeks to halt the build-up in Saudi Arabia and turn the thing around. Unless the troops were heading home by the end of the month, New York would take the consequences. The President looked across at Sullivan again. 'Who do we talk to?' he said. 'These June 7th guys, who are they?'

Sullivan shook his head. 'We don't know.'

'*Nothing?*'

'Nothing.' He paused. 'Not yet.'

'So when?' The President frowned, leaning forward, impatient for news. 'This guy of yours . . . our fireman . . . is he good? Is he doing it for us? Has he . . .?'

Sullivan smiled, a quizzical expression, and looked away, and the President hesitated a moment and then shrugged, an implicit acknowledgement of the pact between them, obliged to accept, for once, an ignorance of the small-print. On this one, the word was deniability. If any hint of Sullivan's operation leaked out, if the shit hit the fan, then it was crucial that none got as far as the Presidency. Sullivan would suffer, sure, but his loyalty had always been beyond question, and he'd be happy to take the fall.

Abruptly, the President got up, folding Sullivan's note into his pocket. Sullivan was on his feet across the table, buttoning his jacket. The President paused by the door, opening it, and then changed his mind and closed it again. With people he trusted, he had a habit of thinking aloud. He looked down at Sullivan, very close. 'We have a problem with the Israelis,' he said. 'You may have gathered.'

'Sir?'

'They've torn up the April deal. They ain't on board any more. They're contemplating a little action of their own.'

Sullivan nodded. Months before the invasion of Kuwait, back

in April, Saddam had sought assurances that neither the US nor Israel would move against him. The President, after a little thought, had twisted arms in Tel Aviv and given the Iraqis the guarantees they wanted. At the time, there'd been no reason to withhold the pledge. Given a choice, the President didn't want to fight anyone.

The Iraqis, four months later, had used the President's assurances for their own ends, throwing the weight of the Iraqi army against Kuwait – in the south – and leaving their western flank unprotected. Even now, there was still no real threat against Israel, but the Israelis had a notoriously short fuse. Year-long rumours that Baghdad was on the verge of producing a nuclear weapon, and now the move against Kuwait, were making them very nervous indeed – and provoked, they tended to favour action and not words. Intelligence reports were indicating a measure of quiet mobilization in Tel Aviv, and Sullivan knew all too well that any Israeli attack against Iraq, however justified, would shatter the Saudi-based coalition the President had so carefully assembled.

Sullivan frowned. 'You're talking to them regularly?'

'Every night.'

'They listening?'

'They hear what they want to hear but the bottom line never changes. If push comes to shove, they'll do it their way.'

'You believe them?'

'No question. They're unilateralists. Always have been.' He paused, his hand still on the door-knob. 'And they have a point. If it was you or me in Tel Aviv, we'd be thinking offensive too. You know the range of a Scud missile? The ones Saddam's had modified?'

Sullivan nodded. *Newsweek* had been publishing the facts for weeks. 'Six hundred kilometres.'

'You got it.' The President grimaced, nodding at the empty conference room. 'The fellas come up here with the maps and the little models. They draw it all out. Scuds are a dime a dozen. Stick a bunch in Western Iraq, out there in the desert some place, and you're in Tel Aviv in a coupla minutes. And remember—' he bent towards Sullivan, his voice low, almost conspiratorial '—you only have to get lucky once, just once, and the coalition's history. Drop a Scud in downtown Tel Aviv, kill women and children, and the Israelis will do the rest.' He snapped his fingers, making the point. 'Can you imagine what a party that would be? Shamir's boys over Baghdad? Our Arabs lining up alongside the Israelis?' He shook his head, leaving the question unanswered, opening the door instead.

In the hall, a woman in grey overalls was bending over the hoover. The President gave her a wave and led Sullivan towards the big swing-doors that led to the lobby. Outside, for mid-September, it was still hot, a light wind off the mountains stirring the tall stands of pine. The President paused for a moment, blinking in the sunlight, then took the path back towards the landing-pad. The helicopter was still there, the fat blue hull visible through the trees. Sullivan fell into step beside him, still listening, still waiting for instructions. The note, he thought. The deadline.

The President glanced down at him. 'You know what the Israelis fear most of all?'

Sullivan nodded. Historically, the answer wasn't hard to guess. 'Gas?'

'Sure. Strap a gallon or two on top of a Scud, and you're back at Auschwitz. That's the line they're taking.' He paused, watching a group of off-duty Marines jogging slowly through the trees. 'You know what one of their guys at the Embassy said to me yesterday?'

'No, sir?'

'He said we wouldn't understand. Couldn't understand. Hadn't been through it. He said we'd be a whole lot more concerned if it was our city, our folks on the receiving end. He said geography made us simple-minded.'

The President paused again. He pulled out Sullivan's note, flattening it against his knee, reading the stark, simple message. Then he glanced over at Sullivan, the worry back in his face, and the impatience. 'I don't want his name,' he said, 'but I hope to God your guy's good.'

*

In Hamburg, Telemann awoke at noon, strong sunlight through the thin calico curtains, the rumble of traffic from the street below. He rolled over and reached for the phone, grunting an acknowledgement to the receptionist.

'Fräulein Hecht,' she said in flawless English. 'Waiting for you in the bar.'

Still numb with jet-lag, Telemann shaved at the tiny basin, scrolling his face with foam, tidying his memories of the last twelve hours. He'd stayed out at the cottage for the best part of the night, picking his way back through the trees to the Mercedes as the sky began to lighten in the east. Klausmann, the German, the one they'd taken him to see, had done most of the talking, sitting in the armchair beside the tallest of the four bookcases, his body bent slightly forward, his arms on his bare knees, the bowl of his pipe cupped in one hand. The man had immense presence. He spoke slowly. He paused often. He took care with the words. He wasn't afraid of silence. He asked for nothing except attention, and by the time he'd finished, Telemann realized that most of what he was saying was probably true. He'd been an industrial chemist, supervising parts of the East German chemical warfare programme. And he had, during his last days in office, developed profound doubts about some of the clients that reunification had brought to the sprawling, ash-grey plant on the northern edges of Halle.

The evening had finished on a strange note. Telemann, notebook in hand, had asked for names, leads, phone numbers. He'd abandoned the fiction that he was some kind of visiting journalist, and substituted a simple list of questions. Who, exactly, were these 'clients'? What, specifically, had they wanted to acquire? How recent, and how reliable, was the best of the Intelligence? These enquiries, terse, hardened by fatigue and a certain impatience, Klausmann had waved aside. His information was at least a year old. His memory for precise details was uncertain. Yes, they were talking nerve gas: constituent chemicals and the ready-made, take-out version. And yes, the clients certainly included Iraq. They'd set up a number of front organizations in Europe. They had addresses in Switzerland, Brussels and the UK, and money – to his knowledge – had never been a problem. They'd used an international bank headquartered in Luxemburg. They'd brought tons of the stuff – hundreds of gallons – and shipped it back to the Gulf. But that wasn't the point.

No? Telemann had stared at him, his eyes playing tricks again, two versions of the German swimming out of focus. No?

At this, Klausmann had sighed, an expression of mild disappointment, a patient teacher handicapped by a slightly backward child. Then he'd looked across the room towards the woman, an appeal for help, and she had stood up and checked her watch, and shepherded Telemann towards the door. Tomorrow, she'd explained in the windy half-darkness outside the cottage, they'd drive east, to Halle. Herr Klausmann was where the story began. Herr Klausmann had been more than generous with his time. Tomorrow would progress events to Telemann's satisfaction.

Now, in the hotel, Telemann checked out and paid his bill. He could see the woman in the mirror behind the reception desk. She was sitting at the tiny bar, a coffee at her elbow, reading a magazine. On the drive back from the cottage, she'd finally offered him a name. 'Inge,' she'd said simply, 'Inge Hecht.' Whether Inge was her real name hardly mattered. What was beyond dispute was the fact that she worked for the Israelis, for Mossad, for Nathan Blum, the *katza* who'd picked Telemann up from the airport. Mossad, as ever, had the inside lane. And for once they appeared to want to share it.

Telemann and the girl drove east out of Hamburg, a hot cloudless afternoon, the sliding roof on the Mercedes wound back, Inge's eyes invisible behind the big Ray-Ban sunglasses. She was wearing a thin cotton dress, low-cut, with a pleated skirt. Her legs were bare. There was a fine silver chain around her neck, and her skin was a dark, tawny gold. Looking at her, aware of her presence beside him, Telemann realized that he hadn't thought about Laura since waking, an almost conscious act of self-defence, the putting away of a bad smell, the shutting of a box and the turning of a key. They drove fast, the promise of Berlin on the big overhead indicator boards, Inge's hand on the leather-rimmed wheel, long fingers, a single ring, perfect nails. From time to time she reached for the radio, changing channels, looking for music, jazz or rock. She seemed happy not to talk.

Ten kilometres short of Wittenberge, suddenly hungry, Telemann reached back for his holdall and rummaged for a bar of chocolate. He peeled back the silver foil and offered the girl a piece. She nodded, smiling, her hands still on the wheel. Telemann broke the bar in half and then halved it again. She glanced sideways at him and opened her mouth. He fed in the chocolate, three squares, licking his fingers afterwards.

'Have you been in Germany long?' he said.

'All my life.'

'Are you German?'

'Yes.'

'Truly?'

She looked sideways at him, the smile still on her face. There were traces of his own accent in her English. 'Truly,' she said.

Telemann looked at her for a moment, an answering smile, aware of how naïve his question must have seemed, an abrupt breach of protocol. There were moves you didn't make in these situations, things you didn't say, and one of them was 'Truly?' 'Truly?' was an act of unpardonable intimacy. It was a casting-aside of the make-believe, and the double names, and the elaborate cover, the bluffs and the counter-bluffs. It was a reaching-out, an act of exhaustion, perhaps even despair, and the girl knew it.

Telemann turned away and broke off another square of chocolate. They were way past the inner German border now, the frontier posts empty and abandoned, part of an older, colder Europe. He put the chocolate into his mouth, letting it melt slowly, savouring the rich, bitter taste. Last time he'd been this way, the autobahn had been empty, the odd Trabant, the occasional convoy of squat trucks out on manoeuvres from one of the huge army camps that dotted the flat wooded country that stretched east, towards Poland. Now, though, the traffic had thickened. West German plates. Hamburg. Lübeck. Dusseldorf. Speeding clots of BMWs, nose to tail, businessmen in dark suits, jowly, unsmiling, pushing 180 k.p.h. on the broken asphalt, West German fingers in the East German pie. Telemann watched them hurrying past and shook his head, a wistful smile.

'*Die sind ja verrückt*,' he said softly.

'*Sprechen sie Deutsch?*'

'*Ja.*' Telemann closed his eyes and yawned. '*Ja.* But I prefer English.'

'OK.'

The car slowed for a moment, then the girl fed in the throttle again and they were back at cruising speed, the tyres thrumming on the road. Telemann swallowed the last of the chocolate, letting it trickle slowly down his throat. He felt curiously light-headed. It wasn't an unpleasant sensation.

'Why are we going to Halle?' he said.

The girl said nothing for a moment. Then she glanced in the mirror. 'You have to meet someone else.'

'Who says I do?' Telemann opened one eye. 'Who says I have to meet this person?' The girl looked at him for a moment, an almost imperceptible movement of her head. In profile, she belonged on the cover of a magazine. She had a classic beauty, fine-boned, generations in the making. Telemann wondered about her mother, her grandmother, where she'd really come from. She didn't look Jewish, but that didn't mean a thing.

'Tell me,' he said softly. 'Tell me why you're here.'

She frowned. 'I'm here to take you to Halle,' she said.

'Why?'

'Because you want to go.'

'Do I?'

'Yes.' She looked at him again. 'You have to go. If you're serious.'

'And am I? Am I serious?'

'Yes.'

'How do you know?'

She shook her head, emphatic, looking away. He'd snared her into this pointless exchange, and she was irritated enough to let it show. Telemann said nothing for at least a kilometre. On the horizon, away to the right, he could see a curl of smoke from a factory chimney. Otherwise there was nothing but pine trees and the huge blue bowl of the sky. He thought, briefly, about Emery, and Juanita, and the offices on 'F' Street. Soon, he knew, he should find a phone, check in, start the wheels turning on the German, Klausmann. All he had so far was a three-hour story, carefully stage-managed, and some fancy stuff about Iraqi links with the East German chemical industry. It was promising enough for starters, but there had to be a whole lot more. He looked at the girl again. She'd taken off the Ray-Bans. Her eyes were green.

'There's a name we ought to mention,' she said, her voice low, her eyes back on the road now. 'You've probably heard of him,' she said carefully. 'His name's Wulf.'

Telemann blinked, staring at her, pure disbelief. 'Otto Wulf?'

She nodded again. 'Yes,' she said. 'Otto Wulf. He kept a mistress in Halle. We're expected at seven.'

*

The note and the Polaroid arrived at 10 Downing Street within an hour of the call from the House of Commons. Ross, as it happened, was privy to both.

The conversation with the MP had been brief. The man had managed to find an empty office. Expecting to be interrupted at any moment, he'd kept the details to a minimum. Listening, Ross had drawn a pad towards him, noting the key points as they emerged. A five-gallon drum of chemical had gone missing from a waste disposal warehouse near Newbury. Overnight tests suggested that the contents might be nerve gas. One man had already died in an incident associated with the drum but knowledge of the analysis results was – as far as the MP understood the situation – still limited to the managing director and one other member of the firm. So far, they'd decided against contacting the police, believing that the public interest – for the time being at least – might be better served by keeping the news in the family. As a board member, the MP agreed with the managing director that the issue was complex. Waste management was a growth industry, and Dispozall was a leader in the field. The company was currently pitching for a major contract overseas. Jobs and exports must be weighed against the obvious risk to public safety. It was a difficult balance to strike. Hence the call to Downing Street.

Ross, listening, understood at once that the issues didn't stop at jobs and exports. Nerve gas was a phrase that would sell a great many newspapers. Any system of waste disposal that permitted 5 gallons of the stuff simply to disappear was clearly flawed. The Government, inevitably, would have to shoulder the ultimate blame, and with the country on the verge of a major war the political consequences would be, to put it mildly, tricky. But what, in God's name, had happened to the missing drum?

Now, the door locked, Ross gazed down at the polaroid. It had been hand-delivered to the police sergeant at the gates of Downing Street some forty minutes earlier. It had come in a plain brown envelope, together with a note, plus a photocopy of a single sheet of paper. The envelope had been addressed to the Prime Minister. In accordance with standard procedures, it had been screened in a small private office in the basement of Downing Street, then added to the pile of other mail in one of the wire trays regularly emptied by the messengers. The word 'Personal' in neat capitals on the envelope's top left-hand corner meant it qualified for Ross's attention.

Ross picked up the Polaroid. The photograph showed a red drum. On the drum was a skull and crossbones and the single word 'Poison'. Ross studied the Polaroid a moment longer and then turned to the note. The message, on a single sheet of white A4 paper, was handwritten in brown ink. Across the top, underlined, was the name of an organization he didn't recognize. 'AAA' went the careful capitals, 'Action Against Armageddon'. Ross scribbled the name on his pad, then read the message. The message was simple. It invited the Prime Minister to read the attached list of companies, together with the numbers, dates and details of the export certificates granted by the Department of Trade and Industry. It then suggested that she refer back to a series of recent speeches in which she had denounced Saddam Hussein and the war-machine with which he was now threatening the entire Middle East.

Frowning, Ross turned to the photocopy. It offered a carefully typed list of companies. Beside each company was a list of goods cleared for export. His eye ran down the list. One

147

company, in the Home Counties, had exported 100 grams of depleted uranium. Another, in the West Midlands, several consignments of gun-ranging equipment. A third, in the North-East, had shipped several thousand gallons of a chemical called thiodyl chloride. At the bottom of the list, under 'Destination', was the single word 'Iraq'.

Ross read the note again, looking for some hint, a ransom demand, or a motive to explain the abrupt arrival of these carefully tabulated hypocrisies. But there was nothing, simply the invitation to read, and absorb, and consider. That, and the terrifying implications of the polaroid. Ross, who admired understatement, gazed at the photograph. The shot was badly lit, the colour far from perfect, but if it was the same drum he'd learned about that very morning, then the folk from 'Action Against Armageddon' could name their price. The political damage implicit in the export list was awesome, an epitaph for any government, while the public order consequences of five stray gallons of nerve gas defied imagination.

Ross studied the Polaroid a moment longer, thinking of the video locked away in the filing cabinet. There had to be a connection. Had to be. Reaching for the phone, he dialled the Department of Trade and Industry and spoke briefly to a contact he trusted in the Export Guarantee section. He read him the listed companies at dictation speed. The voice at the other end chuckled, unsurprised, and promised to call back. Ross thanked him, put the phone down and reached for the polaroid again. Then he leaned back in his chair and gazed out of the window. Before the reorganization, he'd had a fine view of Horse Guards and the plump reaches of St James's Park. Now, though technically more senior, he could see nothing but a newly painted fire escape and a brick wall. He waited a moment longer, wondering whether – for once – it might be better to go through channels, to assign this whole sorry business to the proper agencies. But then he looked at the note again and knew that the old instincts were always the best, and that twelve years in power had proved it. Keep it tight. Keep it private. Trust only those who owe you.

He picked up the phone again and dialled a number from

memory. 'Godfrey,' he said pleasantly, when the number answered, 'something else has turned up.'

*

By late afternoon, his first day in Tel Aviv, McVeigh had located the flat.

It lay in a side-street at the edge of the old town of Jaffa, part of a low-rise block, four storeys of concrete and sandstone facings, shuttered windows and tiny balconies cantilevered out over the busy pavement below. Number seven belonged to Yakov Arendt, the name neatly typed beneath the bell-push on the security phone beside the common entrance on the street.

McVeigh tried the bell through the early evening, watching the entrance from the hire car, parked 50 metres down the street. He rang the bell every half-hour, in case Cela had been sleeping, or perhaps in with a neighbour. Getting no reply, he'd saunter back down the street, smelling the hot, dusty Levantine smells from the open-air cafés, the smells of kebab and fresh mint, the babble of voices from the men bent over tiny glasses of Turkish coffee, the foreign tourists out on the street, monied, wary, sauntering carefully by. One or two of them, McVeigh noted, carried gas masks, slung from their belts or looped casually over one shoulder. Already they'd become almost a fashion accessory, the badge of a certain kind of commitment. Tel Aviv, they said. September '90. Ground Zero.

Back in the car, McVeigh kept a log of comings and goings from the apartment block: a young single woman who hurried up the street and disappeared inside without a backward glance, an older couple who stepped out of a big blue Peugeot taxi and couldn't find their key, a mother with a young child who spent an age trying to collapse her buggy. Each time someone new arrived, McVeigh watched carefully, counting the seconds between the moment when they pushed in through the big glass front door and their reappearance two or three storeys up, throwing open the doors on to the balcony, watering a plant on the kitchen window-sill, pulling a curtain or two, or – when darkness began to fall – turning on a light. By midnight, McVeigh had accounted for all but two of the flats. One, on the second floor, was still empty, the curtains drawn, no lights inside. The other, on the top floor, was also dark, no evidence of movement, no response to the bell-push down at street level. In all there were eight flats. Which meant that number seven was probably the one at the top.

McVeigh, finishing his second kebab of the evening, knew he'd have to break in. Already, he'd studied the adjoining buildings. On the seaward side, separated by the width of a narrow alley, was a low, two-storey tenement, converted at street level to a shoe shop. The distance between the two buildings was modest enough, but the separate roof heights ruled the place out. On the other side, though, there was a taller building, five storeys at least, and although the roof looked tricky, it was physically attached to Yakov's apartment block. At street level, the place housed a restaurant, place-set tables visible inside a long picture window, tapestries on the walls, fancy prices on the handwritten menu pinned to the board beside the entrance.

At dusk, the street nicely shadowed, McVeigh had wandered around the back of the restaurant, gazing up at the rough brickwork, noting the hand-holds, the line of the drain-pipes, and the single route upwards that would shield him from the view of the adjoining buildings. The simplest solution, by far, would have been to scale the back of Yakov's apartment block, but it was overlooked by at least two other buildings. If it was to work at all, then it had to be next door, up the back of the restaurant, and a couple of minutes' careful study told McVeigh that it might just be possible.

At two in the morning, the hire car parked in a cul-de-sac near the harbour, McVeigh walked back to the apartment. He'd stripped down to a dark blue T-shirt and a pair of old jeans. On his feet he wore a pair of newish Reeboks, cut high round the ankle, and he'd french-chalked his hands. Wrapped in a hand-kerchief in his pocket were the two tools he'd need to get into Yakov's flat. The big double doors from the balcony looked the safest route.

Outside the apartment block, as a precaution, he tried the entry-phone a final time, blowing the french chalk off the plastic bell-push and waiting for the voice that never came. As certain as he could be that the flat was empty, he shrugged ostentatiously and sauntered off, walking the length of the street before turning left again, and picking his way back through the warren of houses. The rear of the block was in darkness. The restaurant next door was shuttered and silent.

Hugging the shadows, McVeigh edged carefully round a litter of abandoned cardboard boxes piled haphazardly outside the restaurant's back door. Beside them was the biggest of the drain-pipes he'd seen earlier. He tested it, leaning back on the balls of his feet, feeling the brackets moving uneasily in the crumbling brickwork. Then he was up, climbing quickly, his feet moving left and right, looking for support, finding it, the edge of a window-sill, a brick laid out of true. McVeigh climbed higher, 15 to 20 feet, up to the level of the third floor. To his left was a window, with wooden shutters folded back against the wall. Dimly, through the window, he could see the outlines of a sink and a kitchen range. He began to move again, inching upwards, the foot of the drain-pipe a pool of darkness beneath him. The going was harder here, fewer places to find a foot-hold. The brickwork, too, was rough and he began to worry about the drain-pipe. The last bracket his hand had found had been completely detached at one end, the pipe moving laterally between his knees. Only the tightest of fingertip-holds in cracks between the brickwork kept him anchored to the wall.

Abruptly, beneath him, a door opened in the darkness. Looking down, he saw two figures emerge. They stood beside the pile of cardboard boxes, both smoking. He could smell the burning tobacco. They began to talk softly in Hebrew, chuckling at some private joke. McVeigh closed his eyes for a moment, knowing that a single movement, a single mistake, could give him away. The men might be there for several minutes. Their conversation might go on and on. And his fingers, already, were numb with the weight of his body.

He looked down again. A third man had appeared. He kicked one of the cardboard boxes and then another, as if looking for something. The other men bent into the light from the open door, rummaging in the pile, helping him. McVeigh knew he had to move. Very soon, his fingers would give way. If he should fall, the job would be over. It would be hospital, and the near-certainty of police proceedings. On the time-sheets he was keeping for Friedland, it would look less than impressive.

McVeigh eased his head around. To his left, protruding from the brickwork above the kitchen window, was a ventilation louvre. It was square. It was about the size of a cake tin. It was made of metal. It looked solid. Judging by the smells, and the whirr of a nearby fan, it ducted stale air from the kitchen. McVeigh eyed it for a moment longer. A simple traverse left, a single movement, would put his feet on the window-sill beneath the louvre. The louvre itself would give him ample anchorage. On a rock-face, the manoeuvre would be child's-play. Tight against the wall, he could stay up there all night.

McVeigh looked down again. One of the men was up to his waist in cardboard boxes. The others were laughing at him. He closed his eyes for a moment, concentrating, then he eased his hands away from the finger-holds. For a second or two he hung on the drain-pipe, letting his knees take his weight, flexing his fingers, trying to get some feeling back. Then, as the drain-pipe began to pull away from the wall, he stepped quickly sideways, his left hand reaching for the louvre, his left foot finding the window-sill. For a second, his hand still numb, he couldn't quite place the sensation. Then, as the pain burned through, he realized what he'd done. The louvre was connected directly to the kitchen range. The hot sheet metal had only just begun to cool.

McVeigh clamped his teeth shut, biting his tongue, forcing the instinctive scream back down his throat. Flexing his knees, he crouched against the glass of the window, fanning his hand in the warm night air. Dizzy with the pain, he began to lose his balance, his body tipping out towards the darkness, and he closed his eyes again, knowing that the choice now was all too simple. Either the long drop to the concrete below, or the louvre again, and more flesh shredding from the palm of his hand. He reached up, swallowing hard, tasting the blood in his mouth, knowing in reality that there was no choice, that hot metal was a better friend than gravity.

McVeigh caught hold of the louvre and hung on, both hands,

first one then the other, trying somehow to lessen the pain, telling his mind to ignore it, a simple act of will. Images came flooding back, a decade and a half of serious mountaineering, moments he'd thought he'd long buried. A winter night on a glacier in northern Norway, way up beyond the Arctic Circle, the wind katabatic, the bivvy in shreds. It was worse then, he told himself. Far, far worse. He'd regained consciousness at daybreak, his partner three hours dead, the eyes frozen in his face, the wild stare of terminal exposure. That had been horrible. Ugly, too. This? Now? He opened his eyes and looked down. The men had gone. The door was shut. The light had disappeared. He could hear footsteps receding in the darkness, the sound of a car door, the cough of an engine. He shook his head, hardly believing it, fanning his hands again, trying to relax, leaning back against the window. The worst of the pain had gone now, replaced by a steady throbbing. He held a palm against his cheek. It felt like hamburger, hot and coarse. He swallowed again, fighting the urge to vomit. His only way out now, he knew, was through the window.

The window was metal-framed. One side opened. He could see the catch inside. Leaning against it, he steadied himself and then jabbed hard, backwards, with his elbow. Nothing happened. He moved slightly and tried again, feeling the glass crack, pushing harder, hearing the big shards shatter on a surface inside. Carefully, he reached backwards, feeling for the handle. He found it. Mercifully, the window – designed for exterior shutters – opened inwards. He balanced on the edge of the window-sill for a moment longer, then eased slowly backwards, tiny half-steps, on to a draining-board. He could hear the steady drip-drip of water. He could smell the end of a busy evening, part disinfectant, part stale fat. Lowering himself from the draining-board, he pulled the window closed behind him. In the darkness, he felt for the tap. He turned it on, crying with relief as the cold water sluiced over the raw flesh on his hands.

Ten minutes later, his hands thick with lamb fat from a basting tray and bandaged with strips of rag he'd torn from a washing-up cloth, he was out on the roof of the restaurant. Two flights of stairs and a hatch in the ceiling had given him access. The roof was flat, latticed with pipes from the air-conditioning unit. One end adjoined Yakov's apartment block. The drop to the neighbouring roof was less than 8 feet. Under normal circumstances, it would have taken McVeigh perhaps five seconds. Tonight, it was the work of a full minute, levering himself backwards off the taller roof, using his elbows and his toes, risking his hands as little as possible.

The second drop was trickier. Yakov's roof was also flat. At the front, overlooking the street, there was a raised ledge. From the ledge, McVeigh would be forced to lower himself a full 6 feet, the weight of his body back on his hands, his feet still a 2-metre drop from the floor of Yakov's balcony. Lying full-length on the roof, peering down, McVeigh weighed the odds. His hands, he knew, he could no longer rely on. There had to be a better way.

Behind the air-conditioning unit and the big water tanks, he found an access door to the apartment block. The door was unlocked. Inside, there was a single flight of concrete steps and another door. McVeigh opened it slowly, a single inch. He could see pictures on a wall, plants in big glazed pots, a stretch of hallway. There were doors leading off the hall. The closest, as it happened, was number seven.

McVeigh slipped into the hall, closing the door behind him. His hands had ballooned on the ends of his arms. They no longer felt part of him, gross white bundles of pain, a steady throb-throb that wouldn't go away. So far, he knew, he'd been unlucky. What should have been routine had turned into near-disaster. Now, it had to get better. That god he'd first found in the mountains, that spirit he'd relied on ever since, would surely see him through.

The lock on Yakov's door was old, a three-lever design, and he knew at once that it had been forced before. There were scuff-marks in the wood surround, too deep to be accidental, and when he inserted the thin blade of the knife, feeling for the tongue of the lock, easing it gently backwards, wincing at the pain, he could see the deep gouge inside the jamb. The damage looked recent, thin whiskers of wood still intact. McVeigh gave the knife a final nudge, grunting when the lock gave and the door opened. He was inside the flat in seconds, closing the door behind him, securing the double bolt. In the darkness, his back to the wall, he closed his eyes, letting the air out of his lungs in one long sigh, feeling the sweat beginning to bead on his face. Air-conditioning, he thought. Still on.

He relaxed for a full minute, letting his eyes readjust to the dark. Slowly, the flat began to make sense. At the end of the hall was a half-open door, a carpet oblonged with light from the street, a pile of clothes at the foot of a bed, the quiet ticking of a clock. There was also a powerful smell of perfume, unnaturally strong. McVeigh hesitated for a moment, thinking of Yakov, how little he'd really known about the man, how strange it was to be in his flat, then he dismissed the thought and moved slowly down the hall towards the half-open door. Bedrooms, in his experience, were where you started. Bedrooms were where people kept their closest secrets.

At the door, McVeigh again hesitated for a moment. Then he was inside and across the room, picking his way between piles of clothes, pulling the curtains, shutting out the light from the street. Turning back into the room, he peered into the darkness. The shapes were what he expected: a big double bed, some kind of dressing-table, a long, narrow mirror in one corner. But he sensed something else about the room that didn't quite fit. There was glass underfoot. The smell of perfume was even stronger. That, and something far earthier. McVeigh crossed the room again and felt for the wall switch. Only when the light was on did he realize what had disturbed him. The room, systematically, had been wrecked.

He stood by the open door, staring at it. There were clothes strewn everywhere, sheets ripped from the bed. A built-in wardrobe had been emptied, the contents scattered across the floor. McVeigh knelt amongst them, sifting through layers of blouses, jeans, sweat-shirts, formal suits, realizing that the clothes were all female, all Cela's. The stuff had been torn apart, slashed with a knife, huge rents, nothing left intact. Near by, beneath an upturned drawer, he found underwear – knickers, bras, a beautiful lace petticoat. He examined them one by one, numbed by the careful knifework, unerring, always the same place, the crotch, the cup of the breast, the belly of the petticoat.

McVeigh looked round. The dressing-table had been swept clean, bottles of perfume and toilet water lying on the floor beside it, the glass smashed, liquid blotching the carpet. McVeigh knelt again, fingering the pools of perfume, trying to determine exactly when the room had been wrecked. Perfume evaporated quickly. This stuff was still damp to the touch.

Back on his feet, McVeigh turned to the bed. The mattress, like the clothes, had been slashed, the knife working left and right, an ugly cross-hatching, diagonal wounds. He gazed at it, chilled. He'd seen dozens of wrecked rooms in his time, most recently his own, but there was something intensely personal about this particular tableau. It was a piece of raw violence, murder without a body. There was a smell of shit, too, and he peered more closely at the mattress, wondering about the exact chain of events. Then he looked up and saw the mirror. The mirror was long and slender. Cela must have used it regularly, every morning probably, checking herself out, readying herself for another day at the office. Now, half-ripped from the wall, it was smeared with excrement, a phrase in Hebrew, words he couldn't understand. He looked at it for a long time, committing it to memory, the shape of each letter, turning away from a moment, fixing them in his mind, then checking back, making sure he'd got them right. 'סוד כמוס' it went, 'סוד צלנו'.

Picking his way carefully over the debris, McVeigh left the bedroom. The other rooms in the apartment were untouched. A small lounge. A clean, bright kitchen. A tiny bathroom with a pedestal lavatory beside the hand-basin. In each room, taking his time, McVeigh looked for evidence of Yakov – a photo, perhaps, or a sheaf of old letters, anything that might take him a little further than this flat of theirs, a little closer to the truth. But wherever he looked, he found nothing. No clothes, no correspondence, little sign, even, of Cela. She must be away somewhere, he thought, a posting perhaps, or compassionate leave. And whoever had wrecked the bedroom had probably known it, taking a little trouble in his work, a little pride, making sure that the message was properly understood.

Standing in the bathroom, soaping his swollen hands, McVeigh visualized the mirror in the bedroom again, the single phrase, caked and brown. Translated, it might help. It might be something specific, another hand-hold on the climb, or it might simply be an insult, the foulest of curses embossed in raw shit by someone whose capacity for violence was probably limitless. McVeigh shuddered, glad to have missed the intruder, and bent to the shaving light over the basin. The hot metal had raised huge blisters, and the palms of both hands had blotched an angry red. The throbbing was back again, and when he tried to flex his fingers the pain made him want to gag. He reached down for the toilet seat, pulling it up, and bent towards the bowl. Then, on the point of throwing up, he saw the photo. It was small, black and white, floating face up in the lavatory. He reached down for it, retrieving it carefully, holding it up, letting the water drip from one corner, the urge to vomit quite forgotten.

The photo showed a younger Yakov, a youth in his late teens, a face newly hatched from adolescence. He was wearing an Army beret and an open-necked khaki shirt. He was grinning at the camera, his face screwed up against the sun. Beside him, smaller, was a girl. She had short black hair, a check shirt, big earrings. Her head was inclined towards him, nestling on his shoulder. In the background was a diving-board and part of a swimming-pool. Someone was standing on the end of the diving-board, contemplating the jump.

McVeigh gazed at the photo, knowing at once that the girl was Cela. Yakov had shown him another photo in London, more recent, an older face, but recognizably the same girl. The same smile. The same big eyes. The same wide mouth, one front tooth a little crooked. McVeigh turned the photo over. On the back, at last, was what he'd come to find, the blue biro still legible on the wet, a date and a name. 'August 1975' it read, 'Kibbutz Shamir'. Underneath, in Hebrew, were another couple of words. McVeigh glanced at them, reaching for a sheet or two of paper, meaning to wrap the photo and take it away. Then he stopped, one hand outstretched. The words looked familiar. He'd seen them only a minute earlier. Smeared on the mirror. Beside Cela's bed.

*

Even inside the restaurant, Telemann could still taste the air.

Approaching Halle, early evening, the beginnings of a perfect sunset had disappeared behind a long brown smudge on the horizon. Kilometre by kilometre, the smudge had come closer, yielding its secrets, a black frieze of factories, blast-furnaces, chimney-stacks. The outskirts of the city, a uniform grey, had been blessed with a faint ochre light, the sunset diffused by the smog, the trams packed with workers returning from the day shift, old women wobbling by on ancient bicycles, kids playing football with a rusty can. Cocooned in the Mercedes, the window down, Telemann had watched the city unspooling like a film, yesterday's Europe, embalmed by communism, tasting of sulphur and cheap petrol.

They'd parked on a triangle of wasteland near the city centre, the girl picking her way through a maze of side-streets. The wasteland was flanked by a once grand building, now abandoned. On the street, while Inge locked the car, Telemann had gazed up at the boarded windows. Over the main door, a sculpted head of Marx looked down on passers-by. Decades of pollution had rotted the porous limestone, eating away at the nose and ears. So much for Comrade Karl, thought Telemann, tasting the air again.

The restaurant was small and bleak, half a dozen tables, all empty. A waiter emerged from the gloom at the back and greeted Inge by name, wiping the tiny bar with his sleeve. Inge smiled at him, pulling on a cardigan against the sudden chill, bending to greet a small black cat. The cat walked sideways towards her, mewing a welcome, sniffing at her outstretched fingers, winding itself around her legs. The cat knows her, thought Telemann, the waiter too. She's been here before.

They sat at a table near the bar. The waiter brought two beers and a bottle of white wine. He set a third place at the table and glanced enquiringly at the wine. Inge nodded. He uncorked the bottle and fetched a single wine glass from behind the bar, wiping it with a dishcloth and laying it carefully beside the empty place. Inge glanced at her watch, then looked up at the waiter. '*Fünf minuten*,' she said with a smile.

Telemann looked at her, thinking yet again of Otto Wulf, the name the girl had mentioned, the conversational grenade lobbed into their musings in the car. The details were common knowledge. The man had been a giant in Germany for at least a decade. Too young to be tainted by Nazism, too successful and too rich to be treated with anything less than respect, he'd embodied the very best of Kohl's bustling new Republic. A chemist by training, but a businessman by instinct, he'd never accepted the permanence of the post-war settlement of Germany. As his interests in the West had prospered, he'd looked increasingly across the border, towards the East, for fresh opportunities, and he'd celebrated his fortieth birthday by endowing a million-Deutschmark fellowship at the University of Leipzig. Wulf's contacts in the East had always been extensive, and in Washington he'd long been regarded as Moscow's favourite German. This had cast a certain shadow on his international reputation, but by the late eighties his business interests in the DDR looked like simple foresight. He'd anticipated reunification by at least a decade and now – with the Wall down – he was reaping the profits. Germans, Telemann knew, loved him. Imposing, powerful, eternally tanned, he and his family featured regularly on the front covers of certain kinds of magazine. In middle-class circles, amongst the prosperous burghers of a resurgent Germany, Wulf was '*jemand der's kann*' . . . excellent news.

Telemann sipped at his beer, still watching the girl. She was back at the bar, talking to the waiter. For the last hour, in the car, he'd tried to press her about Wulf, but she'd refused to elaborate, changing the subject, shrugging his questions aside. When he'd pushed her hard – Why the mistress? Why the meeting? – she'd finally turned on him, telling him not to be impatient, telling him he'd simply have to wait.

The door opened. Telemann glanced round. A woman stepped into the restaurant. She was middle-aged, small and blonde, still beautiful, tastefully dressed, a wide, slightly Slavic face. She hung up her raincoat on a hook behind the door, immediately at home, and unknotted a red silk scarf around her neck. Seeing Inge by the bar, she waved. Inge ran across to her, the first real smile Telemann had seen. The two women embraced and Telemann stood up as they turned towards the table.

'Herr Telemann . . . Frau Weissmann.'

Telemann nodded a greeting and extended a hand. The woman's touch was cold. Her smile had gone. She looked wary. They all sat down while the waiter poured a glass of wine. A large plate of black bread had appeared from the kitchen. The waiter left it in the middle of the table. Inge, immediately businesslike, explained briefly that Telemann was a friend. She should trust him. She should tell him everything.

The older woman looked briefly doubtful, reaching for the wine. She picked for a moment or two at a crust of bread, then shrugged. Telemann, wondering whether to seed the conversation with a prompt or a question, decided against it. The two women had already talked. He could sense it. Frau Weissmann glanced at Inge for a last time, then looked down at the table. There was a long silence.

'You know why I'm here?' Telemann said finally. 'You know why I've come?'

The woman nodded. She spoke good English, barely accented. 'Yes.'

'And you think you can help?'

'Yes.'

'How?'

There was another long silence. The bread lay between them on the table. The waiter had disappeared. Telemann looked at Inge again, wondering for the umpteenth time exactly how much she knew. In the cottage, talking to Klausmann, Telemann had never mentioned the threat of New York. The question had never been asked, and he'd volunteered nothing of his own. Yet the direction their conversation had taken made little sense without, at the very least, a suspicion that somebody was on the loose, with access to something chemical. That had been the sub-text. You didn't have to say it to know it. It was simply there.

Telemann looked at Frau Weissmann again. Her fingers were back around the stem of the wine glass. She was having a lot of trouble coming to the point.

Telemann leaned forward. 'You know Herr Wulf?' he said.

The woman nodded. 'I was his secretary. Here, in Halle. There were four of us. I was the most senior. I worked for him for eight years. I knew—' she shrugged '—everything.'

Telemann looked at her, his voice quickening. 'He ran a company here? In Halle?'

'Yes.' She looked up, nodding towards the window. 'Littmann Chemie. He ran it in partnership with the State. Back when . . .' She smiled and shrugged again, an expression of weariness.

'. . . there was a State?'

'Yes. Exactly.'

'You miss all that?'

The woman looked up at him for the first time, the trace of a smile on her lips. 'Yes,' she said quietly, 'in some ways I do.'

'Is that why you're here? Talking to me? Now?' He paused. 'Or is it more personal?'

The woman looked at him for a moment longer, refusing to answer, then she turned to Inge and began to speak to her in German. Her voice was very low yet vehement, her hands clasping and unclasping, the anger evident in her face. As hard as he tried, Telemann could make little sense of what she was saying. It was an intensely private language, gestures as well as words. Finally, the woman stopped, her finger on the table, her last point made. Inge nodded and glanced up. She looked startled, like a child after a surprise scolding. 'Frau Weissmann is happy to talk to you about Herr Wulf and about Littmann Chemie. But nothing else. You understand?'

'Sure.'

'Nothing personal.'

'Fine by me.' Telemann nodded, his hands upturned on the table, a gesture of apology. 'I'm sorry.'

There was another silence, then the older woman leaned

forward again, the hesitation quite gone. She spoke for perhaps half an hour, without interruption. She explained that her relationship with Otto Wulf had been close and that he'd trusted her with a number of sensitive files. Certain of these files related to customers with whom Littmann would not normally have done business. Some of them, she'd come to suspect, were cover names for Middle East terror organizations.

On a number of occasions, she'd accompanied Wulf on three-day trips to the Baltic island of Rugen. There, as well as top names in the State *nomenklatura*, she'd met dozens of young terrorists, Palestinians mostly. They trained for periods of three or six months. They learned about field-craft, explosives, small-arms, surveillance. They were schooled in the ways of the West. They were taught how to lie low in big cities, how to fade into the urban background. These skills they picked up from the DDR's finest, and they then returned to their sponsors to put the theory into practice.

Talking about these eager young recruits, their spirit, their trust, their enthusiasm, Telemann got the impression that she'd rather liked them. The word she twice used was 'Kinder'. Children. Evidently, Wulf had liked them too. Though for different reasons. At this point in the monologue, Telemann had wanted to interrupt her, scenting more detail, but the expression on her face froze the question on his lips, and he smiled, apologetic again, and gestured for her to carry on.

The story returned to Halle. Amongst other chemicals, Littmann produced dimethylamine. With sodium cyanide and phosphoryl chloride, you could make a variety of nerve gases. It was, she said dismissively, a simple process. The company had been doing it for years, supplying thousands of gallons for the armies of the Warsaw Pact. She spoke of Littmann's track-record with some pride. In this particular field, she said, their product was the best. Worldwide, it had an unrivalled reputation. It was very stable, very effective, the kind of stuff you could trust. Telemann listened to her without expression, thinking of the bodies he'd seen in the Bellevue morgue and the grainy shots of mothers and children lying in the dust in Halabja. She might have been talking about lager.

Sitting in the empty restaurant, her body bent towards the table, her fingers endlessly circling the wine glass, she warmed to her theme. Littmann had always been scrupulous about end-users, the customers to whom various gases had been sold. Recently, though, she'd begun to suspect that the rules had been broken. For whatever reason, in an increasingly complicated life, Otto Wulf had decided to supply small quantities of what he termed 'Jaegermeister' to a new outlet. Six months ago, 10 gallons of 'Jaegermeister' had left the factory gates, together with some primitive dispensers. The consignment had been coded as 'industrial detergent' and, to her knowledge, only two men shared the secret of what was really inside the two 5-gallon drums. One of them worked directly for Wulf in West Germany, and the other had been killed in a recent auto accident. At this point, the wine bottle three-quarters empty, she stopped.

Telemann looked at her. Even the remains of his jet-lag couldn't hide his excitement. Otto Wulf. Bonn's favourite businessman. Peddling nerve gas to the rag-heads.

'Three questions,' he said softly. 'Then I go.'

The woman looked at him for a moment, then shrugged. 'OK.'

'One. Do you have any paperwork? A file, maybe? Something I can look at?'

The woman shook her head. 'No. I no longer work for Herr Wulf.'

'OK.' Telemann paused. 'Then I need the name of the guy who works for Wulf. The one you mentioned just now.'

The woman nodded, but said nothing. Telemann hesitated for a moment, then leaned forward again. 'OK,' he said. 'Number three. I need to know what Jaegermeister is.' He glanced up. 'Jaegermeister,' he repeated. 'What is it?'

The woman looked across at Inge and smiled. Then she nodded at the bar, over her shoulder, a private joke. 'It's a drink,' she said finally. 'Curls your toes.'

'I know. But . . .'

'But what?'

'What is it really?'

The woman reached for the last of her wine and raised her glass, a toast. 'It's Tabun,' she said. 'Tabun GA.'

An hour later, back in the car. Telemann settled back into the firm, cool leather. The woman had left the restaurant without waiting for a meal. She and Inge had embraced at the door, an exchange of kisses, a word or two of German, and then she'd gone. Behind her, on the table, she'd left a single sheet of paper with a name and an address. Mahmood Assali. 4/121 Friedrich-strasse, Bad Godesberg. Below it, in large capitals, she'd written the word 'Wannsee'. 'Wannsee', she'd said, was the name they'd used for the file. Mention the word to Mahmood, and he'd know at once what it meant.

Now, in the car, Telemann glanced across at Inge. The meal had been better than he'd expected, and a small celebratory glass of schnapps had mellowed a little of his impatience. What he needed now was access to a secure phone, and that meant returning to Hamburg. He'd go to the US Consulate. He'd talk to Emery, get the story cross-checked and plot the next moves. In the meantime, though, there was still the question of motive. That, in some curious way, still bothered him.

'This relationship Wulf had. With his mistress. What happened?'

Inge looked across at him in the darkness. She didn't reply. Telemann pressed the point. 'He did *have* a mistress?'

'Yes, of course.'

'So what happened?'

Inge shrugged. 'He had an affair with her. He took what he wanted. He made all the usual promises. And then—' she shrugged again '—he left her.'

'How long? How long did this take?'

'Five years.'

'Five years? And he was serious?'

'Very.'

'In love? Bells? Whistles? All that stuff?'

'He said so.'

'Any complications?'

'What do you mean?'

'Children?'

'Ah . . .' She smiled, white teeth in the darkness. 'Is that what you call them? Complications?'

'Well?'

There was a long silence. Then she nodded. 'Yes.'

'How many?'

'One. A little boy. Nikki.'

Telemann looked at her for a moment or two, remembering Frau Weissmann in the restaurant, her hands clasped tight, the private life she'd refused to share. At her age, a child would have been a small miracle, all the more cause for the bitterness and the rage.

'Is that why she told me about Wulf? Because of Nikki? Her child?'

There was another silence. Across the road, two dogs were fighting over a parcel of bones. Inge was watching them, her head turned away.

Telemann leaned forward. 'Well?' he said.

A car swept past and the dogs slunk away. Inge looked at him. She was laughing.

Telemann frowned. 'What's the matter?' he said.

'You think Frau Weissmann was Wulf's mistress?'

'Yes.'

'Truly?' She savoured the word. 'Truly?'

'Yes.' Telemann stared at her. 'She's not?'

'No.'

'Then who is she?'

'She's my mother.'

'Your *mother*?'

'*Ja. Meine mutti.*'

'So who was the mistress?'

Inge looked at him for a moment longer, the laughter quite gone. Then she reached for the ignition keys.

'Me,' she said softly. 'I was his mistress.'

7

The old man, Abu Yussuf, sat beside the water-cooler in the semi-darkness, listening to the machine they called the Regulator. Every hour, throughout the night, it buzzed. The buzz was high-pitched and insistent, impossible to ignore. It lasted for exactly a minute, and it meant that the old man must find his plastic card, and get to the machine, and insert the brown strip of oxide into the slot at the side, a single pass, in and out, less than a second. Then the buzzer would stop, and at the end of his shift, with dawn purpling the sky over Queens, the machine would speak to him again, a long white tongue of paper, proof that he'd stayed all night, the ever-faithful janitor. The paper, his attendance log, he'd leave in a wire tray on a desk in the reception area, ready for collection by the duty secretary. That way, they knew he wasn't cheating them. That way, he kept his job.

Sighing, the old man got up and crossed the corridor. The machine was in a small utility room, beside a drinks dispenser. The old man felt in his dungarees for the card and fed it into the machine. The buzzing stopped. Retrieving the card, he fumbled in his pocket for small change and exchanged a quarter and two dimes for a can of Pepsi. Opening the Pepsi, he crossed the corridor again, a different office this time, one he'd yet to clean. Opening the office with his master key, he reached for the light switch, blinking in the sudden glare of the overhead neon, as awed as ever by the huge expanse of carpet and the crescent of padded leather sofa, and the way that Mr Aramoun had positioned his desk, back to the window, dominating the room.

The old man inched forward, the can of Pepsi still in his hand, his eyes never leaving the desk. There were two phones on the desk, and one of them, he was sure, would carry him through to Ramallah. He glanced at his watch. It was two minutes past three, the middle of a hot New York night. The offices along the corridor were empty. He knew that because he'd cleaned them all. No one would return until the first secretaries at seven, and even then they had to ring the security phone and wait until he shuffled along to the lobby and let them in. No, if he was to do it, if he was to still the voices in his head, then it had to be now, in the dead of night.

The old man put his can carefully on the edge of Aramoun's desk, and crossed to the big picture windows. Outside, Manhattan twinkled in the darkness, block after block. He gazed at the view for a moment, still amazed at the scale of the place, this huge city at his feet. Then he reached for the pull on the venetian blinds. The blinds came clattering down, shielding him from the world outside. Now, he thought. Now is the time.

Beginning to sweat a little, he searched in his pocket for the slip of paper. He'd spent the latter half of the afternoon in the public library over in Newark. The girl at the information desk, Turkish or maybe Armenian, had been very kind. She'd found the international directory for him. She'd written down the number he had to dial. First the numbers for Israel. Then the number for Ramallah. Then, last of all, the numbers for Amer Tahoul. Amer Tahoul worked in the Treasurer's Department in the Municipality Buildings in Ramallah. Amer Tahoul was his wife's brother. He'd know what had happened. He'd know why the letters had suddenly stopped.

The old man found the slip of paper and flattened it on the desk. He reached for the Pepsi and took a sip, wiping his mouth on the back of his hand. His hand, he noticed, was shaking. He looked at the phone for a moment, weighing the odds again, wondering whether they kept some kind of check on the calls, a strip of paper like the Regulator, something they'd confront him with, something that would bring this strange new life of his to an abrupt end.

So far, he knew, he'd done well. Even the boy, in his own way, had been surprised by the job he'd done on the car, the drum installed in the trunk, not a drop of liquid spilled, not a single trace of leakage around the connections to the pressure-hose. The boy had watched him at work in the garage, bent over the trunk, wrestling the heavy drum into place with spanners and a big hammer. Once, just once, he'd looked up, asking for help, an extra pair of hands, surprised to see the youth standing beside him, staring down at the drum, his face invisible behind a huge rubber gas mask. The old man had laughed at him, a small act of revenge for the weeks of scorn and insult, mocking the boy's caution, his timidity. Not even women took such precautions against the Israeli gas, he'd said, watching the boy's eyes, unsmiling, behind the thick discs of ground glass.

Now, standing beside the desk, the old man reached for the phone. He hadn't had a letter from his wife, Hama, for more than two weeks, not since the beginning of the month. Himself, he'd written every day, sitting at the table in the tiny airless kitchen, page after page, the thin sheets of scribble anchored down beneath the tins of chick-peas he bought each week at the corner store. He wrote about New York, the way it felt, this new life of his. He wrote about the heat and the smell. He wrote about the money, how much he suddenly had, how many things there were to buy. And he wrote about home, too, and his family, the two surviving sons, how much he missed them. He wrote about the horses he sometimes exercised, the property of a relative, the long evening rides out towards the refugee camp at Kalandia. He wrote about the other things he missed – the food, the laughter, the endless conversation – and when his wife began to write back, the tight schoolgirl characters, the little drawings of flowers at the foot of each page, it was a little like their first years together.

She missed him, she said. She missed his good humour and his patience, and the respect he'd always won for the family from friends and neighbours. Gone so suddenly, there were whisperings. She'd heard them, heard the rumours. They were saying that the family was *al dam al wisikh*, dirty, stained by the blood of the collaborator killed by the *moharebbin*. The old man going proved it. He'd turned his back on his family, on the *Intifada*. Like his dead son, he was *ameel*, an agent for the

Israelis, a traitor. But she knew different. She knew he was strong. She knew he was *sharafa*, honest, a supporter of the iron man Saddam, who would drive the Israelis into the sea. This she told her neighbours. One day, she said, my husband will come back, and then you'll see for yourself. Openly now, the neighbours disbelieved her. When, they taunted her, when will your husband come home?

At first the letters had arrived regularly, at least three a week. Waiting for the mailman in the street, Abu Yussuf would tuck them into the pocket of his working overalls and take them to the garage, reading them during the break he took for lunch. To her question he could give no answer, but that didn't matter. The letters were a little piece of home. In this strange new city, they reminded him of who he really was. With the letters in his pocket, walking back to the apartment in the hot, dusty evenings, he felt armour-plated, invincible. Without them, he was nothing.

But now, for no reason, the letters had stopped coming, and in his heart, when he was brave enough, Abu Yussuf feared the worst. Hama, like his sons, had been arrested. She was being held without trial in one of the military prisons. The Israelis called it 'administrative detention'. They'd be questioning her day and night, trying to find out what she knew, trying to trace this missing husband of hers. Probably they'd be rough with her, exasperated by her protestations of ignorance, refusing to believe the truth, that she knew nothing.

The old man shuddered, remembering the way his sons had coped with their own spells of administrative detention, the beatings they'd shrugged aside, the hours on their haunches in freezing cells, the way they'd always brought more pain on themselves by dismissing the Israelis as outsiders, intruders, Zionist thieves who'd arrived in the night and stolen their land. One day, his dead son had said, the Israelis will be forced to leave. One day, the rest of the world will wake up to the scale of the thefts. One day, justice will be done.

Now, the old man watched his hand crabbing over the face of the telephone, the thick fingers tapping out the numbers one by one. The dialling tone in his ear changed, became disembodied, and the final digits of the number plunged him into a strange electronic void. For a while, nothing happened. He glanced over his shoulder, imagining footsteps in the corridor. In Ramallah, he supposed it would be daytime already. That, at least, was what the girl at the Public Library had told him. Ten hours, she'd said, ten hours in front. The old man waited, bent over the desk. Ten hours ahead meant one o'clock in the afternoon. Amer Tahoul would be at his desk in the Municipality Buildings, back from lunch, consulting his big leather-bound diary of appointments. He knew the man's hours, knew the way he worked. That was why now was such a good time to phone, a little peace, a little quiet, before the first of the afternoon's meetings. Soon now, any second, he'd answer.

There was a crackle on the line, and then a voice he recognized, cautious, restrained, educated. The old man smiled, reaching for the Pepsi again, relief surging through him. 'Amer,' he said. 'Amer Tahoul.'

*

Godfrey Friedland met Ross, as ordered, on the steamer pontoon beside the Westminster Embankment. The last of the flood-tide was pushing upriver, collars of creamy brown water around the footings of Westminster Bridge.

Ross was standing on the pontoon, his body braced against the rise and fall of the water. He was wearing a dark suit and carried a folded Burberry. There was a small leather overnight bag at his feet. Friedland nodded a greeting. The last of the Librium was beginning to wear off, and try as he might he couldn't rid himself of that final image of his daughter, the face chalk-white on the pillow, the eyes deep-set, following his every move. Afterwards, in the corridor outside, the matron had assured him that it would be all right, that she'd survive, realize how silly she'd been, get better. But the matron had said that already. Twice before.

Ross stepped towards him, scowling. 'You're late.'

'I know.'

The two men looked at each other for a moment, Friedland blinking in the fitful sunshine. Then Ross gestured impatiently at the waiting steamer, and Friedland followed him aboard. The phone call from Downing Street had come through at noon. Ross was due at the City Airport at four. It was already the wrong side of three.

The steamer, half-empty, cast off and edged into the tidal stream. Ross led the way to a small, windswept area at the bow. Two men on the bridge eyed them without comment. Ross lodged his bag carefully against a pile of life-rafts. Since lunchtime, the DTI had confirmed every British order on the list handed into Downing Street. An interesting piece of kite-flying had suddenly become a political nightmare. Five missing gallons of nerve gas had been bad enough, an ample chapter in the Doomsday Brief, but proven complicity in the Iraqi arms build-up made it infinitely worse. Ross had broken the news in a brief series of personal phone calls. The political consensus, at the highest level, was unanimous. The usual Intelligence channels – MI5, MI6, Special Branch, the Military Directorate – were utterly unreliable. Referring the matter to any of them was as sensible as holding a press conference. There had to be a better way.

Ross stood at the rail, pulling on his Burberry and turning up the collar. Friedland stood beside him, waiting. Half an hour ago, for the fourth time, he'd phoned the nursing home. His daughter was asleep again, but her blood pressure was back to normal and the prognosis was good.

Ross glanced across at him. 'We have a spot of local bother,' he said. 'I need your views.'

Friedland said nothing, watching the Ministry of Defence slide past while Ross told him about the missing drum of chemical and the subsequent appearance of a note. They were well past Charing Cross by the time he'd finished. Friedland looked at his watch for a moment, then shrugged. 'Action Against Armageddon?'

'That's what it says.'

'Never heard of them.'

'Quite.' Ross glanced across at him. 'So who in God's name might they be?'

There was a long silence. Friedland said nothing, watching a pair of gulls swooping over a plastic bag. He'd never seen Ross like this before, so chastened, so fearful. It matched his own mood exactly. 'Who says they're not bluffing?'

'No one. But we can't afford to take the risk. The chemicals are definitely missing and the DTI list adds up. Every line of it. We've been arming the Iraqis for years. Raw materials. Weapons. Ammunition. The lot. God knows, we even help them pay for it. Export credit guarantees. With love from London.'

Friedland permitted himself a smile, musing. 'Awkward,' he said quietly.

'Very.' Ross pulled a face, hunching a little deeper inside the raincoat. 'So what do we do? The PM has to keep the country behind her. Has to. It's absolutely vital. The Americans are depending on us. If we don't hold the line, God knows what the rest'll do.'

Friedland nodded, knowing that it was true. Already, the first stirrings of a peace lobby were beginning to surface in the national media. With the PM intent on dragging the country to war, self-interest dressed up as some kind of moral crusade, news of the arms deals would be a real gift. That, of course, plus the nerve gas.

Friedland glanced across at Ross. 'So why me?' he said. 'What do you think I can do?'

Ross said nothing for a while. His bag, Friedland noticed, carried a British Airways Concorde label. It looked recent. Finally he turned away from the rail, his face chilled under the beginnings of a weekend tan. 'Tell me about McVeigh,' he said.

'McVeigh?' Friedland frowned. The last twenty-four hours had emptied him of everything, including patience. 'He's working for Al Zahra. The name came from him, not me.'

'But what do you know about him?'

'Not much. Marine Corps background. Low profile. Keeps himself in work, by and large . . .' He paused. 'Why?'

Ross said nothing for a moment, turning away, gazing down at the brown water folding away from the hull. 'You think he's any good?' he said at last.

'I've no idea.'

'But you think he might be?'

'Yes.' He nodded. 'It's possible.'

Ross said nothing, hunched over the rail, and Friedland suddenly realized what was new about the conversation, what he hadn't seen before. Ross, like everyone else in the world, was finally vulnerable. Friedland turned away, permitting himself a small, cold smile, amused by the thought.

Ross stirred. 'McVeigh was my idea,' he said at last. 'He has a boy called Billy. The child wrote to the Israelis. Evidently he and McVeigh knew Yakov Arendt.'

'Who?'

'Arendt.' Ross turned away from the rail, buttoning his coat. 'The Israeli who got himself shot. Last week. In Kensington.'

'And?'

Ross shrugged. 'There has to be a connection with the video business. Has to be.' He paused. 'So I needed a ferret. To put down the hole. McVeigh's the ferret, hired through our Arab friend.' He paused again. 'It seemed a good idea,' he said wearily, 'at the time.'

Friedland looked at him. 'There are better ways,' he said softly.

'Like what?'

'Like telling me in the first place.' He paused. 'Why use the Arab? Why did you need a cut-out? Why not use me to hire McVeigh?'

Ross shook his head, saying nothing for a moment. Then he shivered, pulling his coat around him. 'Zahra's been offering his services for years. He's happy to pay the bills and he says he'll keep his mouth shut. From where I sit, that's a nice relationship.' He hesitated for a moment. Then he shook his head and turned away, his voice low. 'We're in a mess . . .' he said slowly. 'We're losing ground. Every week we're losing ground. It's been bad for a while. Now it's close to critical.'

'We?'

'The management.' He shrugged. 'Poll tax. Europe. ERM. You name it.' He paused. 'The war will help. But only for a while . . .'

Friedland looked at him, surprised at how quickly the conversation had changed track, curiously flattered that Ross should be so open. As far as Downing Street was concerned, of course, he was right. After eleven years of government by diktat, the stockade was well and truly under siege. Friedland stepped across to the rail. Shooting London Bridge, he could suddenly smell the cold dank breath of the river.

'The key to this thing is the Americans,' Ross said softly. 'There's a man called Sullivan. You may have heard of him . . .'

Friedland shook his head. 'No,' he said.

'He's a White House staffer. Extremely well placed. Pulls lots of serious strings.' He paused. 'His phrase. Not mine.'

'You know him?'

'Yes.'

'Well?'

'Yes . . .' He hesitated. 'It was a social thing at first, but . . .' He shrugged. 'Yes.'

'What does that mean?'

Ross shook his head, emphatic, refusing to answer, and Friedland, studying him, suddenly realized the truth of it, what the man had been up to all these years, guarding the back passage to the White House, bypassing the usual channels, securing for his political mistress what all politicians sought: an independent power-base, free from the deadening hand of the Establishment. Now, of course, the link was all the more important. With Thatcherism dead in the water, Ross badly needed a lifeboat.

Friedland leaned forward. His tone of voice was deliberately light. The best interrogations, as ever, were a conspiracy. 'Why would the Americans need us?'

'Because they're facing a chemical threat. Must be. You've seen the video. That's Manhattan. Not Oxford Street.'

'So what have we got that the Americans might need?'

'Nothing. Yet.'

'But you think that might change?'

'With luck, yes.'

'Because of McVeigh?'

'Yes.'

Friedland nodded. 'You should have come to me,' he confirmed. 'Not the Arab.'

Ross frowned, visibly irritated, his judgement questioned. 'Why?' he said.

'Because Al Zahra works for the Americans too.' He smiled. 'Has done for years.'

*

It was three in the afternoon by the time McVeigh arrived at the bus station.

It lay in the heart of Tel Aviv, an acre or so of oil-stained tarmac off the Petah–Tikvah Road. He'd walked the mile and a half from the hotel where he'd stayed for what remained of the night, the single bag looped over his shoulder. His hands were still swollen and painful, but the American doctor at the clinic three blocks from the hotel had given him two tubes of a special anti-inflammatory cream and assured him that the damage was largely superficial. The blisters would soon burst, and he should be careful of infection, but his hands would be back to normal within a fortnight. McVeigh had thanked him and enquired briefly about the kibbutz named on the back of Cela's photo. The doctor had never heard of it, but the young Israeli nurse who'd tended McVeigh's hands picked up the name and drew McVeigh a map. Shamir was in the north, at the top of the Galilee. You followed the coast road up to Haifa and then you went inland, beyond Rosh Pinna, to a new town called Kiryat Shemona. The journey took about seven hours. With hands like that, she recommended the bus, rather than a hire car.

The bus roared north, along the coast road, the heat bubbling in through the open windows, the driver crouched over the wheel, hunting for news stations on the radio. McVeigh sat at the back, gazing out at block after block of office buildings, stained concrete and crooked lintels, as the city gave way to the suburbs and the traffic began to thin. Tel Aviv had taken him by surprise, the noise and the ugliness, and he hadn't liked it much. There was a jumpiness about the place, a note in the pitch of public conversations too complicated to put into words, though the English-speaking newspaper he'd picked up at the hotel had tried hard enough. 'UN EMBARGO TIGHTENS' went the headline in the *Jerusalem Post*, 'SADDAM THREATENS WAR'.

An hour and a half later, the bus squealed to a halt at the

terminus in Haifa. The city climbed the slopes of Mount Carmel, terrace after terrace of tall apartment blocks, windows ablaze with the late afternoon sun. McVeigh, changing buses, liked the place at once. It had height, space, a certain dignity. It behaved the way a city should.

A second bus, slower, more crowded, drove inland, up into the mountains. Away from the sea and the endless sprawl of the coastal strip, the land began to reassert itself, the bare, stony hillsides shouldering down to the road. The driver swung the long bus into bend after bend, oblivious to oncoming traffic, drawing a long tail of dust across the grey folds of the mountains. Occasionally, at a raised arm or a pointed finger by the roadside, he'd stop to pick up yet more passengers. Some of them were plainly Arabs, the men prematurely aged, the women girdled with sundry baggage. There were kids with them, too, with dirty faces and deeply black eyes, gazing at McVeigh as the bus ground north.

Once, near Safed, the bus picked up a soldier. He fought his way down the aisle and sat down at the back next to McVeigh, sweating, unshaven, dishevelled, his uniform shirt unbuttoned to the navel. He started a conversation at once, loud, heavily accented English, telling McVeigh what a pain the Iraqis had become. Like everyone else in the country, he was liable for military service. He'd done his three years and now he was in the reserve. The last year, he'd been trying to expand his business. He worked as a plumber, self-employed. Prospects, at last, were good. Yet here he was, shuttling back and forth every day from the barracks on the coast to his home in the mountains, trying to do two jobs at once. When the bus stopped again to let him off, some unvoiced arrangement with the driver, the soldier stood up, his hand on McVeigh's shoulder. 'Let the bastard come tomorrow,' he said, 'then we can spend October in peace.' McVeigh grunted, non-committal, watching the man bodychecking his way towards the front of the bus. The back of his shirt was blotched with sweat, and his boots had seen better days, but the shoulder-slung Uzi sub-machine-gun was spotless, the working parts glinting with newly applied oil.

Past Safed, the road descended to a valley floor, dead straight, flanked on either side by rows of dusty trees. McVeigh gazed out of the window. The bus was emptier now, and in the gathering twilight he could glimpse fields beyond the trees, and apple orchards, and the occasional neat rectangle of water. The girl at the clinic had told him about this valley. The land had been settled by immigrants from Eastern Europe. They'd lived in tents for years, working every daylight hour, clearing the stony hillsides by hand, turning malarial swamp into thousands of acres of productive farmland. She'd seen it herself, on trips to her boyfriend's relatives, and it was a fine achievement, though given the choice she infinitely preferred the noisy bedlam of downtown Tel Aviv.

McVeigh wasn't so sure, getting out of the bus at journey's end, shaking the stiffness from his legs. It was dusk now, and beyond the ugly clutter of concrete buildings around the bus station he could see the dark swell of the Golan Heights across the valley. There were lights halfway up the mountain, clusters of them, miles apart. Each one signified a settlement – had to – one of the collective farms they called kibbutzim. McVeigh had learned a little about them from Yakov, afternoons on the touch-line. He'd talked about his own with affection and pride. A kibbutz was one place in the world where socialism went beyond a list of empty phrases. A kibbutz was where you owned everything and nothing. A kibbutz was a way of life that had bred the cream of one of the best armies in the world.

McVeigh left the bus station and began to walk east, out of the town. In his pocket was the map from the girl in the clinic. Cross the main road, she'd said, and look for a signpost. When you find the signpost, you take the secondary road across the valley. This goes on for 5 miles. Maybe you get a lift. Maybe you walk. Either way, at the end of it, up the mountain, is the place you want.

Crossing the main road, McVeigh found the signpost. He looked up at it, grinning. In Hebrew and English, it said 'Kibbutz Shamir'. Shouldering his bag, hearing the cicadas in the orchards on either side, he began to walk, a tuneless whistle in the hot darkness.

*

There was perhaps a second of warning, no more.

Telemann was standing beside the Mercedes on a garage forecourt in the suburbs of Hamburg. The filler hose was in his right hand, the fuel pumping into the empty tank. He was watching the read-out on the pump, wondering why it was so blurred. He stepped towards it, irritated by his own eyesight, trying to force the electronic digits into focus. A figure confirmed, he turned back to the car, reaching for the nozzle, pulling it out. Then the car began to revolve, absurdly, coming up towards him, his feet seeming to slip on the greasy forecourt. He smelled petrol, gusts of it, then it was all over him, his face, his neck, his clothes, the stuff still pumping from the nozzle in his hand. He stared at it, uncomprehending, hearing the soft clunk of the Mercedes door, the girl's footsteps running towards him, a face bent over his. Then the fuel stopped hosing out of the nozzle, and there was only the drip of the stuff on to the tarmac, and the taste of it in his mouth.

Slowly, he got to his knees, looking round, trying to shake the woolliness out of his head. Another car drew up beside the pumps on the other side of the island. A large man got out, holding the door open, staring down at Telemann. Beside him, in the passenger seat, a woman was smoking a cigarette. The girl, Inge, shouted in German at the man. The man nodded, closing the door at once. Telemann looked up at Inge, still on his knees, transfixed by the image, the cigarette in the woman's fingers, his own body soaked in gasoline, a 98-octane accident, the ugliest of deaths.

He got up, stumbling, hopelessly embarrassed. He felt the girl supporting him, her fingers tight inside his upper arm. He sat in the car, the window open, while she paid for the fuel. Only when they were three blocks away from the filling station, heading back in towards the city, did he trust himself to talk.

'Thanks,' he said simply.

The girl looked at him. Her window was open, too.

'You OK?'

'Yeah.'

She looked at him again, shaking her head, supplying her own answer. They drove to an area north of St Georg, turning into a wide tree-lined street overlooking the Aussenalster. They stopped outside a sixties apartment block, big picture windows, generous balconies. They took a lift to the fifth floor, Inge beside him, fumbling for the keys of a door at the end of the corridor. Inside, there were flowers everywhere, stands of flag iris, smaller bunches of freesia, a huge vase of geraniums, exquisitely arranged. All Telemann could smell was gasoline. Inge threw the keys on to a table and led him by the hand into a big lounge. The place was expensively furnished. Outside, beyond the silvered mirror of the lake, a traffic jam tailed back from a minor accident.

Inge unlocked the big french windows. The flowers stirred in the sudden draught. She led him on to the balcony.

'Take off your clothes.'

'Here?'

'Yes.'

Telemann turned to pursue the conversation, but she'd gone. He hesitated for a moment, then slipped his jacket off. The jacket, an old favourite, was made of linen. The fuel, already evaporated, had left blobs of light brown stain. Putting the jacket to one side, Telemann began to unbutton his shirt. Then the girl was back. She had a bucket and a sponge. There was water in the bucket, hot to the touch, and a bar of soap. She left the bucket beside him, a wordless invitation, and returned with a green silk dressing-gown. Telemann looked at it, beginning to sponge his upper body, working up a lather with the soap, hearing the girl in the kitchen, the clatter of china, the sound of water from a tap.

They had coffee in the lounge, Telemann sitting on the low sofa, the leather cold against the backs of his legs. His hair was wet from the sponge, and his clothes were still outside, a small untidy pile, reeking of gasoline. His head was clear now, the woolliness and the bewilderment quite gone.

'I must have slipped,' he said. 'Oil or something. Underfoot.'

Inge was looking at him over the rim of the coffee cup. 'I was watching you,' she said. 'You didn't slip.'

'So what happened?'

She said nothing for a moment, sipping the coffee. Then she

got up, putting the cup on a small occasional table, reaching for an imaginary petrol pump, miming what she'd seen. 'You did this . . .' she said. 'And then this . . . and then you turned towards the car . . . so . . .' She paused, looking down at him. 'And then your face . . .'

'What about my face?'

'You started blinking. You shook your head. You looked—' she hesitated, searching for the word '—very surprised . . . as if . . .'

'Yes?'

She hesitated again, then shook her head. 'I don't know. Maybe you were tired. Confused. I don't know. You looked—' she shrugged '—drunk.'

'*Drunk?*'

'Sure. Crazy. I know. You're not drunk. You weren't drunk. You couldn't have been drunk. So . . .' She shrugged again. 'You don't remember it?'

'Sure. I remember the gas. All over me. And you getting out pretty damn fast. I remember that, sure.'

Inge gazed down at him, nodding, saying nothing. Then she reached for a cigarette from a pack on the floor. Telemann watched the flame of the lighter, still thinking about the garage, the fuel pooling at his feet. Inge sat down beside him and Telemann shivered, knowing how lucky he'd been, the speed of the girl's reactions, the way she'd taken charge.

'Has it happened before?'

'This? At a gas station?' Telemann shook his head. 'Never.'

'Anywhere else?'

Telemann said nothing for a moment, then emptied his cup and returned it to the low table beside the sofa. The table was topped with glass, and the cup and saucer danced briefly on the surface before he withdrew his hand. Telemann nodded slowly, staring at the cup. 'Yeah,' he said.

'Where?'

'In the States.'

'When?'

'Six months back. I'd been working out a lot, weights, repetitions. There'd been some silly episodes, clumsiness I guess, falling over, that kind of stuff, just stumbles. Then—' he shrugged, remembering the feel of the gymnasium mat beneath his body, his arms locked, straight up, the big 20-kg weights either end of the bar. '—I had an accident.'

'Serious?'

'Yeah.' He nodded. 'Could have been.'

'What happened?'

'One minute I was pushing weights. The next—' he shrugged '—I guess I dropped them.'

'You hurt yourself?'

'Yeah. But I was lucky. Couple of broken ribs. Had to give up laughing for a while. Nothing permanent.'

Inge nodded, thoughtful, and Telemann got up, pulling the dressing-gown around him, embarrassed by the direction the conversation had taken. After the accident, at Laura's insistence, he'd undergone a series of tests. The tests had been exhaustive. They'd measured his reflexes, shone lights in his eyes, taken samples of fluid from a lumbar puncture at the base of his spine. The second day he'd spent at a specialist clinic at Georgetown University, climbing painfully on to a motorized bed and succumbing to the attentions of a whole-body scan. The machine had provided metres of print-out information, though nobody subsequently had bothered to explain the outcome of $3000 of hi-tech diagnosis. Twice he'd pushed his own physician for some kind of result, but on both occasions he'd gotten no further than a shrug and a smile. You're in great shape, went the message, so don't worry about it.

He hadn't, letting the intervening months dim the memory of the weights, and the pain, and the odd stumble on the sidewalk. Lately, though, the symptoms had returned. A blur of cities on an airport departures board. Momentary bewilderment at how to access a particular blade on his pocket-knife, the brain quite certain, the fingers temporarily stalled. And now this, several litres of gasoline, liberally applied, all his own work.

Teleman gazed around the room, ready for a change of subject. 'Your boy,' he said. 'Nikki.'

'*Ja?*'

'Where is he?'

Inge smiled up at him, expelling cigarette smoke in a long blue plume. 'In Halle. He lives with my mother. He lived with me for a while, when he was younger, but—' she shrugged, gesturing round the apartment, a neat, well-ordered working life '—it just wasn't possible any more.'

'You miss him?'

'Of course.'

'Wulf ever see him?'

'Never.'

'His choice or yours?'

'His.'

'*You* ever see him?'

'Who?'

'Wulf.'

'No.'

She shook her head, emphatic, grinding the half-smoked cigarette into an ashtray on the table. It lay there for a moment, still smouldering, and Telemann wondered about the logistics of the affair, Wulf with his storybook marriage and his busy schedule, fitting in a relationship or two between meetings.

'Five years is a long time,' Telemann mused. 'Long enough to miss him.'

Inge smiled, saying nothing, and Telemann was still wondering where to take the conversation next when she got up and extended a hand. Outside, in the hall, there were two doors. The first opened into a large, sunny bedroom. A double bed faced the window. There were heavy drapes either side of the window and a small television in the corner. One wall was occupied by a built-in wardrobe, and there were tall mirrors, floor to ceiling, on the sliding doors. Beside the bed was a framed photograph. Telemann picked it up and looked at it. A child of perhaps four was kneeling on a towel beside a half-completed sandcastle. In the background there were pedalos and a circling speedboat on a flawless blue sea. The child was grinning at the camera. He had short blond hair and large dark mischievous eyes. There were traces of Inge in the way he held his head, the chin tilted slightly up. He looked amused and sceptical, as if someone had told him something he didn't quite believe. He was very brown.

'Nikki?'

'Yes. It's very recent. Only two months ago.' She smiled. 'We went to Spain. On holiday.'

'We?'

'My mother. And Nikki.' She smiled again. 'And me.'

Telemann nodded, replacing the photograph beside the bed. Inge looked at it for a moment longer, thoughtful. 'You're married?'

'Yes.'

'Children?'

'Three.'

'Then you understand,' she said.

Telemann looked at her for a moment, thinking of Laura. 'About what?' he said. 'Betrayal?'

Inge glanced up at him, frowning. 'Betrayal?' she said blankly.

Telemann nodded, suddenly exhausted, no longer seeing the point of it all: the shadow-play, the hints and guesses, the careful professional etiquette that had shaped their relationship for two brief days.

At noon, from the US Consulate, he'd at last been able to speak to Emery. He'd told him about Littman and Wulf, and Emery had confirmed that Mahmood Assali was a known player in at least one of the Palestinian terror groups. The Israelis wanted him for a series of outrages in the Occupied Territories, and there was evidence that he'd been responsible for a bus attack in Israel itself. Telemann had noted the details, making no comment, and afterwards he'd enquired about Laura, listening woodenly as Emery had described last night's electrical storms, hours of thunder and lightning sweeping up from the south, a wild twirl from the skirts of Hurricane Dora. Laura had evidently called at midnight from the little house on Dixie Street. She had water coming in through the shingles, buckets of it. The stuff was driving horizontally across the street. Bree was in tears. The cat had disappeared beneath the fridge. She just needed someone to tell her that the end of the world hadn't quite arrived. That dawn would come. That the rain would stop. That it would all be OK. Emery said that he'd done his best, calmed her down, offered to drive over, promised to call by as soon as the next day's schedule permitted, but he knew all along that what she really needed, what they all really needed, was a word or two from the Boss. Telemann was the Boss. A phone call would reach her now. A word or two of comfort might ease her day.

Telemann, listening to Emery's slow drawl, had marvelled yet again at his brazenness, his openly intimate knowledge of Laura's every movement, every fear. That's what they taught you at Langley, he thought grimly. That's what had taken him to the upper reaches of the Analytical Directorate. That, and a nerveless determination to play every scene to the limit.

Telemann had ended the conversation with a non-committal grunt, hearing the noises in his head again, hammer-blows that made him, quite literally, see double. Last time round, they'd spent thousands of dollars looking for a cause. This time round, he'd save them the time and the expense. He knew the cause. The cause was his wife. The cause was Laura.

Now Telemann looked up. He was sitting on the bed. He couldn't remember getting there. Grief, he finally realized, smelled faintly of gasoline.

'Madness,' he said quietly. 'Fantasy. All of it. A crock of shit. Believe me. Twenty years and three kids says I'm right.' He shook his head, looking at his hands, the fingers intertwined, flexing back and forth, whitened with rage. 'Madness,' he said again. 'You think you're in control. You think you're on top of it. You think you *know*, for Chrissakes. Then what happens?' He looked up at Inge, still standing by the bed. 'You find out it ain't that way at all. Probably never was. Not one year of it. One day of it. One second. Shit . . .' He reached up for her, feeling blindly for her hand, finding it. 'You know . . .' He bit his lip for a moment, and took a breath. 'I got a daughter. Bree. She's eleven. She's mad. She can't even spell her own name. Deranged. Always has been. But you know what I think? What I think now? I think she knew all along. I think she knew the

184

secret. About the madness. How mad it all is. Insane. I think she was smarter than we ever were. I think she won. I think she got there first . . .' He buried his head in his hands, his whole body shaking now, under the thin dressing-gown. 'Funny,' he whispered, 'I never figured that before.' He looked up, Inge's face a blur. 'So what does that make me? Even dumber than fucking usual?'

He turned his head away, not wanting her to see the tears, trying to hide them. Then she was beside him, kneeling on the floor, cradling his head in her hands, saying something in German, her voice soft and low, anointing him. She wiped his eyes with a corner of the sheet. Her face slipped back into focus.

'This guy Wulf. He mean anything to you?'

'Everything.'

'And he left you?'

'Yes.'

'Why?'

'Because he didn't need me any more.'

Telemann looked at her, sniffing, digesting the phrase, the simple logic, acquisition, abuse, betrayal, the full circle. 'I'll kill him,' he said quietly. 'That any use?'

Inge smiled, kissing him lightly on the forehead, squeezing his hand.

'I'm serious. Tell me where he is. Where he lives. I'll add him to the list. First the Arab. Then him. Compliments of Uncle Sam.' He made a gun with two fingers and lifted it, arm out straight, aiming for the middle distance. 'Bang, bang,' he said softly. 'Otto's dead.'

Inge looked at him for a moment longer, then got to her feet. She crossed the room to the big fitted wardrobe and opened it. Inside, the wardrobe was full of men's clothing. She sifted quickly through the hangers and produced a pair of slacks, eyeing Telemann for size. Telemann, still on the bed, gazed at the contents of the wardrobe. Many of the jackets were in eye-catching beach colours, blues and lemons and pinks. One was an acid shade of lime.

'Wulf's?' he asked tonelessly.

Inge smiled again and shook her head.

'No,' she said. 'Otto had excellent taste.'

*

Against his better judgement, Emery took the overnight flight to Los Angeles.

The telex from the West Coast had come in during the late afternoon. Juanita, still negotiating with her insurance company about structural damage to her roof from last night's storm, had left the three-line message on his desk. The first two sentences were the ones that mattered. 'Gold inquiry continues,' they went. 'Imperative you attend.'

The message was signed 'A. F.', and Emery had checked the initials with a contact he trusted at IRS headquarters across town. From Los Angeles, he'd so far heard nothing. Two separate inquiries had gone unanswered, a source of some irritation because the body in the morgue at Bellevue was – to date – one of the few tangible leads in an otherwise comfortless picture. When he'd explained this on the phone, the contact over at IRS had volunteered nothing but a chuckle, and a name, and a cryptic aside. 'Andy Fischer,' he'd said. 'Hates to bother folks unduly. Enjoy the man. He's worth the journey.'

Now, five miles above Kentucky, Emery sat at the back of the executive cabin, a tumbler of bourbon at his elbow, wondering how best to trick his body into sleep. Three weeks without meaningful rest had begun to take its toll. Every day had brought more intelligence into the big, shadowed office on 'F' Street, boxes of analysis, raw data, Agency reports, decrypts, ELINT transcriptions, satellite intercepts, top-level stuff sourced from both sides of the Atlantic. Sifting through this material, page by page, he'd sought to detect a pattern, a sequence of events, that would begin to explain the curt ultimata tightening the noose around New York.

The obvious explanation was the best: that a new terror group spawned from the political swamp that had once been Palestine was acting as an agent for Saddam Hussein, carrying the impending war to the enemy's heartlands. That made perfect sense. That was the way the President saw it. That was the theory that Emery had to garnish with names and faces – the key coordinates that would safeguard New York. But it wasn't working. As hard as he looked, there was nothing there. No real evidence of a new terror group. No quiet confirmations from Baghdad. Not a single word from sources which – under normal circumstances – would have been queueing up for a discreet word in some far-flung bar. Only the sign-off on the original note from Amman. The Martyrs of 7th June. Hardly the firmest of leads.

Sullivan, with whom he now met daily, was getting impatient. He could see it in the man's face, in his body-language. He was a politician. His was the currency of means and ends, initiatives and results. He trod the corridor to the Oval Office more often than most Presidential aides, and the message he brought back was no less plain for being unvoiced. We have a problem here, a city we can't afford to lose, damage we can't afford to sustain. We're big players, the biggest. We have a position to protect, a coalition to keep together, a war to fight. The problem's getting outa hand. Solve it.

Sullivan's appetite for progress reports was voracious, and Emery was doing his best to satisfy it with as many titbits as he thought wise. Most of the closely typed digests the couriers hand-carried across to the White House were innocuous enough, the odd peak on the Intelligence trace, the odd anomaly, but in his heart, Emery knew that Sullivan was far too smart to be fooled that easily. So far, he'd offered the man about half a dozen solid leads – some inexplicable messages out of Tripoli, ripples from the murder of a Canadian ballistics expert in Brussels, the name of an English guy cropping up in traffic out of the Israeli Embassy in London – and he guessed that Sullivan would be commissioning a little action of his own. But nothing he'd shared to date offered anything more than another dead end. Of that he was certain.

Even Telemann's latest call from Hamburg was, in his view, of limited significance. Otto Wulf had fingers in all kinds of pies, sure. He ran a huge commercial empire. He boasted openly about his 'achievements' in the East. He was very big in chemicals. But so what? All that gave the guy was an interest in profit, to which – as a businessman – he had every right. On the phone, Telemann had muttered sternly about contacts with the Iraqis, but that, too, was barely past first base. God knows, there wasn't a company in the West that hadn't been queueing for a slice of the Iraqi oil revenues, and if the smell of Saddam's money had suddenly become offensive, then that told you more about political morality than Otto Wulf. The guy had been operating in a democracy. And we, like it or not, were all consenting adults.

No, Ron had to do better than that. An hour in a Halle restaurant, and the name of a burned-out Palestinian terrorist, was hardly pork and beans. The Palestinian guy, Attali, had certainly been front-line and the bus attacks had put him near the top of the Israeli hit-list. But the guy hadn't once looked outside Israel, hadn't once shown any aptitude for running operations abroad. Indeed, in certain circles on the West Bank, he'd earned derision for his decision to cash in, retire to Europe, and spend his winnings on the services of a small army of bodyguards. That was one of the reasons he pissed the Israelis so much. Try as they might, they'd never managed to get near the guy. When they did, they'd doubtless waste him, but so far all the guy was doing was getting older.

Emery inched back his recliner and swallowed the last of the bourbon. The plane was only a third full, a sign of the deepening recession, and he'd had no trouble getting a seat. Laura, when he'd called by in the early evening, had offered to run him out to Dulles, save him the hassle of taking his own car, but he'd turned the offer down, staying only long enough to check that she and the kids were OK. His description of Juanita's place – semi-roofless, three windows out – had served to put her own piece of hurricane in perspective, and she'd begun to apologize for bothering him as they walked back to the car. He'd paused in the driveway, cupping her face with his big hands and staunching the apology with a kiss, and they'd both laughed when Bree appeared at the upstairs bathroom window, a huge grin behind the rain-stained glass, clapping her hands in wild approval.

At the car, in the windless dusk, he'd paused again before

opening the door. She hadn't heard from Ron, he could tell. It was there in her face, an expression that gave the lie to her parting smile. He'd kissed her again and told her that it would be OK, that everything would resolve itself, that the man was strong enough to cope. She'd nodded, unconvinced, and he'd watched her in the mirror as he drove away, the tilt of the head, the farewell wave, the way she turned on her heel and dug her hands in the pockets of her jeans, way deep, walking back towards the house.

The plane bumped a little, invisible cobble-stones in the night sky, and he watched lazily for the seat-belt signs to light over the forward bulkhead, thinking of Laura again, the spaces she'd always cleared in his head for herself, how young she could make him feel. Telling her he loved her had been an embarrassment, and he'd stopped doing it now. The obvious, in any case, had never been his style. Obvious? Style? Me? Laura? He closed his eyes, smiling.

Four hours later, dawn at LAX, Emery met Andy Fischer. He was standing beside the Budget Rent-a-Car counter, the place they'd agreed, a thin, sallow-faced man, younger than Emery had expected. He was wearing a rumpled, ill-fitting suit over a once-white T-shirt. He looked like a refugee from an all-night rock concert.

They drove east against the traffic, the rising sun curtained behind the pall of smog. Fischer chain-smoked at the wheel, grumbling softly about the music on a succession of local radio stations. Emery, whose musical knowledge stopped at Debussy, said very little. Soon, he guessed, they'd get down to business. For now, the guy might as well have been talking Swahili.

Past Whittier, without warning, Fischer pulled the little Honda into a Dunkin' Donuts lot. They went inside, the younger man greeting the black waitress by name, leading Emery to a table in the corner. They sat down, Emery eyeing the door to the washroom. He needed a shave and a mouthwash. It was still barely seven o'clock.

Fischer pushed the menu aside and took out a folded sheet of paper, laying it carefully on the table between them. Emery, uninvited, picked it up. At the top, underlined, was a woman's name, Lola Borg, followed by a series of numbers. Emery recognized a bank sort-code, six digits, plus another number. Beneath the name, neatly tabulated, were more figures, each one prefaced with a date and a dollar sign. Emery ran quickly through the entries. The lowest was $1300. The highest was $270,000. The entries bracketed a period of eleven months. In all, they totalled more than half a million dollars. Emery glanced up. Fischer was talking soul music with the waitress. She touched him lightly on the hand, laughing, and began to pour coffee in Emery's cup. Emery nodded at the figures.

'Who's Lola?' he said.

'Gold's wife.'

'Using her maiden name?'

'Right.' Fischer picked up the piece of paper. 'She's got three accounts of her own. This is the one that matters.'

'Why?'

Fischer looked at him for a moment, and Emery suddenly recognized how tightly wound the springs were beneath the hip banter and the charity-store camouflage.

'Why?' he said again. 'What do these figures mean?'

Fischer leaned forward, expressive hands, long pale fingers, tracing patterns on the fake marble table top.

'Gold,' he said. 'Made a name for himself in ECM. Any idea what that means?'

Emery nodded. 'Sure,' he said. 'The guy designed for the big players. Northrop. McDonnell Douglas. I've seen the file. What little there is.'

'And ECM?'

'Electronic Counter Measures. Keeping the bad guys away.'

'OK. You got it.' Fischer nodded vigorously. 'But the thing to realize about this guy is he's unusual. He's hands-on. He does the stuff himself and he does it brilliantly. Makes all those lateral leaps we all dream about. Ace designer. Computer wizard. Earns himself a great reputation. So . . .' He paused. 'Other firms want him. If this was baseball, we'd be talking megabucks. Big money.'

'Yeah?'

'Yeah. But that ain't all. Because the guy's got a nose for

190

business, too. Likes the smell of money, real money. Knows what he's worth and ain't about to take some dumb fucking offer from the company down the street. No, sir—' Fischer tapped the table, emphatic '—this is one brainy son of a bitch that ain't about to get rolled.'

'So the guy goes freelance?' Emery shrugged. 'Is that what we're saying?'

'Sure. He sets up a consultancy. He's selling his own talents, his own contacts, fifteen years at the cutting edge. The guy has real collateral. He knows what he's worth, and he's got one of those logical minds that tells him who pays top dollar.'

'The Israelis?'

'You got it. Route One. Tel Aviv.'

Emery nodding, looking down at Fischer's sheet of paper, remembering Telemann's description of the body in the morgue. Six hundred and thirty-four thousand dollars, he thought. For a shelf in a fridge. Fischer was looking at him. He was smiling.

'You think that's Israeli money?' He shook his head. 'Gold stopped working for the Israelis last year. Fiscal '89. That's this year's money. That comes from somewhere else.'

'Where?'

'Can't exactly say.' Fischer paused. 'Not for certain.'

There was a long silence, and Emery sat back in his seat, closing his eyes, rubbing his face, letting his dissatisfaction register. It's early in the morning, he wanted to say. I've come a long way. I'm tired. Back home, on the other side of the continent, there are questions to answer, a city to protect. If you have something solid, something real, let's see it for Chrissakes. He opened his eyes. Fischer was looking at him, the young conjuror in the grandpa suit.

Emery nodded at the figures. 'The guy was crooked? Is that what you're saying?'

Fischer shook his head. 'No, sir. Quite the reverse. The guy was straight arrow. The stuff we've been talking about, the Israeli stuff, it's all there in the accounts and returns. I've been through it. It's right to the last cent. Total disclosure. Mr Clean.'

'You sure?'

'Yeah.'

'You sure you can be sure?'

'Yeah.'

'So—' Emery picked up the sheet of paper '—what about all this? You say it's not Israeli?'

'No.'

'Home-grown? Domestic projects?'

'No.'

'Foreign?'

'Yes.'

Emery glanced up, alerted by a new tone in Fischer's voice, excitement. He looked at the figures again. 'Soviet? Would that make any sense?'

'None. I told you. The guy's honest. Plus, he's a patriot. Plus, the Soviets havn't got any money, even if he was for sale.' He shook his head, 'No, we can do better than that. Whole lot better.' He paused, nodding at the basket of doughnuts, newly arrived from the kitchen. 'Which I guess is why you came.'

From Whittier they drove east again, up the San Bernadino Freeway towards San Antonio Heights. By now Fischer had shed the last vestige of his old persona, hunched over the wheel, shredding the cellophane from yet another pack of Winston, intense, articulate, worrying at the theories as they began to emerge from the evidence, qualifying himself time and again in case, in his own words, Emery got the whole fucking thing entirely out of proportion.

What he knew for sure, he said, was that Lennox Gold had made a legitimate business out of the consultancy. He'd taken on the Israelis as bona fide customers. He'd been scrupulous about not sharing US secrets and had dealt exclusively on the basis of technology to which they already had access. Where there was room for improvement on their own production lines, he'd told them so, designing a number of add-on packages that had given the Israelis a significant combat edge. For this they had paid him well.

Then, a year back, the Israeli connection had been abruptly broken. Thereafter, the consultancy accounts reported no appreciable income. At the time of Gold's death, on paper at least, the business was in deep stall, the revenue flows 850 per cent down on fiscal '89, loans unserviced, two separate banks threatening foreclosure.

At this stage, given the figures, Fischer had begun to wonder about suicide. Experience told him that most businessmen had a great deal of pride. Gold wouldn't have been the first to have gone under. Fischer paused here, nursing the Honda into the slow lane, glancing across at Emery. 'You think the guy may have wasted himself?' he said. 'I have to ask.'

Emery shook his head, a grim smile, remembering Telemann's report again, the state of the hotel bathroom, the terrible chemistry of Tabun GA. 'No,' he said. 'He'd have had to be nuts to have done that.'

'Suicides are nuts.'

'No, but *really* nuts. Going the way he went, you'd have to be certifiable.' He paused, shaking his head. 'No,' he said again. 'Definitely not suicide.'

Fischer nodded. He sounded relieved. 'So we're talking homicide?'

'Yeah.' Emery glanced across again. 'That OK by you?'

'Sure,' Fischer said, smiling.

They drove on. The key, Fischer said, was Lola, Gold's wife. At first she'd denied all knowledge of her husband's business affairs. Only lately had Fischer been able to dig deep enough to disinter the evidence he needed to coax her into a real conversation. Using IRS powers of disclosure, he'd accessed thousands of privately held S & L accounts. The search had taken several weeks. Then, a couple of days back, he'd found what he'd been looking for. Lola Borg. The Glendale S & L Association. Account No. 37568498. Stuffed full of her husband's money.

Fischer slowed for the San Antonio exit. It was recent money, he said, recently earned. He knew it was recent because she'd told him so. She'd told him so because he'd arrived on a bad day, and on bad days her patience and her resolve sometimes gave out. Listening, watching the unfenced, ample lots rolling slowly by, Emery became curious, as he was supposed to. Who is she, this Lola? What kind of woman? What kind of wife? He put the question directly to Fischer, realizing the importance of Lola Borg, realizing that this was the point of the conversation he'd flown 9000 miles to conduct.

Fischer sat motionless behind the wheel, the car stopped, the window wound down, a nice view of the acres of lawn and swimming-pools that passed, in Southern California, for suburbia.

'I guess it's a question of motive,' Fischer said softly. 'The last year of his life, our friend stepped outa line. He was an honest man. There had to be a reason.'

'His wife?'

'Yeah. Maybe.'

'Where does she live?'

'Over there.'

Fischer nodded across the street. A low, single-storey dwelling, painted white, big picture windows, drapes inside, blue and white. In the drive stood a big Dodge van, a conversion of some kind, windows in the side, a folding hydraulic hoist fitted beneath the rear doors. Emery had been similar vehicles before, mainly outside hospitals. He turned back to Fischer, remembering the line about the bad days.

'She sick?'

'Yeah.'

'Very sick?'

'Yeah.'

Emery looked at him, beginning at last to understand. 'Since when?'

Fischer smiled, reaching for the door-handle. 'A year ago,' he said. 'I've got the cuttings.'

8

Sullivan took the call mid-morning, Washington time, in the back of a Government Chrysler, en route to yet another meeting. On his lap, open, were the latest updates from the Joint Chiefs. Six weeks of the heaviest staff work he could remember had finally proved, beyond doubt, that the US would be in no shape for a land war in the Gulf for at least two months. Sealift for the heavy M-1 Abrahms battle-tanks had been chaotic. Elderly ships' engines were constantly breaking down. Supply schedules were in tatters, and – even worse – the stuff that had made it as far as the desert was, in the cold prose of the Department of Defense, 'subject to heavy environmental attrition'.

Sand in the goddam helicopter engines, thought Sullivan, reaching for the proffered telephone, irritated that this small moment of peace between the White House and the Pentagon should have proven so brief. Hunched in the corner of the car, he put the phone to his ear. The voice, when it came, was English. The guy from Number Ten. Ross.

'Hi,' Sullivan said wearily. 'How ya doin'?'

Ross spoke for perhaps a minute. Listening, Sullivan reached inside his jacket pocket and began to make scribbled notes on a small jotter. When Ross finished, Sullivan grunted. 'Sure,' he said. 'Al Zahra's a generous guy . . .' He paused. 'So this McVeigh. Who the fuck is he?'

'Ex-Marine. Freelancing in the security business.'

'And where's he gone?'

'Zahra says Israel . . .' Ross paused. 'Evidently the man's a bit of a loner. Only gets in touch when he has something to say. So far we assume he has nothing to say.'

Sullivan, watching a group of tourists rubber-necking the

Lincoln Memorial, frowned. The name McVeigh he'd seen only days ago, a passing reference in one of the digests sent over from 'F' Street. At the time, he'd thought nothing of it. But now he began to wonder. He bent to the phone again.

'You say stuff's gone missing?'

'Yes. Five gallons of nerve gas.'

'How hard are you looking?'

'Hard enough, under the circumstances . . .' He paused. 'The real problem is the threat. Just a rumour would be disastrous. As you may know . . .'

'Yeah?' Sullivan grunted again, refusing to take the conversation any further, refusing the implicit invitation to share the news about New York.

Ross came on again, as persistent as ever. 'You think I should come over again?'

'No point. Unless you've got something to say.'

'That wasn't what I meant.'

'No?'

'No. I was wondering whether a briefing might be in order. You to me. It would certainly help my end. Anything you feel you might be able to share.'

'You bet.'

Sullivan shook his head, scowling. He'd known Ross now for a couple of years, a strictly informal relationship, the product of a Downing Street dinner during one of his frequent trips to Europe. He had no great regard for the man, too ambitious, too eager, too easily impressed, but a presence in Downing Street was a useful asset, certainly a better bet than having to rely on the usual channels. Sharing any kind of information with the Brits had, for years, been tantamount to full disclosure. Their Intelligence services leaked night and day, a steady drip of other people's secrets, and when he'd bothered to think about it properly, to ask himself why it should be so, he'd had to put it down to something in the national character, a by-product of the class system, yet another sign – if one was ever needed – that the place was utterly fucked. He bent to the phone again, assuring Ross that nothing of importance had happened, that he was better off staying his side of the Atlantic, that he'd doubtless be in touch. Then, without waiting for a reply, he rang off.

Minutes later, turning into the huge Pentagon car park, he was still thinking about Ross's news, the missing drum of nerve gas, and he reached for his pad again, scribbling a reminder to himself, the name of the Arab in London, Al Zahra.

*

McVeigh awoke late, some formless dream broken by a sudden pain in his right hand. He opened his eyes, blinking in the sunlight filtering through the mesh door. His hand had become twisted under the weight of his body. He rolled over and sat up, swinging out of bed, planting his bare feet on the cool tiles.

Outside the wooden hut, through a wall of shrubs, he could see grass and the long curve of a cindered path. Further away, out of sight, he could hear the regular ticking of a water-sprinkler. He glanced at his watch. Already, barely seven, it was hot.

He got dressed slowly, standing in front of the mesh door, enjoying the warmth of the sun on his bare flesh. He'd arrived the previous evening, unannounced. The kibbutz had been bigger than he'd expected, dozens of small chalets, windows lit in the darkness, doors open, the sounds of conversation, laughter, music. Shadows trod the paths between the lines of chalets, and he'd walked around for a while, trying to get a feel of the place, before stopping someone, an older man, barrel-chested, hooped T-shirt, ancient shorts. He'd asked the man where a stranger should go, and the man had listened patiently to the question and then, totally incurious, pointed wordlessly to a group of buildings further up the hillside.

McVeigh, none the wiser, had followed the man's directions, taking his time, savouring the rich smells, released by the cool of the evening. It reminded him of expeditions years back, Kashmir, Nepal, the first few days or so when you plodded through the foothills and took your reward in the evening, sprawled by the camp fire, blanketed by the smells of yak dung and wild flowers. It was similar here, the warm, pungent breath of the earth, and he felt immediately at home.

At the top of the kibbutz he'd found a dining-hall and a couple of offices. In one of the offices, a woman in her early thirties had listened to his story. He was a tourist. He had the name of a friend of a friend. He'd like to stay a couple of days, meet the person he'd come to see, find out a little about how the place worked. The woman had listened to him, impassive, and then reached for a pencil and paper. He wrote down the name for her, Cela Arendt, and she'd looked at it for a moment or two before risking a brief smile of recognition. 'Cela,' she'd said finally. 'Cela Eilath.'

McVeigh had apologized at this point, saying he'd known her husband, and the woman had looked up again, the smile gone, an unvoiced question on her lips. McVeigh had shrugged and grinned, offering no further information, and the evening had ended with his occupation of an empty hut in a row reserved for students from the city. The kibbutz, the woman said, had no facilities for tourists. If he wanted to stay, then it would be possible for a few days, but he'd have to work, like everybody else. McVeigh, ever-courteous, agreed at once. If everyone worked, then Cela worked. Perhaps he could do whatever she did. That way, they'd have more time together. The woman had shaken her head and said that wouldn't be possible. Cela helped in the schoolhouse. Newcomers picked apples. Perhaps McVeigh should come to the office again, next morning, when things might be a little clearer.

Now, fully dressed, McVeigh left the hut and took the path up through the kibbutz towards the dining-hall. In daylight, the place was even bigger than he'd thought, spread over the gentle folds of hillside, each row of chalets bedded into the landscape, gloved in creepers and a spectacular mass of flowers. There was little sign of activity, and when he got to the cluster of buildings that housed the dining-hall and administration, the place was nearly empty, five long tables, set with knives and forks, big metal jugs of iced fruit juice, pearled with condensation, bowls of sliced water melon, the flesh pink and glistening.

McVeigh was still debating whether to sit down when he heard the growl of diesel trucks in the dirt yard outside. Then

198

there were footsteps, and the big double doors burst open, and the place was suddenly full of people, all ages, dressed for outdoor work. They sat down at once, without ceremony, reaching for the fruit juice, spreading thick pats of butter on the bread, heaping slices of apple and banana on bowls of creamy yoghurt, and McVeigh watched for a moment before joining them at the furthest table, an empty chair near the end. He was still eating when the dining-hall emptied again, some secret signal, noise outside as the engines restarted, then the crunch of tyres on the dirt road, and the grinding of gears, and the slow receding whine of big trucks heading back towards the valley floor.

An hour later, McVeigh found the woman he'd met the previous evening. She was standing in the shade of a plane tree beside a row of older chalets. She was holding a pen and a clipboard and she was deep in conversation with an older man. Seeing McVeigh, she signalled him over. She nodded at the older man. 'Cela's father,' she said briskly. 'Avram Eilath.'

McVeigh smiled at the old man and extended a hand. The old man shook it briefly. He had big hands, weathered and calloused by years in the fields. Evidently he spoke no English, the woman talking to him in Hebrew. After a while he looked at McVeigh and shook his head, and McVeigh felt vaguely uncomfortable, the victim of a conversation he couldn't understand. He glanced at the woman. 'What did you tell him?'

'I said you were a friend of Yakov. I said you'd come from England. To see Cela.'

'And?'

'He doesn't want to talk to you.'

'Why not?'

The woman looked at the older man for a moment, translating the question, nodding vigorously when the man shrugged and gave her a muttered answer. '*Ney maas, li . . .*' he said, shaking his head. '*Ney maas, li . . .*'

McVeigh stared at him, recognizing the phrase, the shape of it, through the broken shards of Hebrew. Enders, he thought, the little Jew in the antique shop, the conversation he'd overheard the day Yakov Arendt got shot. Same phrase. Same tone of voice. McVeigh didn't take his eyes off the old man, who was still shaking his head.

'What did he say?'

The old woman looked at him sharply. Her English was excellent, barely accented at all. 'I'm sorry?'

'What did he say?' McVeigh nodded at the old man. 'Just then. That phrase he used. What does it mean?'

The woman frowned. '*Ney maas, li*?'

'Yes.'

'It's means he's had enough. It's what people say when they want to be left alone. It's . . .' She paused, trying to find exactly the right words. 'It's just that he's had it. It's become something too much for him.'

'What's something too much for him?'

'All the people coming to see Cela. All the questions.'

'What people? People like me? From England? English-speaking people?'

The old man looked up, shaking his head. He knows more English than he admits, thought McVeigh. The old man turned to go, and McVeigh stepped towards him, wanting him to stay, but then he felt the woman's restraining hand on his arm and thought better of it. The old man walked slowly away, his sandals flap-flapping on the paving-stones. McVeigh watched him disappear into a chalet at the end of the row, making a mental note of the location. Then he turned back to the woman. 'Cela's had lots of visitors? Recently? Since Yakov . . .' He shrugged, leaving the sentence unfinished, and the woman looked at him, not answering, the frown back on her face, and McVeigh knew that he'd gone too far. He was a tourist from England. He'd come to see a friend of a friend.

'The place where Cela works,' he said carefully, 'the school. Where is it?'

'You can't see her there. Not until she's finished.'

'Where does she go afterwards? Where does she live?'

The woman said nothing, but nodded in the direction the old man had taken, the chalet at the end of the row. There was a child's tricycle upturned on the lawn. Draped over it, drying in the sun, was a towel and a woman's one-piece swimming-costume.

'She lives with her father?'

'Yes.' The woman paused. 'Whenever she visits.'

'She's just visiting?'

'Of course.'

'She hasn't moved back? Come home?'

'No.'

'But she could? If she wanted to?'

'Of course.' The woman turned away, bringing the conversation to an end, heading back towards the dining-hall, but McVeigh fell into step beside her, glad that one supposition, at least, had proved correct. Cela Arendt was a kibbutznik born and bred. McVeigh strode up the hillside, thinking of Yakov again, his body sprawled in the Kensington street, the photograph in the evening paper. '*Ney maas . . .*' he mused aloud.

The woman kept walking, saying nothing, refusing to help him out by finishing the phrase, pretending she hadn't heard.

McVeigh persevered. 'What kind of phrase is it?'

'I've told you.'

'You've told me what it means. I want to know why you'd use it.'

The woman said nothing for a moment, still walking. The sun was hot now, and McVeigh was beginning to sweat.

'It's crude,' she said at last.

'Offensive?'

'A little.'

'What else?'

The woman stopped and looked up at him. She was at least a foot shorter than McVeigh, an indoor face, paler than most he'd seen. 'Why do you want to know?'

'It's important, that's all.'

'Is it to do with Cela?'

McVeigh hesitated a moment, weighing the value of an honest answer. Then he nodded. 'Yes,' he said, 'it is.' He paused. 'So why would her father say it?'

The woman looked away again, down the hillside towards

the old man's chalet. Finally, she shrugged. 'He loved Yakov like a son,' she said quietly. 'That's why it's so hard for him. The people who come from Tel Aviv. The questions they ask. How unhappy they make his daughter.' She shrugged. 'It's not a world he understands.'

McVeigh nodded, sympathetic. 'And the phrase?' he said. 'What should that tell me? About someone's state of mind? About the way you have to feel to use it?'

The woman gazed at him, a look of frank appraisal, and for a moment McVeigh wondered whether she, too, might be related to Cela. Perhaps she was. Perhaps everyone was related in these strange collectives. If not by blood, then by some other bond. The woman began to walk again, more slowly, her head down.

'It's not an easy thing to answer,' she said at last. 'It's a phrase people never use. Not here, at least.'

'But?'

'But . . .?' She stopped again. 'It means you're totally exhausted.' She looked up. 'It means you've reached the end.'

*

Emery sat by the bed, his coat carefully folded in his lap. The whole house smelled like a hospital, surfaces scrubbed and bleached, windows curtained against the hot Californian sun. A young Filipino care attendant ghosted from room to room, kind eyes and a permanent smile above the carefully pressed white jacket. Fischer, standing by the window, accepted a third cup of coffee. So far he'd said very little, content to introduce Emery with a deferential wave, the man from Washington, the guy in charge.

Emery looked down at the face on the pillow. They'd been at the house an hour now, going over the woman's story. She'd been married to Lennox Gold for twelve years. She'd known very little about his work. First he'd been in regular employment, salaried jobs. Then he'd gone out on his own. She thought he'd done well. Money had never been a problem. Not, at any rate, until the accident.

Emery hesitated, his finger circling a button on his coat. 'You were drunk,' he repeated, 'when the truck hit you.'

'Yes.'

'You remember anything about it?'

The woman, Lola, gazed up at him. She had a pale, oval face and thick, auburn hair. Her eyes, deep-set, flicked incessantly from Emery to Fischer. She frowned. 'I think I saw something on the freeway. Just before it happened. An animal or something. I dunno.'

'Is that why you stopped? So suddenly?'

'I dunno. Might have been . . .' She grimaced, a small bitter curl of her lower lip. 'Like I said, I was out of it.'

Emery nodded. Fischer had shown him the file of cuttings before they'd left the car. The woman had tested positive at the hospital. The truck had hit her car, a dozen other vehicles had piled up behind the truck, and two people had been killed, one of them a child of three. The subsequent trial had made headlines across the State. Lola had pleaded guilty to causing death by drunken driving, a charge that normally resulted in a lengthy driving ban, a heavy fine, and occasionally a year or so in the State penitentiary. In this case, though, the judge had taken a different view. Her neck broken, Lola Gold would be paralysed for life. Furthermore, with her insurance negated by the police evidence, she'd have to look somewhere else for the hundreds of thousands of dollars the rest of her days would require. That, said the judge, was punishment enough for any human being. And so Lola Gold had been wheeled from the courthouse, free to get on with the rest of her life, trapped in a body that wouldn't work any more.

The Filipino appeared at the door again. He carried a cordless telephone and murmured a name that Emery didn't catch. The woman shook her head, dismissing the call.

Emery bent forward. 'So we're talking how much?' he said. 'Since the accident? Half a million? More?'

'Less.'

'How much less?'

'Not much less.' She hesitated, her eyes on the move again, tallying the costs of this new life of hers. 'Hospital bills, physiotherapy, care attendants, the van out front, alterations to the house, this little bed of mine . . .' Her eyes came to rest on the hi-tech bed in which she lay, with its hoists, and pulleys, and motorized frame. Then she looked up again at Emery, and for a second or two he glimpsed how complicated and helpless her days had become, her every waking need permanently in the gift of other people. Regardless of the circumstances, it was impossible not to feel sorry for the woman.

'This money,' he began, 'it came from your husband?'

'All of it. He paid for all of it. Every last cent.'

'How?'

'I don't know.'

'But he was broke . . .' Emery paused. 'Wasn't he? That last year? Since the accident?'

The woman's eyes flicked towards the window. 'So your friend tells me.'

'You're saying he's wrong?'

'I'm saying Lennox paid for everything. Dollar bills. Hundreds of thousands. He knew what was needed and he found it. You ask me how, I don't know. I just know he did it. He was a good man, a good husband. He looked after me here, after I came out of the hospital, and when things were OK for me, he went off and got the money. Where from, I don't know. How, I don't know that either.' She paused for breath, her voice faint with the effort. 'He was a good man,' she said again. 'And I miss him.'

Emery nodded. 'You know how he died?'

'Yeah.'

'Who told you?'

'Friend of his. Over in New England.'

Emery nodded again, saying nothing for a moment, aware of Fischer watching him from the window. He'd asked the same question, out there in the car, genuine curiosity. Emery looked at the woman. 'So how did he die?' he said softly.

'Heart attack.'

'Yeah?'

'Yeah, for sure. The man never knew when to stop. Never had, never would. He used to go to New York a lot on business. I'd warn him about it but he'd never listen. The man had a real appetite.'

'For what?'

204

'Work.' She paused. 'And sex.' The eyes were back on Emery again. 'Twelve years we were married. Those twelve years we couldn't get enough of it, of each other. I knew the man, believe me. You think all that comes to an end? Because of this? Because of me?' She shook her head, answering her own question. 'No,' she said. 'The man needed it.'

'You knew about it?'

'I knew the man he was. I knew we had a pact. Nothing local. No shitting in the tent.' She looked away. 'So that pretty much left New York. We called it business. It was easier that way.'

'But that's why he went. On business.'

'Sure.' She smiled. 'Work hard, play hard.'

Emery nodded, accepting the point. 'And this friend of his. He told you about . . .' He hesitated. 'What happened?'

'He said Lennox died of a coronary. In bed. In some hotel room. He didn't go into details. He didn't need to. Lennox wouldn't have been reading a book.'

Emery nodded again. Some of the smoke that Telemann had blown around the events in Room 937 had to do with a heart attack. It was down under 'Cause of Death' on the certificate, yet another over-worked executive, struck down at the coal-face of American capitalism.

'You know why he went to New York so many times?'

'Business. He had clients there.'

'Is that what he said?'

'Sure.'

'You believed him?'

The woman didn't answer for a moment. She looked hurt. Then she nodded. 'Sure,' she said again. 'That and the hookers.' She paused. 'He'd buy it. I know he would. He liked to keep things neat and tidy. Emotion bored him. That's why he was such a good businessman. He never went beyond the figures. Never. That's what he used to say. He used to say, "Lola, if it ain't there in the figures, it ain't there. What don't add up, ain't real. The rest is schlock."'

'And you?'

'I was his wife.' She smiled gently. 'The one permitted fantasy. I'd do anything for him. And he knew it.'

There was a long silence. Emery produced a small notebook and opened it. 'This friend of his,' he began, 'the friend in New England . . .'

He glanced down at the bed. The woman had closed her eyes. She was breathing a little more heavily, the sheets rising and falling. When she opened her eyes again, they were filled with tears. She tried to cough, a faint rasp in her throat. She nodded left, towards a stainless-steel trolley on the other side of the bed. 'There's tissues in the box,' she said. 'You get to play mother.'

Emery reached across for a tissue, mumbling an apology, dabbing gently as the tears rolled down her face and on to the pillow. After a while, he started on the question again, the friend back east, but the woman spared him the trouble. 'His name's David,' she said. 'David Weill. He works in Massachusetts someplace. I've got the address. The rest of the time he's back home.'

'Where's home?'

The woman said nothing for a moment, staring up at him, her mind drifting off again, the eyes filling with tears.

'Weill,' Emery said again. 'Where does he come from?'

The woman blinked, making an effort, offering a small, apologetic smile.

'Israel,' she said at last, sniffing.

*

The old man, Abu Yussuf, sat in the tiny apartment kitchen, waiting for the boy to return. He'd cooked himself a meal earlier but he'd barely touched it. It was still on the table, a congealing mound of boiled rice, caked with minced beef and tomato ketchup. Beside it, half-wrapped in a strip of cotton waste, was a heavy adjustable wrench. The wrench he'd fetched from the garage. With the wrench, he'd beat the truth from the boy.

The old man heard a cab rattle to a halt in the street outside. He got to his feet, moving across to the window, peering out, taking care not to show himself. From three storeys up, he watched the cab door open. Two black men got out. The cab

206

drove away, and the old man stepped back into the shadows again as the two blacks sauntered across the street and into a tenement building opposite. The old man checked his watch. He'd been waiting for nearly an hour.

He sat down again, taking another mouthful of warm Coke from the can beside the chair. For two days, he'd brooded on the meaning of the conversation he'd had with Amer Tahoul, his wife's brother, the voice in the darkness, the neat young bureaucrat he'd phoned from the office on 18th Street. The conversation had lasted longer than he'd planned. It had seemed an age, the old man immobile by the huge desk, scarcely daring to move, whispering his story to Amer Tahoul, checking over his shoulder, peering through the open door, listening for the footsteps that never came.

He'd told the Palestinian about the letters he'd written to his wife, the letters she'd written back, and then the long period of nothing, the days lengthening into weeks, no letters, no post-cards, no phone calls, nothing. He knew in his heart that something had happened, something terrible, and he needed, now, to know what it was. Amer Tahoul had listened to his story, interrupting from time to time, sympathetic, wanting to clarify this point or that, and at the end of it there had been a long silence, so long that the old man's nerve had nearly cracked, his hand an inch above the receiver, ready to terminate the call, to bend to the vacuum-cleaner and return to his chores, to the aching void that was now his life.

Then Amer had come back. 'Hala was arrested,' he said. 'Yesterday.'

The old man nodded, already numb. 'Arrested,' he repeated. 'Yesterday.'

'But before that she had been writing to you.'

'You know that?'

'Yes. Some of the letters she gave to me. She has no money for the air-mail stamps. I post them through the Municipality.'

'They went? They definitely went?'

'All of them.'

'How many? Tell me how many this month?'

There was a brief silence. Then Amer came back. He'd never been less than precise. At home. At school. At work. 'Since the end of August,' he said, 'four.'

'To here? To Newark?'

'Yes.'

'You're sure?'

'Yes. I have to keep a record. Hala insisted. She said you'd repay the postage when you got back.'

The old man shook his head. Four letters, he thought. And maybe more, maybe some that didn't come through Amer at all but through some other source. He pictured his wife for a moment, back home, sitting at the table, bent over the pad of lined blue paper she always used.

'Where is she? Where have they taken her?'

'We don't know. We're still trying to find out.'

'Why? Why have they taken her?'

'I don't know.'

'You've been seeing her? Before yesterday?'

'Of course.'

'How was she?'

There was another silence, much longer, and the old man knew that he was close to the heart of it, this terrible mystery, the disappearance of his wife.

'Tell me,' he said, his voice suddenly gruff, 'tell me how she was.'

'She was frightened.'

'Why?'

'Because . . .' Amer paused. 'It's difficult. A woman had been to see her. An Israeli woman. She was confused. Frightened. She didn't know what to do. She asked me to . . .'

Amer stopped again. In the background, the old man could hear voices, men talking, the sound of a door being slammed. Then Amer was back again, asking the old man for a number, some way they could continue the conversation, and the old man panicked, his hand fumbling with the telephone in the darkness, cutting off the call, rearranging the desk, stooping for the hoover, his mind suddenly quite blank.

Now, waiting for the boy, he knew what he must do. He'd

met the mailman in the street. He'd asked him about the missing letters. The mailman, a friendly Greek his own age, had told him that the letters had come. He'd given them to the boy. The boy had always been waiting, eight in the morning, the old man still over in Manhattan. The boy had taken them for the old man. He'd give them to him when he got back. That had been the arrangement.

At the table, the old man heard the door to the street again. The boy had a distinctive way of announcing his arrival. The old man had watched him sometimes. He gave a little half-turn to the key, then kicked the door hard, always the same place, so the door crashed back, pitting the plaster on the wall inside. The old man heard it now, the door crashing back against the wall, and then the boy's footsteps along the hall and up the stairs, stamp–stamp, the rhythm echoing upwards.

There were six flights of steps to the third floor. The old man picked up the wrench, the cotton waste wrapped tightly round the handle. It fitted nicely into the palm of his hand. Standing behind the door, in the narrow hall, he just had room for the one swing that would count, the first blow, the edge of the wrench, hard against the boy's skull.

The footsteps got louder, accompanied by the high piping whistle the boy knew the old man hated so much. The old man closed his eyes for a moment, a simple prayer, the thought of his wife in some damp cell or other, paraded for hour after hour, question after question. At home, they called it *t'azeeb kufif*, light torture. Light torture meant they beat you in the places that never bruised. His sons had shown him how it was done. He knew what it felt like, how much it hurt. The Israelis did it all the time. It meant you were lucky. It meant they'd spared you the real thing, *t'azeeb t'eel*, heavy torture.

The footsteps stopped for a moment outside the apartment. Then the door burst open, a long oblong of dusty sunshine on the greasy linoleum floor, a shadow stepping in, and then the boy himself. He was short and stocky with a thick neck. He had close-cropped hair, and big thighs inside tight blue jeans, and the light, cocky step of an athlete or a male dancer. The old man watched him for perhaps a second and then, as he turned to kick the door shut, he lunged at him with the wrench. The boy saw it coming, some sixth sense, ducking quickly to the left as the wrench smashed into the base of his neck. Then he was on to the old man, his hands reaching for the wrench, twisting it away, tossing it down the hall, his eyes narrow with rage.

The old man backed against the wall, trying to beat the boy off, but the boy was far stronger, seizing the old man by the throat, banging his head against the wall, kneeing him in the groin, then bringing his fist up into his face as the old man folded softly on to his knees. Helpless on the floor, trying to protect his head and belly, the old man gasped with pain. He didn't know there could be so much pain. He didn't know so much pain existed. Every second, every blow, every kick, brought more pain. The boy was like an animal, kicking and kicking, his body, his head, enjoying it, laughing, and then suddenly he stopped and walked away down the hall and into the kitchen, whistling.

The old man slowly unfolded himself, limb by limb, until he was sitting against the wall, his knees up to his chin. His mouth, he knew, was wrecked. He fingered it gently, feeling the sharp edges of the broken teeth, tasting the blood. After a while he tried to move, to stand up, but the colours began to drain from the hallway and he knew he was going to pass out. He collapsed back against the wall again, one hand going to his head. What little hair he had was matted with blood, and when he withdrew his hand and looked at it he saw that the fingers were covered with it. He began to cough, bent double, blood and spittle everywhere, and when he looked up again the boy was standing over him. He was smoking a cigarette. In his other hand was a saucepan full of water. He threw the water over the old man and sauntered back to the kitchen, kicking the wrench as he went. The old man watched him go, trying to steady the fear inside him, the terrible anticipation of another beating, more pain. His sons had told him this, too. How the Israelis played with you, shredded your nerves, left you nowhere to hide, made your body betray you. Of the Israelis, though, it was something you expected. From one of your own, from a fellow freedom-fighter, it was doubly painful.

Minutes later, the boy was back again. He stood above the old man. He offered him the remains of the can of Coke he'd found in the kitchen. The old man nodded, wary, reaching up, putting the can gently to his broken mouth. An hour earlier, it had been simple. He'd beat the boy, cower him into submission, restore a little respect and get to the truth of the letters. It would all have been that simple. Except that here he was, physically pulped, fearful, shamed, hurting everywhere. The boy was looking down at him. From time to time, he rubbed his neck.

'Why did you do that?' he said at last.

The old man shook his head. 'For no reason,' he said thickly. 'I thought you were someone else. I thought you were a thief.'

'A thief?'

The boy bent to him, his face very close. The old man could smell his last meal, the smell of meat and garlic. He knew nothing about the boy. Nothing about his background, his family, where he came from, where he called home. He had a name, Ali, but the way he used it, contemptuous, convinced the old man that it was false. That was the way of it, of course, with the freedom-fighters, but all his life the old man had never met anyone so hostile, so totally devoid of any shred of kindness or humanity. In some senses it was a mystery, something to ponder, but now that mystery had resolved itself into something far darker, simple menace, a quality of violence that made him begin to shake again and turn his head, averting his eyes, taking no more risks.

'A thief,' he said again. 'I thought you were a thief.'

*

After half an hour on the phone to Emery, Telemann was more determined than ever to snatch the Arab, Mahmood Assali.

Back at the US Consulate on Alsterufer, a night's sleep between himself and the incident at the gas station, Telemann had finally renewed contact with Emery at a hotel in Culver City. In Los Angeles, by Telemann's calculations, it was early afternoon. Yet Emery, when he came to the phone, had plainly been asleep.

'Took the red-eye last night,' he explained briefly. 'I'm owed a little rest.'

Telemann said nothing for a moment, wondering whether Laura was with him, then he plunged into his plans for the Arab, keeping the details brief. Involving the Germans, he said, was plainly crazy. Assali was living in Bad Godesburg with their blessing, a tolerated presence. If they'd wanted him off the board, they'd have done it months ago. The fact that they hadn't, the fact that he and his private army were left in peace, was ample evidence that Kohl's Germany, at the very least, had no quarrel with the Palestinians. Add the new Intelligence about Otto Wulf – long-term contacts with Iraq, allegations that he might be supplying ready-made Tabun-GA – and the picture began to look very grim indeed. No, the Germans would never bother Assali with even the briefest list of questions. Nor would they tolerate any interference with Otto Wulf, Greater Germany's favourite industrialist. So if the US had any serious interest in either man, then the time was right for a little free enterprise. The place to start was the Arab. The man should be lifted at once.

Emery, listening to the familiar can-do rhetoric, gently mocked the plan. Germany was a US ally, lynch-pin of the new Europe. Snatching Assali from his legitimate address, even if such a thing was possible, would provoke a major diplomatic incident. At best, it was bad manners. At worst, it could prove very messy indeed. Assali, in any case, was an unlikely source for the threat against New York. Ditto Wulf. Intelligence remained the real key to the puzzle, and to date Emery was unpersuaded. Maybe Telemann had been looking in the wrong trash cans. Maybe the thing was a whole lot subtler than either of them had suspected. Either way, Emery counselled him to try a little harder. Time was moving on. Sullivan's patience was running out. The only currency that now mattered was results, and so far – in Emery's opinion – Telemann had got fuck-all.

Telemann, listening, felt a chill steal through him. He and Emery had always shared a rugged belief in home truths. That had been the basis for their relationship, that plus a great deal of mutual respect.

'Fuck all . . .?' Telemann repeated.

'Yep. What else *is* there?'

'Wulf.'

'We talked about Wulf. Wulf is an industrialist. Big man. *Big* guy. The rest of it's hearsay. Scuttlebutt. He's got too much to lose.' He paused. 'You really believe he's gonna peddle nerve gas to the rag-heads? Put it all on the line?'

'Yeah.'

'Why?'

'Because . . .' Telemann paused, shaking his head, trying to muster the case again: Wulf's limitless appetite for power, his brutal calculations about means and ends, his indifference to the outcome. 'Wulf's got a son,' he muttered. 'Nikki.'

'You think that's it? Some broad spins you a line about kids and promises, and you think that's enough to condemn the guy?'

Telemann closed his eyes. He could see the smile on Emery's face, sitting in his hotel room, playing God, pushing people's lives around. 'Yeah,' he said thickly. 'That's the line. Kids and promises. You got it. Kids and fucking promises . . .'

'It's bullshit, Ron. We're talking evidence here, hard facts, correlations. Not some fairy-tale love affair.'

Telemann shook his head slowly, lost for words. Bree, he thought, and Laura, and Emery himself, with his sailboat on the bay, and his long pianist's fingers, and his love of all that fancy music. He looked at the phone for a moment, holding it at arm's-length, hearing Emery's voice, droning on and on, some other point about Wulf. Then, shrugging, he put the phone down. He looked at it for a second or two, his face quite blank, then he stood up and reached for the jacket he'd hooked on the back of the chair. The jacket had come from Inge's wardrobe. It was lemon, with a light blue stripe, louder than Telemann's normal taste but a perfect fit across the shoulders and around the chest. He left the office quickly, locking it behind him, hearing the phone begin to ring again, knowing it was Emery, not caring. He jogged up the stairs from the basement and tapped twice at the door beside the lobby. The duty officer looked up, and caught the keys that Telemann tossed across the room. Then he reached for the log, making a careful note of the time, asking whether he needed a cab. Telemann shook his head, grinning, thanking him for the facilities, saying he'd prefer to make his own arrangements.

Outside in the street it was nearly dark. The last of the rush-hour traffic had long disappeared and the Mercedes was clearly visible, 100 metres away, parked outside a bank. Telemann crossed the street, whistling, happier than he'd felt for months. His father had once told him, hours from his death, that everyone, in essence, was alone. He hadn't made a point of it, no long speech, no big deal, but the phrase had stuck in Telemann's mind for years afterwards. He thought about it when he remembered his parents' marriage, the dark, loveless house down in Carolina, his father's long absences abroad, the gilt-framed photographs his mother kept for family visitors, and it came back to him now, as the Mercedes coasted to a halt beside him. In his stiff, Marine Corps way, the old man had been right. At the end of it all, sooner or later, you got to be alone. Not anxious. Not fearful. Just alone.

Telemann bent to the window of the Mercedes. He'd expected Inge, the girl. Instead, there was another face behind the tinted glass, curly blond hair, the beginnings of a smile. The window hummed down. Nathan Blum. The Mossad *katsa*. He eyed the jacket for a moment, grinning broadly. Telemann looked down at him. 'Yours?' he said.

Blum nodded, reaching across to open the door. 'Mine,' he agreed.

*

For a second or two, standing in the wet darkness, Sarah McVeigh thought it was a joke. She looked at the proffered address card, then up at the face beneath the dripping brim of the Homburg. 'Mr Friedland?' she said blankly.

The man nodded. 'Yes,' he said. 'May I come in?'

Sarah looked again at the card. Underneath the name, lightly embossed, the card read 'Curzon Securities'.

'Are you selling something?'

'No.'

'Then what do you want?'

'It's about your husband.'

'My ex-husband.'

'Your ex-husband.'

Sarah looked at him for a moment longer. It was quarter-past ten. Billy was in bed. Every instinct told her to shut the door, to keep the man out, to shield herself from the life she'd turned her back on.

'Has something happened to him?'

'He's disappeared.'

'He's always disappearing.'

'We need to find him.'

'We?'

The man looked at her. His face was grey and puffy with fatigue. He tried to smile. 'I work for the Government's security services,' he said patiently. 'I can give you a number. I'm happy to wait here if you'd prefer to ring.'

He reached into his pocket and produced another card. Ross had sent it over by special courier. He'd thought it might help.

Sarah glanced at the card. 'Downing Street?' she said.

'Yes.'

Sarah hesitated for a moment, then stepped back into the house. Friedland followed her, a line of wet footprints up the hall. They sat in the lounge, Friedland's hat and coat draped over the clothes-horse, a steady plop–plop of drips into the plastic washing-up bowl beneath.

'I was doing the ironing,' Sarah said helplessly. 'I'm afraid it's a bit of a mess.'

'My fault. I should have called.'

Sarah nodded, saying nothing, wondering why she felt so disturbed, listening to this stranger talking quietly about a man she'd shared her life with. McVeigh meant nothing to her any more. He was simply another of life's passing irritations, calling to collect his son, eternally late, eternally gruff. His work, what little she knew of it, suited the person he'd become. It was tatty. He dealt with third-rate people, riff-raff, petty criminals. It probably suited him very well. And yet . . . She blinked, shaking her head, trying to concentrate. The stranger, Friedland, was talking about phone calls. Had McVeigh phoned at all? Written? She shook her head, emphatic.

'No,' she said.

'The boy?'

'No, nothing.'

'Isn't that unusual?'

'What?'

'I understood they were very close.'

Sarah looked at him, not answering, not liking the man's use of the past tense.

'They *are* very close,' she said at last. 'Very close.'

'And does he normally stay in touch? When he goes away?' He paused. 'Postcards, for instance?'

'Sometimes.'

'This time?'

'I've told you.' She shook her head again. 'There's been nothing.'

Friedland nodded, looking around, speculative, and Sarah realized that he didn't believe her. For a moment, she wondered whether he had the authority to search the place, whether this house of hers was – after all – as vulnerable to the ebb and flow of McVeigh's life as everything else had always been. But then the stranger was off again, something to do with phoning his office, and she realized that the visit was nearly over.

He left shortly afterwards, collecting his sodden coat from the clothes-horse and bidding her a weary goodnight. Watching him disappear down the street, she fingered the card he'd left for her, the two telephone numbers, the address in Sidmouth Place. Any contact at all, he'd said. Any hint. Any clue. Night or day. Closing the door, she turned back into the hall, aware at once of the figure at the bottom of the stairs, one hand on the banister.

'Billy,' she said. 'You're supposed to be asleep.'

The boy nodded, staring at her, huge brown eyes.

'Who was that?'

'Friend of your father's.'

'What did he want?'

Sarah paused, fingering the card again, trying to keep the anxiety out of her voice. Billy was his father's son, the same tight frown of concentration, the same gruff directness.

'I don't know,' she said at last.

* * *

Stepping back into the office on 'F' Street, Emery knew at once that Sullivan was waiting for him. His coat was folded on top of one of Juanita's filing cabinets. The scent of the small black cheroots he sometimes smoked still lingered in the air. Emery glanced at Juanita, raising an eyebrow, and she nodded.

'He's been here half an hour,' she said. 'He's phoned the airport twice to check your flight.'

Emery nodded, closing his eyes for a moment, running a tired hand over his face. Part of him had anticipated the next half-hour, but that didn't make it any easier. He went into the office. Sullivan was sitting at his desk his shirt-sleeves rolled up, his head buried in a thick sheaf of NSA intercepts. Emery closed the door.

Sullivan didn't look up. 'You make sense of any of this stuff?' he said.

Emergy glanced over his shoulder. Sullivan was halfway through a series of decrypts from Damascus.

'Yeah,' Emery said. 'But none of it's relevant.'

Sullivan grunted, looking up at last. His eyes were red with exhaustion. 'That a judgement or a guess?' he said.

Emery shrugged, ignoring the provocation. 'Neither. It's simple logic. One thing after another. Brick on brick . . .' He paused. 'You give me the bricks, I build the wall.'

'Yeah?'

'Yeah.'

'Then what about London? What about all that stuff I sent over? The gas the Brits have lost? Al Zahra? All that?'

Emery looked at him for a moment, then sank into the chair behind the opposite desk. 'I told you about Al Zahra,' he said. 'We discussed it already.'

'Sure. You told me the guy's a schmuck. You told me he's playing at it.'

'I said he's only interested in influence. Collateral. An hour or two at the top table. That's what I said. Guy wants a few names to drop. That's why he's always on the phone. Offering his services.'

'Is that a crime?'

'Depends.'

'On what?'

'On whether you're buying or selling. Problem with Zahra is he never had anything to sell. I'm telling you, sir, the guy's a waste of time. He never gave us a cent's worth of real Intelligence. Not one red cent.'

'And now?' Sullivan leaned forward, one thick finger stabbing at the air. 'All this stuff about missing nerve gas? The Israeli guy? Shot dead in the street? You're telling me that's not relevant?'

Emery shook his head, weary now, anxious for the conversation to end. 'No, sir. I'm not saying that. I'm saying it's interesting. I'm saying we'll check it out. But we need confirmation. Other sources . . .' He shrugged.

Sullivan was quiet for a moment. 'What if there was confirmation?' he said at last. 'Another source?'

'Then we'd check it out.' Emery paused. 'You've got a name?'

Sullivan looked at him, speculative. Then he shook his head. 'No,' he said, 'I haven't.'

Abruptly, he stood up, crushing his cheroot in the remains of his coffee. At the door, he paused, half-turning. 'You gonna do anything at all about Zahra?'

'Sure . . .' Emery shrugged again, gesturing at the pile of paperwork on the desk. 'It's a question of time, that's all. Just now, we have other priorities.'

'Better than Zahra?'

'Yes.'

Sullivan nodded, reaching for the door-handle. Then he hesitated for a moment, looking back at Emery. 'I'm no expert,' he said softly. 'But you'd better be fucking right.'

*

Late evening, McVeigh went back to the kibbutz school.

It was a low, whitewashed building, flat-roofed with metal-framed windows. He'd found it during the day, following a

218

couple of kids as they wandered back from lunch. They'd taken the path that snaked down through a stand of eucalyptus trees, past the fenced enclosure that contained the swimming-pool, down to the furthest corner of the kibbutz where the hillside dropped abruptly away, offering a fine view of the valley floor and the mountains of Lebanon beyond. The lawn around the front of the school had recently been mowed, and there were kids everywhere chasing each other with handfuls of grass. McVeigh had watched them for a minute or two, wondering whether Cela was inside, knowing it was pointless finding out. The first contact would be all-important. The last thing he wanted was an audience.

Now, though, the school was empty, a single light in the room at the front, a woman sitting at a desk, bent over a pile of paperwork. McVeigh left the shadow of the trees and crossed the grass towards the double front doors. The nights were cool, up from the valley, and he could smell the newly mown grass beneath his feet.

At the door he hesitated, knocking lightly. One of the doors was half-open, and he could see the woman at the desk. She was still looking down, the pencil in her hand moving briskly across a sheet of paper, pausing occasionally, making a note, but he knew at once that it was Cela.

He knocked again, and the woman looked up, the face from the photograph in the Jaffa flat, the high, slightly Slavic cheekbones, the wide-set eyes, the single crooked tooth in the beginnings of an enquiring smile.

'Yes?'

'My name's McVeigh. I knew your husband.'

'You're from London?'

'Yes.'

Cela looked at him for a moment longer, then got up, putting the pencil carefully to one side. She stepped out from behind the desk, her hand outstretched. It was a city gesture, the first time anyone had bothered with a formal greeting on the kibbutz, and McVeigh realized how much he'd missed it.

'*Erev tov*,' she said. 'Welcome to Shamir.'

'Thank you.'

She smiled at him for a moment, then nodded at the row of desks. Her English was fluent but heavily accented. 'You can sit down if you want to,' she said. 'The desks are quite strong.'

McVeigh sat down. Cela was smaller than he'd expected, five two, five three. She was neat, compact, with sturdy outdoor legs and the beginnings of a good tan. She wore an old pair of khaki shorts, buttoned at the front, and the check-patterned shirt was several sizes too large. She saw him looking at it and she smiled again, amused. 'My father's,' she said simply.

McVeigh grinned, caught out, and mumbled an apology. Cela waved it away. She was very direct, no evasions, no games, and McVeigh understood at once why Yakov had talked the way he did about her. 'The best person I ever met,' he'd once told McVeigh. 'Not a lie in her body.'

Now she sat down on the big table opposite McVeigh, her knees drawn up to her chin, her hands round her ankles. She wore a single ring, gold, on the third finger of her right hand.

'You've come about Yakov,' she said.

'Yes.'

'What do you want to tell me?'

McVeigh blinked. Cela had taken command of the situation immediately, without hesitation, the teacher in the classroom.

'I didn't know him that well,' he said at once. 'We used to meet at the weekends. The kids used to play football. He was very keen on football.'

'Yes,' said Cela, 'he was.'

McVeigh hesitated, not knowing quite which way to play it. 'I'm sorry about what happened,' he said finally. 'I read about it in the newspaper.'

'So did I.'

'Here? In Israel?'

'Yes.'

'That's the way you found out?'

'Yes.'

'Must have been a terrible shock.'

'Yes.'

'Terrible surprise.'

Cela said nothing, looking at McVeigh. Her eyes were a deep, flawless green. McVeigh shifted his weight on the desk, wondering about the years with Mossad, what she did for them, how much she knew.

'You worked with Yakov?' he suggested. 'Same firm? Same organization?'

'I worked in Tel Aviv.'

'For the same people?'

'For the Government.' She shrugged. 'Of course.'

McVeigh nodded, aware of how guarded she'd become, a confirmation that she indeed worked for Mossad. 'So why didn't they tell you?' he said. 'About his death? About what happened?'

Cela looked at him, saying nothing.

McVeigh frowned. 'Were you at work? When it happened?'

Cela shook her head slowly. 'No.'

'Were you on leave?'

'On what?'

'Holiday?'

'No.'

'You'd left them?'

For the first time, Cela looked down. There was a long silence. Outside, the night was busy with cicadas and far away, on the other side of the valley, McVeigh could hear the distant rumble of a heavy truck. Cela looked up again. Her face was clouded and McVeigh knew that the easy part was over.

'Who are you?' she said. 'Who do you work for?'

'I'm freelance. I work for myself.'

'No one works for themselves.' She paused. 'Who pays your bills? Who bought your ticket? Who sent you here?'

It was McVeigh's turn to refuse an answer. He shook his head. 'I've come to say I'm sorry,' he said quietly. 'I knew him well enough to miss him. He was a good bloke. In this business, that's not as common as you might think. It was a funny relationship. All we ever talked about was football, but I felt I knew him just the same.'

Cela smiled, nodding. 'He said you knew nothing about football. But he said that didn't matter.' She paused. 'He liked you too.'

McVeigh gazed at her. 'He told you that?'

'Yes. You think I'd be talking to you now if he hadn't? You think I'd be saying these things? Letting you ask these questions?' She shook her head. 'He wrote a lot towards the end. He was very open. And very lonely.'

'He missed you.'

'I know.'

'He wanted to get out. To get back. He never said it but that's the feeling I got. I think he'd have been happier back here. With you.' McVeigh hesitated. 'Was he from this kibbutz too? Yakov?'

Cela pursed her lips for a moment and frowned, feigning an effort of memory, then swung her legs off the desk and stood up, suddenly brisk again, the overworked teacher with an evening's marking to complete. McVeigh glanced down at the desk. It was littered with kids' paintings. Upside down, it wasn't easy to make sense of them. The colours were strong, slashes of blue sky, white bubbles of cloud, heavy browns and greens. McVeigh reached across and pulled one of the paintings towards him, recognizing a child's version of the kibbutz, the hillside blobbed with toffee-apple trees, and cartoon houses, and fat-wheeled tractors with smoke pluming from their exhaust-pipes. Overhead there were aeroplanes, drawn in heavy black. Dart-shaped objects, not small, were dropping from the aeroplanes, and there were stick figures all over the kibbutz. They had guns, pointing at the aeroplanes, and something had gone wrong with some of their heads. Their eyes were too big. Their mouths were too round. They had trunks, like elephants. They looked like visitors from Mars.

McVeigh peered at the painting, at the men with the strange heads, aware of Cela watching him. Finally, he passed it across to her.

Cela didn't even look at it. 'You know what these are?' she said.

'No.'

'Gas masks. The kids here listen to the news. Everyone listens to the news. Some of the kids think it's funny.' She nodded at the painting. 'Some don't.'

'You're expecting gas attacks?'

'No one knows. Saddam could do anything. Not here, maybe. But Tel Aviv . . .' She shrugged. 'Haifa. They want us in the war. They want us to move against them. They want us to break the coalition. That way, the Americans will go home.'

'The kids understand that?'

'Of course not.' She paused, her eyes returning to the painting. 'Why should they?'

McVeigh said nothing. Cela glanced up. 'You're here on the kibbutz for a long time?'

'I don't know. It depends.'

'Depends on what?' She looked at him. 'Me?'

McVeigh nodded. 'Yes,' he said. 'It's your decision, not mine.'

A smile ghosted across Cela's face. Then she began to gather up the paintings, a single pile, quick deft movements of her hands. Watching her, McVeigh thought suddenly of the flat back in Jaffa, the wreckage of the bedroom, the piles of underwear slashed and scissored on the floor, the statement the place made, the photo he'd found in the bathroom. He still had the photo. It was back in the hut where he slept, hidden in his bag. Once or twice he'd thought of transcribing the single line of Hebrew, showing it to someone, getting a translation, but finally he'd decided against it. The thing was too intimate, too personal, someone else's emotional property.

The desk tidied, Cela reached for a sweater, draping it around her shoulders and knotting the sleeves loosely across her chest. McVeigh was still sitting on the desk, still waiting for an answer.

'Well?' he said at last.

She hesitated. Then her hand reached down for the pile of paintings, one final adjustment. 'You know what Yakov said he'd miss most about London?'

McVeigh shook his head. 'No,' he said.

'Your son. Billy.' She paused. 'I think you should stay.'

9

Ross sat at Friedland's desk, quarter to nine on a wet London morning, waiting.

One of the secretaries had let him in, a sodden figure, sleepless, bad-tempered, pushing into the hall and up the stairs without a backward glance. Finding the office empty, he'd hung his raincoat on the back of one of Friedland's antique chairs, watching the drips pooling on the pale grey Wilton carpet. It was a small gesture, but when Friedland finally arrived, it would serve to make the point. Our chair, it said. Our carpet. Our money. Our rules.

A phone began to ring, one of two on the desk. Ross looked at it for a moment, wondering whether the line was routed through the switchboard in the office downstairs. Deciding that it wasn't, he picked it up. A woman's voice came on at the other end. She sounded anxious. She wanted to talk to Mr Friedland. Ross explained that he'd yet to arrive. She could leave a message. All would be well. The woman hesitated, then talked for perhaps a minute. Ross nodded, saying nothing, permitting himself a brief smile. At the end of the conversation he thanked the woman, putting the phone down and checking his watch. Past nine o'clock, there was still no sign of Friedland.

Picking up the other phone, Ross asked for a cup of coffee. Then he opened the brief-case he'd carried up and pulled out a large manila file. Spreading it on the desk, he reached for one of Friedland's sharpened pencils and began to check the draft memorandum he'd drawn up some seven hours before. The memo, intended for circulation to a tiny group of Cabinet ministers, detailed the political fall-out should the press get wind of the scale of recent arms sales to Iraq. He'd drafted it as a contingency, an exercise in damage-limitation, and he'd persuaded himself that sending it was a simple act of political prudence. The arms trade was a mine-field for any government, and this single sheet of paper – three brief paragraphs – was nothing more than a map. Follow this path, and we might avoid injury. Ignore it, and we're probably dead.

Ross read the memo a second time and then leaned back in the chair, revolving it slightly, the pencil still in his hand. Scandals in the arms business were, alas, nothing new. A huge slice of the country's manufacturing industry was defence-related, and exports were its life-blood. Back in April, Customs and Excise investigators had seized a number of steel pipes en route to Iraq. The pipes, allegedly for use in the petro-chemical industry, had in fact been designed as part of an Iraqi supergun. The supergun, potentially, had the range to bombard Tel Aviv. Customs and Excise had been obliged to act after pressure from Mossad, and the resulting scandal had reached higher and higher. Indeed, Downing Street itself was now coming danger-ously close to complicity.

After six months of press speculation, the political lessons of this episode were crystal-clear, and expressed at the top level with characteristic vehemence. There were to be no more surprises, no more invitations for the media to run riot. The country, after all, was preparing for a major war, and war imposed its own brutal logic. A government that went soft would lose. To win, therefore, you had to be firm and coura-geous, and willing to take the odd risk. That was the lesson of history. That was how sovereignty had been restored to the Falkland Islands. Government, real government, brought responsibility, and now was no time to shirk it. It was as simple, and glorious, as that.

Standing in the small, sunlit sitting-room on the top floor, listening to the tirade, Ross had no doubts about the real agenda. The real agenda had to do with keeping the genie in the bottle. Whatever we'd been selling, however lethal, the country at large was best left in ignorance. That was Ross's job. That was what he couldn't afford to get wrong. Unless, that is, he wanted to end up like Friedland, marginalized, pensioned-off, the wet-eyed old retriever brought out for special occasions.

Ross got up and went to the window. Already, he knew, circumstances were working to his advantage. Yesterday's speech by George Habash, leader of the Popular Front for the Liberation of Palestine, had directly threatened Western targets in the event of American action in the Gulf. The threat had galvanized the security services. There was talk of another Lockerbie, or an outrage at some big city railway terminus. Contingency plans had been activated, key points isolated for special attention. There was a rumour that non-travellers were to be banned from all major airports, that armed troops were to be posted to oil installations, that nuclear power plants were to be similarly protected. He'd even seen a memo, yesterday evening, that speculated about the possibility of chemical weapons in terrorist hands.

Ross pondered the thought, wondering what the security chiefs would make of five missing gallons of Tabun GA, watching Friedland in the street below, hurrying in from the rain. Politically, Ross was convinced that the Newbury incident was best kept under the tightest of wraps. Whether that would be possible, whether a deal could be struck with the mysterious authors of the note he'd received, he still didn't know. But any cover-up must start at source, and for that role, at least, Friedland would be perfect.

He heard footsteps downstairs in the hall and a brief, muttered conversation. Then Friedland was at the door, a cup of coffee balanced in each hand. Back in the chair behind the desk, Ross watched him crossing the room, thinking how old the man had become and how tired he looked.

Friedland paused at the desk, giving Ross one of the coffees and putting the other on the blotter. Then he retrieved Ross's coat from the chair and hung it carefully on the hook on the back of the door, and sat down. To Ross's disappointment, he didn't appear to notice the sodden patch of carpet at his feet.

Ross glanced at his watch. 'I've got five minutes,' he said briefly. 'You'll need this.' He pushed a notepad towards Friedland. Friedland made no attempt to pick it up but stirred his coffee instead, inviting Ross to carry on with a polite smile of enquiry. Ross looked at him for a moment, then opened the file. The rapport they'd begun to establish en route to the City Airport had quite gone. Of that one brief moment of weakness there was no trace. Ross was back where he'd always been, standing over Friedland, one foot on his throat.

'Newbury,' he said briskly, 'is where the drum of chemical went missing. Group headquarters is at Basingstoke. The man I want you to see is a Mr Lovell. He's managing director.'

Friedland nodded, sipping the coffee, watching Ross over the rim of the cup. Ross hesitated, one finger still in the file, expecting a reaction of some kind, irritated by its absence.

'Lovell,' he repeated, 'is the boss. He's made the running. He's the one who decided not to go the police.' He paused. 'A week is a long time to have kept a secret like that. I can't imagine he'll take much convincing.'

'Of what?'

'Of this.'

Ross extracted a sheet of paper from the file and slid it across the desk. Friedland reached forward and picked it up. It was a standard form, issued by the Department of the Environment. Across the top, in heavy black letters, it read: 'Notification of Toxic Substances'. Two lines down, beside 'Name of Company', the word 'Dispozall' had been pencilled in, together with a postal address and a phone number. Further down, in the half-page allotted for a detailed description of specific substances, there was a pencilled cross. Only at the foot of the page, beside the word 'Date', did another pencilled entry appear: '26 August 1990' it read.

Friedland glanced up. 'That's last month,' he said mildly. 'It's dated last month.'

'Correct.'

'So what do you want me to do with it?'

'I want you to give it to Mr Lovell. And then I want Mr Lovell to do his test all over again.'

'He can't. The chemical's gone.' Friedland paused, deliberately obtuse. 'It's been stolen. It's disappeared.'

Ross smiled, reaching for his coffee. 'Wrong,' he said. 'The stuff's been destroyed.' He nodded at the form. 'In compliance with the regulations.'

Friedland frowned, his eye returning to the form. 'And the cross? The pencil mark? What does that mean?'

Ross shrugged. 'That's for Lovell to fill in. He's the expert. Not me.' He paused. 'I imagine there are thousands of chemicals that would do the trick. All of them lethal. None of them nerve gases.' He paused again. 'Are you with me?'

Friedland said nothing for a moment. Then he sat back in the chair, crossing his legs, taking his time, making himself comfortable. Through his jacket, he could feel the dampness where Ross had left the wet coat. 'You want me to cover the man's tracks,' he said carefully.

Ross shook his head. 'I want *him* to cover his tracks,' he said. 'You suggest it. He does it.'

'You know nothing.'

'I know nothing.'

'But he falsifies the records.'

'Yes. By redoing the test. On something less ... ah ... newsworthy.'

'Like what?'

Ross looked at him for a moment across the desk. Then he stood up, reaching for the file, snapping open his briefcase. 'The man has a choice,' he said. 'He can either do as you'll suggest, sanitize the record, pretend it was a perfectly straightforward industrial accident, employee negligence. Or—' he shrugged '—we issue a press release, put him in the papers, withdraw his licence, and let the market do the rest. I imagine the commercial advantage lies in remaining in business, though of course—' he smiled '—that would be his decision.'

'And me? My decision?'

'You don't have a decision to make. All you do is get in your car and drive to Basingstoke. Mr Lovell will do the rest. I guarantee it.'

Friedland nodded, hearing Ross spell it out, the classic manoeuvre, stage one of the cover-up, totally deniable. 'Five gallons of nerve gas have gone missing,' he said quietly. 'What happens to that?'

'That's no longer Mr Lovell's responsibility.'

'No?'

'No.'

'And is it yours?'

'No.'

'Then what happens if it turns up somewhere else? Where has it come from?'

Ross looked at Friedland for a moment, not answering. Then he shrugged, nodding at his brief-case, the manila file, the cuttings from yesterday's papers. 'The Palestinians are threatening a second front,' he said. 'Naturally they'll need weapons, ammunition, Semtex—' he shrugged again '—nerve gas.'

'Nothing to do with Dispozall?'

'No.'

'Different source?'

'Yes.'

Friedland nodded, following the logic upstream, the usual rationale, political expediency. Dispozall was a flagship company, a striking example of the new Tory ethic. It was profitable. It was efficient. It was beating the competition worldwide, the hardest commercial evidence that free markets and free enterprise worked. The company had won ringing prime ministerial endorsements, and now was no time to toss it to the wolves. Not, at least, if it could be avoided.

Friedland looked up. 'Do you want it in writing?' he said quietly. 'Or can I just say no?'

Ross paused, halfway across the room, his briefcase in his hand. He looked round. Friedland was still sitting in his chair, facing the window, perfectly still. Ross stepped back towards him, bending down, his mouth to his ear. He spoke very slowly, his voice low, masking the irritation he still felt. 'I took the trouble of answering your phone,' he said. 'Before you arrived. A Mrs Bellingham.' Friedland looked round, a little too quickly, a new expression on his face. Ross smiled at him, back in charge. 'Matron,' he confirmed softly.

'What did she say?'

'She said that Stephanie's gone missing. Evidently she left a note.'

'And?'

Ross straightened, the brief-case still in his hand. 'The note says she's had enough of good intentions. She says she thinks heroin's had a bad press.' He paused. 'We can pick her up. We can put her away. Nice little cell. No drugs. No medication. Would she like that? Would she survive it?' He paused a second time, his hand on Friedland's shoulder. 'Would you?'

*

Telemann awoke at dawn, haunted by images of Laura.

He'd watched her all night in the big cool bed under the eaves on Dixie Street, himself in the shadows, a spectral presence. She'd been with Emery. Emery had made love to her, with limitless stamina and limitless skill. He'd played her like a keyboard, her favourite chords, taking his time, coaxing new tunes, new rhythms, her body arching beneath his, riding the crest of yet another orgasm, the low moan he knew so well, the one that started way down, the tiny gasps of surprise as it built and built, her hands reaching down, pulling him inwards, her breasts flattened against her chest, her eyes huge and wild, her chin back, the veins big in her neck.

Afterwards, saving himself, Emery had folded his long body around hers, and she'd ducked towards his belly, her hair everywhere, her fingertips dancing across the soft triangles of flesh in his crotch, stroking him, nibbling him, making him bigger and bigger, her tongue working up and down, her fingers cupping his balls, her eyes half-closed, catlike, watching him. Soon, when he was ready, he'd begun to withdraw, and she'd shaken her head and taken him way down, her lips around him, up and down, sucking and sucking, that same low rumble in her throat. The rhythm had quickened, and finally he'd pulled out, all of it, and she'd folded her breasts around him, still moving, up and down, still watching his face, the way it crumpled, like a paper bag, when the stuff came pumping out. Afterwards, like babies, like dolls in Bree's cot, they'd lain enfolded, her head on his chest, her hand on his belly, asleep.

Telemann turned over, feeling warm flesh next to his, grief-stricken. It was daylight. He could hear traffic. He opened one eye. Inge lay beside him, her shoulders bare above the sheet, her long body pressed to his. Telemann frowned, confused. He'd gone to bed alone. Of that he was sure. She'd said he could have the flat. She'd be staying elsewhere. He'd watched her leave, walking away down the hall. She'd called goodnight from the elevator, then she'd gone.

Closing the door behind her, falling into her bed, he'd been glad to be out of the hotel. The hotel was no longer secure. Emery had the telephone number, and with the number he'd find the address. With that, he'd send them round, the boys from the Consulate, or one of the special teams from Frankfurt, riding shotgun on his precious operation. He'd feed them some line or other, some pretext to justify the action he'd instruct them to take. Telemann had done it himself, a number of times, other field trips, corralling some luckless maverick, reining him in, returning him to the stockade. The usual excuse was pressure. The guys succumbed to pressure. It was never a question of blame, more a consequence of the job, a risk you took, another sacrifice for Uncle Sam. He never enquired what happened to the guys when they got shipped home, whether they were pensioned off, or quietly institutionalized, or whether – like some of their Soviet counterparts – they simply disappeared. Whatever happened, wherever they ended their days, it had always been strictly academic, someone else's problem. Until now.

Telemann rolled over, grunting, closing his eyes, thinking of Laura again.

'We wanted babies,' he whispered numbly. 'Kids.'

'Ja?'

'Yeah. We tried and tried.' He looked up, aware of Inge behind him, propped up on one elbow, listening. 'What do you think? You think it's me?'

'What do you mean?'

'You think there's something wrong with me? Stuff doesn't work properly? You know? Bad fucking?'

He rolled over and looked at her, curious at how large her breasts were, larger than he'd imagined, big brown nipples, beautiful skin.

'You want to do it?' she said. 'With me?'

Telemann shook his head, saying nothing, and Inge dipped her head, kissing him lightly on the shoulder. Then she drew the sheet back, almost a medical gesture, quite clinical, and knelt before him, her hands running the length of her body, down over her belly to the tight blond curls beneath. She splayed her thighs a little, watching herself in the mirror on the wardrobe door, her fingers curling inward, glimpses of nail varnish, her pelvis beginning to move, backwards and forwards. After a while, not smiling, she splayed her thighs wider still, and Telemann saw her lips, swollen and moist.

Inge's eyes closed. 'You like watching me?'

'Yes.'

'Does it make you think of your wife?'

'Yes.'

'She does this?'

'No. Never. Not with me.'

'With someone else maybe?' Inge opened her eyes again, looking down at him. Her hands were still now. Telemann shrugged, hopeless, saying nothing, and Inge looked at him for a moment longer before bending to him quickly, kissing him, stirring the merest flicker of movement, trying again, her tongue busier, getting nowhere. Finally, she straddled him. He could feel the warm moistness on his chest, caught her eyes for a moment, and she smiled at him, and fitted herself to his mouth, straddling his face, working herself against his upper lip, coming within seconds with a deep groan.

'I'm sorry,' she said, touching his face.

'That's OK.'

She smiled at him, looking down. 'That's not what I meant,' she said.

Ten minutes later, newly showered, Inge was back in the bedroom, sitting on a stool beside the dressing-table, one leg propped on her thigh, painting her toe-nails. Telemann watched her from the bed. He could still taste her.

'You share this place with the other guy?'

'Yes.'

'You sleep with him, too?'

'Yes.'

'He mind me being here?'

'No. Why should he?'

Telemann shrugged. 'Just a question,' he said.

Blum, the *katsa*, arrived for a late breakfast. He looked exhausted and he hadn't shaved for at least a day. Another bedroom, thought Telemann glumly. More mirrors.

They sat round a small table. Inge brought fresh coffee and an assortment of ready-baked pastries. Telemann, his back to the window, ignored them. 'When do I make the call?' he said for the second time.

Blum glanced up. 'Ten o'clock,' he said through a mouthful of Danish. 'He's always there at ten o'clock.'

'You've got the number?'

'Of course.'

'He never changes it?'

'All the time.'

Telemann nodded. They'd agreed the details the previous evening, the three of them sitting at a corner table in a restaurant in Pinneberg. Assali lived behind high walls and a dense picket of electronic devices in a quiet suburban street in Bad Godesberg. He employed at least four bodyguards, working twelve-hour shifts around the clock. To the best of Blum's knowledge, he lived on a diet of videos and take-away meals delivered from a local Korean restaurant. Attempts to get to him through either had so far failed. His one flirtation with real life was an occasional dinner at the Hotel Dreisen, a large establishment on the banks of the Rhine, five blocks from his own street. Evidently he trusted the management there. They reserved a table for him in the main dining-room, and as long as the bodyguards wore jackets and ties, they raised no objections. The clientele, in any case, posed no threat to Assali. Middle-aged, prosperous, overwhelmingly German, they had no quarrel with the Palestinian cause. On the contrary, a number of them appeared to harbour a quiet sympathy with anyone brave or foolish enough to take on the Israelis.

Telemann sipped his coffee. The plan, in essence, was simple. He would phone Assali and offer his credentials. He would then supply a number in Washington the man could contact for the necessary cross-checks. The number was Sullivan's, his desk down the corridor from the Oval Office. Telemann had been in touch with him already, calling him at home, asking for nothing more than support. If a guy called Assali phones, he'd said, just vouch for me. Tell him I'm on the team. Tell him I mean what I say. Tell him I have the authority to deliver. Listening, Sullivan had made no comment, but simply grunted his assent, asking Telemann to repeat the name, getting him to spell it. Telemann had done so, knowing that an extension on the White House switchboard was the best possible collateral, the juiciest of lures to coax the Palestinian out of his bunker.

With Sullivan's endorsement, Assali was sure to meet him. For eighteen months, according to Nathan Blum, the man had been looking for ways of acquiring US citizenship. Every approach, direct or brokered through a third party, had been turned down. Now, for whatever reason, he'd think the tide was at last running in his favour. Telemann, on the phone, would hint as much. But there had to be a meet, face to face, neutral territory. Somewhere local would be ideal. That was where the conversation, this first phone call, would lead. No firm suggestions, nothing specific, just the promise to phone again once the Arab had taken a little time to think about it.

Telemann looked across the table at Blum. Last night, the Israeli had described the hotel in detail: approach roads, escape roads, surrounding houses, the layout of the lobby area, the way the doors worked, the awkward left-hand turn that would take them out of the forecourt and back on to the quiet leafy suburban avenues that led up the hill towards the main north–south autobahn. Listening, Telemann had been impressed. Mossad surveillance, as ever, had been impeccable. Ditto, their operational plan. They'd arrange a modest diversion outside the hotel, enough to detach one or two of the body-guards. Inside, they'd have four agents in the lobby, both men and women. A couple would be guests. All would be armed. All would speak fluent Arabic. Individually, they'd take care of the bodyguards, discreet use of the automatics, whispered advice to stand absolutely still, do nothing, while Assali was escorted quietly out of the hotel and away.

Telemann, a veteran of half a dozen similar snatches, knew all too well that the operation was more fragile than it looked, that few plans survived contact with the enemy. But the Israelis were the acknowledged masters in the field, and if Blum was as good as Telemann suspected he might be, then he had every reason to anticipate a quiet day or two with the Arab, enough time – certainly – to test the Wulf story. What remained unresolved, though, was the whereabouts of the safe house, the location they'd use to quarantine Assali before crating him up and flying him back to Tel Aviv. The latter, for Mossad, was the real prize: the chance to interrogate him in depth, to charge him with the bomb attacks on the Israeli buses, and finally to parade him in a public court of law, living proof that the world was too small a place to hide from the long arm of Israeli justice. They'd done it with Eichmann and countless other Nazi war criminals. They were doing it now with their Arab enemies, an older strain of anti-Semitism, no less dangerous, no less virulent.

Telemann stirred another spoonful of sugar into his coffee. He had cards to play, and Blum knew it. Without him, without the phone call, Assali wouldn't cooperate. Unless it was an American invitation, bona fide, thoroughly checked out, the man would never appear. Not on cue. Not when they were ready and waiting to take him. Likewise, without Blum, Telemann lacked the leverage he needed on Assali. It was a strange collision of interests, a brief marriage of convenience that would serve to answer the needs of both parties.

'Afterwards,' Telemann mused. 'What about afterwards?'

Blum shrugged, a gesture of dismissal, the reaction of a man unused to having his professionalism questioned. 'We switch cars,' he said. 'Twice within a kilometre. The third car takes him to the safe house. He stays there—' he shrugged again '—two days? Three days? How much time do you want?'

Telemann hesitated for a moment. Prominent figures like Assali were never easy to assess. Some broke at once. Others were surprisingly awkward. Either way, sleep was the key. Deprive a man of sleep, keep him awake day and night, disorientate him completely with noise and bright light and random spasms of violence, and sooner or later he'd be yours.

Sleep was the glue that kept most people together. Remove it, and most people fell apart. Telemann looked up. 'Five days,' he said. 'Absolute maximum.'

'OK.' Blum nodded. 'Five days.'

He grinned suddenly and reached for the last of the Danish, a visiting businessman happy with the deal he'd made, and Telemann found himself looking at the girl again, wondering what kind of relationship she'd had with Wulf, and now with Blum, and how she could make any kind of peace with herself afterwards. Aware of Telemann watching her, Inge smiled and then nodded at the telephone. 'It's ten o'clock,' she said quietly. 'In case you'd forgotten.'

*

Emery sat at the wheel of the hired Ford, inching through the Callahan Tunnel. It was rush-hour at Boston's Logan Airport, the exit roads jammed solid, both lanes in the tunnel nose-to-tail, the temperature already in the mid-seventies.

He reached for the radio again, punching his way through the local channels. He'd flown up to Massachusetts at dawn, Weill's parting words still on his mind. 'Face to face, maybe,' he'd said. 'On the phone, no way.' Emery sat back in the big car and scowled at the memory of the conversation, wondering again whether his journey would be worth it, whether he could afford yet another twenty-four hours out of the office. He'd been back from the West Coast for nearly two days now, yet his desk was still invisible beneath the latest carefully sorted piles of data. Juanita, whose appetite for work he'd thought limitless, was visibly wilting from the strain, and she'd stopped even attempting small-talk. Buttressing calls from Sullivan had exhausted her, and she'd warned Emery that after the quarrel about Zahra, the man's patience was definitely running out. He'd been on again the previous evening, demanding an update on the statement from the PFLP. George Habash was threatening to carry Saddam's war to the West. The threat, as Sullivan read it, was quite explicit. The man was promising à la carte terrorism against the coalition partners if they set one foot in Iraq. Nerve gas would doubtless be way up the menu. Didn't this fit the picture? Shouldn't the smart money be on the PFLP? Wasn't Habash the guy to go for?

Emery, eternally sceptical, hadn't answered any of Sullivan's questions, and now he shrugged again, emerging at last from the tunnel, easing the big Ford into the queue for the freeway ramp. Interstate 95 would take him south, beneath the towering cliffs of the downtown area, around the long curve of Boston Harbor, out towards Cape Cod. He'd agreed to meet Weill at a rest area near Plymouth. Weill lived on the Cape. Plymouth was halfway there.

An hour later, Emery found the rest area, an acre or two of cropped grass and wooden picnic tables beside the highway. Of Weill, and the '86 Corvette he'd described on the phone, there was no sign. Emery parked and got out. The sun was hot in a near cloudless sky, but already, mid-September, there was an edge to the wind blowing in from the north. He could smell the ocean in the wind, cool and salt, and soon, he knew, the summer would be gone. Back home, the marina laying-up berths were already filling up with weekend yachts, an early hibernation, and in a month or two he'd have the vast, empty reaches of Chesapeake Bay to himself. That was the kind of sailing he loved best, solitary, physically testing, the short days blessed by silence, and a cold, hard sunshine, and the ceaseless tug of the open sea.

Emery turned on his heel, hands thrust deep in his pockets, walking back towards the car. Lately, the investigation apart, he knew he'd found a kind of peace. Maybe it had to do with Laura, maybe the relief of telling her, of getting it all out in one rich piece and waking up next day to find the relationship still intact. In retrospect, thinking about it, she'd responded the way he knew she always would. With good humour, and tact, and a sense of quiet amusement. She hadn't belittled him by making light of it. She hadn't turned her back on him. She'd simply said she understood. He smiled, remembering the touch of her hand on his arm, anticipating the Bay again, and the huge cloudscapes that curtained the path to winter.

He looked up, hearing the sigh of wheels on the warm

tarmac. A red Corvette stopped beside his own car. He raised a hand, knowing it could only be Weill, seeing the man back-view, thick-set, a heavy square head. The man got out and walked towards him, jeans, T-shirt, sneakers. He looked mid-thirties, a stone or two overweight. He had a full black beard and a pair of rimless glasses. He looked slightly harassed, a man whose schedule refuses to run to time. 'Hi,' he said, not bothering with a handshake. 'I'm Dave Weill.'

They sat at one of the picnic tables. Weill had brought sandwiches, home-made foil-wrapped. Inside thin slices of pumpernickel there was processed cheese and rings of raw onion. He laid the sandwiches carefully on the table between them, indoor hands, telling Emery to help himself. He spoke like a native American, East Coast, the tight nasal Massachusetts vowels. Emery, listening, found it hard to believe he was Israeli.

'I'm not,' Weill said, when Emery asked the question, 'I'm US born and bred. Providence, Rhode Island. I've lived here most of my life. Israel's a recent thing.'

'How come?'

Weill shrugged, demolishing the first of the sandwiches. 'You get to do these things. We have a word for it. It's called *aliyah*. It means homecoming. You make *aliyah*. You go home.'

'And you did? You've done it?'

'Sure. I'm Jewish. My father's Jewish. German Jewish. My whole goddamn family's Jewish. Five, six years back I went to Israel, a tourist for Chrissakes, a face on the bus. But . . . I don't know—' he shrugged again, attacking another sandwich '—when it happens, the trick is to recognize it. Most people don't. The moment comes, you think it's indigestion. It's not indigestion. It's your life changing.' He beamed at Emery. 'My life changed. I made *aliyah*. I went home.'

'But you're still here.'

'Sure. This month. Last month. Most of the summer.' He reached for the rest of the sandwich, his mouth still full. 'I teach. I'm an academic. I go where the work is, where the money is. Also, I'm still studying. People like me don't do degrees, we collect them. Just now, I'm doing the last one, positively the last one.' He grinned. 'You believe that?'

Emery smiled, not answering for a moment. Then he leaned forward, ignoring the proffered sandwich. 'But Israel?' he said. 'You live in Israel? You have citizenship?'

Weill nodded. 'Sure,' he said. 'Plus I have a two-roomed apartment in Haifa. You know about prices in Israel? Real estate? Food? Automobiles?' He shook his head. 'You wanna beer?'

He got up and walked back to the car without waiting for an answer, returning with four bottles of Rolling Rock. The jeans didn't fit properly, too big, too baggy, and the T-shirt was hanging out at the back. He sat down again. 'What do you want to know?' he said. 'You want to know about Lenny Gold? Why I knew him? How I knew him?'

'Yes.'

'He came and talked on a course I ran. I invited him over.'

'Here? In Israel?'

'MIT.' Weill nodded north, towards Boston. 'The IAF people gave me his name. Israeli Air Force. They said he was truly excellent. They were right.'

'These courses you run, you teach. These degrees.' Emery frowned. 'What field?'

'Avionics. Ballistics. Advanced aircraft design. The whole shoot. Research meets business meets technology.' He paused and licked his fingers. 'Tough stuff.'

'And Gold?'

'The best. The very best.' He paused, abruptly reflective, a bottle of Rolling Rock halfway to his mouth, watching Emery carefully. 'Nice guy, too.'

The beer gone, they walked around the rest area. Weill had come to know Gold well. Academically he was a natural. He was tough-minded, witty, and had a rare gift for translating his own commercial experience into a series of brisk one-hour lectures. Weill's students had rated him highly. They liked his lack of bullshit and his insistence on exploring the bottom line. They admired the licence he'd won for himself, two decades of innovatory avionics designwork, the very best guy in the field. And they liked his irreverence, his joky, bitter-sweet asides about the excesses of the defence industry. Invited back for subsequent appearances, Gold had stayed with Weill, sharing the house he rented out at Falmouth. They'd sat up late, summer nights, six packs of Coors and the stir of the ocean through the open patio doors. Though they came at issues from different angles, they'd had lots in common. They were both sceptical about aspects of the US Defence establishment. They both admired what the Israelis had achieved with a tenth of the money and a hundred times the motivation. And they were both able to gauge that point when you stopped talking business or academia for politics and got on to the things that really mattered.

Strolling slowly back towards the car, Emery paused. 'What about last year?' he said. 'After Lola's accident?'

Weill aimed a half-hearted kick at an empty Coke can. He hadn't mentioned Lola at all. Not once. 'She was a lush,' he said, 'the cross he had to bear.'

'Did he say that?'

'Never. The guy was loyal as hell. But I'd seen it. I'd met her. I knew. She was an accident waiting to happen.' He shook his head. 'And it did.'

'And Gold? What did it do to him?'

'Broke his heart. Truly. That's what I never understood about the man. How he could . . . with that woman . . .' He shook his head again, stopping, looking down. There was a long silence. Then they began to walk again, towards the cars.

'He stopped working for the Israelis . . .' Emery said.

'Yeah.'

'Why?'

'They wouldn't pay him what he wanted.'

'How much did he want?'

'Lots.'

'But the Israelis paid him lots.'

Weill looked at him briefly and shook his head. 'Not enough,' he said.

'So where did he go?'

Weill stopped again and looked hard at Emery, one hand up, shading his eyes against the sun. 'Is that what you've come to ask?'

'Yes.'

'Why?'

Emery didn't answer for a moment. Then he shook his head. 'I can't tell you,' he said, 'except that it's important.'

'Sure.' Weill was still looking at him, his eyes shadowed beneath the raised hand. 'So who do you work for? The Government? Some insurance company?' He paused. 'Tel Aviv?'

Emery smiled. 'The Government,' he said. 'Call it the Government.' He paused. 'You knew the guy. You knew him well. You were buddies. You knew the business, too. You knew the options he had. Where a guy like him might go.' He paused again. 'So tell me. Where *did* he go? What happened?'

Weill looked at Emery for a moment longer. Then the hand came down and he shook his head. 'Guy died. That's what happened. Guy died in a hotel room up in New York City.'

'With a hooker.'

'Sure. With a hooker.'

'That make you angry?'

'Yeah.'

'Guy wasting himself like that?'

'Yeah.'

'You miss him?'

'Yeah.'

Weill started walking again, very slowly, his head down. Emery fell into step beside him, saying nothing. Finally, Weill stopped again. 'You know what it is to be close to someone?' Emery smiled, warmed by the irony. 'Yes,' he said, 'as it happens.'

'*Really* close to them?'

'Yes.'

'Then you'll know how I felt about Lenny. He was wasted on the lush. He was wasted on the hooker. Great guy.' He shook his head. 'Totally fucking wasted.'

Weill stooped to the picnic table, retrieving the empty bottles of Rolling Rock. Emery watched him tossing them into a waste-bin, one after the other, crash, crash. 'That last year . . .' he said again. 'Who did he work for?'

The last bottle hit the bottom of the waste-bin. Weill wiped his hands on the backs of his jeans, still staring at the bin. 'I tell you that . . .' he said slowly, 'and I'm . . .' He shook his head, letting the sentence expire.

'But it wasn't the Israelis?'

There was a long silence. A big truck ground past on the highway, the dust settling slowly behind it. Emery put the question again. Finally, Weill looked up. His eyes were puffy behind the thick pebble-glasses. 'I told you already,' he said. 'The Israelis wouldn't pay what he wanted. They never pay that kind of money. I told you. The country's fucked.'

'So he went somewhere else?'

'Of course. The guy had to. Lola like that.'

'Selling the same deal. Selling what he knew.'

'Sure.' Weill nodded. 'Selling himself. Selling whatever.'

'All the stuff he'd picked up on the West Coast?'

'Yeah.'

'And in Tel Aviv?'

Weill looked at him for a long time, tussling with some private decision. Then, abruptly, he extended a podgy hand, a brief sweaty touch, before turning away and lumbering back towards his car. Getting in, gunning the engine, nosing on to the highway, he didn't once look back. Emery stood by the picnic table, watching the Corvette accelerating away. Minutes later, walking back to his own car, he was still smiling.

*

McVeigh, dreaming of Billy, heard the footsteps outside the hut. He opened one eye. It was still dark. He inched his wrist from beneath the single sheet and checked his watch. Half-past three. The footsteps were louder now, heavy boots on the line of paving-stones that marked the path to his door. The footsteps paused, very close, and McVeigh was barely upright, one foot feeling for the tiled floor, when the door crashed open.

McVeigh, crouching on the edge of the bed, squinted into the beam of a powerful torch. Beyond the torch, invisible in the darkness, he heard a soft laugh, far from pleasant. For a moment nothing happened, then something landed at his feet and the disc of light followed it slowly down the line of McVeigh's naked body to the floor. McVeigh looked down. A pair of old working gloves, the ends of the fingers frayed and open.

The torch snapped off. A voice came out of the darkness, guttural, gruff, male. 'Four o'clock,' it said. '*Hader ochel*. You come.'

The figure turned and pulled the door open, and in the faint spill from the security floodlights McVeigh saw someone tall and broad. The face had a beard, and in his left hand, loosely gripped, was a small sub-machine-gun. The mesh door crashed shut again, and the footsteps receded briefly before pausing at another hut, a knocking this time, a word or two of Hebrew and a sleepy acknowledgement from inside. Work, thought McVeigh, reaching for his jeans, letting the adrenalin settle back into his system, thinking again of the man's laugh, and the slow drift of the torch beam, a message all the plainer for being unvoiced.

Twenty minutes later, McVeigh joined the mêlée of sleepy kibbutzniks at the back of the dining-hall. There were trucks parked in the darkness, their engines already running, their headlights on. Someone shouted a name and there was an answering bark of laughter, then figures began to clamber into the backs of the trucks. The trucks were open at the back, and when they began to move, lurching on to the tarmac road that wound down the hillside to the valley floor, it was suddenly colder.

McVeigh stood near the rear of the lead truck, the gloves tucked into the waistband of his jeans, bracing himself with one hand against the constant lurch and sway as the driver pulled the big vehicle round a succession of hairpin bends. The truck was packed with men and women, all ages, rough working clothes, patterns and colours bleached by the sun. No one said very much, no one smiled, and when McVeigh looked slowly around, curious to see whether he could recognize the face with the beard, no one followed his gaze. Central Line, he thought glumly. Just one more working day.

Minutes later the truck picked up speed, following the road across the valley floor. Left and right there were orchards, thousands of apple trees in orderly rows, and when the trucks stopped and the men and women clambered out, it felt instantly warmer. Behind them in the east, the darkness was beginning to lighten, the mountains skylined against a cold, hard dawn.

The kibbutzniks divided into gangs, trudging off into the trees. McVeigh stayed by the roadside, waiting for instructions, recognizing the odd face here and there, finally attaching himself to an older man with a haversack. Amongst the trees the grass was shin-high and wet with dew.

A half-mile walk took McVeigh deep into the orchards. A dozen people stood round a trailer. A canvas tarpaulin was folded back and inside the trailer was half-full of apples. Beside the trailer, on the ground, was a pile of metal baskets. The old man with the haversack began to distribute them, squatting on the ground beside the pile, tossing them left and right without a word. McVeigh caught the last one, copying everyone else, adjusting the diagonal strap across his chest and shoulders, fitting the basket against his belly. The group disappeared into the trees, every man and woman collecting a light aluminium ladder. McVeigh followed them, finding a ladder for himself, and a line of trees laden with fruit. The gloves, when he put them on, were a perfect fit. His hands were nearly back to normal, the blisters burst, the flesh newly pinked beneath.

The work went on for hours, a steady rhythm, top of the ladder, the basket filled and refilled, each new load of apples carried back through the trees and dumped into the trailer. In a curious way, McVeigh liked the work, the monotony of it, the lack of interference, the way the warmth gradually stole back into the landscape, the valley flooding with light, the sun raising the sweat on his back and shoulders. It was, he knew, the price of staying on the kibbutz. To get to Cela, to work towards the conversation he knew he had to have, he was obliged to pick apples. It was as simple as that.

Last night, walking back from the school, she'd agreed to meet him again. The arrangement was loose, they'd probably run into each other at lunch, once the day's work was over. Afterwards, maybe, there'd be time to talk. Knowing there was no point in hurrying the thing, McVeigh had nodded and accepted her whispered 'Goodnight' with a smile. As she'd stepped into her father's house, pushing open the unlocked door, he'd called after her, remembering about Billy. He wanted to get in touch with the boy, tell him that everything was OK, and she'd hesitated for a moment in the darkness, thinking about it, promising to try and find him a phone. The name Billy, the sound of it, for some reason made her smile. McVeigh had noticed the reaction two or three times already. The smile was utterly spontaneous, a sunny, uncomplicated thing, and McVeigh grinned to himself now, thinking about it.

Below, in the orchard, people were beginning to gather by the trailer. There'd been no signal, nothing formal, but the baskets were coming off, and small glasses were being passed around from the old man's haversack, and a boy had appeared through the trees with a metal urn. He joined the group by the trailer, squatting over the urn, filling the glasses with something thick and black.

Smelling the coffee, McVeigh reached for a final cluster of apples. He was up in the very crown of the tree, his feet wedged in the branches below. He dropped the last apple into the basket and began to ease his body down, his feet feeling instinctively for the top of the ladder. Not finding it, he looked down. A face was gazing up at him. The beard was black and the eyes were steady. There was a basket, half-full, around the man's belly, and his left hand held McVeigh's ladder, upright, in the long grass. The two men looked at each other for a moment or two, then the man smiled, a cool, hard smile, a warning, and let go of the ladder. The ladder fell sideways into the grass and the man turned away, walking back towards the trailer, loosening the strap around his shoulder, pulling it over his head. McVeigh, still up the tree, watched him empty the basket into the trailer and then shout across to the boy with the coffee urn. The boy nodded, pouring a fresh glass, getting to his feet, giving him the coffee. As he did so, he gestured towards McVeigh's tree, saying something in Hebrew, a question of some kind, and the man with the beard laughed, shaking his head, his eyes on McVeigh again, the glass tilted in a contemptuous salute. Same voice, McVeigh thought. Same voice as this morning. The torch at the door. The gun slung from the shoulder. He looked at the man for a moment longer, returning the stare, then shrugged and reached for another apple.

*

Heading south on the Hamburg–Bremen autobahn, half-past eleven in the morning, Telemann sat in the back of the big Mercedes, listening to the news.

With US troops still pouring into Saudi Arabia, Secretary of State James Baker had embarked on yet another tour of Allied capitals, touching hands, offering reassurance, pledging aid or trade or credits, as determined as ever to keep the coalition together. To German ears, this tireless American diplomacy carried a special significance. Banned by post-war treaties from any form of foreign military adventure, the Republic's contribution would be solely financial. Given the size of the German wallet, American expectations were high. If Germany wouldn't – couldn't – fight, then at least she could write a sizeable cheque. Chancellor Kohl, though, had other views. Already paying huge sums to return East Germany to the real world, he was determined to limit his country's exposure to the costs of the coming war. Bonn was talking guardedly of a multi-million DM contribution. To Telemann, converting the sum to US dollars in the back of the speeding Mercedes, it seemed a huge sum. But in Washington and London, as the German commentator acidly pointed out, the German offer was regarded as little short of an insult.

The news over, Telemann leaned forward. Blum was driving, the girl beside him. They'd left the apartment in Hamburg an hour earlier, Telemann's big grip in the back. Blum had been evasive about their exact destination, dismissing Telemann's questions with a shrug and a tired yawn, but Telemann knew it must be somewhere in the vicinity of Bad Godesburg. Bonn, perhaps, or even Cologne, or one of the endless dormitory suburbs that dotted the west bank of the Rhine.

Telemann fingered the tightly sewn seams of leather at the back of Inge's seat, looking at Blum. 'Tell me again,' he said, 'tell me the way you think it'll go.'

Blum's eyes found his in the driving mirror. 'I've told you already,' he said. 'I haven't changed the plan. The plan stands.'

'And if he turns up with more guys than you expect?'

'He won't. He never comes with more than three. The people at the hotel get uncomfortable. This is Germany, remember. Bad Godesburg. Not Dodge City.'

Telemann nodded, conceding the point. The phone call to Assali had been simpler than he'd expected. The phone had been answered by a woman, his wife perhaps, or a secretary, but he'd come at once, listening courteously as Telemann explained who he was, making no comment when he touched on Assali's problems with the US Immigration Department and the possibility that there might be alternative methods of acquiring citizenship. At the end of the call, Telemann had given the man Sullivan's Washington number, 456 1414, the main White House switchboard, repeating it twice more when Assali found a pen and paper. Before ringing off, Telemann had promised to make contact before nightfall. Time was a problem, he said. He was running on a tight schedule and had to be back on an airplane before the weekend. Perhaps there was a place they could meet, a local hotel maybe. Somewhere quiet, discreet. He'd call back with a suggestion once Assali had found Sullivan at his Washington desk. Non-committal, but still courteous, Assali had thanked him for the call.

Now, 12 kilometres short of Delmenhorst, Telemann returned to the plan, the moment when the talking stopped and the guns came out, and the Arab slipped quietly into Mossad hands.

'Me.' he said. 'Where do I fit?'

Blum frowned, feigning a moment's bewilderment, his eyes still on the road. 'You?' he said mildly.

'Yeah. Me. You go to the Dreisan. You have the assets in place. The cars. The guys in the lobby. All that I understand. Very neat. Very elegant. But what about me? What do I do? When push comes to shove?'

'At the Dreisen?'

'Sure.'

'You won't be at the Dreisen.'

'No?'

'No.' Blum shook his head, emphatic, the tour guide keen to

spare his clients unnecessary worry. 'You will be with Inge. At the point of delivery.'

'You mean the safe house?'

'Yes.'

'Why's that?'

Blum didn't answer for a moment. Then the eyes were back in the mirror, pure candour, the readiest form of reassurance. 'Operationally,' he said, 'we have control. We never share it. Never. You know that.'

'I wasn't asking for control.'

'It's the same thing. The same issue. You'll be there. It complicates things. It's unnecessary.' He shook his head. 'You'll see him later. Not much later, but later. So—' he shrugged, the eyes returning to the autobahn '—what's the problem?'

Telemann said nothing for a moment, watching the speed-ometer as they slipped past a huge truck, speeding south. At 140 k.p.h., there was barely a whisper from the engine. He glanced at the girl. Her head was back against the leather and she appeared to be asleep. Telemann leaned forward again, his mouth very close to Blum's ear. 'My friend,' he said softly. 'I need to be there.'

'Why?'

'Because I do. Because I've been there before. Because I'm not some eighth-grade bimbo.' He paused. 'Whatever you might think.'

'You don't trust me?'

'That's not what I said.' Telemann paused again. 'You should listen.'

Blum's eyes flicked back to the mirror. He said nothing, but invited Telemann to carry on with the merest nod of his head. Telemann smiled, his hand on the Israeli's shoulder, spelling it out.

'This afternoon you drop me at the Dreisen. I check in. I talk to the Arab again. I tell him I'm staying at the hotel. I suggest we meet there. Most natural thing in the world. We make an arrangement. I phone you with the details, or maybe we meet some place. Up to you. Your call. But whatever we decide,

248

whenever it happens, I'm there, the guy in the lobby, Uncle Sam, the magic handshake. You with me?'

'Of course.' Blum frowned, the irritation plain in his face. 'But you realize it may be dangerous?'

'I thought I told you. I've been there before. Most of my life I've been there.'

'That's not what I meant.'

'No?'

'No.' He shook his head, impatient now, dropping the Mercedes into manual to take another queue of trucks. 'I'm talking politics. You really want to be there? In the middle of it? With your name in the register? Whatever alias you're using?'

'Lacey.'

'OK. Nice American name. Nice American passport. You really want to take that risk? Have them check it all out?'

'Sure.' Telemann shrugged. 'Why not?'

'You don't think . . .' Blum shrugged, something new in his voice, a curious indifference, and Telemann leaned back, content to let it all wash over him. For a kilometre or two there was silence in the car, and when it was finally broken it was by Inge's voice, not Blum's.

'We can say no,' she said, looking straight ahead, her eyes on the road. 'Have you thought of that?'

'Sure.'

'So what do you say? You want the Arab. You want to talk to him. What if we just say yes, go ahead, you and Mr Assali and his three friends. You think he'll talk? You think he'll really tell you what you need to know?'

Telemann said nothing, gazing out at the neatly cropped fields, harvest gathered in. Autumn, he thought. Then winter.

'You have a choice,' he said at last. 'Either we do it my way, me at the Dreisen, me in the lobby, you in operational control. Or—' he shrugged '—I don't make the call.'

'To Assali?'

'Sure.'

'You're serious?'

'I am.'

Blum eased his body in the driving seat, accepting a cigarette from Inge, reaching for the lighter in the dash. The cigarette to his lips, he dipped his head briefly towards the glow of the element. When the smoke cleared, there was a smile on his face.

'Your boss,' he said, 'you think he's sympatico? You think he'll understand this? Your Uncle Sam?'

'Yeah.'

'Forgive you if it all goes wrong?'

'No question.'

'Think you played it all OK? Nothing—' he shrugged, an expansive wave of the left hand, loops of blue smoke '—too subtle? Like shitting on your Uncle Fritz's carpet?'

Telemann shrugged, immune now to the heaviest sarcasm. 'Your choice,' he said again. 'Your call.'

Blum half-turned in the seat, looking directly at Telemann for the first time. The smile, if anything, was even wider. 'OK,' he said, 'we take you to the Dreisen.'

*

The first time the old man, Abu Yussuf, went back to the Public Library, the girl at the information desk wasn't there, replaced for the afternoon by a helpful young black. The old man, disappointed, mumbled his apologies through his broken mouth, his face swollen and livid with bruising, and turned to go. The young black watched him limping away towards the door, another refugee from the mugging statistics. 'She's back tomorrow,' he called. 'Come around four.'

The old man was back next day at four, waiting out the last few minutes in the shade of a drooping plane tree beside the entrance. He hated America now, the hot streets, the garbage, the taste of the air, the pale kids with their begging tins and their dead eyes. He thought he'd seen poverty at home, certain villages on the West Bank, little food, no work, land sold to settlers over the villagers' heads, even the water cut off, hours at a time, days sometimes, no warning, no explanation. But this was different, a different kind of poverty, and for the first time the old man realized that being poor had nothing to do with money. New York was awash with money. It was everywhere, in every shop window. He'd seen enough money on a woman's wrist to feed his family for a year, for two years. Yet still there were the kids with their bowls, and older men, evenings on his way to work, huddled in doorways, knees to their chins, human refuse, discarded by a city too busy to care. Even Tel Aviv, he thought, is better than this. Even the Israelis are kinder than these strange people.

The old man went into the library. The information desk was on the first floor. The girl was there, as the young black had promised. She watched him limping towards her, the expression on her face uncertain, pity and sympathy, but anxiety too. The old man knew it, standing at the counter, trying to muster a smile. New York again, he thought. The city like a germ, spreading its violence and its broken bodies. Should I get involved? Should I take the risk? That's what the girl thought. That's what her face told the old man.

He explained what he wanted. He had money in his pocket. He showed her the thick wad of 10-dollar bills, the dyke he'd been building for himself against the terrible implications of a day like this. He needed to make another telephone call, back to Ramallah, back to his family. He had money to pay for it. It was very important, more important than he had the words to explain. Where he lived, there was no phone. Where he worked, the phone was no longer available. Could the girl help him? Did she have a phone? Here, at the library? Or somewhere else, even?

The girl, embarrassed by the old man's intensity, the way he bent towards her, the wad of money slowly uncurling on the counter, said it was difficult. She'd only been in the job six months. The information desk was a recent promotion. Private use of the phones was strictly forbidden. She wasn't sure who to ask. The old man nodded dumbly at every excuse, repeating his story, knowing it was the only one he had, his sole asset, but knowing too that he'd frightened the girl, and that she was simply looking for the kindest way of saying no. Finally it was the young black who returned from stacking books on a nearby shelf and touched the old man lightly on the arm, bringing the nightmare to an abrupt end. 'Come with me, sir,' he said.

The old man followed him to a small office at the back of the library. The label on the door read 'Duty Librarian'. Inside was a desk and a telephone. Distantly, through the window, there was a view of Manhattan. The young black locked the door behind them and lifted the telephone. He pushed two buttons, listened for a moment, then offered the phone to the old man. The old man, fumbling in his pocket, found the scrap of paper on which he'd written the number.

Amer Tahoul was at his desk in Ramallah. He answered at once. The old man, blinking now, asked about his wife. The young black was at the window, his back turned, staring out at the view, the closest he could get to leaving the room.

Amer Tahoul came back on the phone. 'Hala is still in prison.'

'Have you seen her?'

'Yes. Twice.'

'Is she all right?'

'She's . . . yes.'

'What?'

'Yes. She's OK.'

'What did she say?'

'She said she loved you. She said to tell you.'

'What else? What else did she say?'

There was a silence. The old man sank into a chair by the phone, exhausted already, the young black's kindness, and now Amer.

'Amer?' he said again. 'What else did she say?'

There was another silence, and for a moment the old man thought Amer had gone. Then he was back again, his voice low, almost a whisper.

'She said to be careful,' he said.

'Just that? To be careful?'

'No.'

'What else?'

'She said to get away.'

'Get away?'

'Get away from . . .' The voice hesitated. 'Wherever you are.

Whoever you're with. It was difficult. We couldn't talk. But that's what she meant. I'm sure of it . . .'

The old man nodded, no longer able to understand, his wife in a prison cell, himself in New York. He felt abandoned, lost. He felt like a plant, ripped from the earth. He bent to the phone again. He needed more than news. He needed advice, guidance, an indication that not all was lost. 'So what do I do?' he muttered.

There was another silence, longer this time, then the line went dead. The old man gazed at the phone, betrayed, and put it down. The black at the window was still gazing out at the view. His voice, kind, felt out of keeping with the city. 'I'll walk you down to the street,' he said softly, 'when you're ready.'

10

Billy McVeigh was still in his blazer, half an hour back from school, when his mother answered the phone. She stood in the hall, with a frown on her face, and he knew at once from her tone of voice that it was his father at the other end.

'Dad?' he called from the top of the stairs. 'Is that Dad?'

Sarah nodded. The routine exchange of pleasantries over, she held out the phone, retreating to the kitchen and closing the door, wanting no part of this relationship of theirs, her son and his father.

Billy picked up the phone, sorting quickly through his list of news, what was important, what wasn't. 'Dad?' he said. 'Where are you?'

'Israel.'

'Whereabouts in Israel?'

'On a farm. Picking apples.'

'Is it hot?'

'Very.'

'You OK?'

'Yeah.' McVeigh, sitting on the desk in the secretary's office by the kibbutz dining-hall, grinned, realized how much he'd missed the boy. Billy was talking about football now, the start of the new season, his first sessions with the Hornsey Schools Rep side. In the practice games he'd been picked for the 'A' team. The torrent of news stopped for a moment. 'What about Yakov?' he said. 'What have you done?'

'This and that.'

'What do you mean?' He paused. 'Dad?'

McVeigh shook his head, unable to answer, watching Cela in the corridor outside. She was standing guard in case the

254

secretary came back. Making foreign calls abroad was normally referred to a kibbutz committee for approval.

'Dad?'

McVeigh bent to the phone again, changing the subject, asking about school, friends, life at home, but the boy refused to be deflected, dragging the conversation back to Yakov, like a terrier with the bone.

Finally, McVeigh gave up. 'I'm with his wife, ' he said, 'Mrs Yakov.'

'You mean Sheila?'

'Cela.'

'Yeah. Her. Is she nice?'

'Yes. Very.'

'Does she like football?'

'Hates it.'

'*What?*'

McVeigh laughed out loud, hearing the astonishment in the boy's voice, then he saw Cela's signal, the secretary returning from lunch, and he whispered a goodbye and put the phone down. By the time he was back in the corridor, Cela was deep in conversation with the secretary, taking her to one side and easing her body round, shielding McVeigh. It was a neat piece of work and McVeigh mimed applause before walking past them, back out into the hot afternoon.

*

Telemann sat in the bedroom at the Hotel Dreisen, staring at the phone, wondering why it had been so easy.

He'd phoned Assali minutes after he'd booked in, sitting by the window with his shoes off, his feet on the bed. Outside the window, huge barges pushed up and down the Rhine, folds of grey water feathering behind them, lapping at the stones on the river-bank. Assali had answered the phone in person, unsurprised to hear him again, raising no objection to a meeting face to face. When Telemann explained he was staying at the Dreisen, the Arab had chuckled with genuine amusement. Telemann had asked why, wanting to share the joke, and Assali had said something about Adolf Hitler. Evidently the Dreisen had been one of his favourite hotels. He'd met the Englishman, Chamberlain, there during the Czech crisis. The hotel had been famous, a stepping-stone to war. The Arab was still chuckling when he rang off, agreeing to meet Telemann for drinks and perhaps dinner at half-past six.

Now, Telemann gazed out of the window, still puzzled. If Assali was implicated in the threats against New York, if he was indeed the middleman between the supplier and the point of delivery, why was he so sanguine about a meeting? He had protection, sure, and he'd assume that so public a rendezvous would be doubly safe. But Assali moved in a violent world, and his very survival was a tribute to his refusal to take risks. So why was he so willing to accept the invitation? Why hadn't it been harder?

Telemann shook his head, not understanding. Then the sound of the man's laughter came back to him, that special edge it seemed to have, a knowingness, and he thought again about Adolf Hitler, the meeting with the English prime minister. Telemann was no historian, but he knew that the meeting had been one of a series that had led to Munich and the infamous agreement securing 'peace in our time'. Hitler had been a gambler, tabling demand after demand. Chamberlain, to the world's subsequent regret, had caved in. Telemann mused on the parallels, watching a man in a blue track-suit jogging steadily north on the path beside the river. Maybe that was it. Maybe he had Assali exactly right. Maybe the man was coming to open negotiations, assuming that the Americans had done the thinking, assessed the risk, decided that New York was too high a price to pay for Kuwait City.

Telemann began to smile, following the logic through, testing the theory, realizing that it was a perfect match for the facts. Assali regarded him as a US representative, a proxy empowered to initiate talks. His precautionary call to Sullivan, assuming he'd made it, would have provided ample confirmation. Telemann nodded, relaxing back in his chair, still watching the man in the track-suit, a blue blur receding slowly into the distance. So much for Emery, he thought. So much for all the fancy analysis, twenty years of commuting to a desk and a phone. The man should have been out in the field a little, having to cope with the raw evidence, having to weigh it, assess it, turn it into some kind of operational plan. Maybe, then, he wouldn't have been so damned patronizing, so eternally sceptical. You had to give some to get some. That was Telemann's way. That was what he'd always believed. You had to take risks, trust your instincts. Sometimes you lost out, no question. Sometimes you fell flat on your face, the world on your head, the shit kicked out of you. But other times it could be different. Other times, like now, you got lucky.

Telemann reached for the telephone again, checking a number from a pad at his elbow. The number rang twice before it answered. It was a girl's voice, Inge. She sounded sleepy.

'Half-past six,' Telemann said briefly, 'at the hotel.'

*

Emery met Laura for lunch at a vegetarian café three blocks from the office on 'F' Street. It was her suggestion, her choice. She'd used the place before, always with her husband. It was busy. It was noisy. You could easily get lost there.

He stood up as she came in, her hair wet from a rain shower in the street. She looked tired and preoccupied, scanning the restaurant for some sign of Emery, seeing his raised arm at once, threading a path between the crowded tables. She sat down beside him. He could smell the rain in her hair.

'How long have we got?' she said.

Emery smiled. 'Half an hour.'

'You can spare that?'

'Yes.'

She nodded, reaching for the menu, looking absently through the list of wholefood bakes.

'Ron?' she said at last.

Emery shook his head 'Nothing,' he said, 'so far.'

'Yesterday?'

'I told you. He phoned. Strictly operational . . .' He shrugged. 'I think.'

Laura caught the note in his voice, the provisional lift at the end of the sentence, a code she was beginning to understand.

'You think he knows?' she said flatly. 'You think he's figured it out?'

'I think something's wrong.'

'Same thing, isn't it?'

'Not necessarily.'

A waitress appeared and began to recite the day's specials. Laura shook her head, not listening, still looking at Emery. There was an intensity in her, a lack of patience, that he'd never seen before. The waitress had stopped halfway down the list. Emery glanced up at her and signalled for her to come back later, but Laura reached out, putting a hand on his arm. 'Aubergines,' she said briefly, 'and walnut salad.'

The waitress scribbled on her pad, looking at Emery. 'Sir?'

'Twice.'

'Thank you.'

The waitress disappeared with the order. Laura's hand was still on Emery's arm. He leaned across and kissed her on the mouth. Her lips were dry, without a flicker of response.

'You think he's in trouble?'

'I think he's got a job on his hands.'

'That's not what I meant.'

Emery shrugged. 'I can't say. Either way, nothing's easy.'

Laura nodded slowly, still looking at him. 'He's been my life,' she said at last. 'It's a hard thing for you to understand. It's like a foreign country. If you haven't been there, you don't know. Can't know.' She paused. 'I love the man. I care about him. That make sense?'

'Perfect sense.' Emery hesitated. 'You want *me* to tell him?'

'No.'

'What then?'

'I don't know.' She closed her eyes for a moment, reaching for a napkin, twisting it between her fingers. 'How do you put a thing like this? What do you say? That his life's over? Everything he's been used to? All these years? Is that how you put it?'

'He'll need counselling.'

'Sure. Great idea. Can you see Ron going through all that? Some well-meaning shrink? Some fat analyst from Chevvy Chase, telling him the way it's gonna be?'

'Gotta be.'

'Gotta be.' She nodded. 'Yeah, gotta be.' She fell silent for a moment, pushing the napkin aside, accepting Emery's hand at last, squeezing it, needing it. Then she begun to shiver, thinking again. 'I shouldn't have let him go,' she said at last. 'I should have told him.'

'You did. In a way.'

'No, but properly. I should have told him properly. The whole thing. What it means. Now. Soon. When he gets back. What's got to happen. What might help.'

'We might help.'

'Sure. But—' she shook her head, a gesture of physical revulsion '—this is horrible. The man deserves more than this. He truly does.' She paused again, staring out at the street. The rain had stopped now and sunshine was puddling the sidewalk. 'What about the Agency?' she said slowly. 'Who knows there?'

'Nobody.'

'Nobody?' She sounded incredulous. 'All that money? All those computers? All that brainpower? And *no*body knows?'

Emery smiled, reaching for her hand again. 'It's been a private thing,' he said, 'your decision.'

'I know, but . . .'

'But what?'

'I can't believe they don't know.'

'They don't.' He paused. 'You think they'd have sent him off if they'd have known? Doing what he's doing?'

'What *is* he doing?'

Emery looked at her, saying nothing, the usual rules, never broken. Laura nodded, mute compliance. 'OK,' she said at last, 'I guess they don't know.' She looked at him. 'Was that irresponsible of me? Not telling them?'

'Yes.'

'You know why I didn't?'

'Yes.'

'Because I owed him the truth first. That's why. Not his bosses. Not his mother. Not anyone. Except him.'

'And me.'

'You're different. You're his best friend.'

'Quite.'

There was another long silence. The waitress had reappeared, balencing plates of steaming aubergine on a small tray. Laura watched her, a wistful expression on her face, the flicker of some distant memory.

'We have to do something,' she said softly. 'I have to do something.'

'What?'

'I don't know.' She looked at him again, her face pale under the tan. 'That's why I'm here.'

She reached down for her bag as the waitress began to unload the tray. Beside her plate she put a long brown envelope, sealed at the top. Emery looked at it.

'What's that?'

Laura frowned, picking up her fork, toying with the aubergine. Then she put the fork down and pushed the envelope towards him.

'Trouble with this thing,' she said, 'is it gets worse.'

*

Friedland followed the white Citroën through the thick of the rush-hour traffic. The approach to Crouch End, second gear on the steep hill, was expecially hard, cars and buses nose-to-tail, the boy and his mother clearly visible in the car ahead. He'd picked them up at the corner of their road, parked at the kerbside, watching them emerge from the house in the rearview mirror. The boy was carrying a knapsack, and his mother was wearing a coat. The girl monitoring the telephone tape said the match started at seven. His mother would stay to take him home. It was the regular venue.

Past Crouch End, the Citroën indicated left, plunging into a maze of side-streets, a short-cut to the playing fields up at Hornsey. Hanging well back now, Friedland thought again about Ross, and the real price of the contract he'd struck with the man. He'd known from the start that it wouldn't be easy, yet he'd almost enjoyed the early years. Much of the work had been straightforward – credit checks, covert vettings, the commissioning of occasional break-ins, software thefts, mail intercepts – and even the odd set-piece hadn't, in all truth, demanded a great deal. But lately, everything had changed. Ross had become nervy and slightly irrational, a confirmation, Friedland supposed, that the ruling Tory clique were themselves, at last, under threat. Quite where this would lead was anyone's guess, but he knew already that his own days were numbered. He'd only last as long as Ross lasted, and Ross – he was now certain – was on the way out.

The Citroën pulled to a halt at a T-junction and indicated left. Friedland did the same, recognizing the broad reaches of Hornsey Flats beyond the line of iron railings, still thinking of Ross. The Dispozall business was yet another symptom of the man's desperation. After a great deal of thought, he'd finally made the journey down to Basingstoke, spending an uncomfortable hour with the firm's managing director. The sole merit of Ross's cover-up was its crudeness. It had taken Friedland perhaps five minutes to explain the way it worked, the original analysis destroyed, a new analysis substituted, different substance, same circumstances, same outcome. Lovell, the managing director, a large, bluff man with a warm handshake, had followed Friedland's careful exposition without comment, getting up at the end to tell him that it was madness, that he'd have nothing to do with it, that he'd prefer bankruptcy and disgrace to a role in so daft a conspiracy. Expecting something of the kind, Friedland had devoted the rest of the hour to a carefully pitched confidential briefing, keeping his own role deliberately vague, hinting at membership of the Intelligence services, nothing specific, nothing the man could possibly check. He'd talked about Middle Eastern terror groups, and George Habash, and the endless backstage games of bluff and counter-bluff, games where nothing was quite what it seemed, and where 5 gallons of nerve gas acquired a significance that dwarfed the fate of a medium-sized UK firm. By the end of the hour, Lovell was back behind his desk, an older and wiser man, his company still intact, his pension safe, his family's prospects fully restored. Leaving, crossing the car park in the autumn sunshine, Friedland had mused on his own performance, wondering whether a year or so selling life assurance might not, after all, be so bad. Getting into his car, he'd glanced up at the big office he'd just left, four picture windows on the third floor. Lovell had been standing there, gazing down at him, in shirt-sleeves and braces. Neither man had waved or even nodded, and by the time Friedland had got in and wound down the window, Lovell had gone.

Now, turning into the recreation ground, Friedland watched the white Citroën park beside the line of football pitches. Billy, McVeigh's boy, was out of the car before it had stopped, dragging his knapsack behind him, running towards the distant pavilion that housed the changing-rooms. Ross, he now suspected, would stop at nothing to postpone his own departure from the inner circle. That was what power, real power, did to you. It was a drug. It bred dependence. It warped your judgement. It fed into a long narrow tunnel from which, in the end, there was only one outcome. Either you were prepared for real life again, or you weren't. Friedland, still watching Billy, suspected that Ross wasn't. Real life was no longer of any interest to him. It would be dull. It would be ordinary. It would be routine. All he wanted, all that mattered, was a permanent place in the sun.

Billy at last disappeared into the changing-rooms and Friedland waited a moment longer, enjoying the last of the September afternoon, before reaching for his notepad and his A–Z. He'd heard from the matron that morning. She'd phoned to say there'd been no news. Stephanie might be back in Hastings. She might have come to London. She might even have gone abroad. No one knew. Friedland thought about it, his own flesh and blood, twenty-two years old, adrift and rudderless, consoled only by the contents of a syringe. He'd watched her shooting up. The worst times, he'd even helped her. It had seemed, then, a kind of answer. Now? He shuddered, opening the A–Z. Hornsey Flats was on page twenty-nine. Friedland marked the spot with a neat pencil cross, peering round, looking for other exit roads, committing the place to memory, happy to add it to the growing list of potential locations. In some ways, God forbid, it was better than the school. Less busy. More space. Fewer witnesses.

*

McVeigh let Cela lead, slipping out through the gate in the security fence, finding the path through the rocky scrub, climbing away from the kibbutz. At four in the afternoon it was still hot, the sun high. The heat came bubbling back from the hillside, gusts of it rising to meet them, and McVeigh was soon out of his T-shirt, carrying it in his hand, plodding upwards behind the woman.

They'd spent the early afternoon at the swimming-pool, two towels side by side on the grassy slope. Cela went there every day, a break from the kids in school. She swam for half an hour, length after length, an easy crawl, and McVeigh had found it difficult to match her, settling instead for a series of untidy dives off the high board. Afterwards, dripping wet, they lay together on the towels, talking.

Cela had asked him about Yakov, with genuine curiosity, what he'd thought of the man, what kind of impression he'd made, and McVeigh had stretched out on the towel, shutting his eyes, going back to the wet afternoons on the touch-line in North London, the shouts of the kids in the pale winter light, the half-conversations they'd enjoyed, Yakov's eyes never leaving the game, always watching, sometimes the ball, mostly the players. Cela had smiled at this, recognizing the man she'd known. He played chess as well, she'd said. And he seldom lost.

Now, a mile or so from the kibbutz, Cela paused on the hillside. The walk had been her idea. Up on the mountain, hidden amongst the rocks, was a pool. The pool was fed from an underground stream, ice-cold water, and it was deep enough for swimming. She'd gone there first as a kid, twelve years old, back in 1967, the summer of the Six Day War. Before '67 the kibbutz had been on the old border, 100 metres from Syria, the mountain barred by mine-fields and occasional groups of patrolling soldiers. Sometimes, after dark, there'd been firing in the mountains, and most nights the kids in the kibbutz slept underground in the bomb shelters. In '67, though, everything had changed. She remembered the Army tanks, grinding up the road from the valley floor, and the thunder of jets, swooping low over the kibbutz, bombing the Syrian trenches on the mountainside above. The fighting had gone on for days, the shellfire slowly receding as the Army pushed the Arabs back towards Damascus. After a week, unbelievably, it was all over, and with peace had come the discovery of the pool in the mountains, a private place, an hour's hard walking in the heat of the day.

McVeigh looked down at the kibbutz. A truck from the orchards was turning in the yard behind the dining-hall, coming to a halt in a cloud of dust. People spilled from the trucks, tiny dots, wholly insignificant in the ticking heat. McVeigh wiped his face with his T-shirt.

'Was Yakov on the kibbutz?' he said. 'Was that where you met him?'

'Yes.'

'You grew up together?'

'Yes.' She nodded. 'Down there.'

'Same age?'

'Yes.'

McVeigh smiled, thinking of the photo again, the two faces. He had it with him now, buttoned into his back pocket. They might have been brother and sister, he thought. In some ways they probably were.

They climbed again, the path steeper now, loose shale and low drifts of thorn bush. Soon, the kibbutz had gone completely, hidden by a fold in the landscape. McVeigh called ahead, his breathing faster than he liked to admit.

'You went to the Army?' he said, 'after the kibbutz?'

'Everyone goes to the Army. You have to. We need to. Without the Army there'd be no Israel. Going to the Army is just something you do. It's automatic. It's like helping an old lady across the road.' She stopped, looking round. 'So you do it.'

McVeigh caught up with her. Her face was wet with sweat, but she wasn't out of breath.

'And Yakov?' McVeigh said. 'He went to the Army too?'

'Of course. He went to the tanks. He was in Sinai. During Yom Kippur.'

'He did well?'

'Everybody did well.'

McVeigh smiled, still panting, amused by this strange, tight-knit society. Cela was right. No Army. No Israel. A simple fact of history that did wonders for morale.

Cela peered at him, sensing his amusement. 'You think that's funny?' she said.

McVeigh shook his head. 'No,' he said truthfully. 'I think it's great.'

They reached the pool half an hour later. It was about 10 metres across, overhung by rocks on three sides. The mountain fell away before it, offering a fine view of the patchwork of orchards and fishponds in the valley below. The rocks were hot to the touch, worn smooth by the wind and the rain, and looking down at the pool, McVeigh could sense the magic of the place. The water was crystal-clear, the colour of white wine, and it was difficult to gauge its depth. There were pebbles and small rocks at the bottom of the pool, yellows and browns and daubs of ochre.

McVeigh looked down at the pool for a long time, standing on the rocks, anticipating the taste of the water and the feel of it, cold silk, against his baking skin. He looked up. Cela was standing on another rock, 10 feet above the pool. She'd taken off her shirt and shorts. She wore briefs but nothing else. She ignored him, gazing down at the water. Then she dived, a perfect arc, and McVeigh recoiled instinctively as the water splashed around him, drying at once on the hot rocks. Cela surfaced, her hair flattened against her head. She spouted water from her puckered mouth and jack-knifed down again, two strokes taking her to the bottom of the pool. McVeigh watched, her shape distorted by the broken surface of the water, her small, neat, brown body rippling and rippling. She was looking for stones, he could tell, picking one up, examining it, discarding it, the other hand looking for another, and then a third. Finally she surfaced, the ritual complete, a small white pebble in her hand. 'Here,' she said, offering it. 'For you.'

Flattered, McVeigh reached down for the stone, realizing too late what an old trick it was, her hand grasping his wrist, himself off-balance. Before he hit the water he marvelled briefly at her strength, then the pool swallowed him and he surfaced, gasping at the shock of it, his borrowed shorts ballooned with air, his legs heavy with the weight of the sodden boots. He grinned at her. This must have been the way of it, he thought, with Yakov. Kids all their lives. Tricks and games and treats like this on the hottest afternoons. No wonder he'd been longing to go back. No wonder he'd missed her.

Afterwards, still dripping, they sat beside the pool, McVeigh's shirt and shorts drying on a nearby boulder. The sun was lower now, and the valley was shadowed by the late afternoon haze, but the rocks had kept the midday heat and the air was still. Far away, McVeigh could hear the whine of a bus changing gear and the sound of a dog barking. He looked at Cela. She was sitting back against a rock, her eyes closed. She had the body of a young girl, flat belly, small breasts, shoulders dusted with freckles. Somehow her body matched her candour, her direct-ness, and looking away, across the valley, McVeigh realized how much he liked her. She had qualities he normally associated with men. He could be frank with her, honest. She had strength. Whatever he said, whatever happened, he knew he could rely on her to stay in one piece.

'I went to your flat,' he said carefully. 'In Tel Aviv.'

Cela opened one eye. She wasn't smiling. 'I know,' she said.

McVeigh blinked. 'What?'

'I know you went to my flat. You broke in. It was locked.'

'How do you know?'

Cela looked at him for a long moment. Her body was already dry. 'You tell me,' she said at last.

McVeigh frowned, back in the classroom, pupil and teacher. 'The hut,' he said. 'You searched my bag.'

'Yes.'

'And found the photo.'

'Yes.'

'The one you kept in the flat.'

'Yes.'

McVeigh nodded, reaching for his shorts, extracting the sodden photograph, laying it carefully on the rock between them. Cela glanced at it without comment. McVeigh turned it over. The blue biro was perfectly legible, unaffected by the water. 'What does that mean?' he said.

Cela looked at it for a moment longer. 'It means "our secret". That's the first part. Then there are two other words, "*Zhod k'mous*". That means "Nobody else's". So—' she shrugged '—"Our secret. Nobody else's". It's something you say when you're kids. It's something you grow up with.'

'You and Yakov?'

'Of course. And anyone else. Everyone says it. It's just—' She shrugged again. 'It meant something else too.'

'What?' McVeigh looked at her, the eyes, deep green, unblinking, the steady patience in her voice.

'What do you think?' she said. 'What do you think it means?'

McVeigh reached for the photo, turning it over once more. It was easy to recognize the smile on her face. He'd seen it in the pool, the moment she surfaced, that first dive.

'It means you loved him.'

'Love him.'

'Love him.'

'Yes.' She smiled. 'That's what it means.'

McVeigh nodded, easing his body on the hot rocks, seeing no point in polite evasions, in dressing up the truth. 'The flat,' he said, 'your bedroom was wrecked.'

'Oh?' Cela looked startled.

'Yes. Someone had wrecked it. Taken their time. Done a good job.' He paused. 'Maybe someone who knows you.'

'Why do you say that?'

'Because—' he shrugged, remembering the shredded garments on the floor '—they were making a point.' He nodded at the photo. 'That phrase was on the mirror. I found this.' He picked up the photo, holding it carefully between his forefinger and his thumb. 'In the lavatory.'

For the first time, Cela looked away, out across the valley. When she turned back she was smiling, a small, grim smile. McVeigh watched her for a moment, waiting for a response, some kind of clue, anger maybe, or disgust, but she stayed quite silent, her knees drawn up beneath her chin, her hands round her ankles, her whole body rocking slowly, backwards and forwards.

'What made Yakov want to come home?'

'He was tired.'

'Bored?'

'Tired.'

'Did he like his job? The job he had?'

Cela looked at him, assessing him, openly sceptical, deciding how far to go.

'The job changed,' she said at last. 'And we all began to change with it. Yakov didn't like that. You understand? You understand what I'm saying?'

McVeigh frowned. 'The job?' he said. 'Or the organization?'

'The organization.' She nodded. 'The organization changed.'

'Mossad?'

She looked at him again, not answering immediately, still wary, still uncertain.

'In the beginning it was different,' she said eventually. 'We did what we did, and that was OK. It was good, too. It was fun.' She nodded at the pool. 'We had fun. We laughed a lot. We were good, too. The best.'

'Yakov?'

'The best of the best.'

'So what happened?'

'It changed. Everything changed.' She paused, gazing down at the valley. 'The kibbutz. The country. The organization. Us . . .' She shrugged. 'Everything.'

'And Yakov?'

'They sent him to Lebanon. After the invasion.' She nodded at the mountains across the valley, brooding. 'He went to Beirut. He hated it. What he saw. What was happening. What he had to do . . .' She paused. 'That was the start of it.'

'Of what?' McVeigh bent forward, repeating the question. 'Of what? What did he hate? What made him change?'

Cela said nothing, looking at him with genuine sympathy, shaking her head, reaching for her shirt. She got up, pulling it on.

McVeigh picked up the photograph. 'Who did this?' he said.

'What?'

'Who put this where I found it? Who wrecked your flat?'

Cela looked down at him, shaking her head again, reaching for the photo, wanting it back. She gazed at it for a long time, thoughtful.

'There were three of us,' she said finally. 'Three of us down in the kibbutz. We were together all the time. Every day. Me, and Yakov, and the other one.'

'Who?'

'His name is Moshe.' She paused. 'He took the picture.'

'Where is he now?'

'Moshe?'

'Yes.'

'He's still there, still on the kibbutz.' She smiled. 'He wanted to be in the organization too. Like us. But it was impossible. He was too stupid. Very strong but very stupid. Yakov used to make a joke with him about it. He used to tell him he kept his brains in his backside. So—' she shrugged '—he stayed on the kibbutz.'

McVeigh nodded slowly, thinking of the hut in the darkness, the ladder in the trees, beginning to understand. 'What does he look like, this Moshe?'

'He's got a beard. He's big. Your age.'

'Works in the orchards?'

'Sometimes.' She nodded. 'But mostly he works with the chickens. In the chickenhouse.'

'What does he do there?'

'He looks after them. He's in charge. Every Monday he kills three hundred.' She made a small, neat strangling movement with her hands. 'He's done it for years. It's a horrible job. They go to a place near Tel Aviv. He drives them there. In the truck.'

'How often?'

'Every week. I told you. Every Monday.'

'Every Monday he goes to Tel Aviv?' McVeigh frowned, counting the days backwards. He'd arrived at the kibbutz on a Tuesday. Monday he'd been in Tel Aviv. Monday night, he'd been in Cela's flat. Monday, Moshe went to Tel Aviv. He looked at Cela, and Cela laughed, a soft laugh, shaking her head. 'You think Moshe was in my flat?' she said.

McVeigh shrugged. 'I don't know.'

'But you think he might have been there? Wrecked it?'

'Yes.'

She shook her head slowly, her hand still on the photo, picking it up, slipping it into the pocket of her shirt.

'No,' she said softly. 'Moshe didn't wreck my flat.'

*

The old man, Abu Yussuf, was still trying to decide when the boy came back to the apartment. He came up the tenement stairs without a sound, no kick at the door, no tuneless whistle. He padded silently along the hall and stood at the kitchen door. The old man was sitting at the table, staring at nothing. He looked up. The boy was carrying a holdall. Since the fight, he'd been much quieter, more watchful, less crazy. Now he took the car keys from the pocket of his jeans and tossed them on to the table.

'We have a job,' he said in Arabic. 'This afternoon.'

'What?'

'We need the car. You'll drive. I'm coming with you.'

'Where?' The old man looked alarmed, his reverie broken, his decision unmade. It would be too late now, too late to obey his instincts, to get away from this terrible place. 'Where?' he said again.

The boy didn't answer, but glanced at his watch.

'Have you eaten?'

'No.'

'Then eat.' He picked up the keys again and returned them to his pocket. 'We'll go in ten minutes.'

*

Telemann dressed carefully to meet the Arab, Mahmood Assali.

Late afternoon, he'd taken a cab to the shopping centre in Bad Godesburg. He'd found a small, discreet clothing store and bought a couple of new shirts and a jacket. The jacket was dark blue, a conservative cut, a style much favoured by the diplomatic crowd. With the jacket he chose a silk tie, red and gold stripes on a blue background, not loud. In the mirror in the hotel bedroom the effect was perfect: the envoy from Washington, dressed for an evening's quiet negotiation, briefed to initiate the series of conversations that would doubtless save New York. For those critical few seconds in the lobby, downstairs, Assali would buy it. No question.

Telemann sat on the bed and stooped to lace his shoes, checking his watch as he did so. For a brief moment the dial of the big Rolex swam out of focus, and he found himself shaking it in irritation, as if the problem was some mechanical glitch. Blinking rapidly, he looked again. Six-twenty. Time to move out.

He got up and left the room, locking the door behind him. Downstairs the lobby was busier than he'd expected, three couples checking in, a party of some kind, one of the men arguing with the receptionist about the room rate. Telemann stood by the lift for a moment, watching them, trying to work out whether they were genuine guests or part of the Mossad sting. The lobby was big, a wide, carpeted area with the reception desk built into a shallow alcove to one side. There were armchairs and low tables around the walls, and tall double doors at the rear, opening into a big ante-room. Beyond, through another set of doors, was the dining-room, handsome, vaulted, with big picture windows and spectacular views of the Rhine. Telemann had already booked a table for five, a precaution in case Blum let the Arab get as far as the reception desk. Even now he wasn't sure the way the thing would go. Whether they'd take Assali here, in the lobby, the moment he walked in. Or whether it would be later, with the man a little more at his ease, off guard, Telemann at his side, a conversation under way.

The group at the reception desk resolved their problems and headed for the lift. Two other businessmen concluded a conversation by the door and walked towards the bar around the corner. The lobby, quite suddenly, was empty. Telemann settled briefly into a chair beside the lift, consulting his watch. Six twenty-eight. He frowned, checking it again. Blum was leaving it late, later than good sense would allow. He looked round, wondering if he'd missed something, whether the stake-out was subtler than he'd expected. The man had said at least four operatives, men and women, some of them resident in the hotel. The lift began to whirr, and Telemann glanced up at the indicator board, unwinding from the fifth floor, smiling to himself, the nerve of these guys, their confidence, the sheer class of their choreography. He checked his watch again, the lift doors beginning to open. Six twenty-nine. Less than sixty seconds to run.

Telemann got up, standing aside, knowing the rules, lateral separation. His back to the lift, he heard the doors close. He counted a slow five, his hands in his pockets, studying a print on the wall. The print showed an Alpine scene, three guys in funny hats stalking a distant stag. Berchtesgaden, he thought grimly, remembering the Arab's chuckle on the telephone. He began to turn round, knowing how important it was to get the geography right, who was standing where, arcs of fire, dead zones, and as he did so, the lift doors opened again, permitting a second woman to join the guest already waiting impatiently by the entrance to the ante-room. They were both in their mid-seventies. They began to argue in animated German. They disappeared towards the dining-room.

Telemann blinked, turning round again, his attention drawn to a movement in the street outside. A car had drawn up, a big BMW. Two men got out, one from the front, one from the back, and Telemann knew at once that they were bodyguards, the way they moved, purposeful, alert, the speed with which they had the kerbside back door open and the path to the hotel covered. Telemann began to cross the lobby, realizing that for some reason the plan had aborted. The lobby was empty. The Israelis hadn't showed.

A third man was on the pavement now, short, stocky, a gleaming brown scalp visible beneath thinning hair. He was wearing a dark suit, the jacket open, and he was in the act of securing the middle button when Telemann heard the first shot. There was a blur of movement, the two bodyguards abruptly armed, guns in hands, one crouching behind the car, the other dragging the Arab into cover. Telemann, at the door now, stared down at him. He was barely 5 metres away, sprawled by the car. Blood was pumping from a hole in his chest and there were bone splinters and brain tissue where his left eye had once been. Telemann stared at him, amazed, wondering vaguely why he hadn't heard the second shot, a spectator at a play he no longer understood. He heard voices behind him, someone shouting in German, and then he was pushed roughly aside, just another guest, a small, neat American, halfway to his knees, not knowing quite what to do. He turned to go, looking up, dimly recognizing the shape of the face before him, the blond hair drawn tightly back, the Hermes scarf knotted at the side of the neck, the hand outstretched.

'*Komm*,' Inge said. '*Komm doch mit.*'

*

Abu Yussuf drove north up the valley to the Hudson River, keeping the ancient Oldsmobile to a steady 45 m.p.h. in the slow lane of the big Interstate. The traffic, early afternoon, was light, cars mostly, plus the occasional truck heading up towards Albany.

The boy sat beside the old man, a map on his knee, one finger keeping a tally of the junctions as they sped by. An hour out of Newark he'd barely said a word, and the old man still had no idea where they were going. The best he'd been able to coax from the boy was a shrug and a sour smile. They'd be back before dark, he'd said, and then they'd celebrate.

Past Poughkeepsie, near Kingston, the boy unzipped one of the pockets on the side of the holdall and produced a piece of paper. He peered at it, his lips forming the words. Then he looked up, checking out the next junction indicator board, and tapped the old man on the arm. 'There,' he said. 'Next exit.'

The old man did what he was told, indicating right and following the long curve of blacktop off the Interstate. At the foot of the exit road there was another cluster of signs. One of them read 'Catskill Forest Preserve'.

'There,' the boy said again, pleased with himself. 'Go right.'

The old man hauled the car on to the narrow country road. Ahead, he could see mountains. There were trees everywhere, crowding down to the road, some of them already scorched with the first chills of autumn. It was very quiet, the odd house, the occasional smallholding, and as the road began to climb, the window still down, the old man could smell the damp, resinous breath of the forest.

The boy was back in the map again, a different one this time, bigger scale. He looked up constantly, at each fresh bend in the road, frowning with concentration as his finger kept pace with the car. Finally, half an hour from the Interstate, he told the old man to stop. The old man pulled on to the side of the road and turned off the engine. They'd crested one range of mountains already and were down in the valley again, big, broad-leafed trees, sunshine pooling on the road. It was very quiet, an occasional whisper of wind, the distant whine of a passenger jet, miles above, en route to Canada. Ahead, the road ran downhill for perhaps a quarter of a mile before a gentle left-hand bend. The boy looked at his watch, then picked up the bag and put it on his lap. For the first time, the old man realized he was nervous.

'What now?' he said. 'What do you want me to do?'

The boy glanced across at him. He didn't seem to have heard the question. His breath was coming in tiny, shallow gulps, like an athlete preparing for a race. The old man put the question again, and the boy grunted, opening the bag. The old man looked at the bag. Inside, he could see apples and an aerosol. Beneath was a gas mask, the one he'd seen the boy wearing in the garage, and something else, a garment of some kind, olive green, tightly rolled.

The boy looked at him again. 'Drive round the corner,' he said. 'You'll find a track on the left. We go up the track. Into the trees. Stop when I tell you.'

The old man nodded, compliant as ever, starting the engine and easing the big car on to the road. He found the track at once, hard, rutted earth beneath a thin layer of fallen leaves, and he took the car out of automatic, keeping it in second gear, taking it easy, not wanting to wreck his brand-new plumbing on a tree root or an outcrop of rock. A hundred metres into the trees, the road was invisible behind them. The boy told him to stop and turn the car round. He did so, an awkward manoeuvre, the Oldsmobile pointing downhill again, the engine off.

The boy nodded, saying nothing, getting out and standing

motionless beside the car. For a full minute he stayed there, listening, then he gestured for the old man to join him. 'Give me the keys,' he said.

The old man got out of the car, handing him the keys. The boy nodded up the track. 'Go,' he said. 'I'll follow.'

The old man walked up the track, trying not to look back, trying to hide his own nervousness. Apples, he thought, why apples? At the top of the rise he stopped. Below him, through the trees, was a white picket fence. Beyond the fence was a big paddock, acres of lush grass. There were horses in the paddock, heads down, cropping the grass. He looked at them for a moment, knowing at once they were thoroughbreds. There were four of them in all, and he watched as one of them looked up and snorted and shook his head, making off across the paddock, an easy canter, a joy to watch. The old man marvelled at them, a reminder of the horses he'd looked after back home. He turned round, his finger pointing through the trees, wanting to share the spectacle.

The boy was behind him. His face was invisible behind the gas mask, and he was standing on one leg, pulling on the garment from the holdall. The old man stared at it. He'd never seen anything like it in his life. It was one-piece, gathered at the ankles and the wrists with tight elastic cuffs. There was a hood as well. The boy, quite anonymous now, pulled the hood up over his head, tightening the draw-strings round the black rubber mask, a perfect seal. Bending to the bag again, he produced a pair of rubber bootees and some gloves. The bootees laced around his ankle. The gloves reached halfway up his forearms. Flexing his fingers, he squatted by the bag, feeling inside. Out came the aerosol and the apples. The aerosol was plain, and he handled it gently, at arm's-length, gesturing the old man over.

The old man shook his head, not wanting to move, knowing now that he was in the presence of evil. The boy walked towards him. His voice came through the filter on the side of the gas mask, distorted, a conversation from a nightmare, another world, another planet.

'Stay here,' he said.

'What?'

'Stay here.' The boy pointed at his feet. 'Don't move.'

'Why? What are you going to do?'

The boy ignored him, walking slowly down through the trees, the apples in one hand, the aerosol in the other, held a little away from his body, like a brush dripping paint. At the fence, he stopped. The horses had seen him already. They were young and curious. They loped towards him, stamping and whinnying in nervous excitement, this strange green figure with the rubber face, one hand outstretched, the apples on offer.

The first of the horses, the bravest, nuzzled his hand, worrying the apples, the upper lip going back, the big teeth digging in. The other horses gathered round, huge brown eyes, one apple left, the other hand coming up, the hand with the aerosol. The old man began to run down through the trees but the boy was already at work with the aerosol, a steady spray of droplets, point-blank range. The old man stopped, seeing the first horse begin to stagger, feeling the vomit rising in his own throat, pure revulsion, the deliberateness of it, wholly wanton. Another horse went down, its legs kicking in the air, then a third, before the boy turned away, leaving the aerosol by the fence, running back up the hill towards the old man, his breath rasping noisily through the filter.

At the top of the rise, pulling the old man with him, he stopped and looked back. Three of the horses lay where they'd fallen. The fourth was still on its feet, staggering helplessly round in a tight circle, trying to stay upright, trying to get away. The old man shut his eys, knowing it was hopeless, knowing that this wasn't *drat*, the fart-gas the Israelis used, the stuff that made your eyes sting and your throat burn, but something infinitely more terrible. He followed the boy down through the trees to the car. The boy had the gas mask off now, carrying it loosely in his hand. He was excited. He was grinning. He stopped by the car, stooping to unlace the rubber bootees, his fingers plucking blindly at the knot. He looked up at the old man, abandoning the bootees, tearing open the Velcro pads, pulling the garment off his shoulders. His face was covered with sweat and his T-shirt clung to his body.

'Here,' he said, feeling for the car keys in his jeans' pocket. 'Get me a towel.'

He threw the keys to the old man, telling him to look on the back seat, and bent to the bootees again, still wrestling with the knot. The old man unlocked the car, seeing the towel on the back seat. He reached for it, sickened, a deep hot anger, weeks in the making. He looked through the rear window. The boy was still bent down beside the exhaust-pipes, still working on the bootee. The old man hesitated for about a second. Then he slid the key into the ignition and gave it a short half-turn. He reached for the switch on the dashboard, the single white key that opened the circuit to the tank in the trunk. He flicked it over, hearing the pump engage. Then he slammed the door, himself still inside, winding the window as tight as he could, giving the ignition key another half-turn, thankful that he'd taken such care with the rewiring. The engine fired, and he looked in the rear-view mirror, wondering how long he could afford to wait, whether men were like horses, half-expecting the boy to stand up and smash his way into the car, completing the job he'd started in the hallway, only days ago. But there was nothing, no sign of movement, and he shut his eyes, reaching for the key on the dashboard, killing the pump, engaging gear, slipping the clutch. The car began to move, rolling downhill, and the old man opened his eyes again, hauling on the steering-wheel, trying to avoid the worst of the ruts, his eyes flicking up to the mirror, time and again, making the most of what he'd left behind, the body of the boy, sprawled amongst the leaves, one hand still reaching for the knot on the bootees.

*

Emery took the call from Sullivan in the office on 'F' Street. It was 4 p.m., Washington time, and Emery knew at once that Sullivan wasn't interested in small-talk.

'I'm looking at a Priority One,' he said. 'Came in three minutes ago.' He paused. 'Dripping shit.'

'I'm sorry?'

'Guy called Assali was shot this evening. Broad daylight. Outside a hotel.'

'Where?'

'Germany. Bad Godesburg.'

'Is he dead?'

'Yeah.'

'Is that bad news?'

'It's unbelievable news.'

'Why?'

'Because Assali was a big number with the State Department and no one fucking told me. State have been courting him for months. He's their pet convert. The one Palestinian who was gonna renounce all the violence. The one who was gonna call for peaceful negotiations. The one who was gonna put the fucking Israelis on the spot.' He paused. 'That's why they wanted him so badly. That's why he's on the slab.' He paused again. 'And you know who fucking put him there? Using my good name?'

Emery gazed at the phone, not answering for a moment, knowing it was wiser to permit Sullivan the final word.

'Who?' he said at last.

'Your buddy,' Sullivan said. 'Ron fucking Telemann. Get him back. This is a disaster. The Boxheads'll be all over us. My arse is on the line. I want him here tomorrow.'

*

They were 50 kilometres north of Bad Godesburg, heading back towards Hamburg, before Telemann bothered himself with the obvious question.

'Why?' he said. 'Why did you do it?'

Inge was driving, Telemann beside her. They'd left the hotel through a side-entrance, minutes ahead of the police and the ambulance. The Mercedes had been parked in a cul-de-sac near by, the bonnet pointing uphill, the doors unlocked. Of Blum there'd been no sign. Now Inge glanced across at him. She looked flawless, newly minted. She might have spent a gentle afternoon at the shops.

'I don't know,' she said. 'I don't take the decisions.'

'But you knew. You knew what was going to happen.'

'No. I was only told to pick you up. Nothing else. They told me to make sure you were away from the hotel.'

'Why?'

'I don't know.'

Telemann nodded, watching the lights of the car ahead. He felt wholly detached, a kind of numbness, a compound of exhaustion, bewilderment and a growing sense of indifference. He yawned. 'Who's they?' he said.

The girl looked across at him again, the small private smile he remembered from the half-hour they'd shared in her bed, first thing, before the day had properly started, before they'd shipped him south, and tied him to the end of the trace, and cast him in Assali's direction, and waited for the line to tighten. He laughed, a short, bitter laugh, part admiration, part disgust.

'Neat,' he said. 'Neatly done.'

*

By six o'clock, Washington time, Emery had enough of the detail to warrant another call to Sullivan.

Under the circumstances, the Polizeichef in Bad Godesburg had been remarkably helpful. On the transatlantic line, he'd limited his indignation to a curt sentence or two about unauthorized operations on Federal territory, and had extracted a loose promise from Emery that the entire episode would be subject to an immediate bilateral inquiry. The terms of that inquiry would naturally be settled at a higher level, but in the meantime he was prepared to share what little Intelligence he had.

Assali, the Palestinian, had been dead before he hit the ground. The killing was extremely professional and carried all the hallmarks of a sophisticated Mossad operation. Assali had been due to meet an American called Lacey, a resident at the hotel. The name Lacey was evidently an alias. A search of his hotel room had revealed other documents in the name of Telemann. Herr Telemann appeared to live in Maryland. His wife's name was Laura. The Bureau had acquired three photographs of her from an inside pocket of a holdall. He was looking at them now. For the record, Frau Telemann was in her late thirties, with a nice figure and good legs.

Listening, Emery had tried to hurry the laconic German police chief to a conclusion. Where was the American now? What did they have on the hit squad? How wide were they spreading the net? The German stonewalled each question, telling Emery that the investigation was less than four hours old, that preliminary enquiries were incomplete, that it was far too early to expect anything really solid. Realizing the truth of it, that Telemann and the guys with the guns had gone, Emery had brought the conversation to an end.

Now, hearing Sullivan lift the phone, he did his best to pre-empt the inevitable obscenities. Damage-limitation, he told himself, was a subtle art.

'I've talked to the Germans,' Emery said briefly. 'They've got nothing.'

'Except Telemann's name.'

'Sure.'

'And mine?'

'I doubt it.'

'You'd better be right.' Sullivan paused. 'So where is he?'

'They don't know.'

'Do you?'

'No.'

'But . . .?'

Emery hesitated, remembering his last conversation with Telemann, thirty-six hours ago, the man still up in Hamburg, fantasizing about Otto Wulf. At the time, he hadn't taken much notice. Now, suddenly, it was very different. The Agency's pet bulldozer had thrown a track. Anything might happen.

Sullivan was still waiting. Emery could hear his knuckles drumming on the desk.

'There's a German industrialist,' he began carefully, 'Telemann thinks he might be implicated . . .'

'Is he?'

'I doubt it.' He paused. 'But then he thought this Assali guy was implicated too.'

'The guy in Bad Godesburg? The Palestinian?'

'Yeah.'

'You're saying he had the guy killed?'

'I'm saying he was part of it, sure.'

'Shit.' Sullivan paused. 'So who's this other fella? The industrialist?'

Emery closed his eyes for a moment, knowing where the conversation was headed. 'Wulf,' he said slowly.

There was a moment's silence. Then Sullivan was back, his mouth very close to the phone. Three blocks away, Emery could practically smell the man, the meaty scent of his breath, the big podgy hand wrapped around the phone.

'*Otto* Wulf?' he said.

'Yes.'

'Holy Jesus.' Sullivan paused. 'And you're saying he's next on the list?'

Emery nodded. 'Could be. I don't know.' He paused. 'But yes, it could happen.'

There was another silence, longer this time. Next door, Emery could hear Juanita bullying the coffee machine. Then Sullivan was back on the phone again, the voice softer, intimate, infinitely more menacing.

'Get yourself over there,' he said. 'Go tonight. Take whatever you need. But don't come back without him. You understand me?'

'Yes, sir.' Emery hesitated, gesturing mutely at the mountain of paperwork on his desk. 'But what about—' he shrugged '—the rest of it?'

'Fuck the rest of it.'

'Yes, sir.'

Emery hesitated again, watching the door open, seeing Juanita's hand appear with a brimming cup of coffee. Then he bent to the phone, another question on his lips, realizing too late that Sullivan had hung up.

Juanita crossed the office and left the coffee on a small coaster. The coaster featured a tourist view of Manhattan Island. It had appeared the week they'd moved in, her own small joke. Now, Juanita back outside, Emery stared at it. Key parts of the puzzle he was beginning to understand. Gold, Dave Weill. The absolute lack of any Intelligence from the usual Middle East sources. There were ways these half-clues could just add up, a kind of negative arithmetic, but a result none the less. He looked at the coaster for a little longer, speculative, then reached for the phone again, opening a drawer, taking out a long brown envelope, shaking the contents on to the desk. Laura answered on the third ring. He could hear Bree, singing, in the background.

'It's me,' he said briefly. 'We have to go to Europe. Tonight.'

'Who's we?'

'You.' He scowled, reading the letter from the clinic again, still thinking of the dead Palestinian. 'And me.'

Book three

21 September 1990

11

The two statements lay side by side on the President's desk. Sullivan looked at them. Even upside down, he knew them word for word.

The President picked up one of the two sheets of paper, leaning back in the big chair, revolving it slightly, letting the light from the window fall on the three brief paragraphs. The text was datelined Baghdad, 20 September 1990. It had been in the hands of every major Western media outlet for at least ten hours. Already, on the CNN rolling newscasts, word from the Revolutionary Command had elbowed out every other item.

The President read it for the third time.

'*The mother of all battles*,' he mused. '*Not a single chance for any retreat.*' He looked up, directly at Sullivan. 'Neat phrase, don't you think?'

'Sir?'

'Mother of all battles.' He tapped the news release. 'Who writes this guy's speeches? We have a line on that?'

Sullivan shook his head, grunting, looking down at the note-pad on his knee. Emotionally, he knew, the President was now committed to kicking the Iraqis out of Kuwait. That meant offensive military action – an invasion – and there were power-ful elements in Washington determined to resist him. Neither the State Department nor the Pentagon had any appetite for a real fight. They saw the downside, the risks, the body-bags, the prospect of another interminable war. They wanted to wait for sanctions to bite. They wanted to starve Saddam back to Baghdad. Problem was, Saddam didn't see it that way, and with one of the world's largest armies in Kuwait, he didn't have to. Sullivan toyed with his pen, thinking about the military again, the endless round of briefings, the armfuls of statistics they brought to every meeting, the answers they came up with when they translated Presidential resolve into hard numbers. Retaking Kuwait City would need half a million men. Casualties would number thousands. Public backing for the war might not survive the first week's fighting. Was Kuwait City really worth that kind of risk? Should the President hazard a second term of office for an unelected despot? Was foreign policy to be *entirely* shaped by oil? Sullivan shook his head, glad that the responsibility wasn't his, looking again at the President.

Abruptly, the President stood up, leaving the communiqué on the desk and walking to the window. 'Tell me again,' he said.

'It happened yesterday, sir. Up in the Catskills. Guy runs the stud found four horses dead in the paddock. He called in the veterinary surgeon, and the vet called the police.'

'Why?'

'He found an aerosol. It's down in New York now. Exactly the same as the one the guys found in the hotel.'

'Same contents?'

'We think so.'

The President nodded, turning back into the room again, his face furrowed. Even for a man with his appetite for work, the last six weeks had come close to breaking him.

'We heard anything more from these guys? A note or anything?'

'No, sir.' Sullivan paused. 'But then we don't have to.'

'Why not?'

'The stud's owned by an Arab. The money's Saudi. Fahd's no friend of Saddam, so I guess—' he shrugged '—our friends are sending the same message a different way.'

'But nothing specific? No more dates? Deadlines?'

'No, sir.'

'Why not?'

Sullivan said nothing for a moment, studying the notes on his lap, remembering the last conversation with Emery, his refusal to jump to conclusions, his indifference to the realities of political life. He'd tasked the man to find answers, and all he'd got was a nasty little incident in Bad Godesburg, and the prospect of a major quarrel with the Germans. The consequences of the latter were all too predictable. White House staffers had no business running operations of their own, and if the truth about Telemann ever surfaced, then Sullivan was strictly history. He'd spent most of his career offending the major bureaucracies, and none of them would shed a single tear at his departure. Poaching a guy like Telemann from the Agency was emphatically off-limits. Letting him run with the Israelis was worse. The best he could expect if the media scented the smoke in the wind, if his luck ran out, was early retirement and political oblivion. The worst didn't bear contemplation.

Sullivan glanced up. The President was still looking at him, still waiting for an answer.

'I don't know, sir,' he said. 'We have nothing on that.'

'Why not?' the President said again. 'You wanna tell me?'

Sullivan gazed at him for a moment, old friends, and then shook his head.

'No, sir.'

'OK.'

The President returned to his desk, picking up the other sheet of paper, scanning it quickly. The message from Tel Aviv was twenty-four hours older than the communiqué from the Revolutionary Command Council. In it, Prime Minister Shamir had been concerned to dispel any doubts about Israeli resolve. Israel, he'd promised, would take on Iraq by herself if the US chose to withdraw. Aggression would be met with aggression. An eye for an eye. Survival in the Middle East demanded nothing less. The President pushed the statement towards Sullivan. Sullivan left it on the desk. He'd read it a day and a half ago, understanding at once the dangers it represented. Now he looked at the President.

'Have you talked to them since?'

'Twice.'

'They mean it?'

'Sure they mean it.' He sat back for a moment, staring out of the window again, the message still on the desk. 'You know what that is?' he said at last. 'That piece of paper?'

'Sir?'

'It's Saddam's best shot. Forget ballistic missiles. Forget going nuclear. Forget chemical weapons. Nerve gas. New York. All that stuff. No, Saddam's best shot is that piece of paper . . .' He nodded at the desk. 'The moment the guy drops a Scud on Tel Aviv, this war's over. There'll be another war after it. Right next day. No question. The Israelis will be in, and we'll be in, and the Brits probably too, but the rest of them . . . the Syrians . . . the Eygyptians . . . the Moroccans . . . they'll all be back home . . .' He paused. 'Telling the world what bullies we are, telling Saddam to hang tough in Kuwait, doing all that stuff about imperialism and the Third World . . .' He paused again, shaking his head. 'We can't afford to fight that kind of war any more. Whatever happened on the battlefield, we'd lose it.' He looked at Sullivan again, an air of slight surprise, as if the man had suddenly appeared from nowhere. 'So tell me,' he said, 'how do we do it?'

Sullivan blinked. 'Do what, sir?'

'Rein in the Israelis?'

Sullivan nodded, understanding the logic only too well, thinking of Ross again, the news he'd passed on about the man McVeigh, back in touch, somewhere in Israel.

The President was still looking at him, his head cocked on one side. 'Well?'

Sullivan gazed at the desk for a moment. Then he stood up, bringing the conversation to an end. 'I don't know, sir,' he said carefully. 'Yet.'

※

McVeigh sat in the cab of the big Scania truck, bumping towards Bethlehem, wondering again exactly what Cela had meant.

She was sitting beside him now, her body wedged between his and the big Israeli kibbutznik, Moshe. Moshe was driving, his huge calloused hands gripping the wheel, his eyes never leaving the road or the mirror, cursing in Hebrew and stamping down through the gears whenever a bus or a bend in the road slowed the truck's progress. Since the incident in the orchards, Cela had evidently talked to him, telling him not to worry about McVeigh, telling him the Englishman was a friend.

McVeigh looked down at her. Her eyes were closed, and her

head was back against the greasy seat, and her body swayed and jolted over the rough roads. An hour or so out from the kibbutz, he'd asked her who killed Yakov. He'd shouted the question in her ear, fighting the clatter of the big diesel, confident at last that Moshe spoke no English. At first, Cela had ignored the question, smiling at him benignly, nodding as if he'd made a comment about the weather or the qualities of the coffee from the Thermos they'd just emptied. But then he'd put the question again, his mouth close to her ear, enunciating each word, and she'd looked away for perhaps a minute, thinking about it, watching the sun rise steadily over the fishponds in the fields beyond the roadside. Then she'd touched him lightly on the knee and beckoned him close.

'Is that what you've come to find out?'

'Yes.'

'Who wants to know?'

'Me.'

'And who else?'

'Does it matter? Does it make any difference to the answer?'

'Yes.'

'*Yes?*'

'Yes.'

The truck had juddered to a halt at this point, the beginning of the morning rush-hour on the outskirts of Tiberius, and Cela had paused, looking ahead through the dusty windscreen at the road plunging down towards the Sea of Galilee, a huge bowl of deep blue water, cupped by the haze-brown mountains.

'Answers depend on questions,' she said at last. 'And answers depend also on who asks the questions.'

'I ask the questions.'

'Of course.' She'd looked at him. 'And who else?'

Now, 3 miles from Bethlehem, McVeigh gazed out of the window, still brooding on the conversation. Coming down from the pool in the mountains Cela had told him there was someone he should meet. This person, whom she didn't name, lived on the West Bank. Meeting him would not be easy. She would have to be there, and that would mean they'd have to travel together. Travelling together wouldn't be easy either, but

289

there was a way of organizing it that would get round most of the problems.

Quite what the problems were, McVeigh had never discovered, but his morning had begun even earlier than usual with a knock on the door at half-past two. Outside, in the darkness, he'd found Cela. She was wearing jeans and an old three-quarter-length coat. She had a scarf around her head, tied into a knot at the back. In the light from the hut, once McVeigh had found the switch, she looked like a peasant, a land girl, a first generation import from Eastern Europe or one of the Russian republics. Amused at his surprise, she'd told him to pack his bag. He'd done so, following her through the sleeping kibbutz to a long, low building beside the road. Inside, he'd found Moshe and a handful of other kibbutzniks, crating chickens. The chickens lived in long rows of square pens and they were lifted out one by one, their necks broken with a single movement of the wrist, their twitching corpses packed into plastic crates. Outside, McVeigh had helped stack the crates on the back of the big Scania, his work monitored by the glowering Moshe. They'd left shortly before dawn, no formal introductions, no clues as to where the journey might lead, just the conversation on the descent into Tiberius. Questions. Answers. More questions. And that strange line about who, exactly, was running McVeigh.

All morning they'd driven south. After Tiberius, Nazareth. After Nazareth, the coast again, and the distant brown sprawl of Tel Aviv. Inland, on an industrial estate in one of the suburbs, they'd stopped for an hour and off-loaded the chickens. Cela had worked alongside Moshe, and being with them, McVeigh had begun to sense the shape of the relationship, brother and sister, Moshe gruff and burly and protective, Cela taunting him with her grin and her giggle, and her repertoire of schoolgirl tricks.

The truck empty, they'd headed inland again, joining the big highway that swung past the international airport. Jerusalem had appeared in the late afternoon, back up in the mountains, necklaced with new towns, the sun lancing off the golden domes. They'd skirted the Old City to the north, Moshe taking the wrong turn, wedging the big truck into an interminable traffic jam that inched past the Damascus Gate. The noise had been beyond belief, bus drivers leaning on horns, taxi drivers abusing pedestrians, moneychangers shouting the odds on tight fistfuls of Jordanian dinars. Watching, McVeigh had marvelled at Moshe's nerve, the man losing patience with it all, wrenching the truck into a series of complex turns, ignoring the traffic and the insults, bullying his way back to the Bethlehem Road that wound around the dusty shoulder of the Old City.

South of Jerusalem, on the West Bank, the country had begun to change again, rolling barren hills dotted with olive trees, and now, minutes away from Bethlehem, McVeigh sat back, gazing out at the small stony fields, the donkeys laden with crops, the kids in the soft light of early evening, standing by the roadside, watching the truck roar by. The place was on a different scale to Israel, a smaller, wilder landscape, less productive, poorer, and McVeigh smiled, knowing at once that he infinitely preferred it.

They parked the truck in Manger Square, an acre or so of grimy bedlam in the middle of town. Moshe killed the engine, stretching his huge body behind the wheel and gazing out at the milling crowds of tourists.

'*Eretz Israel*,' he muttered, the contempt thickening his voice.

McVeigh glanced at Cela, not understanding, and she grinned. 'Greater Israel,' she explained. 'Moshe doesn't approve. He liked it before, better.'

'The way you were? Living on the border? In the kibbutz?'

'No. He'd keep the Golan. He likes that. It's all this he hates. He thinks the West Bank's . . .' She shrugged, looking at Moshe, trying to do him justice, putting a question to him in Hebrew. Moshe scowled and grunted, tipping his head towards a ragged queue of sweating pilgrims shuffling towards the Church of the Nativity. They looked American. Some of the women, overweight, wore T-shirts. Beneath a crude drawing of a spaced-out kid, one of the T-shirts said 'I Got Stoned On The West Bank'. Moshe grunted again, giving Cela the answer she needed, and she laughed, turning back to McVeigh, translating it for him. 'A pile of shit,' she said. 'That's what he thinks.'

They got out of the truck, Moshe carefully locking both doors. Parked cars ringed a fountain in the middle of the square. The fountain was dry. They began to pick their way through the cars. One side of the square was dominated by a police station. McVeigh looked at it for a moment. It was heavily fortified with razor wire and grenade screens, and the blue and white Israeli flag hung limply from the top of a recently painted flag-pole. There were armed troops on guard outside. They had visors on their helmets, and they carried sub-machine-guns and the bigger Galil carbines, and they moved slowly back and fourth, eyes flicking constantly left and right, alert, watchful, unsmiling. Belfast, McVeigh thought, following Cela towards a small restaurant wedged between two souvenir shops.

Inside, the restaurant was crowded. There was a smell of cooking oil and cheap tobacco. Cela paused briefly, looking for a face she knew, raising a hand to a small neat man sitting by himself at a table at the back of the room. The man got up. He was wearing a dark suit, and the white shirt beneath was open at the neck. He nodded at Cela and extended a hand. He looked older than he probably was, early thirties perhaps, and he had the measured, slightly grave air of someone used to authority. Cela spoke to him briefly in Arabic, and gestured towards McVeigh. McVeigh stepped forward, shaking the man's hand. His skin was a dark olive colour. He had black, curly hair, greying perceptibly at the temples. He bowed, a neat, formal bow, and pulled out a seat at the table. McVeigh glanced at Cela, gesturing towards the seat, but Cela shook her head, her eyes still on the Arab, completing the introductions.

'Amer Tahoul,' she said. 'He's happy to speak to you in English.'

*

'Yes,' she said. 'That's him.'

Laura sat in the sunshine in the big picture window, fingering the small colour photograph. The man across the table wore the blue uniform of the Schutzpolizei. Thick-set, crop-haired and coldly formal, he'd been sitting in the white BMW police car when they'd arrived at the Dreisen. Emery had seen him at once, stepping out of the cab, surprised that the enquiry was still in the hands of the local constabulary. The Polizeichef had crossed the road and introduced himself, offering Laura a curt bow of welcome, addressing her by name. Now, cold as ever, he looked her in the eye.

'You're certain?'

'Sure.' She shrugged, still looking at the photo. 'He's my husband. I bought him that jacket. It's his favourite colour.'

'And your name's Telemann? Frau Telemann?'

'Yes.'

'So why was your husband using the name Lacey? Why did he call himself that?'

Laura shrugged again, looking helplessly at Emery. Emery was sitting beside her, his back to the window, inscrutable as ever. He'd phoned ahead from the airport at Frankfurt when they'd landed, half-past six in the morning, trying to confirm the arm's-length arrangement he'd made on the secure telex from Washington. The guy he was due to meet was still at home, probably in bed, but the duty clerk at Intelligence HQ in Bonn had agreed a provisional rendezvous at the Hotel Dreisen in time for lunch. The guy's name was Franz Stauckel. He worked for the Bundesamt für Verfassungsschutz, the Republic's front-line agency against terrorism. Emery knew him from way back, a friendship nurtured at a series of international conferences. He had excellent contacts and a mordant sense of humour. He'd been briefed on the Assali shooting, and he'd understand at once what was required. Unlike this man.

Emery reached for the photograph. The damage was worse than he'd thought. In his real name, Ron had left his US passport, his Maryland driving licence, and what looked like a sheaf of credit cards. Offhand, Emery couldn't think of a rule he hadn't broken.

'Herr Telemann is a very private individual,' he murmured, looking up at the Polizeichef. 'He often goes to some lengths to protect that privacy.'

'He's a friend of yours?'

'Yes.'

'What do you do?'

'Me?'

'Yes.'

Emery smiled thinly, knowing there was no point in playing games. The answer was there on the table, the grey plastic card that gave Ron Telemann access to the big car park out at Langley.

'I work for the Government,' he said. 'In Washington.'

'Doing what?'

'Office work.' He shrugged. 'Nothing to get excited about.'

The German looked at him for a moment, and Emery wondered quite where the interview was headed. He'd spent most of the flight worrying about Sullivan. The vehemence of his reaction to the news from Bad Godesburg had shaken him, and for the first time he was beginning to wonder about the real status of the 'F' Street operation. What had started life as a sensibly covert enquiry was fast developing into something far more political. To date, at Sullivan's insistence, he'd successfully insulated the operation from every other arm of government. Officially, the set-up on 'F' Street didn't even exist, a phenomenon known in the bureaucracies as 'ghosting', but when things went wrong, ghosting could give you real problems, and the man in the immaculate blue uniform was currently one of them.

Emery smiled, reaching for his cup again, lightly conversational. 'I thought the investigation had been handed over to the BfV,' he said. 'That was my understanding.'

The Polizeichef shook his head. 'A man was shot dead yesterday,' he said. 'Shooting people is against the law.'

'Of course, but—' Emery shrugged '—sometimes these things are more complex than they seem.' He smiled benignly at the Polizeichef, recognizing at once that he'd made a mistake, questioning his relevance, suggesting that there were areas of public order to which he had no access. He reached for Laura's hand, changing the subject, trying a new tack. 'Mrs Telemann is naturally worried about her husband,' he said. 'She wants to find him.'

'So do we.'

'She has reasons to be anxious about his health. That's why we're here.'

'Oh?'

Emery glanced sideways at Laura, seeking confirmation, and she nodded. The policeman leaned forward, openly sceptical. 'You think he's sick?'

'I think he may be.'

'But why would he disappear?'

'I don't know.'

Laura shrugged, turning a little in the chair and staring sightlessly out of the window. She'd sat awake in the plane all night, no conversation, accepting the barest mouthful of shrimp salad from the four-course Executive Class dinner. Now, her face grey with fatigue, she seemed to have lost interest in the exchange.

Emery returned to the Polizeichef. 'You're looking for Herr Telemann?'

'Of course.' The policeman nodded at the table. 'We have his photograph. His details. Both passports. The photograph will be circulated. People here read the papers, watch television . . .' He offered Laura a thin smile. 'It's simply a matter of time.'

Laura looked at him briefly, saying nothing, and Emery marvelled at how quickly the incident had got out of control. Ron's face at every street corner, Uncle Sam on the rampage. He reached for his cup again, wondering what Sullivan would make of it all, then there was a hand on his shoulder, the familiar squeeze, the smell of Dutch cigars, and he looked up, recognizing Stauckel at once, a big, untidy man, leather jacket, full beard, reddish hair, a face weathered by overtime and alcohol. Emery got to his feet, accepting the damp, meaty handshake, introducing Laura. Franz Stauckel beamed at her, one of life's optimists, ignoring the uniformed Polizeichef. 'Welcome,' he said in perfect English.

Laura nodded. 'Hi,' she said.

There was a brief pause while Stauckel summoned the waiter, then he was sitting down with them, sifting through Telemann's documents, helping himself. The Polizeichef watched him for a minute or two, then stood up and said something brisk in German. Stauckel shook his head, contemptuous, dismissing the point, and when the two men got up and left the room

Emery could see them outside, in the ante-room, arguing. The waiter arrived with a large bottle of schnapps. The Polizeichef turned on his heel, storming towards the street, and Stauckel was suddenly back with them, dispensing the schnapps, raising his glass. They drank to Telemann's health – Stauckel's innocent toast – and Laura found herself looking quickly away, out at the long barges on the river, while the two men drained the glasses and Stauckel's hand reached for the bottle again. By the time Laura was back with them, her eyes dry, the documents on the table had gone. She looked at Emery, the question plain on her face, and he smiled back, nodding at the brief-case he'd left on the floor.

'How come?' she said. 'How come you could get rid of the guy like that?'

Stauckel leaned back in his chair, legs outspread, dismissing the question with a massive shrug, telling her that the man was a fool, a prisoner of his uniform. The problem with the shooting was the lack of evidence. Responsibility, in the first place, lay with the Schupo, the local police, and although everyone knew that Assali's death was the work of the Israelis, they hadn't left a single clue worth the name. On the contrary, the only firm lead was the American, Lacey, and the discovery that his name was an alias made his involvement doubly significant. For the time being, Stauckel had been able to outrank the Polizeichef and reclaim the documentation, but he knew the reprieve he'd won was only temporary. The locals would be back, probably within hours, and at that point anything might happen.

At this, Stauckel roared with laughter, lifting his glass, emptying it, telling Emery that the uniformed guys had a lot to get off their chests, that they hated the BfV, and that the Assali affair might just become the battle that would decide the war. The only sure way of stopping the investigation in its tracks would be an intervention from the Ministry of the Interior in Bonn, and there was, to date, no sign of that.

Emery nodded, listening, then leaned forward, offering his own perspective, nothing too specific but enough to make Stauckel understand the delicacy of his position, the prisoner of an operation so covert that it bypassed every known channel.

Stauckel listened to him with a quite different expression, intent, thoughtful, curious. At the end of it he leaned across, patting Emery on the shoulder, settling back into his chair. He'd dealt with politicians all his life. Their intentions were awful. Their manners were worse. Sensible men had nothing to do with them.

'So how do you feel?' he said finally.

Emery pulled a long face, swallowing the last of the schnapps. 'Abandoned,' he said.

Laura, listening, nodded. 'Sure,' she said quietly. 'Just like Ron.'

*

Telemann sat on the balcony, enjoying the midday sun, watching a young couple in a rowing boat sculling slowly across the Aussenalster. The girl sat in the stern, a plump white dot, while the boy pulled manfully on the oars. His right arm was stronger than his left, and the boat described endless wide circles on the blue water, getting nowhere.

The big french doors to the lounge opened, and Inge stepped out. They'd been back in Hamburg for a day and a half now, and she hadn't left the apartment once, staying with Telemann, cooking him meals he didn't want, washing his clothes, watching him across the lounge when he sat in front of the television, half-asleep. Telemann recognized this new life for what it was, a benign form of imprisonment, but for the time being he was content to accept it. Given the tracks he'd left at the Dreisen – one passport lodged at reception, another abandoned in his room – he knew he'd be a sitting target the moment he stepped back into the street. Better, on balance, to retire for a while, up-wind, out of sight, waiting for the moment when he knew he'd have to make a decision.

Inge settled on the balcony, sitting on a rug on the warm concrete, her back against the door. Around midday, she sunbathed out here, naked except for a pair of briefs, her face tipped up, her eyes closed, a long glass of mineral water at her side.

Telemann reached for the glass and took a sip of the water. He was still watching the rowing-boat.

'That stuff you told me about Wulf,' he said thoughtfully.

'The affair you had. Your son. Nikki. How much of it was true?'

Inge opened one eye. They hadn't discussed Wulf since Bad Godesburg. In fact, they hadn't discussed anything.

'Why?' she said. 'Why do you ask?'

'Because I don't believe you.'

She smiled, not answering for a moment, her eyes closed again. 'No?' she said at last.

Telemann glanced round at her. 'You told me lies about the Dreisen. About Assali. So why should I believe you? Tell me. I'm interested.'

'I didn't tell you about the Dreisen. Nathan told you about the Dreisen.' She shrugged, reaching for the glass. 'So maybe he lied. Not me.'

'OK.' Telemann nodded. 'You and Wulf then. Easy question.'

'What?'

'Prove it.'

'Prove what?'

'Prove you ever knew the man. Even met him.'

Inge looked at him over the glass, saying nothing. Then she got up and disappeared into the lounge. When she came back she was carrying a small wooden box. She sat down on the rug again, the box beside her. She took the lid off and scooped out a handful of photos. The photos were all the same size, four by six, colour. Telemann watched as she began to riffle through them, smiling from time to time. Then he reached forward, his hand outstretched, wanting to see them.

She glanced up. 'You know what he looks like? Otto?'

Telemann nodded. Everyone knew what Wulf looked like. Everyone who read newspapers or magazines. Everyone who'd ever queued at a news-stand, or sat in a dentist's waiting-room. Even in the States.

'Yeah,' he said. 'I know what he looks like.'

Inge laughed, handing him a pile of photos, watching them spill across his lap. Telemann glanced down. The top photo showed a side-view of a large, middle-aged man, tanned, muscular, overweight. He was kneeling on a bed. He was naked. The shaft of a huge erection disappeared into Inge's backside. She was kneeling in front of him, her face turned towards the camera, her eyes closed, her mouth open. Her hands were outstretched, the knuckles white, gripping the rail on top of the bedhead. Telemann recognized the pattern of the wallpaper, the colour of the dressing-gown hung on the back of the door. Her dressing-gown. Her bedroom. He picked up the top photo and looked at the one underneath. Same bedroom, same camera angle, Wulf on his back this time, Inge straddling him, her bum in his face, her mouth and hands wrapped around him. He went on through the pile, the camera angles changing, front shots, back shots, Wulf doing the whole repertoire, every conceivable orifice, a man who never once appeared to smile. Some of the shots looked like snaps from a picnic, the bed littered with discarded fruit and empty bottles of wine and open tubs of yoghurt, spoonfuls of the stuff dripping down Inge's belly, a feast for the hungry industrialist. In some of the other shots, blood was evident on the sheets. Telemann held one up, Inge on her back, her legs apart, each ankle strapped to a post at the foot of the bed. Between her legs, the sheet was puddled with blood, a deep rich scarlet, and Wulf was kneeling beside her, limp for once, his eyes on the television in the corner.

Telemann, revolted, showed her the picture. 'Whose idea?' he said.

She looked at it for a moment, her face quite blank. 'Mine,' she said.

'You *enjoy* that?'

'Yes.'

'Did he?'

She smiled at him, sympathetic, indulging his ignorance. 'Of course,' she said.

Telemann nodded, packing the photos up, returning them to the box. 'You got the place fitted?' he said. 'The bedroom?'

'Yes.'

'I counted three cameras.'

'Four. One never worked.'

'He knew about these?' He gestured at the prints.

'Of course not.'

Telemann nodded, thinking of the set-up again, the trouble

they must have gone to, the Mossad boys, the technical people, installing the cameras.

'Neat,' he said. 'They still there? The cameras?'

'Of course.'

'Working?'

'Yes.'

Telemann nodded again, wondering what his own snaps would look like, where they'd end up, the girl on his face, Uncle Sam well and truly fucked. He shook his head, part wonder, part admiration, part disgust.

'What about the rest of it?' he said at last. 'Did you feel anything for him? Was that true?'

'No.' She shrugged. 'He was good in bed but . . . no.'

'What about him? Was he in love with you?'

'In love with me? The man was an animal.' She shrugged again. 'We fucked a lot. That's all.'

Telemann nodded. 'Sure,' he said.

He looked away, out across the lake. The wind had risen a little and the water was feathered with white caps. Of the rowing-boat there was no sign.

'But didn't he wonder?' he said at last, lifting the photo in his lap, giving it back. 'Exposing himself like that? Taking those kinds of risks?'

Inge shook her head, accepting the photo, putting it back in the box. 'No,' she said, 'why should he? I was a nice German girl. I had a big appetite. A good body. I'd do anything he wanted.' She paused for a moment, fingering the lid on the box. 'He was quite protective in a way. And generous too. He bought the apartment for me. And clothes. And holidays. Anything I wanted. Money was never a problem. It was his way of saying thank you.'

'For what?' Telemann gazed at her. 'For looking after his dick?'

'Yes.' She paused. 'You should remember something about people like Otto. They're often very naïve. Very single-minded. That's why they're so successful. They don't waste time on the difficult things. They don't waste time thinking. They just do it. Get on with it and do it. That's why they get to the top.' She paused again, frowning. 'That's the way Otto was. I told you. The man was an animal. He chased and chased. He never stopped. Not once.'

'So I see.'

'Do you?'

Telemann nodded. 'Yes,' he said.

There was a long silence. Inge was still looking at him, still frowning.

'One thing . . .' she said at last.

'What?'

'Didn't you notice?'

'Notice what?'

She nodded at the wooden box. 'There's a television in the room,' she said.

'I know.'

'Maybe you ought to look at the photos again.'

Telemann gazed at her, not understanding, then he reached for the box and sorted quickly through the photos until he found one with a clear view of the television. Wulf, in the foreground, was sound asleep, flat on his back, his head turned slightly to one side. Inge was sprawled over him, her head in his crotch, her eyes closed. Telemann peered at the photo. The curtains were drawn, and the room was darker than usual, and the image on the television was quite clear. A reporter was standing on a stretch of tarmac, addressing the camera. In the background, neatly echeloned away from the camera, was a line of F-15 fighter-bombers. There were at least ten of them, receding into the distance. Telemann recognized the yellows and sand-browns of the distinctive desert camouflage, and when he looked harder he could pick up the shapes of the ground-crews, bent over the bomb trollies, arming the sleek jets. Telemann nodded, putting a name to the location at last, Dharan Air Base, Saudi Arabia, America standing tall. He looked up. 'That's last week,' he said slowly.

'The week before last.'

'NBC guy.'

'CNN.'

'Yeah.' He nodded. 'CNN.'

He looked at her for a moment, letting it sink in, the implications, the truth.

'He left you a year ago,' he said slowly. 'Wulf.'

'Yes.' She nodded. 'And then he came back.'

'Why?'

She looked at him, that same slow curl of the lip, an expression close to pity. 'Why do you think?' she said at last.

Telemann nodded, his eyes back on the box. 'You still see him?'

'Yes.'

'Regularly?'

'Yes.'

'Soon?'

She didn't answer, but smiled at him, her head tilting back again, her face in the sun, her eyes closed. Telemann studied her for a long time, thinking of the trip to the East.

'The night we went to Halle,' he said slowly. '*Was* that your mother?'

'No.'

'Who was she?'

'A plant. A phoney. Like me.'

'And Nikki?'

'Nathan's boy.' She opened one eye, smiling. 'We took the photo on the beach. At Netanya.'

'Netanya?'

'It's a holiday place. North of Tel Aviv.'

Telemann nodded, looking away, hearing the pieces falling slowly into place, a rattle in some distant outpost of what used to be his brain.

'You did well.' He mimed applause. 'Academy Award.' He glanced down at the box again, the lid half-closed, Otto Wulf contemplating yet another fuck. 'So what about the chemicals?' he said finally. 'Littmann? Jaegermeister? How much of all that is true?'

Inge said nothing, her face still tilted up towards the sun. Then she opened one eye, pushing the box towards him with her foot.

'Help yourself,' she said. 'For these he'll tell you anything.'

*

The old man, Abu Yussuf, found the letters in the boy's room.

He'd been back in the apartment for less than an hour. He'd been looking for money, knowing that he had to get away. They'd find the boy in the woods. They'd trace where he lived, here, back in Newark. And then they'd come calling.

The old man knelt by the grimy window. He'd been on his hands and knees all over the room, looking for the places the boy might have used. He'd torn up the linoleum, first one side of the room, then the other, knowing that the boy had been here already, the stuff brittle and broken round the edges, recent damage. At first he'd found nothing, just a thick, greasy layer of dirt, years old. Then, beneath the window, he'd seen the floorboard, the wood rotten from a leak around the sash. He'd fetched a knife from the kitchen, digging in around the edges, prising the floorboard out, his mind playing the usual games, hearing the boy's footsteps on the stairs, his whistle along the hall. The floorboard had come out at once. Underneath, he found something long and heavy, wrapped in oil-cloth, and a white plastic bag. In the oil-cloth was an automatic pistol. In the bag, with a couple of aerosols and a thick wad of 100-dollar notes, were the letters.

The old man sat back against the wall beside the window, gazing at the familiar script, the carefully shaped handwriting, hearing his wife's voice, remembering her patience and her smile. There were four letters. They'd all been opened, the gum carefully separated, probably by steam from the kettle. The old man peered at the postmarks, trying to read the dates, trying to get the letters in the right order. The first had been mailed three weeks ago, 2 September. He pulled out the letter, three thin sheets of air-mail paper, and began to read, his lips moving as he did so. Hala still missed him. Life was still hard. One of his two surviving sons had been taken by the Israelis. He'd gone to one of the military prisons after an incident with *Al Sawda*, the hated 'blackheads', the black-bereted paratroops who patrolled the streets of Ramallah on days when the authorities expected real trouble. He'd been gone now for three days, no word from the prison, and Hala had been to her brother, Amer Tahoul, asking for help, asked what she could do. The old man looked up, sweating in the heat, wondering why Amer hadn't mentioned it on the telephone. Maybe he was being kind, he thought, sparing me more trouble. Or maybe the boy's already been released.

He bent to the letter again, the second page. Hala was writing about someone else now, a visitor, a woman from Israel. The woman had come without warning or invitation. She'd simply appeared, the previous afternoon, a knock at the door. She was a young woman, pretty. She spoke Arabic well. She'd stayed for half an hour, maybe longer. She'd known Hala's name, and Abu Yussuf's name, and what had happened to their dead son. Hala had been frightened, knowing that the woman could only be from the Shin Beth, the Intelligence people, the Israeli's eyes and ears on the West Bank. And so she'd said nothing when the woman asked about Abu Yussuf, where he was, what he was doing, when he'd be back. The woman had asked the question twice, very sympathetic, very kind, but Hala hadn't been fooled. She knew that was one of the ways they did it, got their information, stole your secrets.

The old man looked up again, the letter at an end, remembering Amer on the phone, and his hand went to the other letters, eager to know what had happened to this strange Israeli visitor, the pretty girl from the Shin Beth. Had she come back? Had she asked more questions? What did she know?

Far away, towards the waterfront, a siren began to wail. It was a sound the old man had come to live with, but even now, after two months in New York, it still made him shiver. It had an animal quality, the tormented voice of this hot, hard city.

The old man got to his feet, the siren closer. He picked up the letters and the money, stuffing them both into the plastic bag. Halfway to the door, he paused, turning, eyeing the gun. He'd never used a gun in his life. He hated violence, what it did to people, how little it ever solved. But then he thought of the days and nights to come, what he might face, and he returned to the window, picking it up, surprised again at how heavy it was.

*

McVeigh frowned, spooning the last of the chick-peas into the envelope of pitta bread, not understanding.

'Al what?' he said.

'Al Kimawiya.'

'What's that?'

'The chemical.' Cela glanced at Amer Tahoul. 'It's the local name for Saddam's rockets. Everyone expects him to fire at Israel. The rockets have poison gas. They call it Al Kimawiya . . .' She smiled. 'The chemical.'

Amer Tahoul nodded. He'd been following the conversation carefully, sitting back in his chair, a cigarette between his fingers. 'That's why they sell us gas masks,' he said quietly.

'Who?'

'The Israelis. For ninety dollars you can buy a gas mask.'

'Do you have one?'

'No.'

'Too expensive?'

'No.'

'Why then?'

Amer shrugged, fingering the edge of the table. 'They don't work,' he said. 'They're old. The design is no good. In Israel, everyone gets a gas mask. The newest. The very best. And free, too. Here?' He offered Cela a smile. 'Here we pay to be gassed. Ninety dollars.' He looked at McVeigh. 'My friend, what kind of bargain is that?'

McVeigh pulled a face, lifting the pitta bread to his mouth, enjoying the sour, sharp taste of the yoghurt and the chick-peas. They'd been in the restaurant for more than an hour, the Palestinian musing about life on the West Bank, how much tougher things had been over the last three years, since the start of the Intifada. Himself, he'd always been a moderate. He worked for the Municipality up in Ramallah. He had an important job. He was Treasurer for the city. He had a lot of contact with the Israelis. He'd got to know some of them, even liked one or two. It was wrong what people said. There were good and bad on both sides, and one day, maybe, they'd all learn to live together. But now? He'd shaken his head, talking again about the *Intifada*, the uprising that had run like a fever through the West Bank. In the beginning, and always, control had been in the hands of the kids. They were the ones who'd known how to taunt the Israelis, how to provoke the violence and the reprisals. They were young, these kids, and they were wise. They understood the power of television pictures: of men and women choking on the streets of Ramallah, of school-kids facing fixed bayonets, of universities closed down, water supplies diverted, houses bulldozed, land seized. Thanks to the kids, it was up there, on the world's agenda, a menu with prices, but still – he'd shrugged – nothing happened.

Listening, McVeigh had warmed to the man at once, the distinctions he made, the careful qualifications, the lack of malice, his quiet sense of humour. Recently, he said, the situation had worsened, both sides going to the limit, refusing to compromise. More and more settlers were pouring in from Israel, grabbing land, putting up houses, fencing themselves in behind dogs, and security lights, and thick coils of barbed wire, concentration camps of their own making. The Americans, of course, were wringing their hands, and issuing declarations, and demanding fair play, but the Israelis spoke a different language, the language of facts, and the facts were there for all to see: a police state, taxed and controlled from Jerusalem, an ugly snarl on the face of *Eretz Israel*. McVeigh had nodded, impressed with the man's quiet passion, asking about the kids again, what they could possibly do, and Amer had nodded, accepting McVeigh's point with a tired smile, confirming the obvious truth of it, that violence bred violence, that the kids had lost patience, that events were fast running out of control.

McVeigh leaned forward, aware of Cela watching him, still unsure quite what they were doing here, mid-evening, a smoky restaurant in the middle of Bethlehem.

'How?' he said. 'How are they running out of control?'

The Palestinian looked at him for a moment, a slight man, prematurely stooped, with elegant hands and an expression of almost infinite patience.

'The kids want to take the war to the Israelis. They want

guns, explosives, anything they can get. They're bored by the rest of it.' He smiled. 'Words don't count any more. Not really.'

McVeigh nodded, trying to follow the argument. His knowledge of Middle Eastern politics was far from complete. 'The PLO?' he said. 'Arafat?'

Amer shook his head. 'The kids think he's a joke. They've no time for him. They think he's gone soft. Too much *barrani*. Too much sitting on his backside in the office. No . . .' He shook his head. 'Arafat isn't the answer. Not to them.'

'And you?' McVeigh smiled. 'What do you think?'

Amer looked at him, returning the smile, not answering, then he turned to Cela and spoke quickly in Arabic. Cela nodded, looking at her watch. Moshe had left the restaurant half an hour ago, wolfing a plate of lamb stew and going back outside to guard the lorry.

Cela got to her feet. 'Moshe's got to move,' she said. 'They clear the square at nine.' She disappeared towards the street, threading her way between the crowded tables.

Amer ordered coffee from the waiter, then turned back to McVeigh. 'You know how many kids we've lost since '87?' he said.

McVeigh shook his head. 'No.'

'Over a thousand. A *thousand*.' He paused. 'And you know who killed nearly half of them?'

'No.'

'We did. Our people did. Because they thought some of these kids were *ameel*, traitors, collaborators. That's what the Israelis have done to us.' He paused again. 'We live under occupation. The Israelis treat us the way the Nazis treated the French. We have identity cards. Road-blocks. Curfews. They arrest us without charge and imprison us without trial. There's *t'azeeb*, too. Torture. That's why the kids in the street are singing for Saddam Hussein . . .' He shrugged. 'But you know why I hate the Israelis? Why I really hate them? Because of what they've done to us, to the way we live. No one trusts anyone any more. Trust has gone. The Israelis have taken it away and buried it.' He leaned back in the chair, nodding quietly, the same careful tone of voice, the same quiet smile. 'Has she told you about my sister? My sister's son?'

'Who?'

'Cela.'

'No.'

Amer nodded, leaning forward again. 'My sister has three children. All sons. Her name is Hala. One of the sons was taken by the Israelis. I forget why. They do it all the time. He went to prison for a while. A month, I think. Maybe longer. Then he came out. They released him. They set him free . . .' He gestured with his hand, opening it. 'My sister is delighted. The boy is OK. Not too much torture. Not too much *t'azeeb* . . .' He paused. 'Two weeks go by. Everything is fine. Then the boy is taken away again, one night, the *moharebbin* this time, our people, my people, *Intifada* people . . .'

'And?'

Amer hesitated for a moment, looking at McVeigh, visibly angry now. 'He was killed. Tied to a car and dragged up and down the street, and killed. It's a form of punishment. Our people do it all the time. They call it justice.'

McVeigh stared at him, imagining it, up and down the road, bone and bare flesh.

'Why?' he said at last. 'Why was he killed?'

'I don't know. Nobody knows. Some people will say one thing. Some another. But that's the truth of it. Nobody knows. And soon, nobody will care.' He paused, shrugging. 'So . . . we kill each other and nobody cares. That's what the Israelis have done to us. That's where we are.'

McVeigh nodded, sitting back, making room for the coffees on the table. Amer didn't move. He was looking away, out into the restaurant, preoccupied. McVeigh eased one of the coffees towards him.

'What about the mother?' he said. 'Your sister?'

'She was in prison, too.'

'Then?'

'Now. The last three weeks.'

'And?'

Amer turned his head, looking McVeigh in the eye for a moment. Then he shrugged, a gesture close to defeat.

'She's dead,' he said. 'She died yesterday. In prison. That's why I'm here. That's what I came to tell Cela.'

*

Laura lay on the bed, staring at the window, rehearsing the scene yet again.

He'd come soon, she knew it. He'd appear unannounced, walking in from the street or along the hotel corridor, a face at the table in the restaurant, a knock at the bedroom door, the big grin, the hug, the restlessness stilled for as long as it took to say 'hi', and catch up on the news, the kids, the house. He'd tell her how pretty she looked, how much he'd missed her, and the compliments would be all the warmer for being genuine.

It wouldn't rest there. It never did. They'd say their hallos properly, share a night's rest, and then there'd be the challenge of yet another day, a brand-new sheet of paper torn from the Book of Life. She smiled, thinking about it, the innocence of the man, his appetite, his energy, the brightness of the crayons in his box. That was why she'd loved him from the start, knowing how rare it was to find someone so utterly uncorrupted, so completely loyal. That was why she'd married him, tried so hard to bear his children. That was what she was doing here now, trying to buffer him from the shock, explaining what would really happen.

She turned over, reaching for the glass of water at the bedside, hearing Emery pacing up and down the room next door. His phone had been ringing all afternoon, long conversations, on and on. She marvelled at his stamina, knowing he hadn't slept on the flight, sensing how complex his problems had become. Like Ron, he never discussed his work with her, and like with Ron, she never asked.

She swallowed the last of the water and lay back on the bed, closing her eyes. Later, around midnight, she'd phone home. The older kids would be back from high school, six o'clock in the evening. It was a new experience for them, her not being there, and she wasn't sure how her sister would cope. Evenings with Bree were seldom easy, and if the child was upset by the change of routine, then it would be doubly difficult. She smiled again as she remembered Bree's parting words as she stepped into the cab for Dulles Airport.

'Daddy,' she'd said. 'Tell Daddy to come home.'

*

In the end, it was Inge's suggestion to make the phone call.

Wulf had a number of addresses. The family home was in Berlin, a handsome eighteenth-century house in its own grounds near the Tegeler See, but he had three other properties dotted around the Republic. Weekdays normally found him in Dusseldorf, where he'd recently established a major presence, and Inge had the number of the penthouse flat on top of the new offices where he spent most evenings. If Telemann was serious, if he needed to meet Otto Wulf, then she would telephone and arrange it. Doing it himself, phoning direct, would be a waste of time. Wulf led a tightly organized life, protected by secretaries and a punishing schedule. Personal introductions were *absolut notwendig*.

Telemann agreed to the arrangement with two stipulations. She wasn't to use his name, and she wasn't to go into any kind of detail. He was to be a visting American, the friend of a friend, a man with a business proposition about which she knew nothing. Inge, listening, shook her head. Wulf never mixed business with pleasure. People with propositions took their turn through the normal channels. No favours. No short-cuts. It was an iron rule and he never broke it. If Telemann was to use the relationship, to take advantage of it, then the pitch had to be a great deal more intimate than that.

Telemann shrugged. 'So what do you suggest?' he said. 'I date the guy?'

Inge knelt beside him, pouring a beer. Outside it was raining, early evening, a hard, steel-grey sky. Inge emptied the last of the beer and stood up. Excitement suited her.

'You're in love with me,' she announced. 'You're crazy about me. You want me. You need to talk to him about it. Man to man. Face to face. *Ja*?'

'You're nuts.'

'No.' She shook her head. 'I'll tell him we've talked about it, you and me. You know everything because I've told you everything. You know about him. You know he comes here. You know the things we do together, how close we are. You know everything. And so now it's time for you both to talk.'

'And what about you? What do you say?'

'Me?'

'Yeah.'

'I tell him the same. I confirm it all. I tell him it's very difficult. I tell him something's got to be done.'

'And he'll see me? Because of that?'

'No.' She laughed. 'He'll want to see you because I'll tell him you're great in bed. He won't believe it. No one's better in bed than he is. So—' she shrugged '—he'll have to see you. Then you're on your own.'

'Thanks.'

'My pleasure.' She looked pointedly at the phone and Telemann nodded, as helpless as ever, hoping his German could cope with the next few minutes. He needed to follow the conversation, be at least half-convinced that he wasn't, once again, being set up. The plan had the sole merit of getting him close to Wulf. After that, as she rightly said, he was on his own.

She dialled a number from memory, reaching for a cigarette from a pack in her bag. After a while, the number answered. Telemann heard a deep voice on the other end, sonorous, beautifully modulated. Inge smiled, murmuring a minor obscenity, provoking a rich bark of laughter. They talked for a while about nothing of any consequence, easy chatter, the tip of a real relationship, and Telemann found himself wondering about the rest of the iceberg, just how possible it might be to share that much time in bed and not establish at least the beginnings of something deeper.

At length, behind a cloud of smoke, Inge said she had a problem. She explained it briefly, matter-of-fact, this other guy, good-looking, funny, hot in bed, a chance encounter turning rapidly into something else. The way she put it, her language, her tone of voice, she might have been talking about the plumbing. She stopped, listening intently, watching Telemann across the room. Then she nodded, frowning, her voice a little higher, a shrillness Telemann hadn't heard before.

'*Warum?*' she said. 'Why?'

She bent to the phone again, listening to his answer, visibly annoyed. 'You think I'm lying? Is that it? You . . .'

She broke off, shrugging, not bothering to complete the sentence, the point made. Telemann heard Wulf at the other end, his voice low, that same rich laugh, and he watched her face soften again, pacified. She reached down for her bag, opening it, sorting quickly through it. Then she bent to the phone again. 'The perfume,' she said. 'L'Orphée. OK?'

Telemann heard Wulf grunt assent, then Inge was blowing wet kisses down the phone, bringing the conversation to an end. The phone back on the floor, she looked up. 'Tomorrow night,' she said. 'He'll see you at eight o'clock.'

'Where?'

'Dusseldorf.'

Telemann nodded. 'And the Orphée?' he said, looking at the bag. 'The perfume?'

Inge's face clouded for a moment, then she shrugged. 'He's a very careful man,' she said. 'You have to take something from me. Something that proves it's you. I said the perfume.' She shrugged again. 'And he said yes.'

12

The old man, Abu Yussuf, looked at his watch again, knowing that he musn't leave it too late. Nine hours, he thought. Ramallah is nine hours ahead. He checked the watch a second time, half-past five in the evening, the traffic pouring out of New York City, a breaking wave of automobiles all round him, flooding up the Connecticut Turnpike towards Rhode Island.

Beside him, in a bag on the seat, was the money he'd taken from the cache in the boy's room. He'd counted it between stop-lights, inching across Manhattan Island. In all, he had 16,000 dollars. For the last hour, he'd been looking at the big billboards along the turnpike, checking the room rates in the motels. His needs were modest: a bed, a lock on the door, a telephone. Sixty dollars would buy him all three, with change for a meal. If he had to, if there was no other way, he could live like that for months.

He saw another sign up ahead, half a mile before the next exit. Ramada Inns. Sixty-eight dollars. He checked the mirror, signalling right, knowing that the last thing he could afford was a traffic accident. If he was shunted from behind, even a minor blow, the tank could unseat, rupturing the pipework, spilling the liquid inside, releasing the deadly vapour. He shuddered, imagining the consequences, somewhere busy, women and children on the sidewalk, his mind's eye returning again and again to the horses belly-up in the paddock, and the body of the boy sprawled amongst the leaves. If the stuff in the tank could do that, he thought, then an accidental spill could kill hundreds. Thousands. His hand reached across to the bag, feeling inside, finding the two aerosols. These too, he thought. These too I must guard.

The motel, when he found it, was brand-new, the contractors

still tidying a corner of the car park. The old man checked in, ticking 'Cash' on the registration form, leaving a 100-dollar deposit with the clerk behind the desk. When he asked her about the phones, whether he could call abroad, she nodded and gave him a small booklet with the international codes and asked him to double the deposit. He did so gladly, peeling off the notes, returning the booklet, telling her he knew the number already. No problem, she agreed, eyeing the white plastic bag as the old man shuffled away down the corridor.

The room was huge, over-chilled, curtained from the sun by a thick blue drape. The old man sat on the bed, the white plastic bag between his feet, punching out the numbers on the phone. The number began to ring. The old man peered at the bedside clock in the gloom, trying to calculate the time in Ramallah, coming up with several different answers, all of them way past midnight. Finally, the number answered. It was a woman's voice. Hala's sister. Amer's wife. She sounded half-asleep.

'It's me,' he said. 'Abu Yussuf. I want to talk to Amer. It's urgent. Hurry.'

'He's not here.'

'No?'

'No. He's away in Bethlehem.'

'Oh.'

The old man blinked, suddenly close to panic. He'd begun to rely on these calls, being able to find Amer at the end of a phone. It was a real comfort. It was like having him in the next room, a conversation he could stop and start at will, sixteen thousand dollars in his pocket, America full of telephones. The old man shook his head, hearing Amer's wife again, asking what he wanted, where he was, how she could help. Amer would be back, she said, back very soon. The old man nodded, muttering his thanks.

'Tell him I called,' he said. 'Tell him I've done what he said.'

*

Peter Emery sat in a corner of the bar at the Hotel Dreisen, half-past ten at night, listening to Stauckel spell it out. The German had been back from Bonn for nearly an hour, ample time to clarify the worst of the news from the Ministry of the

Interior. He'd been pushing all day to get the Assali investigation transferred to the BfV, but after a series of shouting matches and a meeting with the Deputy Minister, the answer – emphatically – had been no.

Emery sat back in his chair, his head against the wood panelling. 'Why?' he said again. 'Just tell me why.'

Stauckel eyed the glass of schnapps Emery had ordered for him from the waiter. So far, he hadn't touched it.

'I don't know,' he said finally. 'I guess it's political.'

'We know it's political. These things are always political. That's why it was a reasonable request. What do the Schupo know about the Middle East? The Palestinians? Peace talks? Mossad?'

'Nothing. But that's not the point.'

'No?'

'No. There's bad blood just now. Bonn and Washington. Baker's been round with the begging-bowl. He came last week. He's due again soon. He wants serious money. He thinks we owe him.'

Emery smiled, fingering the glass of lager at his elbow. US Secretary of State James Baker was criss-crossing the world, raising funds for the Gulf War. It was an interesting proposition, hatched in the White House. You pay. We fight. Emery raised the glass to his lips.

'Maybe you do,' he said quietly. 'Maybe you do owe him.'

'Yeah.' Stauckel nodded. 'And maybe we don't.' He paused. 'You know how much the East has cost us? To date?'

'Millions.'

'Double it.'

'Billions.'

'Closer.'

Emery lifted an eyebrow. 'Really?'

'Yes. And that's just the hors d'oeuvre. The main course is real money. Trillions of Deutschmarks. The way I see it, we end up paying everyone. Even the Russians. So—' he shrugged '—why should we sign up for the Gulf? Pay for your wars as well?'

Emery looked at him. 'Are you serious?'

Stauckel nodded. 'Yes,' he said. 'And so is Bonn. Since you ask.' He paused. 'The Schupo want your friend. They think he has some questions to answer. They believe they have a right to find him.'

Stauckel shrugged again and looked away, his face quite expressionless. There was a function in the ballroom next door, a big formal party to celebrate a wedding, and couples kept drifting in and out of the bar. Emery had been watching them for most of the evening, handsome women, exquisitely dressed, good-looking young men, self-confident, monied, already successful. This was the Germany Emery read about weekly in the heavier Washington magazines. It was Otto Wulf's Germany, the Germany of the nineties, and watching the couples at the bar, listening to the music spilling in from the ballroom, it was impossible not to wonder where it all might end, this energy, this rude vigour. He looked across at Stauckel again, knowing in his heart that the man had tried his best, old debts, old favours.

'So what happens now?' he said. 'With our uniformed friends?'

'They've given it to the Kripo. The Kripo have issued a warrant.'

'What for?'

'Telemmann's arrest.'

Emery frowned, leaning forward. The Kripo were the plain-clothes version of the Schupo. They had an uncomfortable reputation for not giving up.

'Already?' he said.

Stauckel nodded. 'He's all they've got. Apart from the forensic on the Palestinian guy.'

'No witnesses?'

'No.'

'Just Ron?'

'Yes.'

Emery nodded, closing his eyes, running a tired hand over his face. The band next door were playing a march he vaguely recognized, the tempo adjusted for a vigorous quickstep. The bar had emptied in seconds.

'You know who he's after next?' he said quietly. 'Ron?'

Stauckel frowned. 'No,' he said. 'Who?'

'Wulf.'

'*Otto* Wulf?'

'Yes.'

Stauckel stared at him. The music was louder now, the band pushing the tempo even faster. 'Why?' he said. 'Why Wulf?'

'He think he's doing stuff with chemicals.'

'Who for?'

'The rag-heads.'

Stauckel nodded. 'Wulf does stuff with everybody,' he said. 'That's what he trades for power. That's why he's Otto Wulf.' He paused. 'What kind of chemicals?'

Emery looked at him, toying with the remains of his lager. So far, he'd told Stauckel very little about the Washington operation.

'Off the record?'

'Sure.'

'Nerve gas.'

Stauckel gazed at him. Then he shook his head, a quick, emphatic gesture. 'No,' he said flatly. 'Not nerve gas. Not Wulf. The man's got plans for himself. Why wreck them?'

Emery shrugged. 'You might be right,' he said. 'But it hardly matters. The point is Ron. Ron thinks Wulf's involved. And he might just go ask him.'

'He'd never get near him.'

Emery shrugged again. 'Fine,' he said. 'Then Wulf has no problems.' He paused, listening to the band driving hard for the finale. He could feel the floor shaking beneath him. 'What's that music?' he said at last.

Stauckel stared at him, still thinking about Otto Wulf. 'Sorry?'

'The music. The tune they're playing. What is it? Where does it come from?'

Stauckel listened for a moment, saving Wulf for later, reaching for his glass at last, his feet beginning to tap in time with the rhythm. Next door, the music came to an abrupt end, drowned in wild applause.

Emery looked at Stauckel. 'Well?' he said.

The German lifted his glass, a toast. He was smiling again.

'To Marshal Radetsky,' he said, 'our second favourite Austrian.'

*

Moshe saw the Army check-point first, 200 metres ahead, a shallow dip in the road, shadows with guns crouching in the ditch on either side. He began to brake at once, dropping down through the gear-box. Unladen, the big truck had been travelling at speed. At three in the morning, the roads were empty.

McVeigh, sitting by the door, glanced down at Cela. He could feel the tension in her body. She'd stiffened the moment she'd seen the road-block, the moment Moshe had gestured ahead into the darkness, cursing their luck.

The truck squealed to a halt. There was a metal contraption across the road, a metre wide, hinged, with spikes protruding upwards. Soldiers emerged from the roadside, their faces daubed with camouflage cream. They moved slowly, with great care, circling the truck, prodding recesses in the bodywork, making a note of registration, and McVeigh watched them, taking a professional interest, peering into the darkness, wondering exactly where they'd cited the support teams, the guys in the gunpits with the big M-60s. They were good, he could sense it, the way they covered each other, the state of their weapons. immaculately clean. Northern Ireland, he thought again. A quiet night in bandit country, down in South Armagh.

'What do they want?' he said.

Cela shook her head. 'It's routine,' she said. 'It happens all the time. Especially at night.' She shrugged. 'It's nothing.'

One of the soldiers approached the driving cab, signalling Moshe to get out. There was nothing to distinguish him from the rest, no badges of rank, but McVeigh guessed he was in charge. Moshe opened the door and jumped out. In the lights of the truck he cast a huge shadow. The soldier peered at him, making a gesture with his hand. Moshe fumbled in the breast-pocket of his shirt, giving him his identity card. The soldier studied it, saying something in Hebrew, glancing up at Cela and

McVeigh still sitting in the cab. Moshe nodded, walking back to the cab.

'He wants to see our ID,' Cela said quietly. 'Show him your passport.' McVeigh produced his passport from the bag at his feet. Cela hadn't moved.

'What about you?' he said. 'Your ID?'

'I haven't got any. I left it at the kibbutz.'

McVeigh looked at her. She was lying. He knew it. He'd seen her ID card in the restaurant. She'd opened her bag to pay for the meal. It was in there, beside her purse. The soldier was still looking up at them, gesturing for them to join Moshe. They did so, climbing down from the driving cab, standing in the warm darkness. The soldier said something in Hebrew, nodding at Cela, the whites of his eyes visible beneath the rim of his helmet. Cela began to talk to him in rapid Hebrew, using her hands a lot, shrugging. The soldier frowned, saying something sharp to Moshe when the big man stepped forward. Moshe glowered at him, not the least intimidated, then gestured at McVeigh. The soldier stared at McVeigh. McVeigh stared back.

'He's English,' Cela said. 'A friend from the kibbutz.'

The soldier nodded, asking McVeigh his name in broken English. McVeigh told him, offering his passport, spelling the name out, letter by letter, watching while he wrote it down. The soldier looked up at the truck a moment, then turned to another man behind him. The other man began to mutter into a radio. There was silence. The soldier was looking at Cela.

'What's your name?' he said.

'Cela.'

'Cela what?'

'Cela Eilath.'

He nodded, and fell silent again, waiting for some message or other. McVeigh looked at him, wondering why Cela had abandoned her married name, and ID card, and why something as routine as a road-block should have made her so anxious. There was a crackle from the darkness and the sound of a voice on the radio. The soldier listened, staring at the ground, then nodded, handing Moshe his ID card, gesturing mutely to a soldier beside him. The soldier bent to the metal spikes, folding them up, dragging them to one side, and Moshe glanced at McVeigh, jerking his head towards the truck.

Minutes later, bumping through the suburbs of Jerusalem, Moshe began to row with Cela, shouting at her over the roar of the big diesel, his right hand chopping up and down in the darkness. Cela said very little, a word here and there, a shrug, staring forward through the windscreen, her eyes never leaving the road.

Finally, past Jerusalem, the truck began to slow again. McVeigh could see a crossroads ahead. Beside the crossroads a car was parked. The truck coasted to a stop beside the car, and looking down, McVeigh recognized the face behind the wheel.

'Amer,' he said aloud.

The name provoked another gruff outburst from Moshe. He was stabbing the dashboard with his forefinger this time. Cela let him finish, then leant towards him, very quickly, planting a deft kiss on his cheek, murmuring something in his ear. Then she turned away, pushing McVeigh out of the truck. McVeigh jumped down to the road, catching Cela as she did the same. Amer was standing beside the car now, lighting a cigarette. McVeigh nodded at him, peering around. Beyond the road, he could see houses, white cubes in the darkness, dotted at random across the bare hillside. Behind them, a glow in the sky, was Jerusalem. He looked back at the truck. Moshe was revving the engine, making a final point, ignoring Cela's departing wave. He slipped the handbrake and roared away, a cloud of pungent diesel, a pair of red lights receding into the darkness. Soon he was gone, and a kind of silence returned, the chatter of insects at the roadside, the sigh of the wind through the tiny grove of olive trees immediately below them.

Cela was talking to Amer. She glanced back at McVeigh and signalled for him to get into the car. They drove after the truck, same direction, then pulled left at the next junction. Soon they were back in the outskirts of a town, flat-roofed houses in stony orchards, areas of wasteland littered with wrecked cars and abandoned fridges, a half-built block of apartments, a hand-painted sign in Arabic hanging drunkenly from one of the scaffolding poles. Amer slowed at a traffic light and indicated left. He and Cela had been talking in the front of the car, their voices low. The car slowed again, then stopped outside a small, flat-roofed house.

Cela glanced round, unsmiling. 'Come with us,' she said.

McVeigh got out, joining them on the street. Across the road, graffiti reached 7 feet up the store-front shutters. Black paint, spray-canned. Amer ground his cigarette out on the pavement and led the way to the front door. He knocked twice, then knocked again. The door opened at once, a small woman, young. She was wearing a T-shirt and jeans. She looked exhausted. Amer kissed her on both cheeks and said something in Arabic. She nodded, standing aside, inviting Cela and McVeigh into the house with a tired smile. Amer stayed on the doorstep, a few more words of Arabic, then turned and left.

McVeigh followed Cela into a small, low-ceilinged room at the back of the house. There was a table and two small chairs and a sofa in brown vinyl, covered with embroidered cushions. A man sat on the arm of the sofa watching a television in the corner. There was a football match on the television and an empty video-box lying beside it on the floor. McVeigh smiled, recognizing the label on the box. 'Great Wembley Finals' it said. 'Pick of the FA Cup'. Billy had one, exactly the same. The man on the sofa glanced up. He looked the same age as the woman, late twenties. He was wearing an old sweat-shirt over a pair of jeans. His feet were bare. He nodded at McVeigh but said nothing, his eyes returning at once to the television.

Cela touched McVeigh lightly on the arm. 'Come,' she said.

McVeigh followed her from the room. Next door, in another room, she switched on the light. The room was tiny. Most of it was occupied by a big double mattress. There were two blankets on the mattress, no sheets. Beside the mattress, a late addition, were three plastic flowers in a chipped vase. The vase was dark green, and whoever was responsible for the gesture had taken the trouble to fill it with water.

McVeigh smiled, looking at the vase. 'What now?' he said.

Cela nodded at the mattress. She'd already taken off her shirt. Now, she was unzipping her jeans.

'We sleep,' she said.

'Here?'

'Yes.'

McVeigh looked at her for a moment. Then she stepped out of the jeans and reached for the light switch. The window, uncurtained, looked on to the street. In the half-darkness, McVeigh stripped to his underpants and joined her underneath the top blanket. She was lying on her side, her face to the door, her knees up and her back to McVeigh.

'What now?' he said for the second time. 'What's going on?'

Cela said nothing for a moment, then she half-turned, rolling over, looking at him, her face pale against the rough nap of the underblanket.

'We were lucky with the soldiers,' she said simply. 'It could have been worse.'

'Meaning what?'

'It could have been the Shin Beth.'

'The security people?'

'Yes.'

'So?'

She looked at him a moment longer, then reached out, a single finger, touching him on the lips, the gesture you'd make to a child, wanting the questions to stop. McVeigh gazed at her, stirred, knowing that he wanted her, knowing this wasn't the time, then she smiled, white teeth in the half-darkness, and turned over again, telling him to go to sleep. McVeigh said nothing, scenting her body beneath the blanket, an earthy, female smell. Then, next door, there came the roar of the crowd and a high-pitched whirr as the video-machine went into reverse again. McVeigh closed his eyes, sighing. Another goal, he thought. More excitement.

*

Telemann awoke at four in the morning, the bedroom in darkness, the curtains tightly closed. He lay still for a moment, getting his bearings, plotting his route to the door. The girl lay beside him, sprawled on her back, twitching slightly. She slept like a child, limbs everywhere, a physical candour totally at odds with the careful image she presented to the world outside.

Telemann had noticed the contrast before, and put it down to breeding. Now he knew different. The woman was a born actress. What the world saw was a piece of careful fiction. What lay beside him was the real thing. Somewhere in between, he didn't quite know where, lay the animal in the photos in the wooden box.

He shook his head, still disturbed by the rawness of her sexual appetite, easing himself out of bed. Last into the room, he'd made sure the door wasn't properly closed. Now he opened it without a sound, stepping along the hall to the lounge. In the lounge, he collected the telephone, detaching it from the socket in the wall. Furthest from the bedroom was the kitchen. He'd already located the telephone point, a simple plug-in socket next to the fridge. He padded across to it, the telephone in his hand, closing the door behind him. He put the telephone on the side, reaching for a row of recipe books. He pulled out one on oriental cuisine. Amongst a set of glossy photos of Korean stir-fries, he found the slip of paper he'd hidden earlier. He laid the paper on the work surface, memorizing the digits in the number, plugging in the phone, checking the door a final time.

Sullivan answered on the fourth ring. Telemann could hear voices in the background and then the sound of canned studio applause. Game shows, he thought, recognizing the opening bars of the signature tune. After all this, the man spends his evening watching game shows.

'Who is it?' Sullivan said.

'Telemann.'

'Who?'

'Telemann. Ron Telemann.'

Telemann heard a door close. Abruptly, the game show had gone. Then the man was back again, a voice rasping in his ear.

'Where the fuck are you?'

'Germany.'

'I know that. But where in Germany?'

'Doesn't matter. Listen. I need to know what Emery's been telling you. We need to touch base.'

'Who?'

'You and me.'

'Fucking right.' He paused, then came back. 'You had the guy shot. Right?'

'Who?'

'The Palestinian guy. Assali. You had him shot, or you shot him, or some goddamn thing, and now half the fucking world's at my door wanting to know why.' He paused again. 'Any of that sound familiar?'

'Not at all, sir.' He hesitated. 'Is that what Emery's been telling you?'

'It's the goddamn truth, isn't it?'

'No.'

'It isn't?'

'No.'

'What then?'

Telemann said nothing for a moment, holding the phone away from him, listening hard for steps along the hallway, the creak of a door. Hearing nothing, he returned to the conversation, finding Sullivan in mid-flow.

'You talk to him,' he was saying. 'You talk to the guy.'

'Who, sir?'

'Emery, your buddy.'

'Where is he?'

'That hotel. The place you stayed. Bad Godesburg.'

'The Dreisen?'

'Yeah. That's it. He phoned me tonight. Two hours ago. More good news. I told him—'

Telemann frowned, staring at the phone. 'He's at the Dreisen? Emery's at the hotel?'

'That's what I said.'

'Alone? By himself?'

'No.'

'Who with?'

'Your wife. As I understand it.' He paused, then began to talk again, telling Telemann it was time to come back, to return to the States, file a report, help build the dyke he'd need to keep the water out. He was still talking when Telemann put the phone down, unplugging it at the wall, returning it to the table in the lounge, stepping carefully back down the hall towards the bedroom. Inge lay where he'd left her, still on her back, her eyes open, staring at the ceiling.

'What's the matter?' she said, reaching for him.

Telemann got into bed beside her, roused again.

'They've come,' he said. 'They've come across to tell me.'

*

The old man, Abu Yussuf, phoned again at midnight, a different number, Amer's office at the Municipality buildings. He lay in the bed in the motel room, the blanket tucked around his chin, waiting for the number to answer. The plate of food he'd ordered from room service lay where he'd left it, on the floor beside the bed, half-eaten. The sauce on the salad had made him feel sick.

A woman finally answered, Amer's secretary. The old man told her who it was and she recognized the name at once, telling him not to go away, explaining that Amer needed to talk to him and that she would interrupt the meeting he'd just begun.

The old man looked at the phone, pleased and surprised. If life was a queue, he was always at the back. Something must have happened. Something must have changed. He lay in the bed, waiting for Amer. He'd spent the day re-reading his wife's letters. He wanted to know more about the Israeli woman. He wanted to know why she'd made three visits. And most of all he wanted to know that his wife was safe and well and – praise God – back home.

There was a series of clicks on the line as the secretary transferred the call. Then the old man heard Amer's voice, clearer than ever.

'Where are you?'

The old man blinked. Amer sounded anxious. He peered at the pile of promotional literature at the bedside, looking for a name.

'Moosup,' he said. 'I've done what you said. I've left New York.'

'Moosup where?'

'I don't know,' the old man faltered, blinking again. 'I'm

going north. Towards Canada. Things have been happening. Bad things . . .' The old man fell silent.

'OK.' Amer sounded suddenly brisk. 'Abu Yussuf, please listen. You have money?'

'Yes.'

'How much?'

'Thousands. Tens of thousands.'

'OK.' He paused. 'Tomorrow, go north again. Then phone me. Same time. Same number. OK? You can hear me? Understand me?'

The old man nodded. 'Same time,' he said. 'Same number.'

'Good.' He paused. 'You have a car?'

'Yes.'

'What sort of car?'

The old man frowned, confused. He hadn't expected a conversation like this. He wanted to talk about his wife. About Hala. How she was.

'It's an Oldsmobile,' he said.

'What colour?'

'Tan.'

'What's the registration?'

The old man shook his head, swamped by the questions. 'The registration?'

'Yes. The plates. What's the number on the plates?'

'I don't know. RHX I think. Then three numbers.' He paused, trying to picture the plates. He'd had to take them off several times, back in the garage in Newark, making adjustments to the pipework in the trunk. He shut his eyes, frowning in concentration. The plate was yellow. The numbers were white. '781,' he said at last, 'RHX 781.'

There was a silence on the line for a moment and the old man began to panic, knowing that the conversation had got nowhere, that he hadn't had time for a single question about his wife.

'Hala,' he said, the moment Amer lifted the phone again. 'How is she?'

There was the briefest pause, then Amer was back, his voice softer, kinder, less anxious.

'She's fine,' he said.

'Is she back?'

'Back where?'

'Back home.'

'Yes, yes she is. She's back and she's OK.'

'Did they beat her?'

'No, no they didn't.'

'Did they hurt her?'

'No. She's away from them now. They can't touch her. Everything's fine. Everything's OK. Believe me.'

'Thank God.' The old man shook his head, feeling the tears running down his cheeks, the hot salty taste in his mouth. 'Thank God.'

He put the phone down, ashamed of his grief, the way he couldn't contain it, the way it made his voice break, thinking of his wife, back home in the tiny house in Ramallah, safe at last. He looked down the long hump of his body, down to the foot of the bed, the half-eaten tray of food, the dirty plate that was America. Tomorrow, he thought. Tomorrow he'd drive to Canada. Tomorrow he'd start the long journey home.

*

Telemann had never seen himself on television before. He sat in the lounge, half-past eight in the morning, watery sunshine flooding in through the big picture windows. He was wearing Inge's dressing-gown and drinking coffee, freshly brewed, half an eye on the television in the corner.

The photograph had been lifted from his passport, an old shot, the harsh lighting favoured by the Agency's documentation people making him look vaguely Mediterranean. Inge saw it too, coming in from the kitchen with a plateful of hot rolls. She paused in the middle of the room, listening to the reporter's voice-over as the picture cut to shots of the Dreisen. Police in Bad Godesburg were looking for an American. An appeal had been issued for the man to come forward. He might have important information regarding the murder of a Palestinian diplomat. The American was travelling under a variety of names. Two of them were Telemann and Lacey. A telephone number flashed on to the screen. Members of the public were to phone if they had information.

Telemann glanced at the number on the screen, remembering Sullivan's voice on the phone, the man outraged.

'Diplomat?' he queried.

He looked round at Inge. She was stooped over the low table beside the sofa, arranging the rolls on two plates. She smelled like the dressing-gown he was wearing, an expensive scent underscored with something far earthier.

'Diplomat?' he said again. 'The guy was a diplomat?'

Inge shook her head, not looking at him. 'He was a terrorist,' she said. 'He killed women and children. That's why he fled. That's why he left Israel. That's why he came here.'

'But they're calling him a diplomat.'

'They're wrong. They must have their reasons, but they're wrong.'

'How do you know?'

'Because I was in Israel when it happened.' She straightened up from the table, angry now. 'They took the bus near Ashkelon. There was a bomb on board and it blew up. The bomb was on a timer. They were following in a car. Some of the people on the bus managed to get out . . .' She shrugged, tight-lipped. 'They shot them by the roadside. I saw the bodies. There were lots of bodies.'

Telemann nodded, remembering the incident, the headlines worldwide, Israeli politicians vowing revenge.

'You were there?' he said.

'Within an hour.' She nodded. 'Yes.'

'Working?'

'Yes.'

'And you stayed with it. The investigation?'

'Yes.'

'Still?'

She looked at him for a moment, unsmiling, then she nodded at the television. 'No,' she said. 'The case is over. The man is dead.'

She left the room, returning to the kitchen, and Telemann heard her singing, an old James Brown number, word-perfect.

To his surprise, the last couple of hours in bed had been hugely successful, and now she was putting it into words for him. '*I feel good . . .*' she sang. '*I feel good . . .*'

Telemann shook his head, his attention returning to the television. The news magazine had stayed with events in the Middle East. There were shots of masked youths on the West Bank hurling stones at a line of Israeli soldiers. The shots were barely two hours old, and Telemann watched them, fascinated. The soldiers began returning fire, canisters of CS gas, clouds of the stuff drifting down the street. An armoured vehicle appeared. More troops jumped out of the back, running towards the stone-throwing youths. The soldiers were wearing gas masks and carried riot shields and heavy white batons. Most of the youths turned and fled, but the soldiers caught one, clubbing him to the ground, kicking his head and body, then dragging him back towards the armoured vehicle. Telemann turned away, sickened by the endless spiral of violence, the death of some woman in a military prison provoking yet more bloodshed, yet more pain. Where does it end, he thought, hearing Inge in the kitchen, a new song, a different language, lyrics he didn't recognize, couldn't understand.

*

The scene inside the hospital was chaotic. McVeigh followed Cela, pushing through the crowd of women inside the big glass doors. Some of the women had come in from the surrounding villages, weathered brown faces, long flowing cotton *thoubs*, spilling out of the ancient buses, fearing the worst. Now they milled aimlessly around, surrounding first a doctor, then a nurse, anyone in a uniform, anyone who might be able to put a name to the rumours. Who had been injured? Who had been killed? How many had the Israelis taken away?

Cela side-stepped a male nurse guarding a pair of swing-doors and gestured for McVeigh to follow. They plunged down a corridor, ignoring the shouts of the nurse. The corridor was wide. On either side, curtained bays held victims of the riot, broken limbs, bloodied faces, bandaged heads. Several youths were still unconscious, lying on stretchers, their faces turned carefully away from the light. Relatives sat beside them, heads bowed, bodies rocking back and forth, a constant low incantation, hauling them back to consciousness.

In an office at the end of the corridor Cela found Amer. He was standing by the window, arguing with a youth of perhaps nineteen. The youth was half-sitting on the edge of a desk. There was blood on his stone-washed jeans and he was obviously in pain, yet the pain served only to fuel his rage. His face was pale with shock, but his eyes were wild and his voice rose with each fresh outburst. Amer was trying to calm him, his hands flat before him, like a conductor or a priest. He looked exhausted, his suit rumpled, his face shadowed by a day's growth of beard.

The youth saw Cela by the door. He tried to get off the desk, shrieking her name, pushing Amer away as he tried to restrain him. Cela didn't hesitate, crossing the room, putting her arms around him, holding his head to her chest. The youth sobbed briefly, then began to shake, a spasm of his whole body, his rage returning, redoubled. McVeigh caught Cela's eye and went to her side, feeling the youth beginning to collapse, lifting him bodily on to the desk. The youth was still looking at Cela, gabbling in Arabic, his eyes huge in his face, and McVeigh stayed beside him, a target for his flailing limbs, waiting for the worst of the violence to subside. At length the larval flow of Arabic slowed and the youth closed his eyes, his breath coming in shallow gasps, his body beginning to slump on the desk. McVeigh held him for a moment longer, then Cela gestured for him to step away, and he did so, letting a nurse and a doctor in a white coat slip between them. The doctor was carrying a small syringe and a pair of scissors with which he cut quickly up the inside seam of the jeans. The denim parted, peeling back like a banana skin. Above the left knee, where the bloodstains were heaviest, the flesh had been pulped. McVeigh could see bone through the torn sheets of muscle. The doctor examined the wound quickly, calling for something in Arabic, and then injected the syringe into the youth's thigh. The youth screamed, but the fight had left his body, and when the trolley appeared from the corridor, the rubber mattress still wet with someone else's blood, it was a simple job for McVeigh to transfer him.

The trolley disappeared into the corridor and there was a moment's silence before the phone began to ring. The doctor reached for the phone. He was looking at the nurse, signalling for her to clear the office. Cela understood at once, shepherding McVeigh towards the door. Amer joined them in the corridor. Outside, rising and falling, McVeigh could hear the wail of more sirens.

Amer looked at Cela. Some of the women from the hospital entrance had managed to fight their way into the casualty area. They were stumbling from bay to bay, looking for reassurance, sons, husbands, brothers still alive. McVeigh watched them. The noise was deafening. Then Cela touched him on the arm, told him to follow again, herself and Amer, out through another set of swing-doors, leaving the chaos behind them. They turned a corner, then another, Amer in the lead. At a pair of tall double doors, he paused for a moment, looking at Cela. Then he shrugged, and pushed inside.

McVeigh followed, at once recognizing the smell, sweetish, pungent, a mix of bleach and body fluids. He looked around, letting the double doors swing shut behind him. A bank of tall white fridges lined one wall. There were four dissecting slabs, stainless-steel, and a line of basins with the usual instruments laid out ready for use. On the wall behind was a blackboard, with a box of chalks beside it. The room was empty, two big extractor fans revolving slowly overhead.

McVeigh looked at Cela. 'Why here?' he said. 'Why the morgue?'

'It's quiet. We need to talk.'

'We?'

'You and me.' She paused. 'And Amer.'

McVeigh nodded, waiting. Amer had buttoned his jacket, an automatic gesture of respect. He was looking at his feet, shaking his head. McVeigh shivered. The place felt cold.

'Who was the boy in the office?'

Amer looked up. 'His name's Said. He's my nephew. He's

one of the sons of my wife's sister. The woman I told you about last night. The woman who died in prison. That's why—' he nodded at the door '—we have so much trouble.'

'The riot? The gas? Because of your sister-in-law?'

'Yes. I was hoping the news . . .' He shrugged, not finishing the sentence, glancing at Cela.

Cela nodded. 'We didn't need this,' she said. 'Not all this.'

'All what?'

'The violence. The gas. The people from the television.'

'Why not?' McVeigh frowned, remembering the conversation in the restaurant. 'I thought that was the whole point of it. The kids, the *Intifada*. Getting the world to watch.'

'Yes, but—'

'But what?' McVeigh gazed at her, thinking quite suddenly of Yakov sprawled across a Kensington pavement, most of his head blown away. He must have come here, to a place like this, his long body on one of those slabs, ringed by saws, drills, forceps, a pathologist in a white coat. His life would have ended up on a blackboard, a sentence or two of curt anatomical detail, body-weight, vital dimensions, cause of death. McVeigh blinked. Whoever you were, wherever you died, the procedures were just the same.

'Tell me,' he said quietly, 'tell me why he died.'

'Who?'

'Yakov.'

Cela looked at him for a long moment, saying nothing. Then she glanced at Amer. He knows, thought McVeigh. He knows, too. Amer shrugged. He looked uncomfortable.

'We have a problem,' he said at last. 'You must help us.'

'How?'

'You have to go to America.'

'*America?*'

'Yes.'

'When?'

'Tomorrow. Perhaps tonight.' He looked up. 'Please.'

'Why?'

Amer glanced across at Cela. She was studying a row of handsaws. Her face was quite expressionless. Then she began to talk, her voice very low. 'The woman who died was called Hala. Her husband is called Abu Yussuf. Two months ago he went away from this place, from Ramallah. They took him to America. And they gave him gas.'

'What kind of gas?'

'Nerve gas. Tabun gas.'

McVeigh nodded, frowning, trying to follow it. Nerve gas, America, the story ballooning. 'Where is he now?' he said. 'This man?'

Cela looked up for the first time, checking with Amer. Amer nodded. 'This morning,' he said quietly, 'he phoned again this morning. I know where he is.'

McVeigh blinked, then looked at Cela again. 'And he has the gas? This man?'

'Yes. We think so.'

'What will he do with it?'

'We're not sure.' She paused. 'But he's a Palestinian. And we know what the world will think if he uses it.'

'But who sent him? Who gave him the gas?'

Amer was looking at his shoes again. Cela was running a finger slowly along the blade of the nearest saw.

'We did,' she said at last. 'Yakov did.'

*

They were 10 kilometres short of Bremen, late afternoon, before Telemann finally chose the photos he'd use.

He sat in the front of the Mercedes, the wooden box on his lap, flicking through them. Inge, driving, glanced down from time to time, smiling at a particular shot. She'd brought a handful of cassettes with her, British groups mostly, Simple Minds, U2, and she sang along to some of the lyrics, a light, playful voice, her long fingers tap-tapping on the steering-wheel. She'd been singing all day, visibly more relaxed, and when he thought about it properly, Telemann realized what it was. The woman was on vacation. Her work was done.

He extracted a shot of Wulf and propped it on the dashboard. Wulf was sitting on the bed, his back to the wall, his legs stretched out, his belly masking the remains of an erection. His face was shiny with sweat, and his eyes were half-closed, and he was favouring Inge with a benign leer. He looked like a man replete, the gourmet diner at peace with his appetite. It was a photograph that did him no favours. It was neither athletic, nor inventive, nor physically flattering. It demonstrated nothing but greed. Telemann, beginning to despise the man, loved it.

He glanced at Inge. They'd at last established a relationship of sorts, Telemann gruff, Inge taunting, and from time to time he thought he'd detected glimpses of the real Inge, an altogether more complex proposition, almost certainly Israeli by birth, almost certainly German in origin, very definitely known by a different name back home. Once, standing in the bathroom in the Hamburg apartment, he'd tried to guess it, calling out the names he could remember from his days in Tel Aviv, but she'd appeared in the hall, shaking her head at every one, saying only that she'd grown up by the sea and had shared her childhood with her elder sister. Her sister had been her best friend. They'd both been mad about sailing. And they'd both had a passion for animals. Listening, Telemann had laughed, making the obvious joke about Wulf, but when he'd checked in the mirror, scraping away the last of the lather, he'd been surprised to see the expression on her face, angered and hurt.

Now he nodded at the photo. 'You sure you want to go through with this?' he said.

'What do you mean?'

'Taking me to Dusseldorf?' He paused. 'There must be simpler ways.'

She shook her head, reaching for the controls on the radio, turning down the music.

'You'd be stopped,' she said. 'It's in the papers, too.'

'That's not what I meant.'

'Oh?'

'No.' Telemann shook his head. 'Whatever you've got on Wulf, whatever he's done, I'm sure there's paperwork. Evidence. Proof. Just give me that. Then we call it quits and I go home.'

Inge frowned. 'But you want names,' she said. 'You want to know what he's done with the chemical. Where it's gone.' She looked across at him. 'Isn't that what you want?'

'Sure.'

'Then you must talk to him. He's the only one who knows. I don't.'

'And you think he'll tell me?'

She smiled and said nothing for a moment. Then she looked across at him again, an expression he'd seen once or twice before, cool, curious.

'He has an alarm system in the apartment,' she said quietly. 'There's a series of buttons. One of them's under the table in the main lounge. There's another in the bedroom, beneath the top surface of the cabinet, his side of the bed, the side by the window. The disconnect is in the fuse box at the bottom of the closet in the hall. Once you've tripped it—' she shrugged '—I don't think you'll have a problem.'

Telemann nodded, thoughtful, looking at the photo on the dashboard. 'Thanks,' he said drily.

'Pleasure.' She glanced across at him again. 'One other thing.'

'What's that?'

'Pain doesn't bother him. On the contrary, he quite likes it.'

'Ah—' Telemann nodded, still eyeing the photo '—so what does hurt him?'

She smiled for a second time, checking her lipstick in the mirror, then trod hard on the accelerator to pass a long line of trucks.

'Humiliation,' she said.

They reached Dusseldorf at half-past seven, a livid, smoky twilight, the access roads to the autobahn still busy with traffic. Inge drove into the business area, block after block of glass-walled towers and glittering store-fronts. Within sight of the central railway station, she parked by the side of the road. A tram hummed past, a line of heads buried in newspapers. She turned off the engine and nodded down the street. At the corner of the block was a large square building clad in black glass. On the front, five storeys up, in huge red gothic letters, the single word, WULF. Telemann looked at it, not saying anything. The belly, he thought. The appetite. The beast uncaged.

'His idea?' he said at last. 'The décor?'

Inge reached for her bag from the back seat. 'Red and black,' she said. 'His favourite colours.'

Telemann nodded, remembering some of the wilder scenes from the wooden box, the scarlet inserts in Inge's black leather camisole, her blood spilled across the crisp white sheets, the mask he sometimes made her wear, her eyes shuttered, only the mouth visible. Telemann swallowed hard, his hands flexing. He'd picked up the combat skills that mattered in the Marine Corps, nothing text-book, nothing they'd teach you on the mats at Fort Benning, but tricks he'd had to learn to keep the bigger guys at bay. Real violence, he knew, was a matter of will. You had to be motivated. You had to mean it. Fear would do it. That was one way. But this was different. This was hatred. And hatred, face to face, was the best motivation of all.

Telemann stared at the building. The name, the red letters, drifted briefly out of focus, and he blinked, shaking his head, putting it back where it belonged, halfway up the hideous black box, a target for his rage.

'Where do I find him?' he said.

'There's an apartment on top. It's bigger than you think. You go to a side-door. Down the street there. You'll find security guards.'

'Did you give me a name? On the phone?'

'No.'

'Then what—'

She smiled at him, opening the bag on her lap. She reached inside and pulled out a small bottle of perfume. The label on the side said 'Orphée'. She gave it to him.

'Show them this. Tell them you've come from Hannilore.'

'Hannilore?'

'Me.' She smiled again. 'Then take it up. That's what we agreed. Otherwise—' she shrugged, looking away '—you won't get past the door.'

Telemann nodded, looking at the perfume. His hand closed around it.

'And afterwards?'

'I'll be here.'

'Same place?'

'Sure.' She looked at him, savouring the word, giving it the American inflection, then she leaned quickly across and kissed him on the lips. 'Be careful,' she said softly. 'Please.'

Telemann got out of the car, pocketing the photos he'd chosen, and crossed the street without a backward glance. It was nearly dark now, and a light rain had begun to fall. He gazed up at Wulf's building, and counted the storeys to the top. There were nine in all. Next door, on the adjacent site, another building was under construction, gantry cranes towering over the half-clad cage of steel girders. Telemann hesitated a moment, getting the geography right, committing it to memory, then he rounded the corner, looking for the night entrance, finding it at once. The door from the street was unlocked. Inside, a man sat behind a desk. He was flanked by a row of TV monitors and a console covered with buttons.

Telemann bent to the desk, recognizing his own movements on one of the monitor screens. 'Herr Wulf,' he said, not bothering to disguise his accent. 'From Fraülein Hannilore.'

The security guard studied him for a moment. He was young, trim, alert. He nodded, fingering a key on the console, clearing his throat.

'Herr Wulf?'

There was a moment's silence, then a deep voice boomed back from a speaker beside the key. The security guard glanced up at Telemann and passed on the message. There was a bark of laughter and the voice demanded a description. The guard frowned, wrong-footed, and Telemann suddenly realized how nervous he was.

'Middle-aged . . .' he began in German. 'About . . .'

'Big? Is he big?'

'Ah . . . no . . .'

'No?' Wulf laughed again. 'Small? Is he small?'

The guard stood up, looking at Telemann properly, flustered now. 'Sir?'

'Five five,' Telemann said. 'Last time I looked.'

There was a pause, then Wulf came back again. He'd heard Telemann's voice, the accent.

'He's American?'

'Yes, sir.'

'What has he got with him?'

'Sir?'

Telemann produced the bottle of perfume, offering it to the guard. The guard frowned, shaking his head, out of his depth now.

'Orphée,' Telemann said. 'Tell him Orphée.'

The guard nodded, still nonplussed. 'Orphée,' he repeated.

'Send him up.'

'Yes, sir.'

The guard released the key and told Telemann to take the private elevator to the ninth floor. The private elevator was in the lobby, through a series of three doors. Access to the elevator was controlled from the desk. He'd monitor Telemann on the TV screens. The elevator would be waiting for him when he got to the lobby.

Telemann pocketed the perfume and walked to the lobby. There was a series of framed photographs on the walls, all of them featuring Wulf. In one of them he was sharing a joke with Helmut Kohl. In another he was shaking hands with President Gorbachev. In a third he stood on a podium, dwarfing the diminutive figure of Yitzhak Shamir.

Telemann entered the elevator. The doors closed behind him. The elevator was heavily carpeted and virtually soundless. The absence of an indicator panel made it hard to gauge how fast they were going. Telemann checked his pockets. He had the photographs. He had the perfume. The next hour or so was his for the taking.

The elevator stopped. The doors opened. Expecting a corridor of some sort, Telemann was startled to find himself looking at a huge sitting-room. Thick white carpet lapped to the door of the elevator. A wide, shallow semi-circle of black leather sofa dominated one side of the room, a wall of glass the other. There were doors set into the glass, and beyond the patio outside was Dusseldorf, the elegant ramparts of the downtown area, towering blocks of offices, a cascade of neon signs. Telemann gazed at it for a moment, stepping out of the lift, aware of the giant figure lumbering towards him, even bigger than the photos had suggested, a huge man, jet-black hair, heavy jowls, clothed only in a deep crimson dressing-gown, loosely belted at the waist. Telemann nodded, extending a hand, recognizing the smile from the photos on the wall downstairs. It was an expression devoid of warmth, a leer of greeting, wholly animal, simple intimidation. Wulf grasped his hand, squeezing hard, and Telemann withdrew it at once, avoiding contagion.

'You have the perfume?'

Telemann nodded, producing the bottle of Orphée. Wulf took it, looking at it briefly, putting it in the pocket of his dressing-gown. Then he returned to Telemann, stepping closer, towering over him. Telemann felt the weight of the man's arm around his shoulder. He smelled odd, a sour mix of after-shave and something spicy. It was on his breath when he bent to Telemann's ear, whispering her name, Hannilore, then capping it with that same abrupt bark of laughter. Telemann stepped back, walking across the room, producing the photographs from his pocket, sitting down, laying them out, one by one, on the heavy marble-topped table. He looked up. Wulf was in the corner of the room, bending to a drinks cabinet. When he came back, he was carrying a bottle of champagne and two glasses. He uncorked the bottle, sitting down beside Telemann, ignoring the photographs. The belt around his waist had come undone, and now the dressing-gown hung loosely around him, showing his nakedness. He passed Telemann a glass of champagne and lifted his own. 'Krug,' he said. 'For Hannilore.'

Telemann touched glasses. 'Sure,' he said. 'For Hannilore.'

He sipped at the champagne and then put the glass back on the table. There were files on the floor by the table. The labels on the backs of the files read 'Kadenza Verlag'. Telemann glanced up at Wulf. Wulf was peering at the photos, one by one, nodding, deep growls of approval.

Finally he looked up. 'Good fuck, eh?'

'Wonderful.'

'I meant me.'

'I know.'

Wulf looked at him, beaming, then reached for the bottle. 'What do you want?' he said. 'Why are you here?

Telemann hesitated for a moment, then outlined what he knew about Littmann Chemie. He said he worked for the US Government. He said he was investigating a conspiracy to smuggle nerve gas into the US. He had reason to believe the chemicals came from Littmann. Wulf owned Littmann. He had connections in the Middle East. He—

Wulf reached forward, bringing Telemann's little speech to an abrupt end, slapping him on the knee, keeping his hand there, not removing it. The man was full of menace, a curious electricity, part sex, part something darker. Telemann could feel it. It was far from pleasant.

'I have connections everywhere,' Wulf growled. 'Your people too. They talk to me often. They come to me for advice. You should be careful, my friend, with your little stories . . .'

He stared at the photographs, selecting one, then another, coldly assessing each pose, the smile and the good humour gone. Finally, he turned back to Telemann. 'What are you saying, my friend? That I sell nerve gas? To the Arabs? Me? Here? In Germany?'

He looked at Telemann for a while, coal-black eyes. His English was barely accented, as good as Inge's. Telemann thought of her now, out in the car, waiting.

'I want answers,' he said. 'Now.'

Telemann got up. The panic button he'd already located. It was at the other end of the table, a small touch-pad secured in the angle between the leg and the table top. Wulf would have to move fast to use it. Telemann reached for the bottle of Krug. The bottle was two-thirds empty. He poured the rest on to the carpet, then up-ended the bottle, the neck in his hand, and smashed it against the edge of the table. Wulf peered at the table, running his finger along the surface, affecting indifference.

'Take off the robe,' Telemann said thickly.

'Why?'

'Take it off.'

Wulf shrugged, moving his body along the sofa, taking off

the dressing-gown, getting closer to the touch-pad. Telemann stepped forward and kicked him hard, the side of his knee, watching him collapse slowly sideways with a low groan.

'Get up.'

Wulf eyed him, rubbing his knee, struggling into a sitting position. Then he sat back, totally naked, spreading his legs, indifferent again.

'Is that what you want?' he said. 'You and your little bottle?' He gestured down, the huge belly, the triangle of thick black curls underneath. 'Eh?' he said. 'Is that it?'

He reached for one of the photographs, looking at it, establishing his contempt for Telemann. Telemann asked him again about Littmann, the chemicals, keeping the questions simple, wanting a yes or a no, but Wulf ignored him, picking up another photo, then another, murmuring her name, ignoring Telemann completely. Telemann stepped forward again, the bottle outfront, the circle of jagged glass, no ambiguities, knowing with utter certainty that he would do it, and that the man knew it, and that he didn't care. He tried one more question, naming Assali, asking what Wulf knew, what he could tell him. Wulf reached for the dressing-gown and pulled out the bottle of perfume. He looked up at Telemann, a half-smile on his face, that same animal leer, unscrewing the top of the bottle, pressing it against the inside of his wrist, a delicate movement, a single drop glinting in the spotlights, a wholly possessive gesture, deriding Telemann's claims. Hannilore, he was saying. My photos. My property. My woman. Littmann, he was saying. My company. My chemicals. My business. He lifted his wrist to his nose, sniffing it, enjoying it, the bottle back in his pocket, and Telemann edged away, disgusted, watching Wulf as his eyes began to roll, and his lips quivered, and his whole body stiffened on the sofa, the huge legs out straight, the man gasping for breath, reaching up, reaching out, reaching anywhere, the vomit bubbling in his throat, the erection growing and growing, his whole body twisting now, all control gone, his bowels opening, shit falling out of him.

His own vision beginning to blur, Telemann lunged towards the picture windows, willing the neon lights to stay in focus, finding the catch on the sliding door, pulling it open, stepping outside, on to the patio, shutting the door behind him, leaning over the rail, forcing the night air into his lungs, hearing the dull thud as Wulf's huge body rolled off the sofa and on to the floor. Nine storeys down, the face in the Mercedes gazed up for a second longer. Then the car was gone.

13

'I have to phone him.' McVeigh shrugged.

'Why?'

'Because that's the deal. You want me to go to the States, to do whatever, then that's the price. Either I phone, now, tonight, or you find someone else.'

'There *is* no one else.'

'Quite.'

Cela sat crosslegged on the mattress, her head against the wall, a small bowl of yoghurt by her side. Since midday they'd been back in the house where Amer had left them the night before. Ramallah was thick with Israeli soldiers. In the aftermath of the riot, they'd poured in from the big camps around Jerusalem, lorry after lorry grinding down the dusty roads. Sections of men had secured key points – the law courts, the bus station, the market, the main roads linking the city to the rest of the West Bank. An hour before dusk a curfew had been imposed – jeeps with loudspeakers in the streets, incessant announcements on radio and television – and now there were rumours of huge sweeps through the city, of house-to-house searches, the heavily armed soldiers tramping from door to door demanding access, asking question after question. The Israelis were looking for somebody. But no one was quite sure who.

McVeigh had a shrewd idea. Half a day's conversation with Cela had established that Yakov had died because he'd known too much. One of a tiny Mossad command cell, he'd been tasked to set up an elaborate Intelligence sting. Successive Israeli governments had been haunted by the Iraqi arms build-up. They'd been tracking the flow of weapons and know-how to Baghdad for years. They'd known what the stuff could do, and they'd known where most of it came from. One day, they were quite certain, Saddam would use it.

Thus far, Cela had been privy to the Government's thinking. Year by year, the situation had worsened. But what could be done? How could Saddam be dissuaded from using such dangerous toys? Operational suggestions had flowed from the desks in the Research Department at Mossad headquarters. Cela occupied one of them, and she'd helped keep the files as the stakes crept steadily higher. In the early days, the operations had been comparatively crude. Kai Sarut, the network of Intelligence officers at Israeli embassies abroad, had regularly filed the names of key foreign personnel – scientists, businessmen, arms dealers – suspected of helping Iraq. Some of them had been placed under surveillance. The names of a handful were forwarded by the head of Mossad to the Prime Minister's office. Only he could authorize assassination.

Some, Cela said, had died. An Egyptian scientist, his throat slit in a Paris hotel room. A Canadian ballistics expert, shot through the head in the corridor outside his Brussels apartment. A French prostitute, intimately linked to an Iraqi procurement network, run down and killed by a car in the Boulevard St Germain. Each execution had sent a message to the other names on the hit-list, and to some degree the policy had worked. Frightened for their lives, many of Iraq's old allies had backed off.

But money talks, and Iraq had lots of it, and by the end of the eighties the operational suggestions going through Cela's computer were becoming monthly more elaborate. Some of them were wild, and owed more to Hollywood than real life. Others were too long term. Finally, one surfaced which caught the attention of the new head of Metsada, the top-secret directorate in charge of sharp-end operations. The man, said Cela, was very ambitious. He had powerful right-wing friends in the Government. He had equally high-grade assets in Baghdad. He had no doubts about the potential of Saddam's new weapons. And he had no qualms about countering them. Whatever was necessary, whatever it took, Mossad should do it. Otherwise Israel would pay the price.

At this point, abruptly, the operation had gone underground. Cela would normally have been privy to the early planning stages, but all she knew for sure was that the operation was to involve chemical weapons. The Metsada boss, whom she wasn't prepared to name, had identified chemical warfare as the West's waking nightmare. Worst weapon of all was nerve gas. If the West could truly be convinced that nerve gas was a reality, that the technology was simple, that the stuff could be easily smuggled between countries, and that Iraq had hundreds of tons of it ready for use, then Israel might – at last – put an end to the build-up. The chemicals for nerve gas came from the West. Only if the wind blew in their direction would supplies cease.

That, Cela was convinced, was the root of it, an elegant, beautifully crafted plan for holding the West finally accountable for its greed and its hypocrisies and its total lack of responsibility. A cell within Metsada would come up with a plan. The plan would infiltrate nerve gas and hit squads into a number of leading Western democracies. The plan would be code-named 'Looking Glass'. It would, in one bold stroke, discredit the Iraqis, expose Western suppliers, and make the West think twice about any future deals with Saddam Hussein. At this point, Cela's direct knowledge ran out. But the plan went operational, and a year later, only months back, she finally caught up again.

Listening, McVeigh had looked at her. 'Yakov,' he'd said. 'Yakov was part of it.'

'Yes.'

'Because of you? Because you knew so much already?'

'Maybe, yes. But also because he was good. He had a lot of experience. He'd been in Kidron.'

'In what?'

Cela had looked at him, hesitating a moment, and McVeigh had repeated the question, sensing her reluctance, telling her there was no point holding back. If she wanted help, there was a price. And the price was a certain candour.

'Kidron?' She'd shrugged. 'Kidron means bayonet. It's another department. They kill and they kidnap.'

'And Yakov was one of them?'

345

'Yes. For two years.'

McVeigh had nodded, thinking of the gentleness of the man, the way he'd been with the kids, with Billy. Then he turned to Cela again, pushing the story on. Yakov had been part of the Metsada cell, key to the 'Looking Glass' operation. How had she known? How had she found out?

'He told me.'

'When?'

'A month before he died.'

'On the phone? By letter?'

'Of course not. He was being watched. So was I. We both knew it. We met in Ireland.' She shrugged. 'He flew to Paris. Then he went to Le Havre. Then he took the ferry to Cork. I flew to Amsterdam. Then Belfast. Then Londonderry. Then the south.'

She'd smiled, remembering the journey, the three days they'd shared in a farmhouse on the Dingle Peninsula. She'd talked about the wind, and the views, and the smell of the place, peat fires, and soda bread, and the horses the farmer had lent them, away on their own all day, flat out across the huge empty beaches. It had been like the kibbutz, except colder, a world apart. At night, in the tiny annexe next to the farmhouse, they'd huddled together under thick blankets. He'd told her everything about 'Looking Glass', wanting her to know, a precaution in case they pushed him too far, and he did something foolish, and they took the appropriate action, adding yet another name to the Prime Minister's list. At this McVeigh had nodded, remembering how strange Yakov had seemed, those final days, how resigned. He told her about it, the night Yakov had come to the flat in Crouch End to say goodbye to Billy, no travel plans, no posting home, just goodbye. Listening, she'd nodded. 'He knew,' she'd said. 'He knew they'd do it. He knew they'd kill him.'

'But why? Why did they kill him?'

'He'd had enough. "*Ney maas, li . . .*" You know the phrase? Up to *here*?'

She'd raised a level hand above her eye. McVeigh had smiled. 'Sure,' he'd said. 'Well pissed-off.'

'What?'

'Nothing.' He'd paused. 'So where was he off to? Where was he going?'

Cela had shrugged at the question. 'I don't know where he was going. He may have been going nowhere. Knowing Yakov, he hadn't made up his mind. But they couldn't take that risk. I told you. He knew too much. They had to kill him.' She'd paused. 'He was the wrong generation. He had the wrong ideas. He'd do things for Israel of course. For his country. He'd even kill people. But not this. Not gas. He thought it was crazy. The number of things that could go wrong. The number of people . . .' She'd shaken her head. 'He phoned me two days before he was killed. He knew it was going to happen.'

'He say that?'

'Of course not. But I could tell from his voice. Nothing he said. Just the way he talked.'

McVeigh had nodded. 'And you?'

'I was told to resign. Two weeks before, they told me to go. Not to talk. To say I knew nothing. To go back home and be a good kibbutznik. In this country, if you're bad, they send you to pick apples.' She'd smiled. 'There are lots of apples.'

McVeigh had nodded again, thinking of the flat in Tel Aviv, the wreckage of the bedroom. 'So who was in your flat? Who did it?'

Cela had shrugged. 'Someone from the Mossad. Two or three people could have done it. It was a message they were sending. *Zhod shelanu. Zhod K'mous.* Keep our secrets to yourself.'

'But the things they did. Your clothes. *That* personal?'

'Yes.' She'd shrugged again. 'I was alone most of the time. People liked the look of me. Often they tried . . .' She'd shaken her head, turning away, not wanting to discuss it.

Now, past midnight, McVeigh sat back against the wall, still wanting a phone, still waiting for an answer. 'Looking Glass' had gone horribly wrong. The point-man, the man they'd sent, was on the run. He had a car, and a tankful of nerve gas, and a lifelong grudge against the Israelis. His minder, a Mossad plant, was dead. His one point of contact, the one man he trusted, was Amer. Amer had a location in the States, and a description of the car. To date, as far as Amer knew, the old man hadn't heard the truth about his wife. When he did, when he learned that she'd died in an Israeli prison, provoking a riot in his home town, then anything could happen. Someone had to get to him first. And that someone was McVeigh.

'Tell me,' he said slowly, 'why this old man?'

'I don't know. I don't know how he was recruited, why they chose him. He was a car mechanic. That's all I know.'

'Did Yakov know?'

'No.'

'How much did Yakov know about America?'

'Only what I've told you. That's the way they plan these things. Stage by stage. So nobody has the whole picture.'

McVeigh frowned. 'So where did Yakov fit?'

'In England. There was an English plan, too. They put a drum of nerve gas in the sea. They studied the tides. They wanted it to wash ashore.'

McVeigh blinked. '*Nerve gas?*'

Cela nodded. 'That's what Yakov thought. His team had to follow it. Wherever it went. Once the English knew what it was, they had to get it back. Steal it. Make it disappear again. It was a game. They wanted the English to trace it back to the factory. And then they wanted to make them look very foolish.' She paused. 'I told you. Yakov thought it was crazy.'

'But what happened? Where's the stuff now?'

'I don't know.' She paused again. 'Yakov chose good people. Once they'd got it back, it would be very safe. They'd play games with it, political games, but it would be OK. He made sure of that.'

'Where did the stuff come from?'

Cela shrugged. 'I don't know,' she said. 'Europe somewhere.'

McVeigh fell silent for a moment, the decision more pressing than ever. 'A phone,' he said again.

Cela, looking at him, shook her head. 'There is no phone,' she said. 'Not here.'

'Then we find one. We go to Amer's. He'll have a phone. Bound to.'

'There's a curfew,' she pointed out. 'They'll take us.'

McVeigh thought about it for a moment. All evening, he'd heard the Israeli jeeps whining up and down the street outside. They had searchlights mounted on top of the cabs, and they swept the fronts of the houses as they rolled past. The locals had a phrase for it, part of the new language of occupation. They called the searchlights *kamar Israeli*, the Israeli moon. McVeigh looked up, easing his body on the mattress. Cela was watching him carefully, licking the remains of a bowl of yoghurt from a spoon.

'Tell me something,' he said. 'Why have you told me all this? Why all the detail?'

'Because you should know.'

'But why?'

'Because . . .' She shrugged, ducking again as yet another jeep rounded the corner down the street, the searchlight stabbing towards them. McVeigh let his body slide down the wall, lying flat on the mattress. Cela did the same. The room was suddenly bright, flooded with a harsh white light. Then the jeep was past the house, changing gear for the crossroads, and the light had gone. McVeigh looked at Cela in the half-darkness. She was about a foot away. She had yoghurt on the end of her nose. He reached out and wiped it off, licking the end of his finger.

'Tell me,' he said, 'who are they looking for?'

'Me.'

McVeigh nodded, thinking about it. 'And what will they do if they find you?' he said at last.

'I don't know.'

'But you can guess?'

'Yes.'

McVeigh nodded again. He could still taste the yoghurt, creamy and bitter. 'Say the worst happened. Say they took you away and locked you up.' He paused. 'Who'd know then?'

'About what?'

'This.' McVeigh gestured loosely at the space between them, the rumpled blankets, the conversation, the empty bowl of yoghurt, the last half-day.

Cela looked up, a smile on her face. 'You,' she said.

'Which is why you told me?'

349

She nodded, the smile widening.

'Yes,' she said. 'Of course.'

*

Laura was asleep in bed when the phone rang. She woke up, the hotel room in darkness. She rolled over, looking for the digits on the bedside clock. The clock said 01.59. The phone was still ringing. She lifted it to her ear, propped up on one elbow, thinking vaguely of the house in Rockville. Eight o'clock in the evening. One of the kids returning her earlier call.

'Laura Telemann,' she said automatically. 'Who's that?'

There was silence at the other end of the phone, then – unmistakably – the sound of someone breathing.

'It's Laura,' she said again. 'Who is this, please? Can you hear me?' She blinked in the darkness, willing a voice from the silence, frightened. She tried once more, quieter, more matter-of-fact. Then, abruptly, the phone went dead.

Laura lay in the bed for a full five minutes, motionless. She was in a foreign country, a foreign hotel. A man had died here only days earlier. Terrible things were happening, unpredictable things, things she didn't understand. The presence on the telephone could have been anywhere. America. London. Three blocks away. Downstairs even. She lay back, staring at the tiny strip of sky between the curtains, trying to sort her thoughts into some rational order, trying to steady her pulse, trying to keep control.

Finally, minutes later, she drew back the covers and slipped out of bed. She was wearing an old night-shirt, one of Ron's. She padded across the room and tried the handle on the door. The door was double-locked. She eased the lock, frightened again, dreading the moment when she had to open the door and face the five steps along the empty corridor to Emery's adjoining room. She turned the handle, opening the door. The corridor outside was empty. She slipped out, closing the door, realizing – too late – that she'd left the key inside. She swallowed hard, closing her eyes, then she knocked on Emery's door, light taps at first, progressively more urgent. When the door finally opened, he looked terrible, hair everywhere, eyes barely open. Recognizing Laura, he beckoned her inside.

'I'm sorry,' she said at once. 'It's crazy, but I'm frightened.'

He led her to the unoccupied bed, telling her it didn't matter, settling her down, pulling the blankets around her, returning to his own bed, asleep again within seconds.

Lying in the cold bed between the crisp new sheets, Laura heard the phone in the next room begin to ring again, on and on. Even with the blanket over her head, a full minute later, it was still ringing.

*

Telemann stepped out of the phone booth, stumbling a moment in the darkness, reaching out for the rail at the water's edge. The rain had stopped now, and the wind had dropped, and the river was whispering by, only feet away. He could see the bulk of the Hotel Dreisen upstream, the tall picture windows on the ground floor, the bedrooms above, curtained against the night.

He stood by the rail for a moment, leaning against it, trying to ease the pain in his leg. Getting away from Wulf's apartment, returning to street level, was already a blur, a jumble of decisions, taken and half-taken, the product of instinct and adrenalin and something close to panic. On the corner of Wulf's patio he'd found a ledge. The ledge extended the full length of the building. A metre wide, it gave him access to the site next door, a scaffold of huge steel girders, floors already in place, cladding stacked in piles, every working space ensnared with cables and hydraulic feeds and small caches of thick steel bolts. On one of these, in the darkness, he'd tripped, falling heavily, one arm outstretched, narrowly avoiding a nine-storey plunge to the street below. At first, getting to his feet again, he hadn't felt the pain. Only minutes later, climbing carefully down yet another girder, did he realize that his trousers were torn below the knee, his left leg gashed, an ugly open wound still pouring blood.

At street level, behind the cover of the hoardings that ringed the site, he'd done his best to bandage the wound, taking his jacket off and tearing the sleeve from his shirt. Wound tightly round his calf, the bandage had stemmed the blood-loss, but upright again, testing the leg with his body-weight, he'd known at once that walking any distance would be out of the question.

If he was to get to Bad Godesburg, if he was to start the long journey home, then he had to find transport.

At the railway station, he knew, there would be cabs. The station was 500 metres away. He managed it in less than ten minutes, pausing to recover at the end of each block, grateful that the traffic had thinned, glad that the rain was still falling, keeping people off the streets. The first cab in the rank was a newish Opel. He bent to the window. The driver was Turkish, a young man. He asked to be taken to Bad Godesburg. The young man peered at him, nodding towards the station, telling him that the train would be cheaper, quicker even, but Telemann had persevered, producing a thick roll of bank-notes, offering 500 Deutschmarks up front. Looking at them, the Turk had shrugged, reaching back to open the door, starting the engine.

The journey had taken a couple of hours, the autobahn choked with traffic. Telemann had sat in the back, sideways across the bench seat, his leg up, his attention divided between the driver and the road. The driver spoke good English, doing nothing to mask his curiosity, asking Telemann where he'd come from, what he did for a living, what he thought of the new Germany. Bad Godesburg, he said, was the worst place on earth, full of diplomats and old people. Nobody ever went there for a good time. Nothing ever happened. Listening, Telemann parried his questions as best he could, non-committal, gruff, the visiting businessman at the end of an exhausting week.

The Turk had the radio on, low in the background, and Telemann bent forward a little for each newscast, curious to know whether Wulf's death had yet been reported. He'd never seen the effects of nerve gas, not first-hand, but the last month or so had given him all the information he needed, and he was quite certain that the liquid in the bottle of perfume had been Tabun. The symptoms matched, spasm for spasm, the way the man convulsed, the way his muscles had decoupled from his brain, and Telemann shivered, knowing how close he must have come to the same fate. So much for Inge, he thought grimly, remembering the touch of her lips as he'd left the Mercedes. Another betrayal. More bullshit.

By the time they'd got to Bad Godesburg, it was nearly midnight. Telemann had asked the Turk to drop him by the river, a street away from the Dreisen, and he'd added a big tip before the Opel bumped away across the cobble-stones. Alone, the rain gone, he'd limped along the river-bank to the hotel. A band was playing in one of the downstairs reception rooms. He could hear the tramp of feet and the sound of laughter and soon afterwards partygoers began to spill out of the hotel's side-door, arm in arm, calling good night and good luck to the handsome young couple standing inside, nicely framed in the open doorway. Telemann had watched them for a full five minutes, a figure in the shadows, marvelling at their confidence, the way they looked at each other, their fingers loosely inter-linked, the girl's head on her new husband's shoulder. A wedding, he thought bitterly, knowing that the next few hours would be far from easy, knowing that he had to give himself time, keep himself under control. The worst, after all, was over. He'd confronted the news. He knew what it meant. The rest was a mere formality.

He'd waited for two hours, sitting on a bench by the river, watching the occasional barge pushing upstream. Then, near two in the morning, he'd phoned, asking for her by name, asking for the room number, asking to be put through. She'd answered, really there, sleepy, curious, and he'd stood on one leg in the phone booth, feeling like some dumb adolescent, not knowing what to say, scribbling the room number on the palm of his hand, hearing her voice again, puzzled, anxious. Putting the phone down, he'd felt the sweat, cold on his face, knowing that all the clever rationalizations, all the games he'd played with himself, were quite hopeless, that he was as angry, and as hurt, and as confused as he'd ever been. There had to be a resolution, some kind of answer. Picking up the phone again, he'd dialled the hotel's number. This time, he'd tell her who it was. This time, they'd start a conversation. But the phone hadn't answered, and now, limping towards the hotel, he knew that they had to do it face to face, first time, no rehearsals.

The door at the side of the hotel was still unlocked, open – Telemann supposed – for the remains of the wedding party. He stepped inside. To his left, a flight of stairs offered access to all five floors. Telemann knew the route. He'd used the stairs before, only days ago. He began to limp upwards, pausing at each corridor. Laura's room was number 402.

On the fourth floor, Telemann paused again. The corridor ran the length of the hotel. He began to limp along it. Room 402 was at the end. He stopped outside, knocking on the door, waiting for an answer, knocking again, louder this time. Nothing happened. He frowned, peering at the number on the door, checking it against the smudged reminder on the palm of his hand. 402. No question about it. He knocked again, bending to the keyhole, hissing her name.

'Laura,' he said. 'Laura.'

There was a movement in the corridor behind him, a door opening. He looked round. His wife was standing in the corridor. She was wearing his night-shirt. She looked frightened. He stood up. 'Hi,' he said woodenly. 'It's me.'

She nodded, stepping towards him, putting her arms around him, kissing him. She smelled of sleep, a delicious mustiness. She was crying, her hands to his face, her lips to his ear.

'Hi,' she said. 'Hi. Hi. Hi.'

Telemann blinked, losing his place in the script again. He pulled back a little, holding her off, not roughly, and she sensed the hostility in him, and the confusion.

'What's the matter? You hurt?'

'No.' Telemann frowned. 'Yes.'

'Where? What happened?'

He shook his head, letting her take him by the hand, lead him into the bedroom, number 404. She closed the door behind him and put on the light. Telemann gazed round. There were two beds. Emery was in the other, rubbing his eyes, hinging upright. Telemann stepped towards the bed, the rage flooding through him. Not her fault, he thought. Not Laura's. His. Emery's. Oblivious to the pain in his leg, he ripped the sheet off the bed. Emery was naked underneath, his long thin body, his pale skin.

Telemann stood beside the bed, shaking with rage. 'Out, buddy.'

Emery gazed at him, not moving. 'Where've you been?'

'I said out.'

Emery hesitated for a moment, then glanced at Laura and shrugged. Naked by the bed, he reached for his robe. Telemann snatched it from him.

'Tell me,' he said. 'Tell me why you did it?'

'Did what?'

'This. All this.' Telemann gestured round the room, the two beds, Laura. 'Tell me why you've been fucking my wife. Tell me why you did it.'

There was a long silence. Telemann could hear the interminable clatter of a goods train miles away across the river. Finally, Emery sat down on the bed. He was still looking at Telemann. 'That what you think?' he said. 'Me and Laura?'

'Yeah. Sure I do.' Telemann paused, staring at the other bed, the blankets pulled back, the bottom sheet hollowed with the shape of Laura's body. 'Look after you, did she? Full repertoire? Party night?'

He turned round, looking for Laura, finding her behind him, her face white, without expression. 'You disgust me,' he said, 'the pair of you. Ever think about the kids? Bree? Any of that ever occur to you? In between times?'

'Ron . . .' Laura stepped towards him, then changed her mind, sitting down on the other bed, staring at the carpet. Telemann studied them both for a moment, shaking his head, three weeks in the field, three lives changed utterly. 'Hey, guys,' he said softly. 'I'm interrupting. I'm sorry.'

Emery was still looking at him. 'You're not,' he said, 'you're interrupting nothing.'

'Bullshit.' Telemann paused, his finger pointing, his voice shaking with rage. 'You know what I should be doing with you? Here? Now? I should be beating the shit out of you. And you know why I'm not? Because my wife's here. Because she deserves better. Better than me. And better than fucking you.'

He paused for a moment longer, the finger still up, then he threw the robe at him. Emery let it fall to the floor. 'You've got it wrong, buddy,' he said quietly.

'*Buddy*?'

'Yeah, buddy.' He paused. 'I don't know what evidence you've got. I don't know what planet you've been on. But it's all wrong. You hear me? Wrong.'

'You've been seeing her,' Telemann said woodenly. 'I know you have.'

'Sure. She's a friend of mine.'

'She wrote me a note. A letter. You gave it to me. At the airport. Said she couldn't go on much longer.' He paused. 'Remember?'

'Sure.'

'So OK. So what kind of goodbye is that? Dear John. Get this. Fuck off. Yours ever . . . heh?' He paused again. 'You must have read it. You must have seen what was in it. God knows, you probably wrote the thing . . .' He broke off and fumbled in his jacket pocket, producing a rumpled sheet of paper, much folded. 'You wanna read it again? Refresh that memory of yours? Here . . .' He threw the letter towards Emery. Emery let the letter fall to the floor.

Telemann's finger was out again, pointing, his voice thickening with rage. 'Plus my wife comes to New York,' he said, 'way back now. She comes to the hotel where I'm staying. She's very pissed with me. We're not on the beach. I can understand that. Sure. But there's something else, too. She's come to tell me something else. But you know what we did?'

'Sure.'

'You do? She told you?'

'Yes.'

Telemann stared at him in pure disbelief. 'She discusses that kind of thing? How it went? Who fucked who? Who came first?' He paused. 'She tell you all that stuff?'

'She's told me everything.'

'I bet she has.' Telemann stepped closer. 'Every damn time I've phoned, you've been there. Every damn time. And you tell me now I'm wrong? Is that the way it goes? You think I'm some kind of schmuck?'

'Sure I've been there.' Emery nodded. 'She's been upset.'

'Who?'

'Laura.'

'Why?' Telemann bent towards Emery, very close now. 'I want to know why.'

Emery looked at him for a long time, then glanced at Laura. Laura was still staring at the carpet, her hands hanging loose from her knees. She looked up long enough to nod. 'Tell him,' she said quietly.

'You want me to?'

'Sure.'

Emery shrugged. 'OK.'

He got up and went to the closet. His bag was inside. He pulled the bag out and opened it, producing a long brown envelope. He returned to the bed, opening the envelope, extracting a slim file, five or six sheets of paper, stapled at one corner. Telemann peered at the file. It was neatly typed. His name was on the front page, underlined. He recognized the address of the clinic he'd visited up in Georgetown, the clinic with the million-dollar machine. He began to frown, watching Emery's long fingers leafing through the report, lines of dense typescript, figures carefully tabulated, diagrams of the human body.

Emery's fingers came to a halt. He looked up. 'You got checked over,' he said briefly.

Telemann nodded. 'I did,' he said.

'They called you back in April.'

'That's right.'

'They promised to let you have a result.'

'Yeah.'

'This is it.'

Telemann nodded again, still frowning, not saying anything. He looked briefly at Laura. She had turned her back. She was sitting on the other side of the bed, facing the wall, sobbing quietly.

'What's the matter?' Telemann said to her. 'Tell me.'

She shook her head, not looking round, and Telemann's eyes went back to the report, still on Emery's knee. Emery had his finger on a phrase towards the top of the page. He looked up. 'You know anything about myelin?'

'No.'

'It's stuff that coats your nerves. It's like cladding.' He paused. 'Yours is fucked.'

'What does that mean?'

'It means you've got multiple sclerosis. It's to do with the cladding. Your body stops doing what you want it to.'

Telemann gazed at him, nodding slowly. He'd heard the phrase before, multiple sclerosis, but he'd never wanted to know what it meant, someone else's bad news, someone else's tragedy. He sat down on Laura's bed, remembering the gas station in Hamburg, the pumps out of focus, the stuff hosing all over him, the smell of it, days afterwards.

'The eyes?' he muttered. 'Does it affect the eyes?'

Emery nodded. 'Yes,' he said.

'And the balance? All that stuff?'

'Yes.'

Telemann nodded, still smelling the gas. 'So where does it end?' he said. 'Is it lethal? Does it kill you?'

Emery looked up, closing the report, reaching for his robe. 'No,' he said, 'that's the problem.' He paused. 'That's why Laura's so upset. That's what she's been dreading. Having to tell you. Having you understand. That's why she's here.'

Telemann nodded again, swallowing hard, his hand reaching back across the rumpled sheet. 'Shit,' he said softly. His hand found hers. He squeezed it, still looking at Emery. 'You tell the Agency?'

'No.'

'Did she?'

'No.'

'Did anyone? The physician?'

'No.'

'Thank Christ for that.'

There was a long silence. Telemann squeezed his wife's hand again. 'I'm sorry,' he said numbly, 'I guess I got it wrong.'

Emery shrugged, returning the report to the envelope, letting the envelope fall to the floor.

'Question of interpretation,' he said drily. 'Never your strong point.'

*

Next morning, half-past ten, McVeigh finally made the call.

He was sitting in a corner of Amer's office in the Ramallah Municipality Buildings, the phone to his ear, waiting for Friedland to answer. The office was packed with over a dozen people, most of them young men. They stood in a semi-circle around Amer's desk, jeans and track-tops, the uniform of the barricades. Amer sat behind the desk, calm, patient, nodding from time to time, interjecting quietly in Arabic, letting the rhetoric wash over him. Speaking no Arabic, McVeigh hadn't a clue what they were talking about. Only one word did he understand, hurled back and forth, a provocation, a rallying cry. 'Saddam!' someone would shout. 'Saddam!' the others would agree.

The phone at the other end stopped ringing, and a voice answered. McVeigh recognized the voice. It sounded old, and tired, and slightly provisional, the voice of a man unconvinced by what the day might bring.

'Mr Friedland?' McVeigh said gruffly. 'It's me. Your Marine friend.'

There was a silence. Then Friedland was back, slightly more animated.

'Where are you?'

'Israel. West Bank.'

'What are you doing there?'

'It's complicated.' He glanced across the room, wincing at the sheer volume of noise, trying to seal his other ear. 'We've got some of the laughing stuff in Britain and the States. The States I know quite a lot about. Britain's a bit sketchy. Except that the stuff's safe.' He paused. 'You with me? You know about all this?'

'Yes.' Friedland paused. 'You're talking about the same commodity? Here and in the States?'

'Yes.'

'Understood.' Friedland paused again. 'And you're telling me it's safe?'

'Yes.' McVeigh frowned. 'Next, I'm going to the States. Tidying-up job. I've got the story on our Queen's Gate friend, too. Tell the client. OK?'

'Yes. Tell me—'

'No. Listen. Do me a favour. Ring this number. The boy's name's Billy. Tell him his dad sends his love. Tell him I'll be back soon. OK?'

McVeigh didn't wait for a reply but dictated the number, Sarah's place, and hung up. Amer had been unhappy having him use the phone, nervous about Israeli intercepts, asking him to keep the call as short as possible, no names, no mention of nerve gas, nothing obvious. Quite what Friedland would make of 'the laughing stuff', McVeigh didn't know, but the brief had centred on Yakov and he found it hard to believe that Friedland and his Arab client didn't have their suspicions. They must have known the background. Must have. McVeigh got to his feet. Amer was shepherding the young men towards the door. The office empty, he gestured for McVeigh to sit down again. He looked exhausted.

'Three more,' he said finally.

'Three more what?'

'Killed. Yesterday.' He nodded at the door, the departing youths in full cry again out in the corridor. 'They want me to join a strike. Another strike. They're going to close the shops and the factories. They're going to stop the taxes being paid. They want me to withold the monies already collected. Not to give it to the Israelis.'

'Will you? Will you do that?'

Amer looked at him for a moment, then shrugged. 'Maybe,' he said. 'Maybe not. We have a big problem here with Saddam. Everyone wants Saddam to win. Everyone. Saddam wins, the Americans leave the Gulf, and who knows what may happen?'

'Here?'

'Of course. Saddam says he fighting for the Palestinians. That's us. Why not believe him?'

'But what if he loses?'

'Exactly.' Amer leaned back in his chair. 'Then we would lose too. Already the Israelis say we're traitors.' He shrugged again. 'But what choice do we have? The Israelis will never give us our country back. Never. They won't even talk. You hear the kids just now?'

McVeigh nodded.

'You understand them? About the man Assali?'

'No.'

'Assali was a terrorist. He came from Nablus. He blew up Egged buses. He went to live in Germany. Then he had a change of mind about Israel. He was prepared to sit down and talk about Israeli rights. About a peace conference. About living together. And you know what the Israelis did?'

'No.'

'They killed him. Because he was suddenly so dangerous. You understand me? Words, not bullets. That's what the Israelis fear most. Words.' He paused, glancing towards the door again. 'The kids don't understand that. Why should they? All they've ever known is Israeli occupation. Road-blocks. Curfews. Arrests. Beatings. That's their language. The language the Israelis taught them.' He paused again. 'The Israelis took my brother-in-law Abu Yussuf. They had his son killed. They made him believe he was a terrorist. They gave him nerve gas. They wanted to make it look as though we would do anything to win the war. That way, they could turn the West against us, make the West see how dangerous we are, how ruthless we are.' He smiled wearily. 'You know this word? Ruthless?'

'Yes.'

'Remember it. Abu Yussuf still has the nerve gas. I talked to him this morning again. I know where he is. So far, he knows nothing about his wife. Maybe he never reads the papers. Maybe he doesn't watch television. But the moment he finds out about his wife—' he shrugged, fingering the paper-knife on his desk, testing the blade against his thumb '—then the Israelis will have done it. They'll have produced the monster. The monster from the West Bank with his nerve gas. You understand me?'

'Yes.' McVeigh hesitated. 'So what will you do about it?'

Amer sighed, putting the paper-knife down on the blotter, shaking his head. 'I don't know,' he said, 'I'm a moderate. All I want is peace. A decent life. For myself. For my children. I don't want Abu Yussuf gassing anyone. But who knows? Maybe the kids are right? Maybe violence is the only language the world understands?' He paused. 'In any case, that's not the point. The point is far simpler. The point is this. Who took Abu Yussuf to New York? Who gave him the nerve gas? Who had the idea in the first place?'

'The Israelis,' McVeigh said.

'Yes, of course.'

'But how do you prove it?'

'Exactly.' Amer took up the paper-knife again, playing with it. 'We think the Israelis may be looking for you,' he said. 'Cela, too. They're very careful with me, with people who work here. But they listen to the calls.' He nodded at the phone.

'I didn't use any names.'

'I know. I was listening.' He paused, opening a drawer, taking out a large brown envelope, closing the drawer again. 'A man will look after you. A man from Ramallah. He has a truck. He'll take you out of the West Bank. There are places for you to hide in the truck . . .' He paused again, getting up, leaving the envelope on the desk, walking to the window. 'He'll take you to Nazareth. Someone else will pick you up there.'

McVeigh frowned, following the itinerary. 'Why not the Allenby Bridge?' he said. 'Why not straight into Jordan?'

Amer smiled. 'The West Bank is a prison camp,' he said softly. 'You've seen it for yourself. The Allenby Bridge is the only road to Jordan. That's why they guard it so well.' He shrugged. 'Trucks that run to Jordan have to be tied up, like a parcel, everything sealed, special seals. Even the petrol tanks they look inside.' He shook his head. 'No one goes out through the Allenby Bridge.'

'Where am I going, then? Which route?'

Amer looked at him for a long time. Then he smiled again. 'We have a good organization,' he said. 'You must trust us.'

'I do.'

'Good.' He nodded at the desk. 'In two days you'll be with Yussuf. In the envelope are two letters. One is from me. One is from my wife. Give them to him, please.'

'Where is he?'

'There's a map in the envelope. He's in Maine. There's an address. You must phone me from the States when you get there. If he's moved on, he'll have told me.' He paused. 'There's a photograph, too. His wife gave it to me. Before she died.'

McVeigh nodded, eyeing the envelope. 'OK,' he said, 'but what about Cela?'

Amer look at him for a moment, his face in shadow, a small, slight figure, silhouetted against the light. 'Cela will come with you,' he said quietly. 'This morning.'

'And then?'

'She makes her own decision.'

*

Ross was on the M4, travelling west out of London, when he got the call from Washington. Downing Street had given Sullivan the number of his car mobile.

The American sounded even blunter than usual. 'The guy McVeigh,' he said.

'Yes?'

'Where is he? What's he doing?'

'I've no idea.' He paused, eyeing the speedo. Bristol was 90 miles away. With luck, he'd be there in time for lunch. 'Why?' he said.

'The Israelis are crawling about all over the West Bank. Looking for him.'

'How do you know?'

'We've got the ELINT and AWACS birds up from Dharan. We're reading their traffic. We need to know if they're going to pull any stunts of their own.'

Ross nodded. Since yesterday's threats from Baghdad, the world had been waiting for some word from Tel Aviv. Saddam had promised to destroy Israel if the US tried to 'strangle' Iraq. The threat had been quite explicit, the kind of language the Israelis tended not to ignore, and so now the Americans were eavesdropping on their communications.

'McVeigh,' Sullivan was saying. 'Find him. Find out where he is. Talk to him. Before the fucking Israelis do it for us.' He paused. 'Think you can manage that?'

'Of course,' Ross said automatically, signalling left, easing the car into the slow lane for the next exit.

*

McVeigh took the waiting ambulance from the Municipality Buildings to a warehouse on the outskirts of Ramallah. The windows in the back of the ambulance were opaque, and he lay full-length on the stretcher under a cellular blanket, surrendering to the attentions of a young para-medic. The medic spoke reasonable English, assuring him they wouldn't be stopped. If they were, if the Israelis flagged them down, he had instructions to administer gas from the big cylinder strapped in the corner. Unconscious, with the mask pressed to his face, McVeigh would be just another accident statistic en route to the hospital.

The journey to the warehouse took less than five minutes. The ambulance stopped and began to back, and McVeigh heard doors closing behind them. There were footsteps outside, then a murmur of conversation in Arabic, a man and a woman. The back doors opened, and McVeigh struggled upright, glad to have escaped the gas. Two faces peered inside. One he'd never seen before. The other was Cela. McVeigh grinned. She was dressed in a traditional Arab *thoub*, a long blue cotton garment. Her head was covered with a cotton scarf, and she had a pair of slippers on her feet, a garish green much favoured by the local women.

He stepped back for a moment, admiring the effect, trying to guess where she'd been. The outfit suited her. 'Where did you get it?'

Cela smiled briefly. 'It belonged to Hala,' she said.

She introduced the stranger, the truck driver who would take them to Nazareth. He was a middle-aged man, running to fat, large and cheerful. His truck was parked behind him, already loaded for the journey with a dozen crates of apples from the local orchards. McVeigh walked across to the truck. It looked as old as the driver, a Bedford 4-tonner, a survivor of countless accidents. The windscreen was cracked and the tyres were bald. In a country with no rainfall, there was even a problem with rust.

McVeigh looked at Cela. 'Where do we sit?' he said.

She laughed, beckoning him to the back of the truck. The chassis was deeper than usual, a boxlike construction caked with dirt. The back of the box was open, the interior stretching the length of the vehicle, dark, smelling of oil and exhaust.

McVeigh eyed it dubiously. He had a horror of enclosed spaces. 'In there?' he asked.

Cela nodded. It was a technique they'd picked up from Lebanon. It was the securest way for Hizbollah to transport kidnap victims from location to location. They'd lie full-length at the front of the box. The back would be stuffed with oil-drums and baulks of timber, sealing them in. Fresh air would enter through specially drilled holes in the underside. The truck was in use all the time, shuttling human cargoes around the West Bank.

McVeigh shrugged, not wanting to show his fear, stuffing Amer's envelope down his shirt, crawling into the cavity. Inside, the smell was appalling. The floor of the box was thick with oil. Wriggling forward on his belly, he could feel it on the palms of his hands, on his elbows, everywhere. There was no room for manoeuvre, nowhere to lay his head except directly on the metal floor, more oil. He made himself as comfortable as he could, peering down the length of his body, watching Cela crawl towards him. Finally she lay beside him, unwrapping the scarf from her head, folding it several times, each movement the work of a minute or so in the cramped space. McVeigh peered at her, an inch away, as she slid the folded scarf beneath his head, enough material for her own cheek, a cushion of sorts between themselves and the metal.

The driver wedged the last baulk of timber beyond their feet, shutting out the daylight, and hissed something in Arabic, very close, through the bodywork. Cela answered him with a single word, then McVeigh felt the chassis move as the driver clambered into the cab and started the engine. Almost immediately, the space around them was filled with fumes, and McVeigh began to cough, trying to get his hands to his mouth, knowing that he'd never survive the next two hours or so. Claustrophobia had been a nightmare all his life. That, in part, was why he felt so at home in the mountains, with the sense of limitless space. The truck started to move, bumping out of the warehouse, the driver grinding up through the gears, and the exhaust began to thin a little, the taste of the air not quite so sour. McVeigh shut his eyes, willing himself to calm down, hearing Cela's voice in his ear. 'Small breaths,' she was saying. 'Just take small breaths.'

He opened his eyes again, accepting her hand in his, squeezing it, marvelling at her composure, the way she could adapt, the total absence of fear or complaint. Yakov, he thought, had been the luckiest of men, as the truck turned on to the main road, heading north.

*

Friedland had been at his desk for less than an hour by the time Ross arrived back in London. He'd stayed overnight in Portsmouth, summoned by the local police who had grounds for thinking that his daughter had gone missing in the sea. She'd been seen wading into the water at the harbour-mouth, fully clothed. A witness had phoned when she'd failed to reappear.

After a night without sleep, still numb, Friedland had risen early to meet the coastguard, a thin-faced, middle-aged man with a sour view of human foibles. They'd stood together on a tower at the harbour entrance in fitful sunshine, a strong wind blowing from the west. The ebbing tide was pouring out of the harbour-mouth, piling against the rocks at the foot of the tower, and Friedland had no trouble believing the coastguard's gloomy predictions. His daughter's body wouldn't be easy to find. The sensible place to start looking was 6 or 7 miles east. After a month or so in the water, there wouldn't be very much left.

Now, back in London, Friedland sat at the desk in the big bow-window, his chair turned towards the square, wondering about a memorial service. He'd been through the same debate when his wife had died, a long session with the priest down in Carshalton, and he'd never arrived at a real conclusion. Could suicides ever be commemorated? Could the Church ever find room in its heart for those who'd turned their backs on life and elected for oblivion? Friedland gazed down on the square, watching Ross nudge his BMW into a resident's parking space, still none the wiser. His wife, Steph's mother, had chosen pills. He'd found her unconscious in bed, the cats fed, the central heating off, the bills paid, the entire house newly hoovered. The note, when it arrived through the post, had been surprisingly fond, a sentimental adieu that had further perplexed the Monsignor. Friedland shook his head, still staring out at the jigsaw of sunshine in the square, hearing Ross open the door uninvited, unannounced.

Friedland turned back into the room. Ross was standing in front of the desk, his blazer hooked over his shoulder, a busy man distracted from some important task. 'Sullivan's rung,' he said briefly. 'Wants to know about McVeigh.'

'Oh?'

'Where is he?'

'In Israel.'

'We know that.' He paused, impatient, dismissive. 'Whereabouts in Israel?'

'I've no idea.'

'Has he been in touch?'

'Yes.'

'When?'

'This morning.' Friedland nodded at the phone. 'Half an hour ago.'

'He gave you a number? Some point of contact?'

'No.'

'He'll get in touch again?'

Friedland shrugged, leaning back in his chair, half-turning towards the window, still thinking about his daughter. He'd tried to teach her to swim once, in Carshalton Baths. He'd bought her a pair of armbands and a new rubber duck. The child had cried, water in her eyes, the puzzling sting of chlorine. After a second attempt he'd given up. He yawned.

Ross was waiting, more impatient than ever. 'Well?' he said. 'Will McVeigh be phoning again?'

'He may.' Friedland shrugged. 'Or he may not.'

'He *has* to.'

'*Has* to?' Friedland looked up, amused. '*Has* to?'

'Yes.' Ross frowned, one hand in his pocket. 'Otherwise . . .'

'What?'

'Otherwise we'll be looking for other ways of—' he shrugged '—shortening the chain.'

'Like what?'

'Like that son of his.'

Friedland looked up at him, the smile wider, enjoying Ross's impatience, his belief that the world existed to do his bidding. 'What would you like me to do?' he said. 'Kidnap him?'

'Maybe.'

'You were serious?'

Ross looked down, surprised. 'Yes,' he said, 'Of course.'

Friedland nodded. Then he stood up and extended a hand. Ross was staring at him, his own hand still in his pocket. 'What's that?' he said.

'It's goodbye,' Friedland said, advancing around the desk, shepherding Ross towards the door.

The phone began to ring. Friedland paused, glanced at Ross, murmuring an apology, stepping back towards the desk and lifting the phone. He listened for a while, nodding, then thanked the caller and hung up. Ross was back in front of the desk, staring at the phone. 'McVeigh?' he queried.

Friedland looked at him and smiled. 'He says the stuff is safe. He says you have no problems. I assume that means the gas.' He paused. 'You should give your American friend the same message. Evidently they have a similar problem.' He paused again. 'McVeigh says he has the situation in hand. I gather he knows where the gas is.'

Ross stared at him. 'What else?' he said, nodding at the phone. 'What else did he say?'

'Just then?' Friedland smiled again. 'That was the coastguard. At Portsmouth. They've found my daughter. Washed up on a beach.'

*

McVeigh knew the journey was over because Cela told him so, her mouth to his ear, her arm cradling his head. 'Nazareth,' she whispered. 'We're there.'

McVeigh nodded, grunting. He'd been sick three times, vomiting quietly into the darkness. The stench had stayed with them, the sweet-sour smell penetrating the haze of diesel exhaust. Half an hour into the journey, McVeigh had known with absolute certainty that he wouldn't survive. The endless pumps, the endless gear changes, the endless whine of the transmission. Twice they'd been stopped for checks, the truck lurching off the road, the engine still on, the compartment filling with exhaust. Cela had lain beside him, listening intently to the voices of the soldiers circling the truck, her body pressed to his, simple reassurance. On both occasions the stops had been brief, the driver joshing with the troops, an exchange of insults and a warning to take it easy as he engaged gear again, hauling the truck back on to the highway, resuming the journey north.

Once, the journey more than half-done, the truck had slowed on a long hill, the engine labouring down through the gears, the exhaust fumes thicker than ever, curling around them. McVeigh had shut his eyes, gasping for air, the vomit rising again in his throat, and Cela had calmed him, whispering in his ear, telling him that this was the worst of it, that no hill lasted for ever, that the top would come, and the fresher air afterwards, the long downhill stretch, nothing quite so bad any more. Listening to her, concentrating hard on the words, McVeigh had nodded, thinking of the men and women they'd left behind them, the scenes at the hospital, the broken heads and broken lives, knowing that their journey would be infinitely longer than his.

Now, in Nazareth, the truck stopped, reversed, stopped, reversed again and finally came to a halt. The driver killed the engine, and in the silence that followed, McVeigh heard him pulling the key from the ignition. Then he was down beside the cab, the door slammed shut behind him, voices at the tailgate, the sound of oil cans being wrenched out, the first glimmers of daylight penetrating the thick blue haze.

Dazed, McVeigh tried to help Cela slide out, feet first, finally joining her on the concrete outside. The truck had parked in a yard. The yard was surrounded by low, flat-roofed buildings. McVeigh, blinking, looked around, taking his first real lungfuls of air, marvelling at the sensation, an almost liquid taste. He looked at Cela. She was covered in oil and dirt, and parts of Hala's *thoub* were caked in vomit. He reached out, apologizing, meaning to brush it off, but his knees began to buckle and the ground came up to meet him, his fall cushioned by someone stepping quickly forward. McVeigh shook his head, apologizing again, peering up at the huge face, the black beard, the gruff smile.

'Moshe,' he said thickly.

An hour later they were driving north again, back in Moshe's truck, three of them in the driving compartment, the windows open, the hot wind flooding in. Water from a bucket in the yard had returned McVeigh to real life, but even now he could still taste the diesel and the vomit. Getting into Moshe's truck, he'd caught sight of himself in the big wing-mirror, a creature from some horror movie, his hair matted with oil, his face caked in dirt, his eyes bloodshot. Cela, already in the cab, had extended a hand, helping him up, smiling, giving his arm a squeeze. Bucketing north to the roar of the engine, orchards and fishponds flanking the road, McVeigh had let the slipstream sluice through him, emptying his mind of everything but the moment when he could strip off his clothes, and raise his face to the shower, and feel whole again.

They reached the kibbutz in early afternoon, the hottest part of the day. Moshe swung the big truck off the road, bumping down a dirt track beside the chicken-houses. Out of the truck, Cela led McVeigh to a chalet he'd never seen before, a remote corner of the kibbutz. The front door was unlocked. They stepped inside, stirring a brief melody from the hanging chimes beside the door. The chalet was cool and dark after the heat outside. A fan revolved slowly in the ceiling. Cela walked across the big living-room, immediately at home, and disappeared through a door at the back. McVeigh heard the splashing of water from a shower, then Cela was back again, beckoning him, the long *thoub* discarded, clad only in her knickers. McVeigh joined her in the shower, stripping off his clothes, leaving them in a pile on the bathroom floor while she soaped him, head to toe, and then busied herself with a coarse flannel, rubbing and rubbing, loosening the oil and the dirt, massaging his scalp with her fingers, tender gestures, wholly intimate. McVeigh watched her at work, motherly, sisterly, doing what a best friend would do, without embarrassment, and he realized that his was what life must had been like for them all, years back, Yakov, Moshe,

370

Cela, on this same kibbutz. Briefly enrolled, a stranger passing through, he'd joined this strange fraternity.

Clean again, exhausted, he let her rub him dry, more intimacy, her expert fingers, the rough nap of the towel in the smallest, wettest places. Afterwards she led him by the hand through to a bedroom, the single sheet already turned down.

'Sleep,' she said.

McVeigh lay on the bed, still naked, smiling up at her, and she ducked her head, kissing him on the lips, pulling up the sheet, promising to wake him later, promising to be there. The last he remembered, shutting his eyes, was the sound of the front door opening and closing, and that same sweet song from the chimes inside.

*

Abu Yussuf woke late, the curtains still tightly drawn, the motel room in darkness. He lay in the bed for a moment or two, staring at the crack of light down the middle of the big picture window. He could hear the whine of a chain-saw near by. Further away, the growl of a truck, getting fainter all the time. Apart from that, there was nothing.

The old man got out of bed, padding across the room, tugging on the cord at the side of the window, opening the curtains. Arriving in darkness, he'd had an impression of trees and water. He'd heard the water, walking in from the car, and he'd smelt it, the chill breath of a river or a stream. It had been quiet, too, miles from the Interstate, no traffic on the empty country roads.

The curtains open, he gasped at the view, blinking in the sudden light. The hotel was surrounded by mountains. They towered above him, peak after peak, the dark greens of the pine forest turning to bare rock, blacks and browns, above the tree-line. He shook his head, marvelling at the transformation, a day and a half at the wheel, New York to up here, Maine, the very top of the US, the last page on the map. He turned away from the window, reaching for his clothes, remembering the decision he'd taken the previous evening. They might be looking for the car. They might have a description. Time to change the number-plate. Time for a different colour.

He dressed quickly, stepping out of his room, skipping

breakfast, going straight to the car. Driving in the previous evening, he'd noticed a garage and a couple of stores in a village down the road. He'd go there first, find out where he could hire equipment, make some enquiries. Later, midday, he'd phone Amer again, tell him where he'd got to, tell him what was happening.

He drove south, every bend in the road offering a new mountain, a fresh view. The big, broad-leaved trees by the road were ablaze with autumn, a deep russet, the branches stirring in the breeze, the air perceptibly colder through the open window. Two miles down the road, he found the village. The garage was open, an old man in denim overalls pumping gasoline into an ancient pick-up. Two women were talking outside a hardware store next door.

Abu Yussuf parked the Oldsmobile and walked across the road. He hated travelling in daylight now, uncertain what the police might or might not know, aware all the time of the tell-tale exhaust-pipes, one real, one not. He pushed open the door of the hardware store and stepped in. There was a special smell about the place. He could smell wax, and hemp, and wood, a pungent resinous smell. He went to the counter, explaining himself, what he wanted. The woman behind the counter looked dubious. The village was tiny. The garage didn't do that kind of thing. He'd have to go somewhere bigger, Houlton maybe, or even back to Bangor. Best thing to do, buy a paper, look in the classified ads, places offering that kind of service. The old man nodded thanking her, taking a paper, paying for it. The door banged shut behind him, and he walked slowly back to the car, the paper folded under his arm, enjoying the brisk warmth of the sunshine, the smell of the forest in the wind.

He got into the car, sitting back, taking his time, unfolding the paper, looking for the classified ads. Foreign news was on page five. His eye drifted down the page, then stopped. There was a grainy black and white photograph. It showed a line of youths, their faces masked. There were soldiers in the foreground, nearer the camera. They had helmets and shields. Some of them carried guns. The old man frowned, gazing at the photograph, recognizing the building in the background, the chest-high gates surrounding the Court House scrolled with barbed wire. Ramallah, he thought. He studied the photograph for a moment longer, looking for faces he might know, then his eye went to the headline underneath, his lips moving slowly, spelling out of the words, one by one. JAIL DEATH PRO-VOKES RIOT, the headline read.

The old man shut his eyes for a moment, shaking his head, trying to dislodge the headline, trying to make it go away, but seconds later it was still there. He moistened his lips. His lips were dry. He read on through the text, a stranger in the jungle, a path he didn't know, every footfall fraught with danger. Then, abruptly, he saw her name. Hala. His Hala. His wife. The mother of his sons. Dead. Killed. In an Israeli military prison. He stared out through the windshield, seeing nothing, no trees, no autumn, no mountains, hearing the youths screaming abuse, the wailing sirens, the grim-faced Israelis with their megaphones and their broken Arabic, the smack of wood on flesh, the olive-green tide of soldiers, storming forward. He hesitated for a moment, breathless, sweating, then he reached for the ignition key, turning it, knowing what he had to do.

14

Sullivan was outside the Oval Office within a minute, answering the Presidential summons. So far the day's news had been excellent: the United Nations, up in New York, was on the verge of voting for an air embargo of Iraq. Sources within the Security Council were predicting a near-unanimous 'yes'. Better still, Eduard Shevardnadze, the Soviet Foreign Minister, had told the US Ambassador at the UN that Moscow was now prepared to back the use of force to free Kuwait. Nothing, no single gesture, could have pleased the President more. It was the living proof that the Cold War was over and won, the humbled Soviet superstate turning against the regime they had once backed and armed.

Sullivan knocked twice on the door and went in. The President was sitting by the fire, his long frame occupying one corner of the sofa. He glanced up from reading a brief, his forefinger anchored in the middle of the page. 'Hi,' he said 'Take a seat here.'

Sullivan sat down. Over the last four days, the relationship between himself and the President had cooled. It was a difficult thing to measure, but Sullivan, who had a gift for sensing the political temperature, knew it was so. The phone had stopped ringing, the spontaneous calls for advice or a minute's conversation. His mailbag had lightened. His name was suddenly missing from the circulation list of key policy documents. And most ominous of all, he'd been excluded from two crucial meetings in the last twenty-four hours, both of them principals-only, his kind of people, honchos with real clout. His turf, that handful of squares on the gameboard that was Washington, was definitely under threat.

Sullivan sat down and the President smiled at him, nodding

at the coffee-pot, returning to the brief. He read for perhaps five minutes, saying nothing, concentrating on the text. Sullivan poured himself a coffee, not touching it, leaving it on the low table between the two sofas. Finally the President looked up, closing the file, laying it face down on the cushion beside him.

'Good news and bad news,' he said brightly. 'Both from Tel Aviv.'

'Sir?'

'The bad news you'll know. Shamir is off the leash. He's prepared to mobilize against Saddam and he's told him so. More to the point, he's told us too.'

'Meaning?'

The President pulled a face, his eyes going to the buff file beside him. Sullivan could see the State Department seal on the back cover. It was a diplomatic brief, probably sourced direct, from Tel Aviv.

The President leaned forward. 'Meaning he'll pre-empt any moves west by Saddam. If Saddam lifts a finger, pow!' He smacked his fist into the open palm of his other hand, a favourite gesture. 'The guy's history.'

Sullivan nodded. 'But what's he saying? Specifically?'

'Nothing. But you wouldn't expect him to spell it out.' He paused, reaching for the coffee-pot. 'The Pentagon guys are pretty clear about it. In the first place, he'd send airstrikes. He'd go for the airfields. He'd knock out his planes on the ground. Then—' he shrugged '—he'd go looking for the Scuds. The Republican Guards. Any damn thing Saddam could use against him.' He paused again, pouring the coffee. 'You know these guys. When push comes to shove, they're single-minded. You know what matters to them.'

'Tel Aviv? Jerusalem?'

'Sure. And the rest of it.' He shook his head. 'Regardless.'

Sullivan nodded again, reaching for his own cup. The coffee was cold, but he swallowed it none the less. The President was right. The news couldn't be worse. The day the Israelis bombed Iraq, the coalition would be history. The Egyptians would pull out, the Syrians would go, even the Moroccans and the Spanish might send their regrets. Should that happen, it would be a very different war. Without the backing of the UN, without a multinational Task Force, the US presence in the Gulf would be seen for what it really was: naked self-interest, the old battle for cheap oil, the First World against the Also-Rans.

Sullivan looked up. 'And the good news?' he grunted.

The President nodded slowly, thoughtfully, studying him across the table.

'Our friends with the nerve gas . . .' he said at last.

'Sir?'

'The Israelis have found them.'

Sullivan stared at him. '*Found* them?'

'Well . . .' The President smiled. 'I guess not found them. But yes, they know who they are.'

'You're sure about that?'

'They told us. This morning. Fresh stuff. Good stuff. Hot from the oven.'

'What did they say?'

The President looked at Sullivan for a moment, the accusation plain in his face. Then he produced a yellow strip of paper from his pocket. He unfolded it, smoothing it on his knee. 'Two names,' he said slowly. 'Ali Karami. And Abu Yussuf.' He looked up. 'Mean anything?'

Sullivan nodded. 'Sure,' he said. 'The first one. Ali. He was the kid they found up in the Catskills.' He paused. 'We knew that already. It checks out. He was the kid who disappeared from the hotel up in New York. The night the first guy got gassed. We knew that. We had that one already. It's under control.'

'Yeah?'

'Yeah.'

The President nodded, saying nothing for a moment. Then he glanced down at the paper again. 'And this other guy? Yussuf?'

Sullivan frowned, shaking his head. 'No, sir.'

'Nothing?'

'No, sir.'

'Never heard of him?'

'No, sir.' He reached for the paper, still frowning.

The President shook his head. 'I'm pushing it through channels,' he said. 'It's gone to the FBI, the New York State police, every damn agency. Evidently the guy's dangerous. He has gallons of the stuff. We have a description.'

'Of what?'

'The car he's driving. And the guy himself.' He paused. 'Evidently he's some kind of veteran. Old guy from the West Bank. Fanatic. Been a terrorist all his life. He's the one got this 7th June group together. One-man band.' He paused again. 'The Israelis have files on him. They've sent photographs. They came in this morning. They're recommending we shoot on sight.' He smiled. 'The Feds tell me it'll be hours. A day at the most.'

'What will?'

'Getting to this guy. Our West Bank friend. Mr—' he paused, looking down again, musing on the name '—Yussuf ... Joseph—' he shrugged '—whatever . . .'

Sullivan nodded, leaning back against the firm white cushions, abandoning the coffee. He knew a political execution when he met one, the feeling of power slipping away, the eyes turning in his direction, the voices lowered, the quiet invitation to leave the room. It had happened to him once before. It had taken him eight years to repair the damage. Reinstated, his feet under another desk, he'd vowed never to let it happen again. Yet here he was. Well and truly fucked. For the second time.

He mustered a weak smile, still looking at the President. 'Sir . . .?' he said.

'Yeah?'

'Going back to the bad news. The Israelis. Saddam . . .' He paused. 'What leverage do we have?'

The President looked up, his hand reaching for a second cup of coffee. He smiled.

'Right now,' he said, 'we have none. Which is why I thought you might have some ideas.'

*

It was late afternoon by the time Telemann and Emery reached the outskirts of Itzehoe. The town lay north-west of Hamburg, an hour's journey, halfway to the border with Denmark. Still on the autobahn, Emery slowed, easing the rental BMW into the slow lane, eyeing the blue and white indicator boards.

'Here?'

Telemann, sitting beside him, nodded. By his calculation, they had three hours of daylight left. There was no time for a proper search, quartering the local map they'd bought, exploring the minor roads, one by one. No. If they were to find what he suspected they'd find, if it were to happen before dusk, then he had to trust his instincts.

'Left,' he said briefly. 'To Wilster.'

Emery nodded, turning left, back on to the network of local roads that snaked between the flat, neat parcels of farmland. Telemann glanced across at Emery, his finger on the map. They'd left Laura at the hotel in Bad Godesburg. She'd check out, pay the bills, and head for the big international airport at Frankfurt. There were a dozen overnight flights to the US, at least three to Washington. She'd be back home in time for breakfast, getting ready for Telemann's return. Thinking about it, Telemann smiled.

'Crazy,' he said for the third time. 'She should leave me.'

'Bullshit. You were never great at the long words.' Emery smiled. 'Like patience.'

'I never thought.' Telemann looked at Emery again. 'Honest to God.'

Emery shrugged. They'd spent the journey north taking stock, Telemann briefing Emery, telling him exactly what had happened in the apartment in Dusseldorf, himself delivering the nerve gas, duped by Mossad for the second time in a week, Wulf convulsing in front of his eyes, the ugliest of deaths. He still had some of Inge's photos of Wulf, and he'd shown them to Emery in the morning while Laura was taking a shower. Emery had fingered the photos, recognizing Wulf's bull-neck, his paunch, amused at the poses, knowing that the material was priceless, the best possible way of armouring Sullivan against whatever the Germans might throw at him. The man had been an animal. Far more important, he'd chosen a Mossad plant for a mistress. What kind of judgement was that? What kind of other risks was the man prepared to take? At this point in the conversation Laura had returned, intrigued to see what they were studying, and Telemann had changed the subject, suggesting she order coffee and Danish, three huge helpings, palming the photographs into his pocket, part of a life that was nearly over. He and Laura had spent the night in the single bed, very close, nose to nose, scarcely talking. In the morning she'd bandaged his leg, cleaning it thoroughly, wondering when they'd start talking seriously, planning for the difficult years ahead. Saying goodbye, hours later, Telemann had taken her face in his hands, telling her he'd be home in days, telling her he couldn't wait, telling her it would all work out.

'That's my line,' she'd said, kissing him. 'My kind of cliché.'

Now, driving into Wilster, Telemann told Emery to stop, scanning a municipal information board at the roadside, looking for the Fire Department. Finding it, he told Amery where to go. 'Left,' he said, 'then right, and right again.'

They drove into the town. It was compact, old, attractive, streets of half-timbered houses, shops still open in the late afternoon. The Fire Department, by contrast, was a modern building, concrete and glass. Two appliances were parked inside the folding double doors.

Telemann, limping badly, led the way to the office, a door at the side of the building. A uniformed official glanced up as they came in. He was smoking a small cigar and reading an old paperback.

Telemann did the introductions, plucking names from nowhere. 'Mr Stuart,' he said, 'and Mr Wallace. We're touring.'

The official nodded, getting up, shaking hands, listening courteously while Telemann explained what he wanted. He had friends in the area. They had some kind of cottage. He'd heard there'd been a fire. He wondered whether it was true. The official looked at him for a moment, speculative. His English was excellent.

'Fire?'

Telemann nodded. 'Some kind of cottage. Small farm, maybe.'

'When?'

'Recently. This week.'

The official nodded slowly, his eyes going to Emery. He said nothing for a moment. Then he beckoned them across the office. On the wall was a large-scale map of the area. The area was bounded in the north by the Kiel Canal, to the south by the Wilster–Itzehoe road. In between was a lattice of fields and smallholdings, houses marked by tiny black squares. Three of the houses, miles apart, were ringed in red, with dates pencilled beneath. Telemann looked at each of them. The dates went back to the beginning of the year. He looked again, selecting the most recent fire.

'September twenty-first,' he said. 'Four days ago.'

'That's right.'

'What kind of place is that?' He put a finger on the map.

The official peered at the map. 'It's a farmhouse,' he said at last.

'What happened?'

He shrugged. 'Nobody knows. We were called by a farmer—' his finger went to the map '—here.'

'Was it badly damaged?'

'It was burned down. The house. The buildings attached. Everything.'

'Nobody knows why?'

'No.'

'Nobody suspects?'

The official shrugged again. 'Of course,' he said. 'But we are firemen. Not the police.'

Telemann nodded, knowing that his instinct had been correct, looking at the map again, memorizing the route, where the farmhouse lay in relation to the town. Then he turned to the official, extending a hand, hearing Emery muffling a polite cough behind him.

Emery stepped forward. 'Our friends,' he said, 'were they badly hurt?'

The official smiled, still looking at Telemann. 'No, sir,' he said quietly. 'The house was empty. Nobody has been in touch with us.' He paused. 'Strange, don't you think?'

Telemann found the farmhouse in minutes, bumping down a

track from the main road, recognizing the distinctive shape of a copse of trees beyond the hedgerow.

'There,' he said. 'The house is through the trees.'

'This is where you came?'

'Yes. Look . . .' Telemann pointed. Half a mile away across the fields, the top half of an ocean-going freighter was moving slowly across the skyline, smoke bubbling up from the single funnel aft.

Emery nodded, impressed. 'Kiel Canal,' he said. 'You must have been awake.'

They parked in the shadow of the trees, walking the last 100 metres to the farmhouse, the same path Telemann had trodden a week earlier, before Halle, before Bad Godesburg, before his brutal rendezvous with Otto Wulf. The long grass was wet from an earlier rain shower. Telemann could feel his trousers sticking to the bandage on his leg.

They emerged from the trees and paused for a moment. The farmhouse had been razed to the ground, only the walls left, knee-high. Inside, the place was a mess, a black porridge of charred remains, everything either burned by the heat or pulped by the firemen's hoses. Telemann and Emery stepped through it, looking for something recognizable, finding pieces of cutlery, empty bottles, the metal shell of a refrigerator, display panels from an audio stack. Telemann stood over it, poking it with his foot, remembering the German, Klausmann, sitting in his armchair, pipe in his mouth, listening to Brahms. It was Klausmann who'd first told him about Littmann Chemie, about the Iraqi connection. It was Klausmann who'd talked about chemicals, about nerve gas. It was Klausmann who'd sent him to Halle. He shivered in the autumn wind, walking on through the wreckage, the divisions between the rooms unrecognizable, looking round, knowing that the place must have been torched, that the Israelis had been here, covering their tracks, wiping the record clean.

Telemann glanced round, hearing his name called. Emery was 20 metres away, squatting on his haunches, something in his hand. Telemann joined him, stepping round the puddles. They were in a different area now, outside the main farmhouse, the ground still littered with debris and charred wood. Telemann frowned, recognizing the remains of a pump, the outlet pipe open-mouthed, the rubber hose gone. The night he'd been here, he'd heard a motor running in the darkness. At the time, he'd put the noise down to a generator supplying the electricity, but now, looking down, he began to have second thoughts. The farmhouse, after all, might have been mains-fed. In which case, the noise he'd heard could only have been the pump. He peered at Emery, who had something in his hand. He turned it over. It was steel, the length of a milk bottle, the same kind of size. It was open-mouthed at both ends. Emery lifted it to his nose, smelling it carefully. He looked up, shaking his head.

Telemann bent down. 'What's it smell of?'

'Nothing.'

'What is it?'

'God knows.' Emery looked inside, inserting a finger.

'What's that?'

'Some kind of filter.' Emery frowned, measuring it by eye. 'About twenty millimetres.' He stood up, looking round again, stirring up the debris with his foot. The place stank, a sad, sour smell, a soup of thick, glutinous ash. Emery paused, and bent again, reaching down with his fingers, retrieving a length of pipe, fitting it to the object he'd already found, confirming that it was the same bore. He glanced at Telemann.

'You come out here at all? When you visited?'

'No. Only the farmhouse.' Telemann gestured around him. 'Not out here.'

Emery nodded, continuing his search, finding more lengths of pipe. He laid them out on the sodden ash, producing a small camera, photographing them from three angles. Then he began to pace the area of damage, up and down, a step at a time, finding another length of pipe. He took more photographs, with Telemann watching. Finally, he pocketed the camera, joining Telemann on the grass beneath the trees. It had started to rain, a thin drizzle, misting the fields. Emery grimaced at Telemann. He'd wrapped the object he'd found in a handkerchief.

Telemann nodded at the pipes, still neatly latticed on the ashes. 'What would you find in the pipes?' he said.

Emery shrugged. 'Nothing,' he said. 'Fire destroys everything. They'd know that.'

'And that thing?' Telemann eyed the filter.

'I don't know.'

Telemann nodded, none the wiser, limping after Emery as he walked back through the trees towards the car.

Twenty minutes later, rejoining the autobahn for Hamburg, Telemann glanced across at him. In an hour they'd be outside Inge's lakeside apartment, another locked door, another neat piece of houseclearing, another dead end.

Telemann thought of Wulf again. 'She meant to kill him,' he said quietly. 'I know she did.'

Emery said nothing for a moment, adjusting the wipers to the rain. Then he glanced across at Telemann. He was smiling.

'Yeah,' he said, 'That or suicide.'

∗

By the time McVeigh awoke, it was dark. The wind had risen, and he could hear the trees stirring near by. There was a draught, too, and now and again he caught a faint tinkling from the hanging chimes by the front door. He struggled upright. Even now he still had the taste of diesel in his mouth, a sour, slightly metallic taste, and he swallowed a couple of times, trying to get rid of it.

He peered round, suddenly aware of a presence in the room, someone else sitting in the low wicker chair by the door, looking at him. He blinked. It was Cela.

'It's late,' she said. 'I have food for you. Soon we must go.'

They ate together in the tiny kitchen, a salad of eggs and tomatoes and feta cheese. Cela had brought bread from the dining-hall, newly baked, and McVeigh piled the salad between thick slices, surprised at how hungry he was. There was a jug of juice, too, and sluicing down the last of the salad, he could taste plums and apples and pears, windfalls from the orchard, pulped and chilled. Finishing the meal, washing his plate in the sink, McVeigh called to Cela. She was in the next room, laying out fresh clothes for him, a shirt, jeans and a pair of heavy boots.

'Where are we going?' he said.

'Lebanon.'

'*Where?*'

'Lebanon.' She looked up, squatting on the wooden floor. 'Moshe will take you to the border. Up in the mountains. He knows the paths through the mine-fields. Amer's people will meet you there. We must go soon. They have a car. They want you in Beirut by dawn.'

McVeigh nodded, drying the plate, joining Cela in the next room. 'Moshe do this often?' he said.

Cela looked away, still folding the shirt, not answering. McVeigh stood beside her. She was wearing shorts and a thin T-shirt. Hardly the clothes for a hike in the mountains.

'What about you?' he said. 'You coming too?'

Cela looked up.

'Well?' he said.

Cela shook her head. 'I'll come with you part of the way,' she said. 'Then you're on your own.'

McVeigh frowned, not understanding. 'You're staying on the kibbutz?'

'Yes.'

'And they're still looking for you?'

'Yes.' She shrugged. 'Of course.'

'But won't they come here? Isn't this the obvious place to look?'

'Of course,' she said again, gesturing round. 'But it's a big kibbutz. It's easy to hide. No one talks. And there are other places to go, too. Other friends I can stay with. They can look for ever. They won't find me.' She paused, fingering a loose button on the shirt. 'It's my home,' she said. 'It's where I belong.' She smiled. 'Maybe that's hard for you to understand?'

'Yes.' McVeigh nodded. 'Just now it is.' He took the shirt from her, pulling it on, over his head. It smelled newly laundered, a soft, clean smell. He reached for the jeans and put those on too, surprised at what a good fit they were. Dressed,

384

he helped Cela to her feet. 'You can't hide for ever,' he said. 'If they want to find you, they will.'

She looked at him for a moment, inspecting him, very close, and then she licked a finger and touched his face, high on the cheek-bone, a blemish of some kind, something he'd missed in the shower. Then she smiled, her face tilted up, and kissed him lightly on the chin. 'If you get to America,' she said softly, 'they'll never dare touch me.'

They left the kibbutz half an hour later, Moshe driving a small jeep, a relic from the '73 war. The jeep was open at the back, and McVeigh sat sideways on the metal floor as it bucketed along. Getting into the jeep, Moshe had produced a gun which he had handed to him with a dark smile. The weapon was an Uzi, an Israeli-made sub-machine-gun. McVeigh had used them before, in and out of uniform, and rated them highly. It was a beautiful gun, perfectly balanced, reliable, accurate, capable of absorbing infinite punishment. Now he had the weapon on his lap, the two spare magazines wedged in his belt. Quite why he'd need it, neither Moshe nor Cela had made clear. Maybe he was expected to fight his way across the border. Maybe the travel arrangements were less than perfect.

Off the mountain, back on the valley floor, they turned right and headed north along a narrow track through mile after mile of orchards. Moshe drove fast, dancing the jeep round the worst of the pot-holes, growling from time to time as one or other of the wheels left the ground. The night air was cool in the valley and McVeigh sucked hungrily at the slipstream, forcing it deep into his lungs, still haunted by the memory of the morning's journey. That he'd survived at all was a miracle, and he knew it, one hand on Cela's shoulder, a gesture of gratitude and admiration.

At the head of the valley they turned right again, a bigger road, a dusty white ribbon winding up the mountainside. Moshe dropped through the gear-box, urging the jeep ahead, cursing softly when he misjudged a particularly vicious hairpin, the jeep slewing sideways on the loose gravel, McVeigh bracing himself for the inevitable impact, Cela motionless, unperturbed. The jeep came to a halt in a cloud of dust and they were off again, whining up the mountain, the lights of another kibbutz straddling the hillside above them. They turned off again, plunging down a narrow track, the lights suddenly gone. It was abruptly colder, and lifting his head, peering forward, McVeigh could smell the damp, resinous breath of a forest.

Amongst trees, they stopped, Moshe killing the engine. In the silence, McVeigh could hear the splash of water falling on to rocks. Cela glanced around. She'd produced a small bottle from a bag at her feet. The bottle had a screw-top. McVeigh could see it in the light from Moshe's torch. Cela motioned for him to get out of the jeep. He did so, joining her in a small clearing beneath the trees.

'What now?'

'Come with me.'

She led the way down a path through the trees, sweeping left and right with the beam of Moshe's torch. McVeigh could hear Moshe turning the jeep round behind them. He wondered for a moment whether they'd arrived at the border, whether it was Cela's job to pick a route through the mine-fields. Then, suddenly, they were out of the trees and standing on the edge of a narrow gorge. Cela angled the torch down. Water was bubbling over a series of ledges. McVeigh could see it tumbling over a longer drop downstream. He shivered. For the first time in Israel, he felt a sense of physical chill.

Cela handed him the torch, telling him to shine it on the water. He did so, pooling the beam on a spot a metre or two in front of her. Cela squatted at the water's edge, filling the bottle, sealing it tight, putting it to one side. Watching her, McVeigh knew she'd been here before, doing this very same thing. Her movements had an element of ritual, of something semireligious. She hesitated for a moment, gazing upstream, then she cupped both hands, filling them with water, raising them to her mouth, drinking. She did it again, retrieving the bottle, standing up, rejoining McVeigh. She gave him the bottle.

'Here,' she said.

'For me?'

'No. For Yussuf.'

McVeigh nodded, feeling how cold the water was through the glass. 'Yussuf?' he said. 'You want me to give this to Yussuf?'

'Yes.' She looked at him, then nodded back at the stream, invisible now in the darkness. 'That's the River Jordan. Where it begins. Every time Yakov went abroad, I came up here. To give him the water too.' She hesitated, touching McVeigh lightly on the hand. 'Please. For Yussuf. Tell him what it is. Tell him it comes from me.'

'Will he understand?'

'No.'

'Did he know Yakov?'

'No.' She paused. 'Tell him it comes from an Israeli wife. An Israeli widow.' She paused again. 'And tell him that some of us are ashamed. We shoot and we cry.' She reached for his hand and pressed something else into it, a small square of cloth, edged with tassles. 'And give him this, too.'

'What is it?'

'I cut it from Hala's scarf. It's his wife's. It's for him.'

McVeigh nodded, pocketing the material, turning away from the river. Cela had the torch now, the beam probing the path back. As she began to move away, he caught her arm, the gentlest touch. 'What about me?' he said.

Cela stopped and looked up at him, her face just visible in the spill from the torch. 'You?' She smiled. 'You'll come back. I know you will.'

'You want that? You'd like that to happen?'

Cela looked at him for a moment longer, still smiling. Then she leaned up for him with both hands, her eyes closing, the beam of the torch spearing wildly into the trees. Her lips were still wet, with the sweet, chill taste of the Jordan.

'You know what we say,' she whispered, 'here, in Israel?'

McVeigh shook his head, holding her. She opened her eyes, looking at him.

'We say *shalom*,' she said. 'It means Peace.'

*

It took Telemann less than a minute to get into Inge's apartment. He did it with a tempered-steel pick, Emery's credit card, and a final kick from his one good leg. For a moment, the two men stood in the open doorway, listening. Four rings on the doorbell had produced no response, but Telemann had been caught like this before. The favourite trick had you inside too quickly, anxious to avoid enquiries from the neighbours. Off-guard, unbalanced, that was when they took you. Telemann waited for a moment longer, his leg beginning to throb again. Then he stepped inside, gesturing for Emery to follow.

The apartment was empty. They moved quickly from room to room, confirming the obvious, that Inge and Blum had decamped, leaving behind them nothing but soiled bedding, cupboards of food, and a small saucepan on the stove, stone-cold, the milk covered with a thin film of whey.

Telemann returned to the bedroom. The wardrobe was empty, the drawers too. On the dressing-table were a couple of discarded hairclips and an old brush. Telemann lifted the brush, inspecting it closely, recognizing the long blond hairs. He sniffed it once, eyeing the bed in the mirror, then he circled the room, remembering the photographs, the angles they'd captured, looking for the hidden cameras. According to Inge there'd been four, and he found them one by one, neat, effective installations, the cavities masked by hanging pictures, or curtain drapes, or one or other of the huge mirrors. The cameras themselves had gone, but Telemann was able to trace the tiny cable runs which had linked them together, the cables forming a junction at floor level, another cable laid beneath the carpet, emerging on the inside of one of the legs of the bed. Telemann lay full-length on the bed for a moment, reaching down, his fingers finding the button at once. He smiled, the simplicity of it. This was how she'd triggered the cameras, either shot for shot, or – more likely – a single pulse initiating a sequence of shots, carefully timed, offering her a chance to choreograph the action, the circus ringmaster with her mask and her whip and her repertoire of animal tricks. He closed his eyes for a moment, wondering again whether she'd bothered to waste any film on his own brief appearance, realizing for the first time that he didn't care.

He opened his eyes again to find Emery in the doorway, watching him.

'Stay here long?'

Telemann nodded, rueful. 'Three days.'

'Worth it?'

Telemann considered the question for a moment longer than he should have. Then he shook his head. 'An education,' he said quietly, 'like you wouldn't believe.'

They went back into the living-room, searching carefully, on hands and knees, every square inch of carpet, every ashtray, every book on the shelf beside the kitchen hatch. They took the back off the television, peering inside. They took the pictures off the walls, dismantled the telephone, emptied the fruit bowl, tipped out the waste-bin, eliminating all the obvious places, one by one, finding nothing.

They repeated the procedure in the kitchen, going through the cupboards, piling up sachets of soup, removing crockery, emptying the refrigerator, wrestling the washing-machine into the middle of the floor, examining the alcove behind, knowing all the time that the effort was probably worthless, that no graduate of the Mossad Academy would leave anything of any value.

Finally, empty-handed, they shut the internal doors and made their way out of the apartment. Twenty-four hours after the event, the German media were at last reporting the death of Otto Wulf, and Telemann paused in the hallway, picking up the name in the blur of sound from the television in the next-door apartment. So far the reports had made no mention of foul play or police involvement. On the contrary, a terse statement from the administration at the Dusseldorf Hospital had blamed a long-standing coronary condition. The man had been over-wrought and under stress. He'd suffered a major heart attack. The funeral, in a church in Berlin, would be in a week's time. End of story.

Now, reaching for the front door, Telemann saw the package on the floor. It was wrapped in brown paper, neatly taped, with his name stencilled across it in large black letters. Coming into the flat, the kick perhaps over-eager, the package must have disappeared behind the door. Telemann bent to the carpet and retrieved it. It wasn't heavy. Back in the living-room, he put it on the table. Emery was beside him.

'What do you think? We open it? You wanna take the risk?'

Emery shook his head. 'The Consulate,' he said briefly. 'Put it through the analyser.'

They left the apartment and drove to the Consulate. The duty officer, recognizing Telemann, signed them in. It was late for the mail-room, but the duty officer had the key and knew how to work the analyser. The analyser was at the end of the mail-room. It was the size of a rabbit hutch, matt grey metal, the technology adapted from similar machines in use in US airports. The duty officer switched it on, lifting the swing-lid on top and putting the parcel carefully inside. The three men stood around the small TV screen. In various shades of grey, it showed the outlines of the parcel. Inside was something folded. Telemann could see buttons. He frowned.

'It's a jacket,' the duty officer said. 'Someone's jacket.'

'Anything else?'

'Yeah. Some kind of envelope. Here.' He indicated a shape in the middle of the parcel.

Telemann peered at it. It didn't look very big. 'Any hazard?' he said.

'Not that I can see.'

Telemann glanced at Emery, who shrugged. Telemann lifted the parcel out and began to open it. Inside he found his jacket, the one he'd been wearing the day he'd collapsed at the gas station. He lifted it, sniffing it, remembering his own bemusement, utterly helpless as the gas splashed all over him.

'Dry-cleaned,' he muttered. 'She must have dry-cleaned it.'

The duty officer was looking at him. He was black, and faintly laconic. 'You got a problem there?'

Telemann glanced up at him, acknowledging the comment with a terse grunt. 'Yes,' he said, 'since you mention it.'

'Jacket doesn't smell too good?'

'Jacket smells great.'

'Then what's the problem?'

Telemann looked at him, wondering how long it would take for the full speech, what the disease was called, where it might lead, what it might mean after a lifetime of taking his body for granted.

The duty officer was still gazing at the jacket. 'Looks great to me,' he said.

Telemann smiled. 'You want it?'

'Sure.' He looked up. 'You serious?'

Telemann gave him the jacket. The duty officer shook out the creases, and an envelope dropped out, falling on the floor between them. The duty officer bent to retrieve it. 'You wanna smell this, too?'

The duty officer gave him the envelope, then held the jacket up against himself, trying it for size. It looked a little small against his chest. He shrugged. 'Man gets older,' he said, 'man shrinks.'

Telemann nodded, thoughtful. 'Maybe,' he said softly. 'Maybe not.'

Back outside in the BMW, Telemann opened the envelope. Inside he found a photograph and two folded sheets of paper. Telemann extracted the photo and examined it in the overhead light. It showed two men standing together, their faces clearly visible. They were both wearing heavy coats. One of the men dwarfed the other. He had his arm around the smaller man and he was beaming down at him. In the background, half a kilometre away, black dots were trudging up a line of sand-dunes. Some of them, on closer inspection, appeared to be carrying rifles.

Telemann returned to the two men in the foreground. He recognized both of them, faces from the recent past. 'Otto Wulf,' he said quietly, 'and Mahmood Assali.'

'Where? When?'

Telemann frowned, looking at the two men, shaking his head, turning the photograph over. On the back, in careful blue script, he found the answer to both questions.

'Rugen,' he said. 'June. This year.'

'Whose word do we have for that?'

'Theirs. Hers.'

'Whose?'

'The Israeli girl. Inge.' He nodded at the back of the photo. 'That's her writing. I've seen it before.'

'So where did she get it?'

'Maybe the woman I met in Halle. The one she said was her mother.'

'The woman who worked for Wulf?'

'Yes.' Telemann paused. 'She said she'd been to Rugen. She may even have taken the photo.'

Emery nodded slowly, looking out at the darkened street. The commercial area had long emptied, the windows of the offices barred and shuttered.

'So Wulf did know Assali,' Emery mused.

'For sure.'

Emery nodded again, reaching for the photo, examining it closely. Anything, Stauckel had said. The man will do anything for power, anything for influence. That's what fuels him. That's what's taken him to the top. He has this image of himself, wheeling and dealing and solving the world's problems. That's why he's moving into the media. That's why he's buying up radio stations, television channels, even newspapers. The guy can't get enough of himself. He wants to coat the world with mirrors. He wants to show us how big he is, how important he is, the ultimate power-junkie, the man who can't get enough.

'Kadenza,' he said quietly.

Telemann frowned. 'What?'

'That's the name of the conglomerate he was setting up. Kadenza Verlag. Print. Electronic. You name it.'

Telemann nodded, remembering the pile of documents on the floor in Wulf's apartment, the name embossed on the backs of the files. 'So?' he said. 'Where does that take us?'

Emery glanced across at him. 'Wulf,' he mused, 'here's a guy needs recognition, fame, glory, all that stuff. So what's the way you make sure you get your name in the papers?'

'Buy your own.'

'Sure.' He nodded. 'But then you need something to sell, something to boast about. So what do you do? You get up there on the world-stage and you look around. You want the big one.

The one that no one else can solve . . .' He paused, looking at Telemann.

Telemann nodded. 'The Mid East,' he said slowly.

'Sure. The Israeli problem. The Arab problem. Whichever way you cut it. So—' he put the photograph on the dashboard between them '—supposing in the end there's a deal? Supposing there *has* to be a deal? What kind of prize . . . what kind of headlines . . . go to the guy that brokers that deal? And what kind of guy would want it?'

Telemann looked away. 'Wulf?' he said. 'That kind of guy?'

'Right. Wulf. So what happens? It's the mid-eighties. He's big in West Germany. He's big in East Germany. He sees what's going to happen. Honecker, Gorbachev. Reunification. And he sees where he can fit in to all this. He can be the bridge between the two worlds, the East and the West. Lots of Deutschmarks there, lots of *geld* . . .' He paused, choosing his words carefully. 'But here's a guy with even bigger ideas. *Geld*'s not enough. He wants glory, too.'

Telemann nodded, remembering the photos in Wulf's apartment, a parade of world statesmen framed and hung, set dressing for Wulf's wilder fantasies.

'Gorbachev was there,' he said.

'Where?'

'In Wulf's place. A photo. Him and Gorby. Old pals.'

'Who else?' He paused. 'Shamir?'

Telemann frowned, thinking. 'Yes,' he said at last. 'In the lobby.'

'So OK. He knows Shamir.' He paused again, tapping the photo. 'And he knows Assali, too. He puts the two together in his head, a concept, a plan. He works on the Palestinian a little, gives the guy what he wants.'

'For what? In return for what?'

'In return for a gesture. A public gesture. The guy has to renounce violence. The guy has to turn his back on all that. The guy has to recognize Israel.' He smiled. 'It's called peace. The guy has to talk peace.'

Telemann nodded, following the logic. 'And he did that?'

'Yeah. That's what all the grief's about. Assali approached the

State Department. They were working him up nicely. He was exactly what they wanted. He was the guy gonna put the Israelis on the spot.'

'Which is why they had him killed?'

'Of course.'

Telemann said nothing, his eyes returning to the photo. The man in the gutter outside the Hotel Dreisen had been wearing exactly the same coat, a close-weave herringbone, expensive, fashionable.

'OK,' he said slowly. 'So what did Wulf offer him? Why did he do it? What was in it for the Arabs?'

Emery leaned back behind the wheel and took off his glasses for a moment, running a tired hand over his face. Then he smiled. 'Look in the envelope,' he said quietly, 'and we'll find out.'

Telemann looked at him for a moment, marvelling at how the relationship always acquired the same shape, Emery the conjuror, himself the stooge. Just once, he thought, it would have been nice to have produced the white rabbit for himself, no tricks, no fancy analysis, just good fieldwork and honest graft. He shrugged, reaching for the envelope, pulling out the two sheets of paper. He unfolded them, holding the first up against the light. It was a photocopy of an invoice. The company name on the top of the invoice was Littmann Chemie. The date was 6 June 1987. The invoice was made out to a firm in Zurich. Under 'Goods Supplied' there was a typed list of chemicals. They included dimethylaminophosphoryl dichloride and sodium cyanide. A note on the bottom of the invoice indicated compliance with an international export protocol. The chemicals, the note concluded, were designated for use as a pesticide. Telemann frowned, noting the sum billed on the invoice. In all, Littmann was asking DM 95,000.

Telemann hesitated for a moment, then passed the invoice to Emery. He scanned it quickly, then nodded, putting it to one side. Telemann unfolded the second piece of paper. It was another photocopy, this time of a cheque. Dated nine months later, it was for an identical sum, DM 95,000. Telemann gave the cheque to Emery. He glanced at it, then nodded, picking up the invoice again.

'OK,' he said. 'Number one, Littmann is under-quoting. Ninety-five thousand is bottom dollar. Even in 1987. Two, these guys in Zurich are a front organization. It's a procurement outfit, run from Baghdad.'

'Yeah?'

'Yeah. You want proof? Collateral?' He picked up the cheque. 'That's a BCCI account. I know these accounts. I've spent goddamn weeks crawling all over them. That one is Iraqi. Put my life on it.'

'OK.' Telemann nodded. 'So what do they do with the chemicals?' He peered across at the invoice. 'Dimethyl—'

Emery smiled, looking down at the invoice. 'Easy,' he said. 'You put this guy with this guy. Do it in the presence of ethyl alcohol. And . . . hey . . . you know what you get?'

Telemann looked at him, nodding, remembering the German's huge body contorting on the long black crescent of sofa.

'Orphée,' he said quietly. 'You get Orphée.'

*

The old man, Abu Yussuf, sat behind the curtained window, finding some succour in the darkness, the phone to his ear, listening to Amer Tahoul. My brother-in-law, he thought bitterly. The man who lied to me.

'What are you going to do? Yussuf?'

The old man shook his head. There were no more tears. He'd wept all the tears he had, the pillow still damp, his heart broken. 'I don't know,' he said for the second time. 'I don't know.'

'Yussuf. Tell me. Where are you?'

'At the motel.'

'Which motel? Where?'

'Somewhere. I don't know.'

'The same motel as last night? Is that the one?'

'Yes.'

'Will you stay there? Will you phone me again?'

'I don't know.'

'Yussuf. Listen to me. There are things we can do, you and

me. Someone will come. Someone will be with you . . .' He
paused. 'Yussuf? Yussuf?'

The old man sniffed. His throat ached. His head ached.
Everything ached. He reached for the glass of water on the
cabinet beside the bed, hearing Amer's voice again, telling him
to stay at the motel, not to move, not to go away. Everything
would be all right, he kept saying, everything would get better.
He'd seen his sons. Today, he'd seen them. They were fine.
They were looking foward to their father's return, to seeing
him again, to being with him. They needed him. They depended
on him. He owed it to them to come back.

'Yussuf?' he said. 'Yussuf?'

The old man shook his head, sipping the water, knowing that
his sons were probably dead too, or in prison, next to dead, and
that Amer would never tell him. It was very simple now, too
simple for argument or even discussion. The Israelis had done
it. They'd killed his wife. They'd imprisoned his sons. And now
they must pay for it. He sighed, lying back on the bed, the
phone abandoned. The boy had been right, the boy he'd left in
the woods. The best the Jews deserved was gas. That was the
lesson of history. That was the only, the final, solution. He
sighed again, getting up, pulling open the curtains, admiring the
job he'd done on the car, the neatness of it, the two exhaust-
pipes. For now, he'd find another place, somewhere up here,
somewhere in the mountains. He'd take his time, lay his plans,
make as good a job of it as he could. He smiled, a positive
thought at last, and reached for the car-keys. Leaving the room,
he could still faintly hear Amer, half a world away, a voice from
the telephone on the bed.

'Yussuf?' he was saying. 'Yussuf?'

*

McVeigh walked steadily on through the darkness, following
the massive shape of the big Israeli. The river and the gorge
were an hour behind them, and when he had time to look back
he could see the lights of the kibbutz, faint and shimmering in
the heat still rising from the valley. Up here on the mountain it
was cooler, a keen wind blowing from the north, a smell he
recognized from countless climbing expeditions. Cela had given

him a small haversack, Army issue, and he wore it now. Inside, amongst his own possessions, was the envelope from Amer and the bottle of Jordan water. Saying goodbye beside the jeep, Cela had wished him luck, kissing him again.

'For Yussuf,' she'd whispered, leaning into him, 'and for you.'

Moshe strode on, his bulk filling the narrow path. There were loose stones underfoot and the path continually twisted left and right, but the man obviously knew it well, pausing from time to time, grunting phrases McVeigh didn't understand, indicating some kind of hazard up ahead. On these occasions McVeigh would nod, equally gruff, telling him to press on. He'd been here before, he wanted to say, a hundred night route-marches, 120 pounds on his back, Dartmoor, mid-winter, a decade of tramping up and down the world's highest mountains. Compared to that, compared to his journey from Ramallah, this was a stroll in the park.

Another hour took them higher still, sweating now, the wind much stronger. Once, they stopped to rest, squatting amongst the rocks, Moshe producing a water flask, telling McVeigh to drink, watching him swallow long mouthfuls of the pulped fruit juice. The one thing they had in common was Cela, and McVeigh regretted that he couldn't talk about her, find out more, what kind of kid she'd been, what kind of childhood they'd all shared. The woman was beginning to obsess him, a feeling he couldn't remember before, not like this, not as strong, as overwhelming. The fruit juice gone, Moshe shook the last drops into the darkness and clipped the flask back on to his belt. Then he reached out, a big warm hand, hauling McVeigh upright, peering into his face, then roaring with laughter at some private joke before setting off again up the mountain.

At last, past midnight, Moshe stopped, waving McVeigh into cover. McVeigh dropped silently behind an outcrop of rock. He still had the Uzi and he slipped it carefully off his shoulder, thumbing the safety catch foward. He could see nothing ahead. Moshe waited, motionless, then whistled, two notes, high-pitched, distinctive. He repeated the call, and far away McVeigh heard an answering whistle, exactly the same two notes. Moshe grunted, looking back for McVeigh. They began to move again, more cautious this time, McVeigh off to a flank, lateral separation, the Uzi ready. Moshe stopped, and dropped on one knee. McVeigh did the same. Three men stood on a ledge of rock immediately below them. They were looking up, faint shapes in the windy darkness. Moshe whistled again, and one of them called his name softly, Moshe. Moshe stood up, revealing himself, and then they were down on the ledge, exchanging greetings, stiff handshakes. Two of them were very young, no more than boys. The other was in his late twenties, short, watchful, wearing trainers, jeans, a thick bomber-jacket. The boys were carrying guns, and McVeigh recognized the sturdy shape of the AK47, Soviet-made, the Third World's favourite weapon.

Moshe began to talk to the older man in Arabic, gesturing at McVeigh, and the older man nodded, impatient, looking twice at his watch, tapping it forcefully, making a point. Moshe shrugged his huge shoulders, turning away, back to McVeigh. 'You go with them,' he said. 'They take you.'

McVeigh stared at him. He'd been told the man spoke no English. Another of Cela's little jokes. 'OK,' he said.

Moshe looked at him for a moment longer, then held out his hand. McVeigh took it. He wanted to say a thousand things. He wanted to know who these guys were. He wanted to know what might happen next. He wanted to say he was grateful. Instead, he shook Moshe's hand.

'Cela,' he said. 'Look after her.'

Moshe frowned, making sense of the phrase, then laughed again, that same abrupt bark of laughter.

'*Shalom*,' he said, turning away.

15

McVeigh was still trying to make sense of *L'Orient – Le Jour* when the flight was called. He'd found the newspaper on a seat in the departure lounge. On the front page were two photographs, Saddam Hussein and Yitsak Shamir counterposed beneath a baffling headline in French. *'La Drôle de Guerre'*, it read. Beneath the photo were columns of text and a smaller photo of George Bush waving from the steps of a helicopter. McVeigh looked at it for a moment longer before folding it into his haversack and getting up. He was no linguist, but the phrase seemed simple enough. *Drôle* was some kind of joke. *Guerre* was war. The joke war? The war of the jokes? He shook his head, shouldering the haversack and crossing the concourse towards the lengthening queue for security checks.

The imminence of war seemed all too real. You could smell it in the air. You could see it in the faces of the women still sitting around the concourse, their luggage piled at their feet, their heads buried in other newspapers, other headlines, looking up from time to time, checking for their kids. People with sense and money were abandoning the Middle East. The area had become a combat zone, ground zero for Saddam's Scuds, for marauding Israeli bombers, for the hit-squads of journalists and TV news crews, scenting blood and treasure.

McVeigh joined the back of the queue for security checks, one hand to his mouth, stifling a yawn. It was early afternoon. The journey from the border had seemed interminable, hour after hour in a clapped-out Datsun, McVeigh in the back beside one of the youths, the older man driving. There'd been no attempt at conversation beyond an exchange of cigarettes, and McVeigh's occasional questions had met with no response at all. The youth beside him had been nervous, sitting foward in his seat, peering into the darkness, the AK47 held awkwardly across his lap, useless if they were to hit real trouble. Dawn had revealed a series of cracks in the windscreen and a landscape of rich physical beauty. Beyond the dusty roadside were dark fields of tobacco and tall stands of poplars, and later, when the sun came up and they wound down the windows, McVeigh could smell the sweet, tangy scent of oranges. By this time most of the tension in the car had gone, and as they bumped slowly up the Bekaa Valley, one of the men in front had taken to humming a tune. After a mile or so, McVeigh had recognized it. It was a seventies number, the New Seekers, 'Got To Teach the World to Sing', and McVeigh had smiled, the irony of it, the fatuous lyrics, the nervous young man with his dangerous toy, the images he'd left behind on the West Bank: the drifting clouds of tear gas, the squalling women in the hospital corridor, the purpled faces, the broken limbs. At Beirut's International Airport, without ceremony, they'd dropped him outside the terminal. Standing at the kerb, he'd ducked into the car, shaking each of them by the hand, three wooden smiles and a paper bag produced, like an afterthought, from the glove compartment. He'd opened the paper bag as the Datsun drove slowly away, shaking out an airline ticket. The ticket had been made out in his name. Under 'Destination' the issuing agency had typed 'Montreal'.

He reached for the ticket now, opening the haversack. The newspaper fell out and he stooped to retrieve it. The queue shuffled forward again, a single step, and McVeigh shook the newspaper open, aware of the man behind him, tall, well dressed, blazer, slacks, silk tie. The man was glancing at the front page of the newspaper, reading the headline, smiling. At length he looked at McVeigh, one hand appearing from beneath the folded raincoat.

'Mr McVeigh?' he said.

McVeigh nodded, the newspaper still open. 'Yeah.' he said.

'My name is Ghassan. I'm a friend of Amer Tahoul. I shall be with you. On the flight.' He smiled again. 'And perhaps afterwards.'

McVeigh looked at him for a moment. 'You can prove that?' he said. 'Your name? And about Amer?'

'Of course.' The man nodded, a nod of approval. Reaching inside his brief-case, he produced a Lebanese passport and a neatly folded letter. McVeigh glanced at the passport. Mr Ghassan came from Tyre. He was thirty-one years old. A thin black moustache adorned a younger face. McVeigh turned to the letter, reading it quickly, the single typed paragraph. Mr Ghassan was a friend of the organization. He was carrying a great deal of money. He was at McVeigh's disposal. The letter was signed 'Amer Tahoul'. McVeigh read it again, wondering why Amer hadn't mentioned the man. Maybe it was a late development. Maybe something had happened, over in the States, something that McVeigh should know about. McVeigh shrugged, folding the letter, returning it with the passport.

Ghassan was looking at the newspaper again. 'You speak French?' he said.

'No.'

'You know what that means?' He pointed to the headline.

McVeigh frowned, hesitating for a moment, then shook his head. 'No,' he said again.

Ghassan looked up. '*La Drôle de Guerre*,' he said. 'It means "The Phoney War".'

*

Later the same day, 16.48 Eastern Standard Time, Telemann and Emery landed at Dulles Airport, Washington. They took separate cabs from the pick-up area, Telemann going north, towards Rockville, Emery heading in towards the Beltway. Against the rush-hour traffic flooding back to the suburbs, he made excellent time. By half-past six, the cocktail hour, he was sitting at his desk on 'F' Street, gazing at the messages from the West Coast.

There were three of them. Ever blunter, they asked him to contact a Los Angeles number. The name at the end of the yellow priority form was Andy Fischer. Emery reached for the telephone and punched in the numbers. Fischer answered at once and Emery smiled, imagining him at the spotless desk in

Century City, shaping up to the computer, a battle he seemed to wage day and night.

Emery glanced at his watch. 'Just back from lunch?' he enquired.

'Emery? That you?'

'It is.'

'Listen. Get a pen.'

'Got one.'

'We're talking Gold here. You with me?'

'Yes.'

'OK. I finally got a trace on the payments. The last set. The last payments he got before it all went zip.'

'Yeah?' Emery frowned, reaching for a pad. 'OK,' he said, 'shoot.'

'The payments came in three tranches. Two hundred and fifty thousand dollars twice. And one of one hundred and thirty-four thousand dollars. That was the final instalment. Dates, we're talking October '89, November '89, and June '90.'

Emery nodded, scribbling the dates first, the most important items, sitting back, doing the arithmetic, smiling to himself. June, '90. Six hundred and thirty-four thousand dollars. Perfect.

'OK,' he said. 'So what's the source?'

'No problem. It's a New York Corporation. Ready?'

'Go.'

'Vivace International. Got that?'

'Yeah.' Emery was frowning. 'What do they do?'

'It's a media conglomerate. They do everything. Publishing. Television. Co-productions. It's Arab money. Not Japanese.'

Emery, busy writing again, grunted. Then he bent to the phone. 'You been through their drawers too?'

There was a brief silence, and Emery could hear Fischer chuckling at the other end. 'Yeah,' he said, 'what do you think?'

'You tell me.'

'Well now ...' He paused, pure effect. '... This wouldn't stand up in court because it's three per cent supposition, but I'm telling you it's rock-solid.'

Fischer paused again, a longer silence. Emery, examining his pen, suddenly realized how excited he was.

'Well?'

'The money came into Vivace in three equivalent tranches, a week in advance of each payment to Gold. Vivace washed it.'

'OK.' Emery sat back. 'So what was the originating currency?'

'You tell me.'

'Deutschmarks?'

'You got it.'

Emery nodded, plesed with himself, the pen in mid-air. One question to go, he thought, one space left on the board.

'OK,' he said again. 'And the source company?'

'Kadenza,' Fischer said, 'Verlag.'

There was a long silence. Then Emery heard Fischer chuckling again. 'That surprise you?' he said. 'The big bad Wulf?'

Emery shook his head. Kadenza had been preparing a bid for Vivace. It made perfect sense. 'No,' he said, 'not at all.'

He glanced at the pad at his elbow, checking the figures, then Juanita appeared at the door, five fingers outspread, her private code for a priority incoming call. Emery bent forward towards the desk, muttering a hasty goodbye, and hung up. Juanita was still at the door.

'Who is it?'

'Sullivan.' She smiled. 'He's waiting in the limo downstairs. Threatening cocktails.'

*

It was nearly dark by the time Telemann stepped back into the house on Dixie Street, taking his sister-in-law by surprise. She was sitting at the table, playing the usual game with Bree's food, cutting the broiled fish steaks into bite-sized pieces. Telemann coughed politely, the watcher by the door. Bree looked round, recognizing him, swallowing the fish whole, running across the room, arms out.

'Daddy,' she said, 'Daddy . . .'

Telemann hugged her, squeezing her, big fat kisses, the kind she loved.

'Me,' he agreed, wiping her face.

'Mummy said . . .'

'Mummy said what?'

'Mummy said you'd be back. She promised. Mummy's in

bed. Quick.' She caught Telemann by the hand and began to drag him across the room, and Telemann semaphored a greeting to Laura's sister, still sitting at the table, a fork in her hand, the last cube of swordfish speared on the end. 'Asleep,' she mouthed, 'she's asleep.'

Telemann nodded, understanding, already on the stairs. The bedroom was across the landing at the top. The door was shut. Bree half-fell against it, singing already, a hymn she'd learned only recently, her voice high and pure.

'*O Sabbath rest by Galilee . . .*'

One of the cats was asleep on a chair in a corner of the landing. It woke up, disturbed by the noise, arched its back, stretching lazily, and disappeared into another room.

'*O calm of hills above*
Where Jesus knelt to share with thee . . .'

Bree wrestled open the bedroom door, ignoring Telemann's whispered plea to be quiet, and tugged him inside. The bedroom was small, built into the eaves. Light from the street spilled in through the single window. Telemann stood at the foot of the bed, gazing down at Laura. She lay like a comma under the sheets, her knees up, her body curled. She was still asleep.

'*The silence of eternity . . .*'

Laura opened one eye, the beginnings of a frown, trying to make sense of the shapes in the middle of the room. Then Telemann was sitting on the bed, the back of his hand against her cheek, her breath warm on his flesh. He smiled in the half-darkness, and Laura reached up, pulling him down, his body beside hers. It was an old greeting, a hug they'd shared for two decades, and Telemann began to murmur something, an apology for waking her up, but she shook her head, her fingers tracing the shape of his mouth.

'Hi,' she whispered, 'soldier boy.'

*

Emery studied the photograph, his Michelob untouched. Sullivan sat beside him in a discreet corner of the bar, his jacket hanging open, his belly barely contained by the bulge of striped grey shirt. They'd been at the Four Seasons for half an hour, quite long enough for Sullivan to establish the political consequences of the hunt for Abu Yussuf. Three days in Europe hadn't warmed the relationship one degree.

'Disaster,' he muttered again. 'Grade fucking A.'

Emery was still looking at the photo. 'Where did this come from?'

'Tel Aviv.'

'When?'

'Three days ago.'

Emery nodded, plotting the chronology in his head, testing the dates, one against the other. Sullivan was watching him closely. In the back of the limo, driving up Pennsylvania Avenue towards Georgetown, Sullivan had said his piece about Emery's failure to deliver. He'd given him the inside track on every other federal bureaucracy. He'd given him limitless freedoms, limitless scope, yet all he had to show for it was a stack of unreturned phone calls and the makings of a major diplomatic incident with the Germans. What had happened over there? Had Telemann got some kind of problem? Narcotics? Senile dementia? Was it true that he was off the case? At home with a headache? Emery, surprised that the fall had come so soon to the trees around Washington Circle, had said very little, knowing that Sullivan had a reputation for outbursts like these. Like any politician, the man demanded an early return on his investment. Notions like time and patience meant nothing to him. Now, the photograph face-down on the table, Emery asked about the scale of the manhunt. How wide was the net being cast? How fine was the mesh? And most important of all, who was in charge?

Sullivan shook his head, miserable, reaching for the last of his bourbon. He had the air of a child after an especially bad Christmas, his favourite toy already broken, in pieces on the playroom floor. 'Feds,' he said wanly. 'FBI.'

'Whose decision?'

'The President's.' He glanced up at Emery. 'The business with Assali shook him badly. He's having enough trouble with the Germans already. The last thing he needs is more blood on the sidewalk.' He shrugged. 'So we're back in channels. I guess he thinks it's safer. God knows. Maybe he's right . . .' He signalled the waitress and ordered a refill, and Emery watched him as he sank back in the chair, physically diminished, a favoured courtier resigned at last to exile.

Emery reached for his beer and sipped it. 'What about the Israelis?' he said thoughtfully. 'They still on the leash?'

'No way. Bastards have mobilized. They're talking first strike again. It's in the papers. You can read about it. Top billing. Front page.'

'Isn't that a problem? For our new Arab friends?'

Sullivan shot him a look, part contempt, part despair. 'I asked you to find the guys with the gas,' he said, 'not run the fucking State Department.'

There was a long silence. A group of senators across the lounge were swopping gossip. Emery, still toying with his Michelob, looked up. He'd been wondering about his feelings for Sullivan, whether or not he cared about the man. To his surprise, he discovered that he did. Sullivan was watching him, his huge hands cupping the tumbler of bourbon as if seeking warmth. 'Well?' he said.

Emery frowned. 'The Israelis have found the guy with the gas.' He shrugged, glancing down at the photo on the table. 'You've got a name. A face. Why look any further?'

'That's what they're saying. Word for word.'

'Who?'

'The Israelis.'

Emery nodded, smiling, lifting his glass, a mock toast.

'Surprise, surprise,' he said.

*

The old man, Abu Yussuf, saw the sign amongst the trees. 'Sugarloaf Mountain Ski Resort' it said. 'Houses and Condos for Rental'. He hesitated a moment, his foot easing off the accelerator. He wanted somewhere safe, somewhere with a telephone and a garage, somewhere he could hide for a couple of days and lick his wounds. The newspaper still lay open on the seat beside him. He'd been looking at it from time to time, playing tricks with himself, willing the photo to change, willing the names to disappear from the text, willing Hala back to life again. Anything, he thought grimly, anything would be better than this. Even another spell in prison. Even a night or two with the Shin Beth people. Anything. In return for Hala.

He indicated left, pulling off the highway up into the trees. The road was new. He could see wooden houses through the trees. They looked big, safe. Further up the road he found an office. A pleasant young man in a plaid shirt listened to his faltering English. He wanted a house for a week, maybe longer. He'd pay cash. He had lots of cash. The young man said the minimum rentals were a fortnight. Six hundred and fifty dollars would buy him three bedrooms, a double garage, colour television, and a fully automated kitchen. Low-season rates still applied because the snow had yet to fall, but there were hiking trails, and white-water rafting, and rumours of a black bear in the woods over towards Peaked Mountain. Abu Yussuf nodded, numb, giving the young man his roll of bank-notes, letting him take what he needed, following him outside. The young man asked for a lift up to the house. He'd show him over the place, talk him through the facilities. The old man nodded, not thinking, opening the passenger door for him, realizing too late how interested the young man might be in automobiles, the things you could do to customize them, the nice new switch on the dash, the mysterious twin exhausts.

They drove back down the mountain, the old man sweating gently behind the wheel. The house was in a clearing amongst the trees. It was brand-new, the earth freshly turned in the small plot out back. Inside, the place smelled of cedarwood and sunshine. Abu Yussuf followed the young man around, half-listening to him explaining everything. Finally, the tour over, the young man extended a hand and left, taking the wooden steps two at a time, pausing by the car, looking back with a cheerful wave.

*

McVeigh landed at Montreal at midnight, Eastern Standard Time. The flight had been twice delayed, held on the ground in Beirut and again in Paris. Standing up, stretching, McVeigh nodded across at the Arab, Ghassan Azrak. They'd travelled at opposite ends of the Business Class compartment, Ghassan asking for a smoking seat, McVeigh glad to be left alone. Once, somewhere over Greenland, the Arab had slipped off his seat-belt and walked forward down the aisle, but McVeigh had seen him coming and pretended to be asleep. Now, filing off the big 747, the Arab was as affable as ever. 'I'm with you,' he confirmed, patting the wallet in his breast-pocket. 'We stay together.'

Travelling with hand-baggage only, McVeigh was the first through Customs. He completed his Immigration Form, had it stamped, and stepped through on to the Arrivals concourse. So late, the place was deserted, an acre or two of polished marble floor. Shouldering the haversack, McVeigh crossed the concourse to a cluster of telephones arranged in pairs of kiosks. McVeigh chose the farthest. Using the phone, he could still see the exit channels from the Customs and Immigration areas. Soon, he knew, the Arab would appear.

Checking his watch, McVeigh dialled Amer Tahoul's office number. In Ramallah it would be ten o'clock. By now the man would be at his desk. The number began to ring, and McVeigh piled the 25-cent coins beside the slot. With luck, the conversation would be brief. Just two pieces of information, both of them vital.

The number answered, Amer's voice, a poor line. McVeigh began to shout down the phone, his voice uncomfortably loud, his eyes still on the exit channel. So far, no one had appeared. 'Yussuf?' he said for the third time. 'Where is he?'

There were more crackles down the phone, then Amer's voice broke through. He had a new address. It was some kind of ski resort. McVeigh grunted, scribbling the details on the pad at his elbow. He read the details back, Sugarloaf Mountain, somewhere in Maine. Then he returned to the phone. The first passengers were beginning to appear on the concourse, trailing huge suitcases.

'There's a bloke called Ghassan,' McVeigh shouted, 'Ghassan Azrak.'

'Who?'

'Ghassan Azrak.'

Amer said something, then something else, but his voice was breaking up on the line again. McVeigh cursed, bringing his knee up beneath the phone console, shaking it, doing it a second time. The line got worse. 'Ghassan,' he said again, 'Ghassan Azrak.'

Across the concourse, the Arab had appeared. He carried a small overnight bag and a larger grip. He was looking around. McVeigh moved sideways into the cover of the phone kiosk, his eyes on Ghassan. He could still hear Amer, his voice faint. It was impossible to make any sense of what he was saying. It was like listening to a man in a high wind. McVeigh fed another three dollars into the console, praying for the line to get better, watching the Arab's every move. The Arab was still looking round. Then he signalled, a barely perceptible movement of his right hand, and McVeigh saw another man crossing the concourse towards him. He'd come from the front of the building. He was wearing a big coat. He looked local, white-skinned, not an Arab. Ghassan had retreated a little into the mêlée of arriving passengers, making himself less conspicuous, and McVeigh watched as the two met, a small brown package changing hands, the work of a couple of seconds before the newcomer turned on his heel and made for the big sliding doors that led to the pick-up area. McVeigh watched him disappear into the night, then his eyes went back to the concourse, looking for Ghassan, finding him almost at once, standing slightly apart from the crowd, still looking round. The package had disappeared into his bag. Abruptly, Amer's voice came through the static. 'You can hear me?' he kept saying. 'You can hear me?'

McVeigh smiled, his body in full view now, the Arab spotting him, waving, walking over towards him. 'It's OK, Amer,' he said, 'I think I get the picture.'

*

Next morning found Emery back in Boston. He stepped off the Eastern shuttle and phoned Juanita from a call-booth in the baggage hall.

'I found him,' she said briskly. 'He's at home.'

'Where's home?'

'East Falmouth,' she said. 'There's a neat little plane goes out to Hyannisport. You're booked for 9.45. Terminal D.'

Emery thanked her, checking his watch, sprinting for the

transfer bus. Fifteen minutes later, he was in the air again, gazing down at the brown waters of Boston Harbor as the ancient DC-3 droned south-east, towards the long curve of Cape Cod. At Hyannisport, Emery walked through the tiny terminal building and stepped into a cab. By midday he was in Falmouth.

Weill lived out on the coast on the edge of town, a rented place, one of a row of white timbered houses facing the sea. Paying off the cab, Emery stood on the sidewalk for a minute or so, smelling the air. The place had a quiet, low-rise, end-of-season feel to it. The wind blew in off the ocean, bowing the stands of maram grass on the sand-dunes, driving a fine yellow dust across the road. There was a good sea running, the deepest blue, the tops of the waves white-laced by the wind. Nice place to live, thought Emery, turning his back, pushing in through the broken gate, thinking again about Sullivan.

Weill, when he came to the door, looked terrible. He was wearing the bottom half of a pair of pyjamas and an old white T-shirt. His hair was tousled, and his eyes were bloodshot, and his face was the colour of putty. He peered into the strong sunlight, trying to make sense of the stranger at the door. Emery stepped inside, introducing himself. The house was a wreck. Empty flagons of wine stood in a row by the kitchen door. Plates of decaying food were piled on the draining-board. One of the taps needed mending, dripping noisily on to an upturned saucepan. Weill stared at it. 'Washer's gone,' he said hopelessly. 'Been fucked for months.'

They went into the living-room, ancient rugs on a bare lino floor. The place was unheated, and Weill sank on to the vinyl-covered sofa, pulling a blanket around himself, settling back into the corner, his knees drawn up to his chin, shaking visibly.

'You cold?' Emery asked. 'Or sick?'

'Both.'

'What's the matter?'

Weill shook his head, not answering, and Emery looked pointedly at the bottle of Jack Daniels on the floor by the window. The top was off and the bottle was three-quarters empty. Weill pulled the blanket a little tighter around himself, only his face and toes visible.

'Gold,' Emery said. 'I want to know what happened.'

'I told you.'

'You told me zip.' He paused. 'This can take ten minutes or ten years. Your choice.'

Weill blinked. 'Is that a threat?'

'Yes.'

'You serious?'

'Yes.'

'You really do work for the Government? One of those guys?'

'Yes.'

'OK.' He shrugged. 'Try me.'

Emery nodded, getting up, crossing the room, heading for the bottle, replacing the top. For some reason, it bothered him. He put the bottle on the table. Weill shut his eyes. For a moment, Emery thought he was going to be sick.

'Gold stayed here a couple of times,' he suggested, 'before he died.'

'Sure.' Weill nodded, his eyes still shut. 'Place was better then. Things were OK. You know—' he shrugged, hopeless again '—OK.'

'He'd picked up a contract.'

'Yes.'

'Big money. Six hundred and thirty-four thousand dollars.'

Weill opened his eyes. Surprise put colour in his face. 'You know that?'

'Yes.' Emery paused. 'And I know where the money came from. I know who paid him.' He paused again, leaning back against the table. 'You speak German?'

'Yes.'

'Read it well?'

'Yes.'

'Technical standard?'

'Yes.'

'OK,' Emery said. 'Then tell me what Gold was paid for.'

411

There was a long silence. Gulls swooped and soared in the sunshine outside, and Emery could hear the wind pushing in through cracks in the shingles. Emery shifted his weight slightly, still looking at Weill. Weill was mustering the courage to say no.

'Gold brought documents here,' Emery suggested. 'Stuff in German. Scientific stuff. You knew the science. You understand German.' He paused. 'Don't bother telling me you don't know what he was selling.'

Weill gazed up at him, the rabbit on the pike at midnight, transfixed. He began to blink, rapid blinks, then he shook his head. 'Can't,' he said, 'can't do it.'

'Won't.'

'Sure. Won't. Same thing.'

Emery shrugged, reaching for the bottle, picking it up, looking at it. 'I can do you a favour,' he said slowly. 'I can have you out of here within the hour. I can have you behind bars. I can save your liver. I can save your life. Like I say, I can guarantee you ten years. Maybe more.' He shrugged. 'After that, you're on your own . . .'

Weill swallowed a couple of times, then licked his lips. His eyes hadn't left the bottle. 'I loved the guy,' he said quietly. 'You pick any of that stuff up? Amongst all the other shit?'

'No,' Emery said coldly, 'I didn't.'

'It's true.' Weill nodded. 'He didn't need it. He didn't want it. We never did it. But he let me touch. Just sometimes.'

'Often?'

'No.' He smiled for the first time, a bitter-sweet curl of the lip. 'Twice, if we're counting.'

Emery shrugged again, indifferent. 'OK,' he said.

There was another long silence. A car drove past. Emery felt inside his jacket and produced a small black and white photo, Abu Yussuf, a copy duped from Sullivan's print. He held it up, inches from Weill's face. 'Ever see this guy?'

Weill frowned, looking at it. The sunlight glinted off the thick pebble-glasses. 'No.'

'Never?'

'No.' He looked up. 'That's an Arab guy.' He looked up. 'You think Lennie was some kind of terrorist? Is that it?'

'You tell me.'

'Lennie was an engineer. Pure and simple.'

'So what was he selling?'

'You know. You've gotta know. You know the rest of it, you know what he was selling . . .' He paused, blinking, then his face collapsed and he started to sob, his whole body shaking under the blanket. Emery said nothing for a moment, letting the sobs subside. Then he uncorked the bottle and offered it. Weill looked at it, sniffing, shaking his head.

'I told him they'd kill him,' he said, 'I know those bastards. I know the way they work. I told him. He didn't believe me. He said he'd worked for them all those years. He said he had the right contacts. He said they'd leave him alone.' He shook his head, still sniffing, wiping his eyes with the back of his hand. 'And I was right, wasn't I? They did kill him . . .'

Emery nodded, saying nothing, and Weill looked at him for a long time, his eyes bloodshot, his cheeks wet. Then he produced a box of Kleenex from under the blanket and blew his nose. 'How did they do it?' he said at last.

'They gassed him.'

'*Gassed* him?'

'Yeah. Nerve gas.' He paused, 'You want the pictures? Him and his lady friend?'

Weill shook his head, shutting his eyes. A shudder went through his body. 'Over there,' he said at last.

'Over where?'

'There.' He nodded at a sideboard across the room. 'Middle drawer.'

Emery went to the sideboard and pulled open the drawer. It was full of gay magazines, some colour, some black-and-white. One or two were folded open, explicit poses, not much left to wonder about.

'What am I looking for?'

'A Jiffy bag.' Weill smiled weakly. 'German stamps. Dusseldorf postmark.'

Emery began to rummage in the drawer. The Jiffy bag was at the bottom, under a photo feature on bondage. He pulled it out and shook the contents on to the table. There were documents inside, closely spaced lines of typescript, scientific equations, half-page diagrams. The documents were in German. The science meant nothing to Emery. He glanced at Weill. His eyes were closed again, his head back against the tan vinyl.

'I'm taking these away,' he said, 'but you could still save me a day or two.' He paused. 'Yeah?'

Weill nodded. 'Sure.' He reached down for the Kleenex and wiped his eyes. 'We're talking Israeli radar frequencies. Missile locks. ECM. Everything he'd ever done for them.' He smiled weakly. 'You want the full lecture?'

*

McVeigh slept the night at a hotel beside the airport at Montreal. He awoke at four, again at six, and finally got up at eight, unrefreshed. He dressed, ordered a hire car and breakfast from room service, and put a second call through to the Arab's room. 'We leave at nine,' he told him. 'See you in the lobby.'

McVeigh was in the lobby ten minutes early. He paid for his room and filled in the form for the rental car. When he asked about taking the car into the States, the girl said no problem. She left him with the keys and a set of maps. The maps he'd ordered specially. By the time the Arab appeared, they were back inside the envelope.

They drove east, through the downtown area and over the bridge across the St Lawrence River, leaving the suburbs behind them. Soon they were deep into rural Quebec, a plump, prosperous countryside, rolling hills, small towns, neat, white-fenced farms. Ghassan sat beside McVeigh, the window down, a cigarette in his hand, pushing the conversation along, nothing obvious, none of the questions McVeigh might have expected, simply a raft of small-talk floating on the unspoken assumption that they were comrades-in-arms, fellow combatants in a shadowy war, best left undescribed. Only once did he mention Amer again, and then only to confirm that he'd known the man for years, an old friend, a trusted ally. The big grip he'd stowed in the boot of the hire car, but the smaller holdall he kept at his feet.

Beyond a small village called St Gérard, McVeigh saw a sign for the border. The US was 57 miles away. He glanced at his watch. It was half-past eleven. He drove on a couple of miles, the countryside emptier, the traffic light. He checked in the mirror, waving on a big truck, frowning. The truck thundered past in a cloud of dust, and McVeigh began to weave the car across the road, fingers on the wheel, shaking his head. Ghassan had just lit another cigarette. His English was near-perfect.

'What's the problem?'

'I think we've got a flat.'

McVeigh checked the mirror again. The road behind was empty. He braked and pulled the car on to the broad dirt-strip at the side of the highway. Then he got out, circling the car, kicking each tyre in turn, grunting. When he got to the Arab's side, he paused, bending quickly, his hands on the front wheel, shaking it. He heard the front door open and stood up as the Arab stepped out.

'It's fucked,' he said, hitting him hard with the heel of his hand, taking no risks.

The Arab collapsed back against the car, his nose spouting blood, and sank slowly to the ground. McVeigh kicked him as he fell, a single kick with the point of the foot, midway between his armpit and his waist. He gasped with pain, reaching for the bag in the front of the car, and McVeigh stepped quickly over him, grabbing it. Inside, a gun lay under a fold of scarf. McVeigh recognized it at once. It was a Beretta, the high-powered version, .22 calibre. Security services used it worldwide for close-quarters work. It was a favourite for assassinations because it didn't need a silencer. McVeigh took out the Beretta and threw the bag into the car. Then he knelt beside the Arab, the gun nuzzling the tight curls of black hair beside his ear. The Arab was nursing his nose, dabbing at it, staring at the blood.

'Who gave you this?' McVeigh said, pressing the gun against his temple. 'Who met you at the airport?'

The Arab looked at him and McVeigh knew at once that he

was in for a long wait. He glanced down the road. The road was still empty. He looked at the Arab again. There was a certain calculation in his eyes. It had to do with fighting back. McVeigh grunted, standing up very quickly, taking half a step back, kicking the Arab again, catching him on the top of the thigh as he rolled sideways, trying to struggle to his feet. McVeigh let him get halfway there, an awkward crouch, then he kicked him again, hard this time, the centre of the chest. The Arab fell back and McVeigh drove in a third kick, lower, Ghassan's groin unprotected, his hands way too high. The Arab screamed with pain, doubling over, his face in the dust, and McVeigh knelt beside him, repeating the question, the Beretta an inch from Ghassan's eye.

'Are you Mossad?' he said. 'Israeli? Is that it?'

The Arab spat blood into the dirt, still fighting for breath, shaking his head, mumbling in Arabic. McVeigh waited a moment longer, knowing that it was hopeless, that the man could be anything – Mossad, PLO, Iraqi, even CIA. They'd all have an interest in getting to the old man, and they'd all have their own ideas on what to do when they found him.

McVeigh stood up, abandoning the questions, knowing that the next logical step was unconsciousness. He hauled the Arab away from the car, propping him up by the side of the road, wiping away the worst of the blood with the broad end of the man's tie. Pocketing the Beretta, he returned to the car. Thirty seconds later, checking in the rear-view mirror, the Arab was still slumped against the fence, his head down between his knees, a small black dot, receding into the distance.

＊

Early afternoon, back in Washington, Laura took the wheel of the old Volvo and drove her husband to the Outpatient Clinic at Georgetown University. Telemann sat beside her, numbed by this new role of his, a passenger in the family car. Heading south through Rock Creek Park, he gazed out of the window, his hand on Laura's knee, neither fretful nor morose, simply thoughtful.

Laura glanced across at him. 'The name's Laing. You've met him before. Scots guy. Neurologist.'

'And you've had this fixed for a while?'

'Yes.' Laura nodded. 'He needs to talk to you, to explain one r two things. I said that was fine. Just so long as I talked to ou first.'

'Yeah?' Telemann smiled, amused at this small act of disloy- lty, his wife keeping him out of the hands of the medics until he'd been able to break the news. The right time. The right lace. The right circumstances.

'What about the Agency?' Telemann said. 'Who tells them?'

'Pete. He has it in hand.'

'Sure.' Telemann nodded again. 'Once he's saved the world.'

'What?'

'Nothing.'

They drove on, leaving the Park, turning into the grid of :reets that led to Georgetown University. Telemann had always ked this area. Lately, it had been spoiled a little by money and tidal wave of Yuppies, but the essence of it had survived: the eat little houses, the sense of neighbourhood, the sense of an lder, quieter, more reflective America, a nation less wedded to iolence and wealth. Sometimes, leaving one or other of their vourite bars, mid-evening, another day spent, he'd talked to mery about it, musing aloud on what it might be like to retire ere, he and Laura, serving out a gentle dotage amongst the :ademics and the politicians. Emery had laughed. Georgetown as a big fat duvet. Someone like Telemann would suffocate eneath it. At the time, Telemann had protested, but now he new that Emery had been right. What they'd look for, very >on, was space, and big skies, and horses for the kids, and >ok-outs in the summer, and Laura in her element, nut-brown, arefoot, the pole in the very middle of their tent. It wasn't hat he'd ever planned, not at this age, but it would do.

The University complex loomed up. Laura indicated left, lging into the middle of the road. Telemann gazed out, wistful.

'What's the matter?' she said.

Telemann frowned, trying to put it into words.

'I'd have liked to have seen this thing through,' he said at last. Ie and Pete. That's all.'

*

Emery phoned Juanita again from the airport at Hyannis. The next flight to Boston was an hour away, and he had time to pause for breath.

'The pipe I brought back from Germany,' he said. 'You got it to the lab?'

'Sure.'

'They come through with anything yet?'

'Yes. They say there's nothing worth analysing.' She paused. 'You tell them it had been in some kind of fire?'

'No.'

'Well, I guess they figured that for themselves. They found evidence of ash. But that's all.'

'No chemical?'

'Nothing.' She paused again. 'But the guy still said you might be right. It fits the process. It's what you'd need. There's just no proof. That's all.'

'OK.' Emery nodded, juggling a styrofoam cup of coffee in his other hand. 'I need a translator,' he said. 'Someone with good German. Someone who knows science. Someone in the loop.'

Juanita laughed, a deep, rich laugh. 'You kidding?' she said. 'There is no loop. There's you and me and Ron and that nice Mr Sullivan. Some loop.'

Emery grinned, sipping the coffee. Juanita had a point. With Telemann out, the loop was even tighter. Tight enough to hang them all.

'Sullivan been on again?'

'Yes. He dropped by this morning. High excitement.'

'Why?'

'He's talking about the English guy again.' She paused. 'He wants you to run checks.'

'McVeigh?'

'Yes.'

Emery winced, remembering the last time the name had cropped up, Sullivan sitting in the office on 'F' Street, telling him about Zahra's news from London, how important it could be, a kid with a big fat candy-bar that Emery had never wanted to share. He bent to the phone, wondering why the name should suddenly have become so critical, putting the question to Juanita, realizing too late that she'd gone.

*

It was mid-afternoon before McVeigh found the Sugarloaf Mountain Ski Resort. He spotted the sign at the roadside, newly painted, and began to slow, looking for a road. Finding it, he left the highway and drove up through the trees. The office lay back from the road. He parked outside and got out of the car, locking the Beretta in the glove-box. The Arab's bag had yielded two spare clips of ammunition and another 100 rounds in a square cardboard box. The box was Canadian in origin, standard .22 snubnose. Nothing else in the bag had been of any interest: three packs of Winston, a tablet of soap, still wrapped, from the hotel, a packet of chewing-gum and a toilet bag. With the stuff carefully laid out across the passenger seat, McVeigh was no closer to knowing who the Arab had been working for. Leaving him at the roadside had been untidy, but under the circumstances, McVeigh wasn't sure he'd had much choice. A man carrying 140 rounds of .22 snubnose clearly had debts to settle. McVeigh didn't want to be one of them.

Now he walked across to the office. The young man inside glanced at Amer's photo of Yussuf and confirmed that he'd taken a rental. McVeigh looked pleased. The old man was his father-in-law. Tomorrow was his birthday. The trip up to Maine had been a present from the family. They'd recommended that he stay at Sugarloaf, and now they wanted to surprise him. McVeigh asked for directions, telling the young man not to bother showing him in person. Surprise was the key. Surprise would make the old man's day. He'd find the place for himself.

Back in the car, McVeigh drove slowly down the mountain. Finding the road to the old man's house, he parked out of sight amongst the trees, retrieving the Beretta from the glove-box and checking the clip. Then he reached back for the haversack, feeling inside for the letters from Amer and the bottle of Jordan water. Out of the car, the haversack on his back, he slipped into the trees. The house was about a quarter of a mile away, timber-built, Scandinavian design. The ground had been cleared around

419

it, but the trees pressed down to the edges of the turned earth, and there was plenty of cover.

McVeigh circled the house, moving carefully from tree to tree, stepping around the puddles of sunshine on the carpet of fallen leaves. Directly above the house, looking down on it, he settled himself. From here he could see two sides of the building. The big picture windows gave him clues to the interior layout. He could see a kitchen and what appeared to be a big open-plan lounge. Upstairs were the bedrooms and a bathroom. Of the old man there was no sign.

McVeigh waited for an hour before he spotted him, a flicker of movement in the downstairs lounge. He peered through the trees. The old man was standing near the window, a mug in his hand. He was staring out, immobile, a broad, well-built figure, not much hair. He was wearing a short-sleeved sports shirt and baggy jeans. He sipped at the mug once or twice, then shrugged and turned away. Analysing the movement, McVeigh couldn't be sure whether he had company. Either way, it was best to be sure. McVeigh settled down again, still waiting.

*

Telemann sat in the tiny office, listening to the neurologist spelling it out. He was a small, round man with a ruddy outdoor face and an almost permanent smile. A decade or two of American medicine hadn't quite erased the soft Scottish brogue.

'Here,' he said. 'And here. And here.'

A folder lay open on his desk. Inside the folder were a series of black-and-white scans. They looked a little like early NASA pictures of the moon, whorls of grey, nothing distinct, nothing recognizable. They were print-outs from a Magnetic Resonance Imager, and each one represented a slice of Telemann's brain, but in anatomical terms they made no sense at all. The only bit Telemann recognized was his own name, neatly typed on the top left-hand corner of each scan.

He looked up at the neurologist. He remembered the face from his previous visits to the clinic, the afternoon when they'd fed his body into the scanner, answering his questions with a series of soothing one-liners about precautionary checks. Since then, he'd thought no more of it. The problems with his vision, the general feelings of fatigue, the occasional moments when he dropped his car keys or spilled his coffee, all these symptoms he'd attributed to overwork. After fifteen years in the field, to no one's surprise, his body was slowing down. Nothing scary. No long names. Just simple wear and tear.

Now, thanks to science, he knew better. He bent to the last of the scans, frowning. 'And these?' he said, pointing to a series of white flecks.

'More damage to the sheath. Your nerves have this fatty stuff covering the fibres. The stuff's called myelin. When it gets damaged, the messages don't conduct so well.' He paused. 'Your story about the gas station? In Hamburg?'

'Yeah?'

He nodded, returning to the scan, tapping the cluster of white flecks. 'Something like this would have been enough to have done it. Your brain says put the gas nozzle back in the pump. Your hand's ready and waiting. But the message doesn't get through properly.' He shrugged. 'You were lucky. It might have been worse.'

Telemann nodded, remembering Inge running from the car, how quickly she'd taken control, how well she'd done.

'Yeah,' he said, turning away. 'It might.'

There was a long silence. Laura was still outside in the waiting-room. She'd offered to come in, be with him, but Telemann had shaken his head. However bad the news, he was the one – in the end – who had to cope. Best to get a little practice. Best to start rehearsing.

He looked at the neurologist. 'It doesn't kill you?' he said.

'No.'

'It's not infectious?'

'No.'

'So—' he shrugged '—what's the problem?'

The neurologist reached for the file again, leafing slowly back through the scans, his eyes flicking quickly from one to the other.

'You have a lot of damage,' he said at last. 'Frankly, I'm surprised you've kept going for so long. That's why ...' He gestured towards the waiting-room repeating what he'd said earlier about Laura, the letter he'd had to send her, how strongly he'd advised her that her husband should be told, how important it was for him to know, to understand, and to begin to come to terms with it all. Telemann nodded, mutely compliant, accepting the gentle reprimand. The doctor leaned forward again, an ally, a friend. 'The science isn't exact,' he said, 'not as exact as we'd like.'

'But?'

'But—' he shrugged '—I'd expect more attacks. I'd expect difficulties with your vision and your balance. I think you're going to have a lot of trouble walking. I think you might find talking hard. Your memory might go. Plus—' he shrugged again '—you may become incontinent.'

Telemann looked up. '*What?*' he said.

'You may . . .' The neurologist hesitated, picking over the words. 'It's a question of control. Your brain decouples, you see. It decouples from the motor functions. Gaps develop. The body takes over—' he smiled bleakly '—develops a mind of its own.'

Telemann stared at him, shocked, suddenly aware of the way it would have to be. Not guesswork. Not maybes. But the real thing.

'So what's time-scale here?'

'Years.' The doctor reached forward, a hand on Telemann's shoulder. 'The rest of your life.'

Telemann nodded, saying nothing, looking away. A wheelchair, he thought, and that silly fucking bag you keep between your thighs under the blanket. The one with the tube. The one you have to empty every two hours or so. The one that spares you all that social embarrassment. He got up and walked to the window. It was a beautiful fall afternoon, students crossing the road outside, walking, talking, laughing. He shook his head slowly, hearing the doctor closing the file.

'Sounds like nerve gas . . .' he said quietly. 'Only slower.'

※

An hour before dusk, the old man came out of the house. He locked the door and pocketed the key, looking carefully down the road towards the highway. Then he rubbed his face a couple of times and took a deep lungful of air. Watching, McVeigh could hear the long sigh as he breathed out again and began to walk, very slowly, away from the house.

McVeigh grinned, scarcely able to believe his luck. No need to break into the house. No need to ring the doorbell and risk a confrontation on the stoop. No need to worry about anyone else, some mystery guest, some minder he'd yet to spot. He stood up, stepping quickly back into the trees, then set a course for himself that would intersect with the old man. He could see him now, on a path below, his head down, pausing from time to time, picking things up, fir cones, examining them, tossing them away. McVeigh walked a little further, moving silently. He wanted to meet the old man face to face. He wanted to cause him as little grief as possible.

Minutes later, he was in position, the old man coming towards him, head still down, the trees in deep shadow now. McVeigh waited a moment longer, then began to walk, whistling to himself, plenty of noise. He saw the old man stop and look up. His face had changed since the photograph. He looked thinner, older, more gaunt. McVeigh kept going, stopping three or four yards away. The two men looked at each other. McVeigh could see the fear in the old man's eyes. He held out his hand. 'My name's McVeigh,' he said. 'I've come from Amer Tahoul.'

The old man studied him for a moment longer. '*Salaam*,' he said. 'Amer promised you'd be here.'

They went back to the house. The old man made coffee. They sat together in the big lounge, the lights on, the curtains drawn, and McVeigh told him everything he knew, bits of the story stitched together, some from Cela, some from Amer. He told him how the Israelis had built the hatred in his heart, taking his son, selling his life to the *moharebbin*; how an Israeli had appeared at his door, pretending to be an Arab, pretending to recruit him for the cause, sending him overseas, giving him the key role in a plot to poison the streets of Manhattan. Whether or not the strike would ever have taken place, whether the threat was real or not, McVeigh didn't know. Far more likely, the Israelis would themselves have unmasked it, earning the gratitude of the Americans, saddling Iraq with the blame, stiffening Washington's resolve, exposing Saddam for what he really was.

McVeigh did his best to simplify the plan but he could tell from the old man's face that the depth of the treachery was too much for him. He didn't understand power politics. He couldn't fathom the subtlety of the play the Israelis had tried to make. He kept shaking his head, looking away, his hands knotting and unknotting, the mug of coffee untouched. 'My wife,' he said at the end. 'Hala.'

McVeigh nodded, reaching for the haversack, looking for the square of cloth Cela had given him by the river. Finding it, he laid it carefully on the table between them. The old man stared at it, uncomprehending.

McVeigh took his hand. 'She's dead,' he said.

The old man looked up. 'You're sure?'

'Yes.' McVeigh nodded. 'I'm sorry.'

The old man got up and left the room. When he came back, minutes later, McVeigh knew he'd been weeping. It was there in his face. He stood by the table, looking down at the tasselled square of cotton, roughly cut from his wife's scarf. He made no attempt to touch it. 'I hate them,' he said. 'I hate the Israelis.'

McVeigh nodded, reaching in the bag again, producing the bottle of water. He put it on the table beside the cloth, uncertain what to say, how to put it. Finally, he looked up at the old man.

'This comes from an Israeli,' he said. 'Her name is Cela. She was the wife of one of the men behind the—' he shrugged '—plan. He gave the plan away. He betrayed it to his wife. The Israelis killed him for that.' He paused. 'His wife asked me to give you this. She took it from the the River Jordan. She hoped you'd understand.'

He offered the old man the bottle of water. The old man shook his head, ignoring it, his eyes wet again, the talk of death, the talk of bereavement. 'What about you?' he said at last. 'Are you Israeli?'

'No, I'm British.'

'Then why . . .' He shrugged, nodding at the water.

McVeigh thought about the question, the bottle still in his

and. He remembered the darkness by the river, how cold it was. He looked away.

'Because of her,' he said simply. 'Because of Cela.'

*

Emery, stepping out of the cab from Washington's National Airport, recognized Sullivan's limo, still parked by the kerb outside the 'F' Street office. Personal visits were becoming a habit, he thought, crossing the sidewalk and heading for the door.

Juanita met him in the tiny reception area on the fourth floor. 'He's been here nearly an hour,' she said. 'He's still on the computer.'

'Doing what?'

'Getting into NID.'

'You give him the pass codes?'

'Yeah.' She nodded. 'In the end I did.'

Emery looked at her for a moment. NID was the National Intelligence Databank. It held details on a huge range of intelligence contacts worldwide. Unlimited access depended on a set of pass codes, issued to no more than a couple of hundred people in the Washington area. Despite his position at the White House, Sullivan probably wasn't one of them. Ordinarily, he'd have gone through someone like Emery for hands-on Intelligence. Emery shrugged and gave Juanita the envelope he'd taken from Weill. 'This is the German stuff,' he said. 'Absolute priority.'

Emery walked into his office. Sullivan was sitting at his desk, bent over the computer. The blinds were down on the window and the room was in semi-darkness. Even from the door, Emery could read the name on top of the computer file. 'McVeigh,' he said aloud.

Sullivan looked up. He'd spilled coffee on his shirt-front. The empty styrofoam cup lay on the desk. 'English guy,' he said. 'Ex-Marine. Seems to do a lot of work for the Arabs. London-based.' He paused. 'You wanna read the rest for yourself?'

Emery shook his head. He circled the desk and pulled up a chair on the other side. 'No,' he said. 'Just tell me why you're interested.'

'You know why I'm interested.'

'I know that Al Zahra passed on the name.' He paused. 'Zahra's not a source we can trust.'

'Who says?'

'Ten years of dealing with him says. He fabricates. He lies. Guy lives in fairyland. Should work for Disney.' He leaned forward across the desk. 'Plus I checked with London. No one's heard of any missing nerve gas.'

'Who did you talk to?'

'MI5.' He paused. 'And they should know.'

Sullivan shrugged and bent to the computer again, scrolling out another line of text. The entry on McVeigh ran to a bare three lines. Emery could see Sullivan struggling to control his temper.

'McVeigh went to Israel,' Sullivan said finally.

'How do you know?'

'Guy in London told me.'

'Who?'

Sullivan looked up. The smile was icy. 'Guy I happen to know. Well placed. Someone I trust.'

'Not Zahra? Not the Intelligence people?'

'No.'

'Who, then?'

Sullivan shook his head, refusing to impart the name, and Emery shrugged, peering at the screen again. 'So where is he now? This McVeigh?'

'He's here. In the States.'

'Whereabouts?'

'I don't know. Yet.' Sullivan frowned. 'But he's in touch with our friend with the gas. Word is, he'll deliver.'

'*Deliver*?'

'Yes.'

'When did you hear this?'

'Last night. Late.'

Emery sank back in the chair. There was a long silence. 'Ever think of sharing the news?' he said drily.

Sullivan removed his glasses for a moment, then ran a hand over his face. 'You were too fucking busy,' he said, 'not listening to me.'

The two men looked at each other for a moment over the computer. Then Emery shrugged. 'Might have been easier, that's all.'

'Sure, buddy.' Sullivan reached for the empty styrofoam cup, lifting it in a mock toast. 'And here's to Mr Assali.'

Emery looked at Sullivan for a moment longer. Then he got up and went to the window. The blinds up, daylight transformed the room. He turned round. Sullivan had switched off the computer. Emery walked back to the desk. 'The Israelis killed Assali,' he said quietly. 'And Ron was part of that. Another guy's dead, too. Otto Wulf.'

'Heart attack. It was on the wires.'

Emery shook his head. 'No,' he said. 'He died of poison gas. Nerve gas. Either murder or suicide. The evidence isn't clear.'

Sullivan blinked, leaning forward. 'How do you know?' he said. 'How do you know that?'

'Ron was there. He saw it. In fact he delivered the stuff in the first place.' He offered Sullivan a cold smile. 'Federal Express.'

'Shit.' Sullivan shook his head. 'Who gave it to him?'

'Wulf's mistress.' The smile faded. 'An Israeli.'

'Why?'

'Two reasons. One, he'd been supplying gas to the rag-heads. Not the final product, but constituent chemicals. Once you've got that, the rest is simple.' He paused. 'In fact I suspect Wulf supplied the stuff that came here. It was either ready-mixed or synthesized at a place near Hamburg. Out in the country. Then shipped through Antwerp.'

Sullivan nodded. 'And two?'

Emery looked down at the desk, wondering whether he should wait for confirmation, the transcript of the German material he'd hand-carried back from Cape Cod. Finally he decided against it, looking up, smiling again. 'Wulf was a broker,' he said. 'He had connections everywhere. He traded favours for influence.' He paused. 'One of the items on Saddam's list was data on Israeli ECM. The frequencies they use. What he'd need to know to knock the IAF out of the sky.'

'And Wulf?'

'Found him the data. Guy on the West Coast. Avionics guy. You might remember the name. Lennox Gold.'

'Guy in the hotel? Guy that got gassed?'

'Right. Gold needed the money. The Iraqis had the money. And Wulf was the go-between.' He shrugged. 'The Israelis settled both debts. Wulf's and Gold's.'

Sullivan was frowning now, following the smoke upwind, trying to find the bonfire.

'You're saying the Israelis killed Gold?'

'Yes.'

'With poison gas?'

'Yes.'

'And the rest of it?' He paused. 'The horses up in the Catskills?'

'Same message.'

'From the *Israelis*?'

'Sure.'

'Why?'

Emery sat down at last, the smile quite gone, spelling it out, explaining the motive, describing the plan, Sullivan leaning forward across the desk, following it all, word for word.

'You're saying it's a scam?' he said finally. 'The fucking Jews leading us to water?'

'Leading us to war,' Emery suggested drily. 'In case we were under-motivated.'

Sullivan sat back, nodding, going over the analysis. At length he permitted himself a broad grin, infinitely benign. 'I need proof,' he said. 'Evidence. Then the rest is just beautiful.'

'Beautiful?'

'Sure.' He reached for a cigar. 'We get the evidence. We give it to the Israelis—' he shrugged '—and our problems are over.'

'Whose problems?'

'The President's—' he lit a cigar '—and mine.'

Emery nodded, fingering the intercom, checking with Juanita. The German material was en route to a translator, security cleared. It should be back by midnight. He thanked her and sat back again. Sullivan was still waiting, the cigar clamped between

428

his teeth. He reached for the empty coffee cup and began to crush it in one hand, then another.

'We have some of the evidence already,' he said. 'Wulf is rock-solid. Even the Germans know it. That's why they've been trying to bury the truth.'

'And the rest of it?'

Emery hesitated for a moment. Then he nodded at the computer.

'Your friend McVeigh,' he said lightly. 'Who else?'

16

Three days later, McVeigh picked up the telephone in the lounge of the rented house on the slopes of the Sugarloaf Mountain. The old man, Abu Yussuf, was in the garage, repairing a broken bracket on the car. After seventy-two hours together, they had a plan. The plan was simple. With a couple of maps and a tankful of Tabun GA, they were going to avenge two deaths: the murder of Hala and the murder of Yakov. The old man had shown him the car, the way it could be done. At his insistent invitation, McVeigh had lain on the cold concrete in the garage and admired the pipework, how neat it was. He'd seen the pump, the fake exhaust. He'd fingered the switch on the dashboard. He had absolutely no doubt that the system would work, and when he checked the distances on the map he concluded that two nights of steady driving were all that separated Manhattan from 5 gallons of Tabun GA.

Now McVeigh began to punch in the digits for a London number. Beside the phone was the letter from Amer Tahoul. The letter was in Arabic. the old man had read it once, grunted, and put it down. He'd never discussed it, never shared its contents, never looked at it again. Whatever it said, however hard Amer had tried, the old man had put himself beyond reach. His grief had turned to rage, and his rage had consumed him, like a fever. Nothing would touch it.

McVeigh sank into a chair, waiting for the number to connect. In three hours, once darkness had come, they were moving south, he and Abu Yussuf, sharing the Oldsmobile. The London number began to ring, then a voice came on. It sounded sleepy.

McVeigh glanced over his shoulder, checking the path to the front door. He'd wrenched the exhaust bracket out of shape. It would take a while to fix.

'Mr Friedland?'

'Yes?'

'Pat McVeigh.'

'Ah ...' McVeigh heard the click of a recording-machine. Where are you?'

'I'm in the US.' He paused. 'Is that thing recording OK? You want to check it?'

He heard Friedland laugh, the sleepiness gone. 'Go ahead,' he said. 'It's Japanese. It's foolproof.'

McVeigh smiled, glad of the joke. The role he'd been playing for the last three days hadn't left much room for laughter.

'Listen,' he said briskly, 'this is the plan. This is what's going to happen. But I need one guarantee.' He paused. 'OK?'

'Where are you?' Friedland said again.

'It doesn't matter.'

'Do you have the gas?'

'Yes. And the bloke that goes with it.'

'OK.' Friedland paused. 'So what's the condition?'

McVeigh bent to the phone, speaking slowly, no ambiguities, nothing left to chance. He'd spell out every detail of the plan as long as Abu Yussuf was left unharmed. There was to be no violence, and no legal proceedings.

'You got that?'

'Yes.' Friedland paused again. 'Anything else?'

'Yeah. He gets citizenship. If he wants to stay in the States. Otherwise he gets enough to settle somewhere else. With me?'

'Yes. I'll have to check all this. Phone me again.'

'Sure.'

There was a long silence. McVeigh could hear the old man hammering at the bracket outside in the garage.

Then Friedland came back. 'So what's the plan?' he said.

McVeigh laughed. 'You get the guarantee,' he said. 'I'll give you the plan.'

'Otherwise?'

'The deal's off.'

'Meaning?'

McVeigh shrugged. Across the room, on the television, CNN were showing yet more pictures of the American build-up in the Gulf, Navy F-14s, blasting into a pale blue sky. The set had been on for three days solid and McVeigh was sick of it American muscle. Arab despots. No mention of the kids he'd left in Ramallah, the broken bodies en route to the mortuary fridge.

He bent to the phone again. 'Meaning I leave him to it,' he said, 'my friend with the nerve gas.'

*

Emery phoned Telemann the same afternoon. He'd deliberately left him alone for three days, knowing that the homecoming would be difficult enough without interruptions from the office Now, sitting at his desk, he heard the phone answer. It was Laura

'Hi. Me.'

Laura said nothing for a moment. Emery heard a door close in the background. Then she was back. She said she was glad he'd called.

'How is he?'

'Quiet.'

'Has he seen the doctor?'

'Yes. We went Monday.'

'How was that?'

'I don't know. He won't talk about it. He didn't want me there. Said he preferred it one on one.'

'But what about afterwards? How was he afterwards?'

'I told you. Quiet. He doesn't talk too much. Not about that.' She paused. 'Not about anything, actually.'

Emery nodded, wondering what he could do, wondering what to say, relieved when Laura came on the phone again breaking the silence.

'There's one thing, Pete . . .'

'Yeah?'

'I don't know whether it's possible, but . . .'

'What? Say it. Go ahead.'

'He just . . . I guess . . . wants to be on the end of this thing.'

'What thing?'

'Whatever it is . . . you and Ron . . .'

'Yeah.' Emery nodded, non-committal. 'Sure.'

'I don't know whether . . .'

'Is he there now?'

'He's asleep.'

'*Asleep?*' Emery looked at his watch. 'Shit.'

There was another silence. Emery reached for a cigarette. The material from Weill, sourced from one of Wulf's companies, had turned out to be a detailed specification for the required Israeli ECM data. The invoices from the Hamburg flat had checked out as genuine. The German connection could now meet any standard of legal proof. But quite where the thing would end was still a mystery.

'I dunno,' Emery muttered down the phone. 'It's not too easy just now.'

'Sure. I understand.'

'But if there's any way . . .' He shrugged. 'No question. I promise.'

'Yeah . . . well . . . whatever . . .' Laura trailed off.

There was another long silence. Emery lit the cigarette, pulling it deep into his lungs, letting it rest there, then expelling a long plume of blue smoke. 'You sound really miserable,' he said quietly.

'I am.'

'Hey . . .' He smiled, picking a shred of tobacco from his lower lip. 'I love you. If that helps.'

'Thanks.'

'I mean it.'

'I know you do.'

Laura began to say something else, but there was another disturbance in the background, a door opening this time, and Emery heard Bree. She wanted to ride her bike. The back tyre was flat.

Laura returned to the phone. 'Call again,' she said. 'You should talk to Ron.'

*

It was nearly eight in the evening by the time McVeigh and the old man left the house. The bracket had taken longer than Abu Yussuf had expected, and he'd cut his hand while he was making a washer from a sheet of spare cardboard. The cut was deep, at the base of the forefinger on the left hand. McVeigh had bound it tightly, but it was an awkward place to apply pressure and the slightest movement made it bleed. Driving was out of the question, and McVeigh had taken the car-keys from the old man's hand, helping him into the passenger seat, sliding himself in behind the wheel.

They headed east, back down the country roads towards the Interstate, the big old car wallowing on the corners. After the conversations of the last three days – wild passionate outbursts from the old man, spasms of intense debate – there was little left to say, and McVeigh was content to drive in silence, reaching for the radio from time to time, retuning between channels, trying to find something that would ease the pain on the old man's face. Nothing did, and nothing could, and finally McVeigh switched the radio off, leaving them with the low murmur of the big engine and the steady thrum–thrum of the tyres on the road.

Beyond Shin Pond, for the first time, McVeigh noticed the lights behind him. They belonged to a car, too low for a truck. The car was travelling fast. McVeigh adjusted his speed a little, easing his foot on the throttle. The road was straight for at least a mile, a ribbon of tarmac flanked by trees. The car was behind them now, no more than 10 metres, and McVeigh flicked the right indicator, signalling it on. Nothing happened. He did it again. Still nothing. The old man, visibly alarmed, looked back, turning in his seat. Beyond the glare of the headlights there was only darkness.

The two men exchanged glances, and McVeigh accelerated again, returning the car to cruising speed. For half a mile they drove in tandem, one car behind the other, then the headlights suddenly swerved out into the middle of the road, and McVeigh felt the car on his shoulder, very close, slowing again. He glanced across, certain now that something was wrong. Two faces were looking at him. On the nearside was a woman, sharp-featured, her hair drawn tightly back from her face. Behind the wheel was a man, a little older, curly blond hair, a day's growth of beard. McVeigh stamped on the accelerator, pulling the car left, hitting the other vehicle. The old man, leaning forward, looking across at the other car, was thrown on to McVeigh by the impact. McVeigh pushed him off, fighting for control, ducking instinctively as the first bullet tore through the body-work. The old man was on his knees under the dashboard, his body half-twisted. 'Shlomo,' he kept saying. 'Shlomo.'

'Who's Shlomo?'

'In the car. The one driving the car.'

'But who is he?'

'He's—'

The two cars collided again, side on, and McVeigh knew he had to get ahead before the next bend. The Beretta he'd stored in the glove-box. The two seconds he'd need to get it out was time he didn't have. These people were pros. They'd done it before. They meant it.

McVeigh reached down the gear-shift, taking the car out of automatic, dropping into second gear. The transmission screamed, but the big old engine responded at last, kicking the car forward, putting a metre or two of space between the two vehicles. McVeigh glanced at the dashboard. The needle on the speedo was nudging eighty. A shallow bend was approaching. The car behind was dropping back a little but soon, McVeigh knew, they'd make another run. He heard glass smash behind him, another bullet, and he braced himself against the seat as the corner came at them, a blur of pine trees, the Oldsmobile beginning to drift sideways as McVeigh applied even more power.

Safely through the corner, he checked on the old man. Abu Yussuf was looking back over his shoulder at the other car. One hand was on the dashboard. The other was on the back of the seat. The car behind was gaining again, getting closer. 'Don't stop,' he said. 'Don't stop.'

McVeigh frowned. 'What?'

'Faster. Go faster.'

McVeigh looked in the mirror. The other car was very close now, 5 yards, maybe less. The road ahead was straight. Any minute, he thought. 'In the glove-box!' he shouted. 'There's a gun.'

The old man was concentrating on the car behind. He didn't appear to be listening.

435

'A gun!' McVeigh shouted again. 'In the glove-box.'

The old man looked at him briefly. His right hand moved to the switch on the dashboard. McVeigh stared at him, hearing the faint purr as the auxiliary pump cut in, then he realized what the old man had done, and his eyes went to the mirror again, and he was wondering how long the stuff in the tank took to work, and whether Billy would ever get to hear the truth of it, his father a chemical warfare statistic, gassed to death on a remote country road in the middle of nowhere. The lights in the mirror began to waver, the car swerving from side to side, then – abruptly – it had gone, a squeal of tyres and a sickening thud and the sound of breaking glass as it disappeared into the trees.

McVeigh looked at the old man. The pump had stopped now and his hand had left the switch, but he was still looking back, wild, exultant. 'Shlomo!' he shouted in Arabic.

'Who's Shlomo?'

'*Mish bani admeen.*'

'Speak English.'

'The one who came to see me. In Ramallah. The one who betrayed my son.' He shook his fist. 'The devil take him.'

'Yeah?'

'Yeah.'

The old man beat his fist on the dashboard, cursing him again, and McVeigh nodded, the car still topping 80 m.p.h. He had the window down now, the cold night air sluicing through the car, and for the first time he began to wonder whether they might get away with it. The gas couldn't linger, not vapour, not at these speeds. A small town was coming up, Patten, a handful of clapboard houses, but McVeigh swept through, taking no risks, determined to put as many miles as he could between themselves and the cloud of Tabun GA. In the Marine Corps, he'd attended lectures on nerve gas. They'd always said it didn't hang around. 'Non-persistent' was the word they'd used. But McVeigh had never fully trusted them. Not then. Not now. A lot of what they told you was bullshit, stuff to make you feel better, and he had no intention of putting it to the test. Only when he saw the signs for the Interstate, only when he got there, would he truly relax.

He drove on, looking at the old man from time to time, shaking his head, part-admiration, part-disbelief.

'Daft old fucker,' he muttered, grinning at him.

*

Sullivan eventually found Emery at home. He bent to the security phone outside the apartment block, half-past one in the morning, a thin rain drifting in from the Bay.

'I'm in the car,' Sullivan barked. 'Come on down.'

Emery joined him minutes later, an old pair of yachting waterproofs thrown over his pyjamas.

'Afraid of heights?' he enquired drily, climbing into the big Lincoln. 'Didn't want to come on up?'

Sullivan ignored him, waiting until he'd closed the door. The night was cold, the first real chills of autumn. 'I'm grateful,' he said, 'that's why I'm bothering with all this shit.'

'Yeah?'

'Yeah.' He paused. 'My Brit friend has been on. About the fella McVeigh.'

'You talked to him?'

'No. But he's here somewhere. He wants a deal. He has the old guy. The guy in the photo. The guy with the gas.'

'A deal?'

Emery nodded, thinking about it. New York saved by a bucket of money. In four busy weeks, he'd never once considered something so obvious. He looked at Sullivan. 'How much does he want?'

'Nothing.'

'*Nothing?*'

'No. He just wants a deal for the other guy. The Palestinian.'

'What sort of deal?'

'Freedom. No violence. No rap. Just citizenship.' He shrugged. 'Why not? We've done it before . . .'

'Sure.' Emery nodded, looking away. 'When?' he said at last. 'When will all this happen?'

'Soon. I'll call the fella in London when I get back . . .' He paused. 'There's another thing, too.'

Emery lifted an eyebrow. He was cold. He felt empty. He wanted to go back to bed. 'What?' he said.

Sullivan gazed at him for a moment, then laid a land on his arm. Emery gazed at it, uncomprehending.

'The President's grateful,' Sullivan said at last. 'He wants you to know that.'

'He does?'

'Yeah. We were having a little problem with the Germans. Question of financial help. For our boys in the Gulf . . .' He paused, smiling, squeezing Emery's arm. 'Appears the problem's gone away.'

*

McVeigh and the old man got to Portland an hour before dawn, driving slowly into the city suburbs, looking for the right kind of motel. They found it almost at once, half a mile off the Maine Turnpike, 70 dollars a night with security parking. McVeigh went to the desk, paying cash for a double room, apologizing for the lateness of the hour. The woman said no problem, giving him the key to the room and confirming that there were three lock-up garages out-back, residents' use only.

McVeigh parked the car in the furthest of the three garages. Later, he told the old man, they'd buy a replacement rear-screen. The old man nodded, agreeing. He could fit it. Then the car would look normal again, just another run-down Olds, a little rusty, a little tired, nothing special.

They went to the room. The old man lay down on one of the beds with a sigh, not bothering to undress, and fell asleep at once, his eyes closed, his hands folded over his chest. Watching him from the other bed, McVeigh thought of the handful of corpses he'd seen, men who'd died of natural causes, the same pose, the same sense of peace. Since the incident with the other car, some of the rage had gone. He'd been quieter, less fretful, less tense. Once they'd got to the Interstate, he'd even managed the beginnings of a normal conversation. He'd wanted to know about London, whether it was as bad as New York, whether it had beggars, kids sleeping in the streets. McVeigh had said yes to both, and the old man had shaken his head, wistful, not able to understand. Amongst such wealth, he muttered, such poverty.

McVeigh waited another half-hour, making sure the old man was asleep, then he rolled quietly off the bed and let himself out of the room. The woman at the desk was asleep in front of the television, her head lolling on her chest. McVeigh found a payphone in the lobby and dialled Friedland's number. Friedland answered at once. McVeigh asked about the guarantee. Friedland said it was watertight. McVeigh said that was fine, but he had a gun and he'd use it on the tank in the boot if the old man was harmed. Friedland said he understood. McVeigh repeated the threat, then gave Friedland the details that mattered. Where they'd be. What time they'd arrive. The precautions the authorities should take. He wanted no grand opera, nothing dramatic, just a sensible low-key operation. That way, the thing would work. Any other way, it might get tricky. Friedland asked if there was anything else he needed, any other requests. McVeigh thought about it briefly, then nodded. 'Yeah,' he said. 'Tell them not to shoot me. Tell them it wouldn't be in their interests.'

'No?'

'No.' He grunted. 'Not if they're interested in the Israelis.'

*

Telemann, hearing the knock at the bedroom door, looked up. No one knocked at bedroom doors. Not unless they were guilty. Or needed help.

'Come in.'

The knocking went on. It sounded like a foot. Telemann swung out of bed and opened the door. Bree stood on the landing. She had a tray in her hands. Expecting breakfast, Telemann found himself looking at a huge mountain of jelly.

'Mine,' she said. 'I made it.'

Telemann looked at the jelly. He hated jelly. He took the tray from her and went back to the bed. He got in, the tray on his knees. Every time he moved, the jelly wobbled. Bree was at the foot of the bed. She hadn't taken her eyes off him. 'Eat it,' she said. 'It's get-better jelly. It'll make you well again.'

Telemann smiled. There were two spoons on the tray. One was clearly for him. He picked it up and pushed it into the jelly.

Scooping out a spoonful, the jelly made a soft, sucking noise. He put it in his mouth, swallowing it whole. It was green. It tasted of nothing.

'Nice,' he said. 'Clever girl.'

Bree grinned. She liked nothing better than praise. It was the fuel that got her through the day. She could never have too much of it. She watched him take another mouthful. Then another.

'Mummy says you might be in bed a lot,' she said at last.

'Did she?'

'Yes. She said you might be very sick.'

'Oh.' Telemann nodded. 'I see.'

'Doesn't matter, though.'

'No?'

'No. I can make lots of jelly. Every day, if you want.' She grinned again. 'Then you'll *have* to get better.'

Telemann nodded, returning the grin. Three spoonfuls had made little difference to the jelly. It still looked huge. Bree nodded absently, losing the thread of the conversation, her eyes finally leaving his face, going down to the newspaper spread on the bed, the bits and pieces lying across it. She bent down, curious, picking up a piece of heavy grey metal, weighing it in her hand, looking at her fingers afterwards, covered in a film of oil.

'Daddy?' she said, frowning.

'Yes, darling?'

'What's this?'

She picked up another piece, the same curiosity, looking at him, the bowl of jelly long forgotten.

Telemann smiled woodenly, putting down his spoon.

'It's a gun,' he said. 'We call it a revolver.'

*

Friedland phoned Ross at midday on the private Downing Street line. A woman answered, curt, unhelpful. Mr Ross had been relocated. She gave him another number.

Friedland tried again, finding Ross on the point of leaving for lunch. He heard him sitting down again. He heard him ask someone for a pen. He heard a door close. Then Ross was back on the phone again, eager, abrupt, impatient. Relocation had done nothing for his manners. 'Well?' he said. 'What's the plan?'

Friedland relayed the contents of his conversation with McVeigh. He detailed the location, the times, and McVeigh's parting advice about leaving him unharmed. When Ross came back on the phone, checking the small-print, the impatience had gone. Instead, he was audibly excited, even euphoric.

'You think we can rely on this?'

'I imagine so.'

'You're sure?'

'Under the circumstances . . .' Friedland shrugged. 'Yes.'

There was a brief silence. Then Ross came back. 'Any of your Curzon Street chums been on?'

'No.' Friedland frowned. 'Why should they?'

'Someone's been telling MI5 about missing nerve gas.' He paused, laughing. 'Would you believe a story like that?'

*

McVeigh told Abu Yussuf to be ready for eight o'clock. It would be dark by then, and the traffic southbound would be light. With luck, without busting the regulation 55 m.p.h., they'd be in New York City by 3 a.m. The old man looked at him, sitting on the bed, newly showered, newly shaved.

'They'll come at that hour?' he said. 'The press?'

'Of course.'

'So late?'

'For sure.'

The old man shrugged, another mystery, and collected the handful of belongings he'd brought with him. McVeigh had already been through his bag. Amongst the litter of 100-dollar notes, he'd found an automatic and two aerosols. He'd emptied the magazine of the automatic and peered hard at the aerosols. Neither had any markings, and he'd been on the point of giving one a trial squirt when the old man had shown signs of waking up. Now, his bag packed, he waited patiently for further orders.

They drove back to the Interstate, McVeigh at the wheel again, settling the car to a steady 55 m.p.h. The old man had spent most of the afternoon fitting the replacement rear window and McVeigh sensed that the way the work had gone had pleased him. Now he sat quietly beside McVeigh, his hands on his lap, gazing ahead, seemingly at peace. When it was all over, he said, he'd go back to Ramallah. That was the decision he'd made. He still had two sons. His sons needed him. Ramallah was where he belonged.

McVeigh nodded, said it sounded a great idea, knowing that it was possible. After New York, after the exchange, the old man would be free to go. Courtesy of the US Government, he'd be able to fly anywhere in the world. That was what they'd agreed. That was the deal.

The old man was looking at him. The last twelve hours or so, McVeigh had sensed the beginnings of a real friendship in his face, something in the eyes, something in the slow curl of his smile. The old man liked him. The old man trusted him. Together, they'd seen off the Israelis. Together, they'd finish the job. From tragedy, the truth.

'How many?' the old man said. 'How many from the newspapers? The television?'

McVeigh shrugged. 'Dunno,' he said. 'Hard to tell with those bastards.'

*

Emery picked up Telemann from the house on Dixie Street. Telemann was waiting for him on the stoop, the beginnings of a fine sunset pinking the wooden shingles. Emery saw him turn and kiss Laura. Then Bree. The other kids were upstairs, and they hung out of their bedroom windows, waving. 'Daddy . . .' they called. 'See you tomorrow.'

Telemann waved back to them, saying nothing, shouldering a small overnight bag, walking down the path towards the gate. He got into the car without a word, lifting a hand in farewell as they drove away.

'Where are we going?'

'Andrews.'

'Yeah?' He smiled for the first time. 'Then where?'

'New York.'

Emery headed south, then east on the Beltway. Within an

hour they were turning into Andrews Air Force Base. Emery stopped at the first of the security check-points and produced a letter with his CIA pass. The guard scanned the letter, then bent to the window, giving Emery directions, snapping a salute as he drove away.

Sullivan was waiting in the ten-seat executive jet, sprawled in a rearward-facing chair at the front of the cabin. All three men shook hands, Emery and Telemann settling themselves into seats facing Sullivan. The doors closed and the pilot started the engines. Five minutes later they were airborne, a steep left turn, climbing out of Andrews, setting course for New York.

Level at 28,000 feet, Sullivan chaired the brief conference. McVeigh, the Brit, was driving the Arab point-man to New York. Where from, no one knew. The car had several gallons of nerve gas on board and some kind of diffuser but the Brit seemed to have everything under control. A key group of New York people had been briefed, and they'd been conferencing all day on a range of contingency plans. The car was to appear in the vicinity of the UN building on East River Drive. The Brit would be at the wheel. The guy Yussuf would be with him. To the best of their knowledge, he wasn't armed. The meet was fixed for 3 a.m.

Emery, gazing out of the one of the windows, nodded. He could see most of Baltimore, necklaced with street lights. 'What then?' he said.

'The Brit hands him over.' Sullivan paused, his fingers outspread, tallying the items one by one. 'We have helicopters, NYPD, Fire Department, para-medics, and a non-specific all-hospitals alert. Beyond that, New York isn't prepared to go. They say it'll be counter-productive.' He paused. 'Plus there's an issue of pyrido bromide all round.' He smiled. 'Had trouble finding enough of the stuff. Most of it's gone to the Gulf . . .'

Emery nodded again. Pyrido stigmine bromide, taken every eight hours, offered a little protection against nerve agents. Supplemented with other chemicals, immediately after exposure, a man might even survive.

'Sounds good,' he said. 'What's our interest?' He looked at

Sullivan. Then at Telemann. Telemann was sucking a cube of barley sugar, the bag in his lap, his eyes half-closed.

Sullivan smothered a cough. 'McVeigh,' he said simply.

*

McVeigh saw Manhattan first. 'There,' he said, pointing through the windshield. 'Straight ahead.'

The old man awoke with a jerk, rubbing his face, peering forward. They were still on Interstate 95, skirting the Bronx, the black waters of Long Island Sound on the left. Ahead, plainly visible, were the towers of Manhattan Island, a city from another world, a Hollywood fantasy, millions of lights. McVeigh slowed, checking his watch. It was 02.12. He'd said 3 a.m. Looking at the map, and the near-empty freeway, it would take twenty minutes at the most. He began to slow, signalling right, taking the next exit.

The old man stared at him. 'What are we doing?' he said.

McVeigh smiled, patting him on the arm, reassuring him.

'We're early,' he said. 'We need to kill a little time.'

*

Emery and Telemann sat in the back of an unmarked police car in the shadow of the UN building. The building was ablaze with lights, yet another round of Security Council meetings, focus for the world's attention. Across the East River Drive, the lights danced on the black surface of the water, and through the open window, Emery could hear the faint buzz of a helicopter, high in the darkness.

Telemann was talking to the man behind the wheel, small, dark, wistful. He'd recognized him at once, Benitez, the guy he'd met last time he'd been up here, getting the brief on the body in the fridge in the Bellevue morgue. Benitez was talking about him now, wondering aloud where the investigation had led, too experienced to push for real detail, too curious to leave it alone. Telemann told him what he could, what little Emery had been prepared to share, knowing all too well that there was much, much more.

Benitez smiled. 'Aerospace guy, eh? One of those?'

'Sure.'

444

'Didn't do him any good, though, eh? Trip to Bellevue? Couple of days in the fridge?'

'No.'

Telemann nodded, falling silent. He had a pair of night binoculars in his bag, Marine issue, and he lifted them from time to time, scanning the shadowed recesses on the north side of the building. So far, to their credit, Telemann hadn't spotted a single player in the stake-out. Benitez, monitoring the radio net, glanced at his watch. 'Twenty before three,' he said. 'They give you any of that bromide stuff?' He licked his lips and made a face. 'Tasted lousy. Tasted of rusty nails.'

Emery nodded. 'We had some,' he said. 'On the plane.'

Telemann looked at him briefly, then lifted the night glasses again as Benitez began to unpack his gas mask.

'Correction,' he said quietly. 'You had some.'

*

McVeigh emerged from the tangle of freeways at the foot of Interstate 95 and eased the car on to the Bruckner Expressway. From here he could cross the East River and head south, down the eastern shore of Manhattan Island, a route that would take him directly towards the UN building. He had the radio on now, scanning the local stations, curious to know whether the authorities had made any kind of announcement. In their place, he wasn't at all sure what he'd do. A life-time of Hollywood movies told him that 5 gallons of nerve gas was the Doomsday scenario. Just the threat of it would be enough to empty most major cities, and this one was surely no exception. He sat back as the old car rumbled west, watching the cliffs of steel and glass get closer, the buildings taller, the sheer scale of the place more unlikely. He glanced at his watch again. 02.46. Exactly on schedule.

*

A NYPD helicopter saw them first, 500 feet, flying slowly up the East River. The observer, in the left-hand seat, motioned the chopper down, his glasses trained on a car travelling south down the Roosevelt Driveway. He fumbled for the switch that gave him access to the command net.

'OK,' he said quietly. 'We have them.'

*

McVeigh, watching the helicopter as it dipped towards the river, flicked his lights twice, the agreed signal. Beside him, the old man was staring at the bulk of the Queensboro Bridge.

'You think they'll understand?' he said at last.

'Who?'

'The people. When they read the papers. When they watch the television. When they see what we've done. When we tell them about the gas, and the Israelis.'

McVeigh glanced across at him. Choosing the UN building for the rendezvous had been his idea. After two days of listening to the old man, of letting his rage break like a wave around them, he'd suggested that they call a press conference, middle of the night, as private a time as any in New York. At first the old man, still bent on vengeance, had shaken his head. He wanted bodies on the sidewalk, Israeli bodies, Jewish bodies. He'd heard that New York was a Jewish city. Jews everywhere. Hala was dead. The Jews must die. He'd do it himself. Broad daylight. Rush-hour. Dying himself in the process. Who cared? Who cared what happened? As long as the Jews finally understood that they, too, must suffer. An eye for an eye. A tooth for a tooth.

McVeigh had nodded, making the obvious points. Many of the people on the street wouldn't be Jews at all. Some of them would be women and children. Some of them, even, might be Palestinian, immigrants, exiles. Was that the kind of justice the old man believed in? Was that the kind of death they deserved?

At this the old man had faltered, not quite so sure any more, retiring to his bedroom to rest and think, and hours later, when he re-emerged, McVeigh was able to talk about a different kind of justice, the Israelis exposed, forced to account for themselves in front of the entire world. The old man had been right. The place to go was New York. But not Broadway or Park Avenue. Not six o'clock in the evening, the middle of the commuter rush-hour. Somewhere quieter. A place where they could meet the press and the cameras, a place where they could show the world the evidence, the car, the tank in the boot, the gallons of

446

waiting nerve gas. The UN building, somewhere close, some-where near by, would be the perfect spot. That was the nerve centre. That was where the world had decided to solve its problems. How better to punish the Israelis?

Now, McVeigh looked across at the old man. He'd promised him the media. He'd promised they'd be there. Operationally, it was a lousy combination, a mixture of showbiz and armed force, and after some thought he'd made a private decision to defer the press conference, to call it later, once the car had been impounded, once the danger had gone. The old man would be disappointed, sure. He might even try and take a little unilateral action of his own. But McVeigh was prepared for that, too. He had the Beretta tucked inside his belt, the mechanism checked, the magazine full. If necessary, if it had to be, he'd separate the old man from the car at gun-point.

*

Telemann, sitting in Benitez's car, leaned foward, listening to the exchanges on the command net. The Oldsmobile had made contact with the helicopter. The car was two blocks from the UN. The Englishman was at the wheel and the Palestinian was sitting beside him. The observer in the helicopter estimated visual contact with the ground units in two minutes. Telemann lifted the glasses again, twisting round in his seat, sweeping the stretch of highway that fed traffic south into the underpass in front of the UN building. Even at three in the morning, the road was busy, a succession of cabs and private cars, none of them Oldsmobiles. He racked the focus, panning right again, the route they'd probably take, the feeder road that looped in towards the giant shadow of the UN building. With luck, they'd come here, journey's end, half an acre of tarmac barely 100 metres from where he was sitting. Telemann smiled, scan-ning left again with the glasses, back towards the road.

*

McVeigh began to slow, remembering the details on the map. Before they got to the UN building, there was an exit. At the end of the exit road, near the Douglas MacArthur Plaza, was the spot he'd chosen. He peered ahead, ignoring the driver of the cab behind, his hand on the horn, his fist raised. Up ahead was the UN building. The old man was staring at it, shaking his head again, awed.

McVeigh saw the exit road at last. He indicated right, hauling the old car off the highway, looking already for the tell-tale signs of a stake-out. The Plaza was coming up now, empty except for a car in the shadows. There were three figures inside. Two of them were wearing gas masks. The one in the back had a pair of binoculars. The binoculars were trained on the Oldsmobile.

McVeigh smiled, pulling the Oldsmobile into a tight turn, applying the brake, switching off the engine. Beyond the underpass was the river. Beyond the river, the lights of Queens. The two men sat in silence for a moment, waiting. On the phone, McVeigh had stipulated that the Americans must make the running. Their operation. Their first move. The clock on the dashboard read 03.02. The old man was frowning. The bag was on his lap. 'Where are they?' he said.

Telemann steadied his elbows on the tops of the front seats, the night glasses to his eyes. The man behind the wheel had a lean, square face. His hair was cropped short. He was talking to the other man but not looking at him, his eyes scanning the Plaza, left to right. The other man was much older, smaller, balding. His skin was dark. He was wearing an open-necked shirt. He looked nervous. He kept shaking his head.

On the command net, Telemann could hear the units reporting their readiness, one after the other, their voices distorted by the gas masks they were wearing. The officer in charge was querying the wind speed. Evidently the wind had dropped. Under the circumstances, it seemed utterly academic. What did the wind speed matter when the guys were here? Waiting?

'Go,' Telemann muttered. 'For Chrissakes, go.'

The old man was angry again. The darkness and the silence had unnerved him. McVeigh knew it, easing the Beretta, loosening it in his belt, hearing the whump–whump of a big helicopter, somewhere off to the right, flying low up the river.

'They'll come soon,' he said, trying to sooth the old man. 'They're always late.'

'You said three.'

'I know.'

'It's important, this story.'

'Of course it is.'

The old man looked at him a moment, the accusation plain in his face. 'You lied to me? About them?'

'No.'

'Then why . . .?' He gestured out at the darkened Plaza and as he did so the car was suddenly flooded with light. It came from everywhere, high-intensity, the beams criss-crossing in the darkness, pooling on the car. The helicopter was much louder now, the noise of the rotors coarsening as the pilot flared into the hover. The car was beginning to rock in the downwash, and McVeigh peered up through the windscreen, shielding his eyes against the blinding light, seeing nothing. They're doing it to disperse the gas, he thought. They're doing it in case we hit the pump.

He looked across at the old man. Abu Yussuf was terrified, his eyes huge in his face, the noise, the lights, the voice on the megaphone, harsh, metallic, booming across the Plaza.

'Get out of the car,' the voice said. 'Get out of the car. Put your hands on your head.'

The old man looked at McVeigh. His hand went to the switch on the dashboard. McVeigh got there first, stopping him, leaning over, opening the door, pushing him out of the car. The old man rolled on to the tarmac, still holding his bag, and McVeigh followed him, drawing the Beretta, falling on top of him, shielding his body from the downwash of the helicopter.

Watching, Telemann shook his head.

'Shit,' he said. 'Holy Jesus.'

The two bodies on the ground were motionless for a moment. Then the younger man struggled upright, pulling the Palestinian after him, fighting to stay on his feet in the turbulence. They began to stagger towards the shadows. The Palestinian seemed to have hurt his leg. He was pulling away from the younger man. He had a bag. There was something else in his hand. Telemann stared at it through the binoculars, hearing Benitez talking rapidly into a microphone, recognizing the shape of the canister. 'Shit,' he said again. 'He's got an aerosol.' He dropped the binoculars, wrenching open the door, beginning to run, his body in the half-crouch, a revolver in his hand.

McVeigh knew they were in trouble. Semi-blind, deafened by the helicopter, buffeted by the downwash, he headed into the light, hauling the old man after him. Abu Yussuf was resisting now, fighting back, his lips moving, the words impossible to catch. He had something in his hand, an aerosol of some kind, and he kept waving it, shouting some question or other. McVeigh shook his head, wading on through the squall, the old man in one hand, the Beretta in the other.

Abruptly, ahead, a figure appeared, small, silhouetted against the light. It dropped to one knee. McVeigh faltered for a moment, confused. Then he saw the arms come up, both hands out, and he was still turning back towards the old man, trying to shield him, when his body went suddenly limp, a dead weight. He looked at him for a moment, sprawled on the tarmac. His left eye had gone, and bits of the back of his head lay glistening on the tarmac. McVeigh turned, dropping into a half-squat, a mix of training and rage, bringing up the Beretta. The figure in the searchlights hadn't moved, the arms still out, pointing at the old man. McVeigh's first shot dropped him, and he ran forward, crouching over his body, emptying the rest of the magazine, point-blank range, into his head.

Watching from Benitez's car, Emery heard Sullivan's voice on the command net. 'No one shoot,' he was saying. 'No one shoot. Anyone shoots, I'll have them off the fucking planet. You hear me?'

Abruptly, the lights went out. The helicopter dipped its nose and then climbed away into the darkness over the East River. Emery got out of the car. He could hear footsteps on the tarmac. He began to walk towards the Oldsmobile. The Englishman was kneeling beside the Arab, taking off his jacket, laying it gently over his face. The footsteps got louder, Sullivan appearing, flanked by two policemen. They were both armed, pump-action shotguns. Sullivan was taking off his gas mask, smoothing his hair. The group paused for a moment by Telemann, looking down. Emery joined them. There was nothing left of Telemann's face. Emery knelt quickly, loosening the ring on Telemann's finger, taking off his own jacket. Then he stood up.

Sullivan was standing over the Englishman. 'McVeigh?' he grunted, extending a hand.

The Englishman nodded, saying nothing, turning away.

Epilogue

10 June 1991

Nine months later, the Gulf War won, America held a Victory Parade in New York City. Brass bands led column after column of marching troops up Broadway. Streamers and confetti whirled in the wind. Secretaries cheered from office windows. Kids in Stormin' Norman T-shirts waved paper flags. Crowds at street level clambered on to news-stands, cars, soft-drinks trucks, anywhere to get a better view.

Laura watched the parade on television, Bree an untidy tangle of arms and legs on her lap. Every time the soldiers appeared, Bree clapped. There was a lot of clapping. Finally, after the soldiers, came the floats. Each float had a theme. The Israeli float featured blitz scenes, Tel Aviv under bombardment, Scud missiles falling out of the night sky, brave faces amidst the rubble.

Bree, quiet for once, asked about the float. Laura shrugged, deflecting the question. 'Ask Uncle Peter,' she said. 'He'd know.'

Bree wriggled off Laura's lap and ran across the room. Emery was sitting by the window, his long body sprawled in the armchair. Bree asked him about the float, what it meant, all that pretend mess, and Emery told her, history simplified, the facts made easy.

Laura, half-listening to him, glanced across. 'You're saying they would have attacked the Iraqis?'

'Sure.'

'But didn't? For some reason?'

'Yeah.'

Laura looked at him for a moment, frowning, then turned back to the television. 'Thank God for that,' she said, watching the float roll on.

*

The same week, McVeigh flew back to Israel. Billy went with him, sitting in the window seat, his nose pressed against the perspex. At Ben Gurion airport, McVeigh hired a car. They drove north along the coast to Haifa. Then they cut inland, up into the mountains, past Safed, past Rosh Pinna, down into the Hula Valley, the long white road through the orchards.

They reached the kibbutz at dusk, the light golden, the temperature still in the eighties. McVeigh parked the car and they walked down the hill, following the path to the schoolhouse, McVeigh nodding to faces he remembered, risking the odd word of Hebrew, raising a smile. Outside the schoolhouse, the kids were playing football, and Billy stopped, tugging at his father's hand, wanting to know how to ask for a game. McVeigh smiled, wading in, intercepting the ball, passing it to Billy. Billy trapped it, flicked it into the air, juggled it from foot to foot, aware of the other kids watching him. Bringing the ball down, he chipped it to the nearest boy, someone his own age, and McVeigh left him there, walking into the schoolhouse, glad to get out of the heat.

Cela was in the classroom. She was writing on the blackboard, big round characters, a teacher's script. Hearing the door open, she glanced round.

McVeigh stood by the door. He was bathed in sweat. He grinned. 'Hi,' he said.

Cela looked at him for a moment, her hand still on the blackboard. Then she turned round and stepped towards him, picking her way between the desks. She had chalk on her hands. She rubbed them on her shorts, then reached up and touched McVeigh's face. 'You,' she said, smiling.

McVeigh nodded, putting his arms around her, holding her. Outside, he could hear Billy calling for the ball.

'Me,' he agreed.

All Pan books are available at your local bookshop or newsagent, or can be ordered direct from the publisher. Indicate the number of copies required and fill in the form below.

Send to: Pan C. S. Dept
              Macmillan Distribution Ltd
              Houndmills Basingstoke RG21 2XS
or phone: 0256 29242, quoting title, author and Credit Card number.

Please enclose a remittance* to the value of the cover price plus: £1.00 for the first book plus 50p per copy for each additional book ordered.

*Payment may be made in sterling by UK personal cheque, postal order, sterling draft or international money order, made payable to Pan Books Ltd.

Alternatively by Barclaycard/Access/Amex/Diners

Card No.   `[ ][ ][ ][ ][ ][ ][ ][ ][ ][ ][ ][ ][ ][ ][ ][ ][ ][ ]`

Expiry Date   `[ ][ ][ ][ ][ ][ ]`

———————————————————————————

Signature:

Applicable only in the UK and BFPO addresses

While every effort is made to keep prices low, it is sometimes necessary to increase prices at short notice. Pan Books reserve the right to show on covers and charge new retail prices which may differ from those advertised in the text or elsewhere.

NAME AND ADDRESS IN BLOCK LETTERS PLEASE:

....

Name _____

Address _____

_____

_____

_____

6/92